CUTTHROATS

Look for these exciting Western series
from bestselling authors
William W. Johnstone and J.A. Johnstone

The Mountain Man

Preacher: The First Mountain Man

Luke Jensen: Bounty Hunter

Those Jensen Boys!

The Jensen Brand

MacCallister

Flintlock

Perley Gates

The Kerrigans: A Texas Dynasty

Sixkiller: U.S. Marshal

Texas John Slaughter

Will Tanner, Deputy U.S. Marshal

The Frontiersman

Savage Texas

The Trail West

The Chuckwagon Trail

Rattlesnake Wells, Wyoming

KENSINGTON BOOKS are published by

Kensington Publishing Corp.
119 West 40th Street
New York, NY 10018

Library of Congress Card Catalogue Number: 2018952813

ISBN-13: 978-1-4967-1859-4
ISBN-10: 1-4967-1859-3
First Kensington Hardcover Edition: February 2019

10 9 8 7 6 5 4 3 2 1

Printed in the United States of America

CUTTHROATS

WILLIAM W. JOHNSTONE
and
J.A. JOHNSTONE

KENSINGTON BOOKS
www.kensingtonbooks.com

CHAPTER 1

In the early morning hours, the bounty hunters gathered around the remote mountain cabin, crouched in a shadowy clearing. They were thirteen in number—a dozen-plus wolves on the blood scent.

Ray Laskey walked up to where Jack Penny crouched in the pines roughly fifty yards from the cabin, running an oily rag down the barrel of his Henry repeating rifle.

"All the boys are in position, boss," Laskey said, slicing a hunk of wedding cake tobacco onto his tongue and chewing.

Penny turned to Laskey and winked in acknowledgment with the rheumy blue eye that always seemed to roll to the outside corner of its socket and that always made Laskey feel vaguely uneasy, for some reason. That wandering eye seemed like some separate living thing, rolling and bobbing around in Penny's ugly, bearded head . . . like some ghastly thing that lived inside a log at the bottom of a murky lake and only came out to rend and kill. . . .

Both men crouched lower behind their covering pine when the cabin's front door latch clicked. Laskey drew a sharp breath as he turned to see the door open. He squeezed his Spencer tightly but then eased his grip when he saw that the person stepping out onto the cabin's small stoop was a woman with long, thick, copper-red hair.

The woman, nicely put together and clad in a man's wool shirt and tight denim trousers, turned toward the split firewood stacked against the cabin's front wall. When she had an armload, she straightened, turned back to the door, and stopped abruptly.

No, Laskey thought. *Don't do that. Keep goin'. Get back inside the cabin, dearie. . . .*

The woman turned ever so slowly to stand staring straight off into the trees, directly toward where Laskey and Penny crouched behind a stout ponderosa.

Laskey's gut tightened.

Had she heard or in some other way sensed the killers crouched in the forest around the cabin? Had she smelled their unwashed bodies made even whiffier from their long, hard ride over the course of the long night lit only by a small and fleeting powder-horn moon?

Penny glanced at Laskey. The bearded bounty hunter smiled darkly, then raised his Henry to his shoulder. He slid the barrel up over a feathery branch and leveled his sights on the woman. He crouched low over the long gun, resting his bearded cheek up snug against the stock.

Slowly, almost soundlessly, he ratcheted back the hammer with his thumb.

Laskey looked at the woman. His heart thudded. She appeared to be staring straight at him. Straight at Penny steadying his sights on her chest.

No, no, no, dearie. You didn't hear nothin'. You didn't smell nothin'. No one's out here. A coyote, maybe. A rabbit, maybe—up and out too early for its own damn good . . .

That's all.

Go on inside, stoke your stove, start cookin' breakfast for them two cutthroats in there. It's them we want. Not you, purty lady.

We got other plans for you . . . dearie. . . .

As though obeying Ray Laskey's silent plea, the woman turned slowly, stepped back toward the door, nudged it open, and stepped inside. She turned to look outside once more, then closed the door and latched it with a soft *click*.

Penny eased his Winchester's hammer down against the firing pin.

Laskey released a breath he hadn't realized he'd been holding.

Penny turned to him, spreading his ragged beard as he grinned. "She almost joined the angels."

"When, uh . . ." Laskey said, pressing the wedding cake up tautly against his gum, "when do you want to . . . ?"

"Start the dance?"

"Yeah, yeah. Start the dance."

"As soon as they show themselves. Best odds, that way. Won't be too long now, most like. We got time."

"What, uh . . . what about the woman?" Laskey said.

"What about her?" Penny asked him.

Laskey shrugged, toed a pinecone. "She's too purty to kill. Outright, I mean . . ."

Laskey grinned, juice from the wedding cake bleeding out from between his thin lips.

Penny scowled down at the shorter man. "We came here to kill, an' that's what we're gonna do, Ray, my boy. She's with them cutthroats, so she dies with them cutthroats. Hell, there's a reward on her head, too. Dead or alive. Same as them."

"Oh, boy," Laskey said. "The woman, too, huh? Seems a shame's all."

Penny placed a big, strong, gloved hand on Laskey's shoulder and squeezed. "The woman, too, Ray. We ain't here for none o' that nonsense you're thinkin' about, you randy scoundrel."

Penny brushed his gloved fist across Laskey's pointed chin.

He winked his weird fish eye again, and it rolled like that living thing in the dark lake, fleeing back to its log after feeding.

CHAPTER 2

"What you two old cutthroats need is a job," said Jaycee Breckenridge.

James "Slash" Braddock lifted his head from his pillow, frowning at the pretty woman forking bacon around in the cast-iron skillet sputtering atop her coal-black range. "Jay, honey, please don't use such nasty language so early in the morning. Pecos an' me got *sensitive ears*!"

"What'd she say?" asked Melvin Baker, better known for the past thirty years of his outlaw career as the Pecos River Kid.

He lay belly down on the cot on the far side of the small cabin from Slash Braddock. His blue eyes were open, regarding his longtime outlaw partner in shock and disbelief. "I didn't just hear her use the bad word again—did I, Slash?" He closed his hands over his ears. "Oh, please, tell me I didn't!"

"Now, look what you done, Jay! Poor ole Pecos is beside himself over here! He's likely ruined for the whole dang day! I might have to hide his guns from him, so he don't blow his brains out!"

Pecos buried his face in his pillow and pretend bawled.

At the range, one hand on her hip as she continued to

flip and shuttle the bacon around in the same pan in which potatoes and onions fried, Jay shook her long, copper-red hair back from her hazel-eyed face and laughed. "Look what time it is, you old mossyhorns!"

She glanced at the windows behind her through which slanted the crisp, high-altitude sunlight of the Juan Valley of southern Colorado Territory. "It's nigh on midmorning and you two are still lounging around like a pair of eastern railroad magnates on New Year's Day!"

"Lounging around—nothin'!" Pecos lifted his head from his pillow and looked over his shoulder at Jay. "I was dead asleep not more'n two minutes ago. You done woke me up with your foul language. You oughta be ashamed of yourself, woman. What would Pistol Pete think of such talk?"

"Ha!" Jay threw her head back, laughing. "Whenever I mentioned the word 'job' to that old rascal—as in he might want to quit ridin' the long coulees and try an honest job for a change—he'd howl like a gut-shot cur an' skin out of here like a preacher caught in a parlor house. He'd run clear across the yard and throw himself in the creek. Didn't matter what time of year it was. Spring, summer, winter, or fall—that's just what he'd do, Pete would."

Jay threw her head back again, laughing.

But then she turned a thoughtful look over her shoulder, gazing out the window toward the lone grave standing on a knoll about sixty yards out from the cabin, in a little pocket of ponderosas and cedars. Jay's shoulders, clad in a plaid work shirt tucked into tight denims, rose and fell slowly, heavily. Her lower lip trembled. She stifled a sob, clamping her hand over her mouth, then wheeled from the range and hurried to the cabin's front door.

"Excuse me, boys!" she said in an emotion-strangled voice as she opened the door and stepped out onto the small front stoop. She slammed the door behind her.

Through the door, Slash heard her sobbing.

He turned to his partner, scowling, and said, "Pecos, what'd you have to go and do that for?"

"Ah, hell!" Sitting up now, clad in his wash-worn long-handles that clung to his big, rawboned frame, Pecos slapped the cot beside him and hung his gray-blond, blue-eyed head like a young man fresh from the woodshed. "I reckon Pete's name just slipped out. I mean, hell, he *was* her man. And, hell, we rode with him for nigh on thirty years before he . . . well, you know . . . before he got himself planted over there in them trees."

Pecos turned a disgruntled look at Slash. He kept his voice down so he wouldn't be heard on the stoop from where Jay's sobs pushed softly through the door. "Come on, pardner, Pete's been dead almost five years now. We should be able to mention his name from time to time."

"Dammit, Pecos." Slash tossed his animal skin covers aside and dropped his bare feet to the timbered floor still owning the chill of the crisp mountain morning. "You an' I both know Pete didn't get himself planted in them trees over there. *I* did!" Slash jabbed his thumb against his chest that bore the hooked knife scar that gave him his nickname. "I'm the one that got him planted. My own damn carelessness did."

"It was a bullet from the gun of one of Luther Bledsoe's deputies that killed Pete, Slash, you stupid devil. Don't you start in with all this old Pete stuff now, too!"

"I didn't," Slash said, rising in disgust and grabbing his brown whipcord trousers off a chair. "You did!"

"Ah, hell!" Pecos twisted around and flopped belly down on his cot, burying his head in his pillow. His big Russian .44, snugged inside its brown, hand-tooled leather holster, hung by its shell belt hooked over elk horns mounted on the wall above his head, within an easy grab if needed. Such a move had been needed more than a few

times in his and Slash's long careers as riders of the long
coulees, or the owlhoot trail, as some called the life of a
professional western outlaw.

Slash quickly stepped into his pants. Then his boots. He
left his blue chambray shirt on the chair but he strapped
his twin, stag-butted Colt .44s around his waist, which was
solid as oak at his ripe age of fifty-seven, which he was not
above crowing about to Pecos, who'd grown a little fleshy
above the buckle of his own cartridge belt.

Slash rarely walked more than five steps without either
the revolver or his Winchester Yellowboy repeater. As he
grabbed his hat off the kitchen table his bone-handled
bowie knife, also strapped to his shell belt, rode high on
his left hip, behind the .44 positioned for the cross-draw
on that side. He swept a hand through his dark-brown
hair, still thick, he was proud to know, but well streaked
with gray—especially up around the temples and in his
long sideburns that sandwiched a broad, strong-jawed,
brown-eyed face—the face of a handsome albeit middle-
aged schoolboy.

One who'd spent the bulk of his life out in the blazing
western sun.

That he was no longer a schoolboy, however, made itself
obvious once again as it always tended to do upon his first
rising. As he tramped across the kitchen, his hips and
knees and ankles popped and cracked, stiff from too long
in the mattress sack after too many years forking a saddle
and sleeping on the hard, cold ground of one remote outlaw camp or another. An old back injury, the result of
being thrown from a horse during a run from a catch
party nearly twenty years ago, made Slash curse under his
breath as he lifted the popping skillet off the range and slid
it onto the warming rack, so the vittles wouldn't burn.

He pulled a couple of heavy stone mugs down from a
shelf near the range and set them on the table. He dumped

two heaping helpings of sugar into one, because he knew Jay liked her mud a little sweet—"Just like her men," she often quipped—then used a deer hide swatch to lift the hot black coffeepot from the range, and filled both mugs to their brims.

"Is Jay gonna be all right?" Pecos asked, his chagrined voice muffled by his pillow.

"Of course, she's gonna be all right," Slash said, heading for the door. "She's Jay, ain't she?"

He fumbled the door open and stepped out, drawing the door closed behind him with a hooked boot. Jay stood ahead and to his right, her back to him, staring out over the porch rail toward the lone grave on the knoll.

The sun glowed in her hair. Birds flitted about the sunlit yard around the cabin ringed with pine forest. Tall, stone escarpments flanked the place. The cabin, originally built by a hermetic, now-dead fur trapper, was situated here on this mountain shoulder in such a way that it couldn't be seen from any direction unless you rode right up on it. And the only way you were likely to ride up on it was either by accident or if you'd already known it was here and you were headed for it.

That's what had made the place such a prime hideout over the years. After a bank or train job, the Snake River Marauders, as Slash and Pecos's old gang called themselves, often split up their booty and then separated themselves into small groups of twos, threes, and fours, scattering and holing up till their trail cooled. They'd meet up again later at some far-flung, prearranged place to plan their next job.

Sometimes Slash, Pecos, and Pistol Pete, the old outlaw from the far northern Dakota country, would meet Jay in Mexico, and they'd spend their winnings in Durango, Loreto, or Mazatlán. Sometimes they'd sun themselves on the beaches of the Sea of Cortez, drinking pulque and tequila and feasting on spicy Mexican dishes like tortas ahogadas and chilorio.

Sometimes they'd hole up here for weeks or months at a time, hunting in the San Juans and the Sawatch to the north, and fishing and swimming in the pure, cold mountain streams. It was the time between jobs spent either here or in Mexico that Slash had always preferred over the jobs themselves, but he could never deny his almost primal attraction to the danger and excitement, as well as the money, that had always lured him back to the outlaw trail.

Now he set the cup of sugary coffee on the rail in front of Jay and kissed her tear-damp cheek. "Cup o' mud for you, darlin'," he said. "Put hair on your chest."

Staring toward the grave atop the knoll, Jay laughed at the old joke she and her old friend Slash had shared all the years they'd known each other—going on fifteen now—and offered her usual retort, "I don't want hair on my chest, Slash. That doesn't sound appealing to me at all!"

Slash gave a wry snort and sipped his coffee. "How you doing?"

"Look at me," she said, still staring toward the grave. "It's been how long, now? Going on five years? And I'm still pining for that man turned to dust under those mounded rocks over there."

"That's all right. He was a good man. He deserves pining for."

"Yes, he does, at that." Jay hardened her voice as well as her jaws as she turned to her old friend. "But it's time for me to move on, dammit, Slash."

"You're right on that score, too, Jay." Again, Slash sipped the rich black coffee.

"I'm still young . . . sort of," she said with proud defiance. "I still have my looks. Or most of them, barring a few crowfeet around my eyes and a little roughness to my skin . . . as well as to my tongue," she added drolly.

Slash looked at her, which was one of his favorite things to do. She was a slight, petite woman but with all the right female curves in all the right female places. She wore each of her forty-plus years beautifully on a face richly tanned by the frontier sun. The lines and furrows had seasoned her, refining her beauty and accentuating her raw, earthy character. Her hazel eyes were alive with a wry, frank humor.

She was the most sensuous and alluring woman Slash had ever laid eyes on, and he'd first laid eyes on her when she was well past thirty.

"Hellkatoot," he said. "You're still a raving beauty, Jay. There's not many women over forty who've kept their looks as well as you have. You'll find a man. You just gotta start lookin' for one, that's all."

Jaycee Breckenridge drew a deep, slow, fateful breath. "I'm not gonna find one out here, am I? The only men who come around here anymore are you and that lummox lounging around inside like Jay Gould."

Slash smiled.

"And you two don't deserve me," Jay said with another laugh.

"We sure don't!" Slash chuckled and shook his head.

Besides, he knew, they shared too much history. Good history and bad history. He'd once gotten his hopes up about Jay, a long time ago. But then she'd tumbled for the older, wiser "Pistol" Pete Johnson, five years Slash's senior, old enough to have been Jay's father.

She'd preferred the astuteness and assuredness of the older man. She'd been taken by the burly Pete's rough-sweet ways and his bawdy humor. Mere days after she'd met the man at the country saloon she'd been singing in, she never looked back. At least, not as far as Slash knew, and he thought he knew her as well or better than anyone on earth, now that Pete was gone.

"I'm so sorry, Jay," he said, looking off in frustration. She frowned at him, puzzled. "For Pecos? Don't be silly. He only mentioned his old friend's name."

"No, not for Pecos." Slash turned to her. "For me."

Jay looked at him askance, with sharp admonishment. "Let's not go down that trail again, Slash."

CHAPTER 3

"Pete's death wasn't your fault," Jay said. "It was the fault of the man—that deputy U.S. marshal riding for Chief Marshal Bledsoe—who shot him from that ridge. Cowardly devil!" she added hatefully, tears glistening in her eyes once more.

Slash shook his head. "I led us into that trap. I knew those mountains we were riding in. I knew 'em like the back of my hand! At least, I thought I did."

"It was a box canyon," Jay said. "The box canyons are filled with lunatics."

"I took a wrong turn. I was hungover from the night before. I shouldn't have been drinking the night before a job, but I did. I took a wrong turn and led Pete an' Pecos an' Arnie and Devlin into that box canyon and couldn't find my way out again before that no-account lawdog that was shadowin' us fired down at us from that ridge.

"To put the cherry on it, that bullet wasn't even meant for Pete. It was meant for me! That marshal wanted to cut the head off the snake, to take me out, the gang's leader, but Pete rode in front of me when we were all looking for another way out of that canyon. He's the one whose ticket got punched when it should've been mine."

Slash gritted his teeth and shook his head as he stared toward the grave, the old sorrow and self-recrimination having returned full-blast. "Dammit!"

"Slash, now—"

"No." Slash shook his head defiantly. "I reckon I should've retired back then, nigh on five years ago. I got careless in my old age. Overly confident. If I'd called it quits, let one of the others take over—one of the younger men that was *qualified* to take over—Pete might still be alive today." He turned to the woman, placed his hands on her arms. "I hope to God you can find it in your heart to forgive me one day, Jay."

She studied Slash thoughtfully. Slowly, a sad smile stretched her lips and she placed a gentle hand on his cheeks, staring deeply into his own sad eyes. "I'll make a deal with you, Slash."

He cleared emotion from his throat. "Anything . . ."

"I'll forgive you if you forgive yourself." Jay's smile grew, and warmth filled her hazel-eyed gaze. "How 'bout that? Oh, and I'll add one more thing. I promise not to break down like a damn weeping fool every time I hear his name. Maybe *sometimes*, but not every time," she added, chuckling. "All right, Slash? Do we have a deal?"

Slash gazed back at her, his heart lightening ever so gradually. He removed her hand from his cheek and kissed it. "All right." He chuckled with genuine relief. "All right. We got ourselves a deal."

"Good!" Jay picked up her coffee and sipped it, gazing through the steam at Slash. "Now, tell me what brought you both here last night, looking so raggedy-heeled and hang-headed."

Slash and Pecos had pulled in so late the previous night, having awakened Jay from a dead sleep, that once they'd tended their horses, they'd all headed off to bed, Slash assuring the woman he'd explain their unexpected visit first thing in the morning.

Now Slash glowered as he turned to stare out over the porch rail again, holding his coffee up close to the scar on his chest, the top end of which was exposed by the V opening of his unbuttoned longhandle top. "Another foolish mistake, Jay. Just another in a long line of 'em."

"Tell me," Jay prodded, rubbing her hand on his shoulder. "Can't be all that bad."

"Oh, yes it can, darlin'. It sure as hell can!"

Leaning forward against the porch rail, coffee in his hands, Slash told her in a tone of deep chagrin about how he and Pecos got hornswoggled by their own gang—or by the two upstarts in the gang who decided to take over the gang's leadership.

"Loco Sanchez and Arnell Squires?" said Jay. "You can't be serious? Why, they're . . . they're foolish young firebrands!"

"They're both damn near your age," Slash said, chuckling. "They ain't schoolboys no more."

"No!"

Slash chuckled again. "I know—where does the time go? I still see 'em as pimply-faced brats myself!" He shook his head. "All I got to say for 'em is at least they didn't shoot us. They could have, sure enough."

"Instead, they shamed the hell out of us!" Pecos said, barreling out the cabin's door like a bull from a chute, tucking the tails of his white cotton shirt into his black broadcloth trousers. "They got us drunk the night before we was to rob the bank in La Junta—"

"*Good* an' drunk!" Slash said, shaking his head in self-disgust.

"*Good* an' drunk," Pecos agreed, leaning against a porch post, his own mug of freshly poured coffee in his big right hand, "while most of the rest of the gang must've stayed purty damn sober. They was up at the crack of dawn the next morning, and lit out to rob the bank without us."

Slash gave a dry, sheepish snort. "They rode off to rob the bank, leaving me an' Pecos three sheets to the wind in Doña Flores's place down by the Arkansas River. As they rode into La Junta, they told someone to tell the marshal that none other than Slash Braddock and the Pecos River Kid was sawing logs over at Doña Flores's place by the river."

"Oh, no!" Jay said, snapping her eyes wide in both shock and amusement. "They didn't!"

Slash and Pecos both shook their heads in unison, flushing to the tips of their ears.

"Well . . . ?" Jay said. "Don't leave me hanging, boys!"

Slash looked at his partner, who was a good four inches taller than Slash's six-two, and a good sixty pounds heavier, though Pecos could carry that much weight on his broad, ham-boned frame and not look fat. Long blond hair tumbled down from the snuff-brown, broad-brimmed, bullet-crowned hat on his head. His graying blond mustache and goatee, as well as the fair hues of his face, set off the lake-blue of his eyes.

"Jay's enjoying this tale way too much, Pecos," Slash said.

Pecos chuckled despite himself and brushed a big fist across his nose. He gave his head another wag and said, "Well . . . we got arrested. While our own gang was robbing the bank in town, the lawdog and his two deputies . . . well, they snuck into our rooms along the river, an' . . . they cuffed us. . . ."

He glanced at Slash as though for help.

Flushing an even brighter red, Slash said, "They cuffed us while we was both passed out. Out cold. I didn't even know I'd been cuffed and arrested until a good hour, maybe two hours later when I came out of the whiskey fog in the jail cell!"

"Yeah," Pecos said, nodding with chagrin, eyes on his boot toes. "Me, too." He winced and clamped a hand to the back of his neck. "Damn, that was one of the worst hangovers I've ever endured. Leastways, north of the Mexican border!"

They all laughed at that.

Jay said, "Well, how did you two get out of jail? I'm surprised they didn't hang you both from the nearest cotton-wood!"

Slash looked at Pecos. Pecos looked at Slash. They both flushed in unison once more. Slash chuckled.

Pecos toed a weed that had grown up between the porch boards. "Um . . ."

"Go ahead," Slash said, grinning at his partner. "Tell the woman, Pecos."

Turning to Jay, staring at him expectantly, Pecos said, "Well, I uh . . . I know this girl from Trinidad, ya see."

"A girl from Trinidad, hmm?"

"Yeah, a girl from Trinidad," Pecos said. "She just happened to be in La Junta. She travels with this theatrical troupe. Plays in all the opry houses in Colorado and northern New Mexico, an' . . . well, she sorta helped us out a little, Slash an' me."

"Her an' her actress friend," Slash added. "A coupla fine-lookin' young ladies."

"Very upstanding, I bet," Jay said, grinning, eyes bright with humor.

"Oh, very upstanding," Slash said.

"Well, they normally are," Pecos said. "But the one, Evangeline Kinkaid, she took a shine to me a while back in Taos, ya see—"

"A very big shine!" Slash added, snickering.

"Understandable," Jay said, chuckling. "Pecos is a big man!"

Flushing but otherwise ignoring the ribbing, Pecos continued with, "When Evangeline seen me an' Slash led over to the jail in cuffs an' leg irons, she decided to offer a hand, an' she got her actress friend to help."

"What kind of a hand did these two *actresses* offer?" Jay asked.

"They waited until the town marshal had organized a posse to go after the gang and its new leaders," Slash said, speeding up the story. "When he and the catch party left town, he left two older fellas on guard duty in the jailhouse. A pair of old widowers. Apparently, neither widower had known the pleasures of a woman in a lot of days. So it was no hard trick for Evangeline Kinkaid and her friend . . ."

"Magdalena St. Charles," Pecos filled in, toeing the weed again.

"Yes, yes, Magdalena St. Charles," Slash said. "It was no hard trick for those two good-lookin', upstandin' girls to distract the old-timers long enough to squirrel the cell block key away from 'em . . . as well as a pistol, an—"

"Oh, good Lord in heaven!" Jay's laughter peeled. "You two old cutthroats were saved from a sure-fire hanging by two girls of the fallen variety!"

"Give the lady a cigar!" Slash said, grinning despite his embarrassment.

All three had a good laugh over two of the frontier's most notorious outlaws, Slash Braddock and the Pecos

River Kid, having been arrested while drunk on whiskey and then being freed by two young ladies named Evangeline Kinkaid and Magdalena St. Charles.

Slash and Pecos didn't laugh as long or with nearly as much vigor as Jay, however. Pistol Pete's pretty widow had a good long laugh over the old outlaws' latest escapades.

For Slash and Pecos, however, the whole drunken experience had been quite sobering.

"So," Slash continued when Jay's laughter had all but died, "we got our horses out of the livery barn and rode hell for leather. We covered our trail pretty good, I think," he added, glancing cautiously around the cabin, "before we drifted up this way. I don't think we were followed. Honestly, Jay, we didn't know where else to go. We been rode hard an' put up wet, Pecos an' me."

"You know you boys are welcome here anytime," Jay said. She frowned at each man in turn. "Why such long faces?" she asked. "At least you evaded the hang rope. You should be stompin' with your tails up!"

Pursing his lips, Slash shared another incredulous look with his old trail partner Pecos, then shook his head. "We're all washed up, Jay. We burned the candle at both ends for too damn long. We're done. Through."

"We're gettin' out of it," Pecos said. "Before we embarrass ourselves further or, worse, get our necks stretched for our stupidity."

"Getting out of it?" Jay said, arching her brows hopefully. "You mean you *are* going to leave the long coulees and actually get *real jobs*!"

"There she goes again!" Pecos yelled, pointing a mock-accusing finger at the pretty woman, who was once again laughing delightedly. "There she goes again, Slash! Make her stop!"

Slash chuckled and threw back the last of his coffee.

Tossing the dregs over the porch rail, he said, "I reckon you could say we're gonna get ourselves jobs, sure enough. But we'll be workin' for ourselves."

"Oh?" Jay's curiosity was piqued.

"Sure," Pecos said, grinning. "Me an' Slash done thought it through over the past year or so. We're gonna go up to Camp Collins, north of Denver, an' buy a small freighting company from this old man we know up there. Emil Becker. We been through that country a few times, and we both took a shine to it.

"Last time we was through there, after robbing the bank up in Laramie"—Pecos added with a devilish wink— "Emil took us aside and said he'd sell his freight outfit to us for ten thousand dollars. Four big Pittsburg freight wagons, heavy-axled for mountain trailing, and a dozen big Missouri mules. Emil wasn't in no hurry to sell at the time. He told us to think on it for a year and then get back to him. He figured in that time, he'd be ready to retire and go live with his daughter in Denver."

"Well, it's been a year," Slash said. "So . . . since our minds about retiring from the owlhoot trail were sort of made up for us . . . by Sanchez an' Squires . . . we decided to go ahead an' pull the trigger on our new careers."

He smiled winningly and threw an arm around Pecos's broad shoulders. He doffed his low-crowned black hat and held it over his chest. "Miss Jaycee Breckenridge, meet the new proprietors of Front Range Freighting—James Braddock and Melvin Baker!"

"Oh, so you've already bought the business?" Jay asked.

Slash and Pecos shared another conferring glance.

"Ah . . . well, no," Pecos said.

Slash winced. "You see . . . we, uh . . . we're flat broke. I might have a gold eagle rolling around in the hollowed out heel of my boot, but . . ."

"I got a couple of nickels in my vest pocket," Pecos put in sheepishly. "But mostly lint. I reckon I spent the last of my jingle at Doña Flores's place." He winced as he raked a thumbnail along his unshaven jaw. "I was really countin' on the takedown from that bank in La Junta, gallblastit!"

"So you're gonna need a stake," Jay said, crossing her arms on her chest and drawing her mouth corners down, knowingly.

"Yeah," Slash said, dropping his gaze to the porch floor and toeing the weed that Pecos had been toeing before. "So we're gonna pull one more job. Just one more! Then . . ."

He wagged his head, sighed with resolve, and shuttled Jay a direct, open gaze. "Then we're gonna take our cold hard cash up to Camp Collins an' plunk it down on old Emil's barrelhead. We're gonna be freighters. We're gonna haul goods from Denver to the mining camps up high in the Rockies. A good, honest life of hard work an' clean living—ain't that right, Pecos?"

Pecos grinned and rose up onto the balls of his boots as he draped his long, thick right arm around Slash's shoulders. "Gonna be a life of peace an' quiet from here on out for old Slash an' Pecos!"

"Uh, make that James Braddock an' Melvin Baker," Slash corrected.

"Right you are, partner. Ole Slash an' Pecos is dead as fence posts. Long live James Braddock an' Melvin Baker, proprietors!"

Just then the clay water pot hanging beneath the porch roof exploded.

Clay shards and water rained down over the porch and onto the toes of Slash's and Pecos's boots.

For a half second, they and Jay just stared at the frayed rope jostling from the ceiling, where the pot had been hanging a moment before. Pecos swiped his left hand across the side of his neck and stared at his fingers, dumbfounded at the greasy blood from the bullet burn.

As the shrill, echoing report of the rifle reached the trio's ears, Slash grabbed Jay and shoved her through the cabin's open door, bellowing, *"Ambush!"*

CHAPTER 4

As Jay lay sprawled on the cabin floor, just inside the front door, Slash clawed both his .44s from their holsters and swung back around, crouching in the open doorway to stare off into the trees and rocks bordering the cabin's broad yard, carpeted in dun-brown grass.

He held both pistols barrel up, hammers cocked, waiting.

Pecos stood crouched to Slash's right, also aiming his cocked Russian straight out into the yard.

The silence after the bullet and the wailing report was deafening.

Sunlight splashed the yard. The smell of summer-cured grass and warm pine resin and mountain sage peppered Slash's nose. Birds flitted in the pine branches.

That was all there was out there now. Slash almost wondered if he'd imagined the bullet, but the frayed rope hanging from the porch ceiling and the shards of the clay pot lying on the wet floorboards were all the proof he needed that they had, indeed, been shot at.

But from where?

By who?

Pecos swallowed nervously and, keeping his cocked

Russian aimed straight out from the porch, said, "You see the devil?"

"Nope." Slash paused, raking his gaze slowly across the yard and the furry green of the pines and cedars bordering it, roughly fifty yards from the cabin. "I sure don't. But he's out there . . . somewhere."

"Who, you thinkin'?" Pecos asked, his low-pitched voice strained with anxiety.

"I don't know—Pattinson?"

Lew Pattinson was the La Junta town marshal who'd been off trying to throw a loop around the Snake River Marauders while the gang's former, aging leaders were breaking out of his jail with the help of two comely show-girls. Slash and Pecos hadn't ridden directly to Jay's hide-out cabin from La Junta. As was their custom, they traced a circuitous route, taking their time to make sure they weren't being shadowed.

At least, they hadn't *thought* they'd been shadowed.

Pecos jerked with a start, swinging his pistol to the right. But the thud he'd just heard had only been a pinecone tumbling from a branch at the forest's edge. "Uh-uh," he said. "I don't think so. Pattinson ain't cagey enough to have tracked us from La Junta."

Jay's voice rose quietly behind Slash. "You boys see anything?"

"No," Slash said, his heart thudding in his chest. He felt a tingling sensation just over his heart, as though someone were drawing a bead on him.

"Why don't you two get your tails in here?" Jay urged, keeping her voice down.

Just then a deep, rumbling male voice vaulted out of the forest fronting the cabin. "Slash Braddock and the Pecos River Kid?"

Slash and Pecos shared a quick, dubious look.

Slash lifted his chin and, tightening his grip on both his aimed Colts, yelled, "Who's out there an' what do you want?"

"It's Jack Penny!" the deep voice rumbled back from the tangle of green, breeze-jostled branches. "And me an' the boys is here to burn you fellas down!"

"Penny!" exclaimed Pecos, hardening his jaws and flaring his nostrils.

"Goddamn bounty hunters!" lamented Slash. "Penny and his raggedy-tailed sons of Satan have been after us for years!"

Penny bellowed even louder, "Burn 'em down, you men!"

Instantly, chunks of hot lead sizzled through the air, slamming into the porch's ceiling support posts and into the front of the cabin. One curled the air a cat's whisker wide of Slash's left ear to clang against an iron skillet hanging on a wall in Jay's kitchen.

Jay screamed.

The cacophony of a good dozen or so rifles followed a wink later, smoke and flames stabbing out of the pine forest where the shooters crouched, hurling lead from the cover of the trees. As soon as Slash saw the first smoke puffs, marking the bushwhackers' positions, he began triggering his own Colt. Pecos fired his Russian, standing sideways atop the porch, revolver extended out from his right shoulder, trying to make himself as slender as a man his size could.

"Boys, get your asses in here!" Jay screamed above the din of thudding bullets, several of which were breaking the glass out of the cabin's two front windows.

Slash emptied his right-hand Colt and glanced at Pecos. "Jay's got a point, partner!"

"Don't she always?"

Slash backed into the cabin, firing two more shots. At the same time, Pecos triggered a couple more rounds at the smoke puffing between the pine branches, then backed up and swung around, cursing, as the ambushers' bullets plastered the front of the cabin to both sides of him, one nipping the bullet-shaped crown of his snuff-brown hat.

Pete and Jay had put a large window in the cabin's front wall, so they always had a good view of the hideout's front yard. It was through this window that the big, lumbering Pecos plunged head first, yelling, more lead tearing slivers from the frame around him. As Slash slammed the cabin's front door outfitted with loopholes through which to return fire from inside, he turned to see his partner landing on Jay's kitchen table in a rain of shattering glass and wood slivers from the frame.

"Damn you, Pecos!" Jay shouted, crouching down in front of the range, poking two fingers into her ears against the din. "Do you know how much that window cost me—not to mention the work it took Pete an' I hauling it up here and installing the blasted thing?"

"Blasted is right," Slash yelled, crouching against the front wall between the door and the ruined window. "Jesus, Pecos!"

The bigger cutthroat rolled across the table, grunting and groaning, losing his hat but managing to keep a firm hold on the big, silver-washed Russian in his right fist. He dropped over the table's far side just as two more bullets slammed into the halved-log table's thick surface, and he hit the floor with an enormous thud.

"*Ohhh!*" Pecos grunted as the air was hammered from his lungs.

Slash emptied his second Colt out the front window, then holstered both revolvers and dropped to his hands and knees, keeping his head beneath not only the front window but all four windows in the cabin, as bullets were being hurled at the cabin from all sides.

Jay raised her own head to cast a cautious glance out

the broken front window. "Bounty hunters, you say? Those SOBs!"

"What I want to know," said Pecos, "is how the hell did they find us here?"

"We're too damn old an' stupid not to keep a better eye on our back trails—that's how they trailed us here!" Slash snaked across the floor to where Pecos lay between the table and Jay, who was still crouched in front of the range. Pecos was groaning and clutching his right shoulder, bits of glass from the window glistening in his long, stringy, gray-blond hair as well as in his mustache and goatee of the same color. "You hit, pard?"

"My neck!"

Slash ran a finger through the blood along the left side of his partner's thick neck. "Pshaw—I've cut myself worse shaving!"

Slash crawled across the glass- and sliver-littered floor toward where his Winchester Yellowboy repeater leaned against the back wall, near the elk horns from which Pecos's gun rig had dangled.

"My shoulder!" Pecos groaned behind him, wincing as more lead stitched the air over his head. "I think it's dislocated! Or . . . maybe it's broke. Galldangit, Slash, I think my shoulder's broke!"

"My wonderful window is broke!" Jay screeched, cowering low against the floor.

Slash grabbed the Yellowboy and, sitting on his butt on the floor, swung around toward Pecos and levered a cartridge into the action. "Stop your caterwauling, partner! Ain't seemly in front of the lady!"

"I remember Pete talking about a bounty hunter named Penny!" Jay yelled above the *zing* and whine of bullets threading the air inside the cabin, slamming into the walls and furniture and banging shrilly off pots and pans hanging from kitchen rafters.

"We sure are sorry about leadin' 'em here, Jay!" Crawling past his partner, wincing as broken glass nipped his knees, Slash said, "Stop lollygaggin', now, Pecos. We're gonna have to hold these SOBs off before they . . . oh, *crap!*"

Slash had just pressed his shoulder up against the front wall, to the right of the big window, and edged a look through the broken glass poking out of the frame.

"What is it?" Pecos asked, crawling toward the wall against which both his Colt revolving rifle and his sawed-off, double-barreled, twelve-gauge shotgun leaned.

"Trouble," Slash said. "Big trouble!"

He turned his wide brown eyes to Jay and said, "They got your wagon—the one you haul wood in."

Jay scowled, deep lines etched across her forehead. "It's not the wagon I care about. It's the cabin I care about, Slash, you corkheaded fool!"

"Yeah, I know." Slash raised the Yellowboy, planted the sights on a stocky gent in buckskins just then making a run toward the cabin, zigzagging between large rocks that pocked the yard. He was heading for the stone well coping over which a shake-shingled roof angled, housing a winch and a wooden bucket.

The stocky man was triggering a Winchester from his hip as he ran, his face shaded by a floppy-brimmed, leather hat. A red neckerchief billowed across his broad, lumpy chest.

"That's Ray Laskey," Slash said, a devilish glint in his eyes.

He squeezed the trigger. The stocky man dropped to the ground and rolled, clutching his right knee on which dark red blood shone, yelling to beat the band. Quickly, Slash ejected his spent cartridge, seated fresh, and fired again.

Laskey stopped yelling.

"*Was* Ray Laskey, the black-hearted devil!" Slash pulled

his head back behind the front wall as several bullets tore into the frame just inches from his nose.

"Ah, hell!" Pecos had just edged a look out the front window from where he stood near the door, which jerked in its frame as bullets pelted it. "They're gonna burn us out!"

He'd just seen the wagon that several of Penny's men were pushing toward the cabin. They'd piled brush into Jay's old buckboard and set it on fire. There must have been three or four men at work pushing the burning buckboard, but they were staying down behind its far end, rolling the wagon ever closer toward the cabin's east front corner.

"Burn us out?" Jay bellowed. "Those devils can't do that!"

"You're preachin' to the choir, honey!" Slash triggered his Winchester toward the wagon but had to jerk his head back behind the wall again as more bullets tore into the frame. He glanced at Pecos, who tried to snake his Colt revolving rifle out the window but had to pull it back down or get himself perforated.

"They're laying down covering fire for the wagon!" Slash yelled to his partner. "They're not letting us get any shots off!"

Pecos swiped his hand across another bullet graze—this one on his right jaw—and turned his blue-eyed, frantic gaze to his partner. "Don't I know it! We gotta do somethin' fast, though, Slash, or we're gonna—!"

Just then there was a crunching *boom* that made the whole cabin lurch. The front wall and the heavy door shuddered. A couple of ceiling beams sagged, groaning, threatening to give. Thick smoke billowed just outside the broken front windows and slithered through the cracks between the door's halved timbers.

"I do believe the wagon has arrived," Slash said wryly,

coughing against the smoke now billowing through the window—thick, cottony tufts of the stuff, making his nose burn and his eyes water.

Outside, the ambushers laughed.

"Gonna be gettin' mighty warm in there mighty soon, Slash an' Pecos!" bellowed Jack Penny from somewhere outside, now hidden if not by the trees, then by the smoky fog. "You best come out here an' let us finish you quick! You're worth as much dead as alive, an' we don't want you to suffer none!"

"Or not so quick!" yelled one of Penny's men. "I'm gonna shoot you two cutthroats real *slowwww*! Then we're gonna saw your heads off, toss 'em in a croaker sack, and take 'em to Marshal Bledsoe in Denver for the *ree*-ward!"

"That's disgusting!" Jay said.

"That's Bart Antrim," Slash told her. "Penny's first lieutenant."

"You go to hell, Antrim!" Pecos shouted through the window, but then jerked his head back as several rounds plunked into the frame, threatening to blow off his broad, sunburned nose.

He turned to Slash. "Any ideas, pardner, or is it time to get right with the Lord?"

"Jay, is there a back door to this place?" Slash had turned toward the range, but Jay was no longer there.

"What the hell good is a back door gonna do us, Slash?" Pecos shouted above the flames' roar as the fire from the wagon spread onto the cabin's roof and east front corner. "They got us surrounded! There must be a good dozen bounty hunters out there—and they do seem to have plenty of ammo, in case you hadn't noticed! Ouch!" he added as another bullet grazed him—this one streaking across the outside of his upper left arm.

"Jay, where in the hell are you?" Slash called.

Just then he saw her running down the stairs that ran along the cabin's far side, behind the front door. She crouched beneath a window over there, above the stairway, and then dropped into the kitchen. She wore a large Stetson and she had Pistol Pete's twin Colt Navy .44s strapped around her waist. She held his old Spencer repeating rifle in her gloved right hand.

She ducked with a scream as a bullet from the far window almost blew her head off.

As she dropped to all fours and crawled toward the rear of the cabin, she glanced at Slash through the thickening smoke. "You asked about a back door?"

"Yeah, but it's no use," Slash said. "Pecos is right, we—"

"Come on!" Jay yelled.

She threw up a braided and dyed hemp rug near Slash's cot, abutting the cabin's rear wall. She rose to her knees and, coughing on the thickening smoke, tugged on the ring of what appeared to be a trapdoor that had been built into the floor. She tugged several times, grunting, but the door wouldn't budge.

Jay cast her bright, fearful gaze toward Slash and yelled, "Help me!"

Slash and Pecos shared a wide-eyed look of eager anticipation and then both men scrambled like oversized rats to the back of the cabin.

CHAPTER 5

"Pete dug this escape tunnel in case the hideout was ever discovered and attacked," Jay said, her voice disembodied in the musty darkness beneath the cabin. "I've never had to use it . . . till now."

Slash and Pecos crouched around her. They'd both quickly grabbed their saddlebags after Slash had pried the door up out of the floor, and now they held the bags over their shoulders in the cool, damp darkness. Slash couldn't see anything except the stygian black pushing up close around him.

He heard the muffled shooting through the cabin's floor above his head, smelled the smoke licking through the cracks in the trapdoor.

A scraping sound. A match flickered to life in Jay's hand. "Hold that."

She handed the match to Pecos, then plucked one of three tree branches, whose ends were wrapped in old flour sacks, from a small vegetable crate. She tipped a rusty can over the flour sack end of the branch, and the acrid odor told Slash that the liquid she poured into the burlap was pine tar.

She tipped the branch to the match in Pecos's hand, and

the flames grew into a ragged orange ball around the sacking, shoving the coal-black shadows farther back away from the trio hunched there in a tight group beneath the closed trapdoor. Now Slash could see the earthen sides of the tunnel, which was only about five feet high and five feet wide. Wooden steps to his right, coated with grime and spiderwebs, angled up toward the trapdoor through which smoke continued to slither, fouling the tunnel's pent-up air.

Jay pushed between Slash and Pecos and, holding the flaming torch out in front of her, began crawling on hands and knees. In her right hand was Pistol Pete's Spencer rifle. His old Colt Navys bristled on her lean hips.

"Has this been here all the time?" Pecos asked as, crawling, he fell into line behind Slash, both men following the torch-wielding woman along the musty tunnel.

"Pete dug it the year after we moved into the cabin. Be glad you never had to know about it," Jay said, adding dryly, "till now."

"We sure are sorry, Jay," Slash said, crawling and sort of dragging his Winchester along beside him, his saddlebags hanging off his left shoulder. He kept his head low so his hat wouldn't rake the tunnel's low ceiling. "I don't know how in the hell Penny followed us here, but—"

"Forget it, Slash," Jay said, breathing hard ahead of him, keeping the flaming torch raised in front of her.

Slash followed her, staying close on the heels of her high-heeled, high-top leather boots. His embarrassment and self-revulsion at having led bounty hunters here to burn the woman's home were equaled only by the rage burning just behind his heart. He could feel it tingling in the fingers wrapped around his Winchester's neck, in his eyes, in his toes.

He could tell from Pecos's grim silence that his partner shared his sentiment.

If they made it out of here and could circle around behind the bounty hunters, Jack Penny would die hard.

Finally, after about sixty yards of crawling on their hands and knees, they came to what appeared a wall.

The end?

Jay glanced over her shoulder at Slash and Pecos coming up behind her. "We just have to hope nothing has blocked the door over the years." She hammered the back of her fist against what sounded like wood.

"Pete only came down here a few times after he dug the tunnel, to make sure it was still open. If a tree or rocks or something has fallen down over the door, we'll be trapped in here. The only way back is . . ."

"Through the burning cabin," Slash finished for her. "Then, thanks to me an' Pecos, you'll die with us . . . in Pete's escape tunnel."

"I told you to shut up about that!"

Jay rammed her shoulder against the door. As far as Slash could tell, the door didn't move.

"Let me try."

Slash slid around her, and Jay drew back. Slash rammed his left shoulder against the door.

Nothing. It felt solid.

He rammed his right shoulder against the door.

Again, nothing. A dark dread began oozing into his belly, making him feel sick. He was suddenly starting to feel as though they'd all been buried alive.

He turned sideways and drew back away from the door, glancing at Pecos.

"Get over here, you big lummox. Your turn."

"No need for name callin'." Pecos's deep voice sounded brittle, betraying his own anxiety.

He sidled up to the door and, on his hands and knees, bunched his lips and rammed his right shoulder against the door.

"Harder," Slash said.

Pecos rammed his shoulder harder against the door.

"Harder!" Slash said.

Again, Pecos rammed his shoulder against the door, this time with a grunt.

"Oh, come on, Pecos," Slash berated him. "You can do better than that. You're embarrassin' yourself in front of the lady!"

"Yes," Jay said, chiming in. "Why don't you put a little muscle into it, Pecos? Put those shoulders to good use!"

Pecos glared at them both, then pulled farther back from the door, giving himself some room with which to build up some momentum. With another fierce grunt, he slammed his shoulder against the door.

"Ahhh, *helllll*!"

The big man disappeared into a sudden explosion of lemony sunlight.

Slash blinked against the light, blocking the glare with one hand. As his eyes adjusted, he saw that the door had given way. In fact, it had totally disappeared.

Along with Pecos himself.

Slash crawled forward to poke his head out the tunnel's back door, which opened onto the side of a ravine gaping thirty feet below. Pecos was on the slope directly below the yawning doorway, rolling . . . rolling . . . rolling down the slope until he piled up with a grunt at the ravine's bottom.

During the roll, he'd lost his rifle as well as the sawed-off shotgun that had been hanging down his back. He'd also lost the Russian, which rolled down the slope to land beside him now on the ravine's floor covered with flood-scalloped sand, rocks, and sun-bleached driftwood.

Jay shouldered up to Slash to poke her head out of the doorway.

Gazing down at Pecos, she made a face and said, "I

reckon I should have told you the door opened out over an arroyo!"

Pecos sat up stiffly, grunting. Dirt and other debris clung to his long hair. In fact, it covered nearly every inch of his big frame. He shook his head as if to clear the cobwebs from his brain as well as the dirt from his hair, and glared up the slope at Slash and Jay staring down at him.

"I might've broke my neck!" he said.

"Oh, come on," Slash said, grinning as he stepped gingerly out of the tunnel, placing one foot and then the other firmly down on the gravel-carpeted slope. "You couldn't break that thick neck of yours with a sledgehammer!"

He offered Jay his hand. "My dear?"

"Why, thank you, kind sir," Jay said, as though a royal gentleman were helping her out of a golden carriage. "Your chivalry knows no bounds."

She dropped the torch in a mound of sand, and the flame sputtered out.

Slash led her down the slope, following the scuffed track that Pecos had carved with his body. Once on the canyon floor, where Pecos groaned and flexed each brawny arm in turn, working out the soreness and the stiffness, Slash leaned his rifle against the bank of the arroyo and then walked back up the slope, retrieving Pecos's guns and hat.

When Slash gained the arroyo floor again, Jay was standing over Pecos, massaging his shoulders while Pecos grunted and groaned and spat dirt and sand from his mouth.

"Here you go, pardner," Slash said. "You look a little worse for the wear."

Pecos glared up at him. "I feel a little worse for the wear!"

"Now, don't get your neck in a hump, ya sissy!" Slash stared up the slope, at the gray-black column of smoke unfurling against the sky far above. The gunfire had died.

The bounty hunters likely figured their quarry had burned up in the cabin.

Hardening his jaws, Slash picked up his rifle and loudly racked a cartridge into the action. "Time to hunt us some rats. Those rats we let shadow us here to burn Jay's house down!"

"I hear that!" The notion of revenge appeared to snap the big outlaw from his stupor. Pecos placed his hands on the ground, heaved himself to his feet, and shoved his pistol into its holster. He slung his double-barreled shotgun behind his back and picked up his Colt rifle. "I'm ready, dammit! Let's go, Slash! You best wait here, Jay."

Jay grabbed Pecos's arm. "Fellas?"

"What is it?" Slash asked.

"Before you go, you have to know something."

Slash turned to her, concerned. "What is it?"

She kept one hand on Pecos's arm and closed her other hand over Slash's. She looked up at both men. "It wasn't you who led those men here. I did."

"You?" Pecos said in shock.

"What're you talking about, Jay?" Slash asked.

"Oh, I didn't mean to, of course. But I . . . I got careless." Jay backed up a step, crossed her arms on her chest, looked away in shame. "I . . . got lonely. One day I was riding through the mountains and I came across the man who owns a ranch near here. I . . . I got to know him. From time to time, when I knew he was working in the area, I took him picnic lunches. Eventually . . . I . . . I brought him here. Cooked him meals. Sometimes . . . sometimes he didn't leave until after breakfast. The next morning."

She hardened her jaw and shook her head in disgust. "Like a fool, I brought him here, to our hideout!"

"You don't need to explain, Jay," Slash said gently.

"Yes, I do."

"No, you don't," Pecos said. "You're a pretty woman, Jay. Pete's been dead nigh on five years. You've been livin' alone up here for five years. No one could blame you for . . ."

"That's not the part I'm ashamed of. Of course, I was lonely. You two don't come around all that often anymore, and since Pete died, you're about the only two men I ever keep company with. I hardly see anyone at all between trips to town for supplies. I have no friends . . . except you two."

"The only part I don't get," Slash said, "is . . . how did you lead Penny here?"

"I rode to town one day and I saw Ed—he's the rancher I got to know, Ed Ritter—talking to a big, bearded man out front of one of the saloons. Ed didn't see me—there was a lot of traffic on the street that day, but I had a strange feeling about the man he was talking to. Ever since that day—it must have been six weeks ago now—I've had the strange feeling someone has been keeping an eye on me and the cabin. When I've taken my horse out for rides around the mountains, I've sensed someone keeping pace with me, watching me.

"One day, I saw someone from a distance. He was just a man-shaped shadow, watching me from some trees just below a ridgeline. I didn't put it together until a few minutes ago, but I think the man who was shadowing me must've been one of Jack Penny's men. I have a strong feeling that the man Ed was talking to in town that day was Penny."

"Penny is a big, bearded hombre for sure," Pecos said to Slash.

"Tall, lanky man with a ratty beard," Slash said to Jay. He gestured toward his left eye. "With one wandering eye."

Jay nodded slowly, darkly. "That was him." She drew a deep breath, released it slowly. "He probably knew that Ed Ritter ranched in these mountains, and that's why he was talking to Ed that day. He probably offered Ed money for information about you two. He might've even offered him a cut of the bounty on your heads."

Jay paused, then added, "I haven't seen Ed anywhere near the cabin since then. He's been staying away from me out of shame, no doubt, for informing Penny where the cabin is." She glanced at the dark smoke unraveling against the sky. "Was."

Slash thought about Jay's story, then asked, "How would Ed have known you were connected to me an' Pecos?"

"He wouldn't have. I certainly didn't tell him. He just suspected, most likely. Suspicion based on rumors, probably, though he never let on to me about those suspicions. Those suspicions were likely confirmed when he spoke to Penny. After talking to Ed, Penny posted a spy to keep an eye on me and the place."

Jay's cheeks colored with rising emotion as she shifted her angry gaze between Slash and Pecos. "They were setting a trap for you two. They were biding their time, waiting to spring it. The spy must have seen you two ride up here yesterday—he was probably well hid, on a distant ridge, no doubt—and then rode to town to inform Penny. His gang probably rode all night to get here. To spring their trap."

Jay grabbed each man's arm again and squeezed. "I'm so sorry, boys! This was all my fault. It wasn't *you*. It was *me*. I got careless!"

"Good to hear," Pecos said. "For a while there, I thought me an' Slash were the only careless ones." The big brigand kissed Jay's cheek.

Slash kissed her other cheek. "Pecos is right. That may be the first time in his life he was right about anything."

Pecos grunted.

Slash set his rifle on his shoulder. "Stay here, Jay. We've got bounty hunters to hunt."

"No, I'm going with you." Jay grabbed her own repeater

from where it had been leaning against a rock. As Slash and Pecos began to object, she held up a hand to shush them both. "I'll stay back when the lead starts flying. But I want to be close, in case you boys need tendin'."

Slash looked at Pecos and shrugged. "Good enough."

He swung around and began striding along the arroyo, Pecos and Jay falling into step behind him.

CHAPTER 6

Ten minutes later, Slash and Pecos climbed a rocky, brushy slope, Jay following from ten feet behind them, her red hair glowing surreal copper in the crisp, midday sunshine.

Slash slid a glance around a low escarpment ahead and above him, and then pulled his head down sharply and gave a low hiss. He dropped to a knee, and then Pecos did, as well, the big man questioning Slash with his gaze.

"Horses on the other side of the scarp," Slash whispered.

"Anyone with 'em?"

"One man as far as I could tell." Slash glanced at Jay, who dropped to a knee just down the slope from him and Pecos. Slash said, "You two wait here. There's a man with the horses. I'm gonna take care of him."

"Be careful," Jay whispered.

Slash handed Pecos his rifle. Rising from his knee, he moved slowly up to the scarp and stepped around to its far left edge.

He doffed his hat and then leaned his head forward, casting a glance around the scarp to where a dozen or so horses were tied to a long picket line in the pines about thirty feet up the slope. The man Slash had glimpsed was sitting on a rock to the right of the horses, nearly directly above the scarp.

His back faced Slash. He was hunkered forward over his knees, and he appeared to be whittling. Slash recognized him by the grisly scar on his sun-seared neck, showing below his brown, ragged bowler hat and his close-cropped, gray-flecked hair.

Rex Schmidt.

When the no-account ex–mule skinner had been working with another, smaller team of bounty hunters six years ago, they'd set up an ambush against Slash and Pecos on the dry plains of western Kansas. They'd shot up the gang, killing four Snake River Marauders and wounding two others including the young man Slash had come to love as his son, Clayton Henry. Young Clayton had suffered badly from the two bullet wounds over the next two weeks until, when the gang had ridden clear down into southern Colorado, he'd finally died late one night, sobbing in Slash's arms.

Schmidt had been the only one of those three cowardly, back-shooting bounty hunters who'd made it away alive that day, fleeing hell for leather on a dapple-gray gelding, leaving a clear trail of blood in the bromegrass and sage. Slash had heard that Schmidt had been seen lately walking with a pronounced limp, and he'd assumed with satisfaction it had come from one of the Marauders' own bullets that day of the bushwhack.

That had made Slash smile. But it hadn't been enough.

He'd longed to avenge the cowardly killing of Clayton Henry.

Slash smiled now as he slid his bowie knife from its sheath on his right hip, where it rode behind the holstered .44 on that side, and took several quiet steps straight out from the escarpment. He glanced toward the horses cropping grass and switching their tails ahead and on his left, the sunlight glistening in their coats.

A couple of the mounts had winded Slash. He could tell that one, whose ears were twitching, was about to whinny a warning to Schmidt, so he dropped to a knee and let it happen. The copper bay whickered as expected. Schmidt dropped the stick he'd been whittling and, rising and grabbing the rifle leaning at his side, quickly turned—awkwardly, due to his stiff left leg

"Wha—huh?" he grunted, holding his pocket knife in one hand, the rifle in his other hand.

"Hidy, Rex," Slash said as he flicked the bowie from just behind his right ear, thrusting it forward.

He watched in satisfaction as the twelve inches of tempered steel jutting straight out from the staghorn handle flew end over end, flashing in the sunshine filtering through the forest canopy.

Rex saw the flashing bowie as well, and he grimaced suddenly, as though he'd swigged sour milk.

Knowing he was doomed and there wasn't one damn thing he could do about it, his eyes grew wide, crossing slightly as the bowie vaulted toward him, whistling softly, arcing upward and then downward before, just as the blade turned forward from the handle again, it disappeared into Schmidt's chest with a resolute, crunching *snick*, splitting his breastbone and impaling his heart.

Rex had opened his mouth to call out a warning to the rest of the bounty hunters, but words failed him. As the bowie sliced his heart in two, he only showed his teeth in an agonized grimace and stumbled straight backward, wobbling like a drunk.

He dropped his pocketknife and his rifle and slapped both hands to the bowie's blade. He tried desperately to pull the knife out of his chest, staring down at the silver blade in horror.

But then he weakened. His arms dropped to his sides. He flopped backward against the ground.

Slash straightened slowly, looked around. None of the other bounty hunters appeared to be in the close vicinity. Another horse whickered nervously but not loudly enough to alert the rest of the gang near the cabin, sixty or seventy yards beyond. Or so Slash hoped.

He moved forward quietly and stared down at Rex Schmidt dying hard on the ground before him. Schmidt had a long, horsey, unshaven face from which all the blood had drained. He stared up in mute horror at Slash, his mouth forming a dark O between thin, chapped lips.

Slash crouched over the man, smiling.

"Hi, Rex. How you doin', pard?"

He placed a boot on Schmidt's belly and jerked the bowie knife free of the man's chest.

"Not feelin' too good, Rex?" Slash cleaned the bowie's blade on Schmidt's grungy broadcloth coat. "Yeah, well, Clayton Henry wasn't feelin' too good either, all those days he lingered with your lead in his back."

The bounty hunter's mouth moved, but he only groaned as he stared up at Slash, his coyote-yellow eyes cast with both fury and raw terror.

Slash glanced over his shoulder as Pecos walked up behind him, staring down at Schmidt, grunting with satisfaction when he recognized him.

Pecos glanced at Slash. "Gonna finish him?"

Slash shook his head as he continued to stare down at the shivering Schmidt. "Let him die slow. It's better'n what he deserves."

"I hear that."

Jay came around from behind the escarpment, and Slash walked quickly over to her, taking her arm and leading her wide around the hard-dying bounty hunter. "You don't need to see that."

Despite the warning, Jay looked around him at Schmidt and, as Slash led her ahead through the pine forest, she said, "You're rather efficient—aren't you, Slash?"

"Schmidt and me got history." As Pecos moved up behind them, Slash turned to Jay once more. "You wait here, now, Jay. Pecos and I are gonna go on ahead. If all goes well, we'll fetch you in a few minutes."

"Should be able to take 'em by surprise," Pecos said, gazing off through the pine branches as he held his rifle up high across his chest, his shotgun bristling behind him. "They're prob'ly just waitin' for the fire to die down so they can sift the ashes for our bodies. They'll be wantin' somethin' to take to Bledsoe. Somethin' he can identify."

Jay nodded. "I'll stay here. Be careful, you two. You're badly outnumbered."

"We been there before," Pecos told her.

Slash gave her a reassuring smile, then squeezed her arm. "Remember—stay here. No matter what you hear. If it ain't us that comes back through these trees, you light out on one of them horses."

"I heard you the first time, Slash. I will stay right here. I promise." Jay's plump, red lips shaped a smile beneath the broad brim of her brown Stetson.

"Okay."

Slash nodded at Pecos, and they moved off together through the pines.

As they approached the cabin's yard, they split up, Slash angling left, Pecos angling right. Slash saw a large rock at the edge of the forest, abutting the clearing in which the cabin sat. As he headed toward it, tracing a meandering route between the trees, he could hear men talking and laughing.

Anger blazed in him.

He dropped to a knee behind the rock, which slanted sharply downward on one side, and peered over the slanting top toward the cabin that had all but collapsed in on itself. Only the left wall remained partly standing, flames licking up from its base. The fire still burned but it had already done most of its destructive work and was beginning to die.

The old, dry timbers that the now-dead fur trapper had constructed it from offered the flames one hell of a feast.

The sight of the old hideout diminished to flames and charred rubble sickened Slash. The men gathered around in front of it, passing bottles, talking and laughing, fueled his fury the way those old timbers had fueled the fire.

His own inner conflagration burned even hotter when he saw one of Penny's men urinating into the flames at the edge of the cabin, where the stoop had stood only a few minutes ago. Another man, obviously drunk, laughed and pointed out the urinating man to the others, holding a bottle in one hand, a rifle in the other.

There were thirteen bounty hunters. They stood in three loosely bunched groups around the front of the cabin. They were talking and laughing like men at a barn dance who'd stepped out to get a drink and a smoke.

Slash swept the rough bunch with his enraged eyes and picked out the big, fat, bearded Penny. Clad in greasy, smoke-stained buckskins and a calico shirt, the bounty-hunting leader stood to the far left of the bunch with a shorter man whom Slash didn't recognize. Even from this distance of fifty yards, Slash could see the white around Penny's wandering left eye as the man threw his arms up and tipped his head back, laughing.

They were all reveling in the supposed demise of Slash Braddock and the Pecos River Kid along with the widow of Pistol Pete Johnson. To their minds, believing Slash and Rio dead, they'd cleaned up well. Several thousand dollars worth of well. Not to mention the prestige they'd acquired by taking down two of the West's most notorious cut-throats.

Their names would be mentioned in all the eastern news-papers and even in some history books, most likely.

Not a bad haul even given all the time the bounty hunters had spent waiting to spring their trap. Now they just had to hope there were enough remains of the two outlaws for Luther "Bleed-'Em-So" Bledsoe to identify.

Heart thudding, Slash quietly levered a round into his Yellowboy's action. He was about to rise from behind the rock and show himself when he heard the soft crackle of footsteps to his right. He turned that way, expecting to see Pecos walking toward him.

But it wasn't Pecos. It was Jay.

Unable to stay away from the burning cabin, no doubt irresistibly attracted by the thought of witnessing the bushwhackers' demise, she stepped up to the edge of the forest, holding Pistol Pete's old Spencer in her right hand.

"Jay!" Slash hissed.

Beyond her, he saw Pecos turn toward him. When the big, blond outlaw saw Jay, he looked beyond her at Slash, widening his eyes and throwing out his left arm in exas-peration.

"Jay!" Slash hissed again. "Get back, dammit!"

But then she must have seen the bounty hunter urinating on the cabin's ruins, for her mouth opened wide in shock and fury and she bolted forward, striding stiffly out of the trees and into the clearing, yelling, "You son of a bitch!"

The fire and the bounty hunters' own voices must have been loud enough that they'd drowned Jay's yell. Those few who had heard it turned toward the woman as she raised Pete's rifle to her shoulder, quickly aimed down the barrel, and fired. The bullet sent the urinating man plung-ing straight forward into the flames with a scream.

He screamed louder—much louder—when he hit the flames and flopped around, rolling as the flames engulfed him.

The other bounty hunters had heard Jay's rifle report as well as their cohort's screams. They wheeled, bringing weapons to bear on the redheaded woman storming toward them. Jay paused only to work her Spencer's trigger guard cocking mechanism, sliding another cartridge into the old rifle's breech.

"Dammit!" Slash bellowed, heart racing as he frantically ran out from behind the slanting rock, raising the Yellowboy to his right shoulder and going to work hurling lead toward the bounty hunters.

As he ran, he automatically triggered the Yellowboy and worked the cocking lever, the Winchester leaping in his hands, stabbing flames toward the bounty hunters, who were just then dropping their bottles and cigarettes as they realized their quarry had flanked them.

"Oh, hell!" Slash said mostly to himself as he ran.

Several bounty hunters had raised their own weapons and were triggering shots toward Jay.

CHAPTER 7

"Jay, dammit, get down!"

Slash bulled into the woman, and they hit the ground together, Slash sprawling on top of her, shielding her from the bullets that now screeched through the air above them.

"Fool woman!" he bellowed, rising to a knee and picking out targets.

To his right, Pecos had gone to work with his own rifle, and several bounty hunters were jerking and dropping. Slash planted a bead on a long-haired man in a cream duster, and fired. His target screamed and inadvertently shot one of his brethren as he twisted around and fell.

Slash finished the man the long-haired man had drilled in the knee, then swung the Yellowboy to the left and quickly laid out two more of the bushwhackers, his spent cartridges arcing up and over his right shoulder, his own powder smoke wafting around him. Two more men fired on him from his left, off the burning cabin's west front corner.

The slugs thudded into the dry grass around Slash and Jay, whom he could feel jerking with frightened starts beneath him.

Slash ejected another spent cartridge, then planted a bead on the chest of one of the men ahead and on his left, and squeezed the trigger. The man's head jerked back, lower jaw dropping, eyes widening. A quarter-sized hole shone in the dead center of his forehead. He opened his hands and dropped his Winchester '73 and flopped backward in a patch of fire-scorched grass, small flames licking around him, causing his shirt and greasy denims to smoke.

The other man triggered his Spencer, and Slash felt a grinding burn across his upper left arm. He cursed as he returned fire, but he'd jerked to one side with the force of the bullet slamming into him, and his bullet nudged wide. It struck the back of the head of a wounded bounty hunter trying to crawl away, to the right of his intended target.

Slash's intended target tried to fire another round toward Slash but his rifle clicked, empty. The bounty hunter cursed, threw down his rifle, rose, and turned and ran straight out to the west of the cabin, leaping over several of his dead cohorts.

Slash lined up the sights on the fleeing man's back, but when he squeezed the trigger, he discovered that his own rifle was empty.

Pecos must have emptied his Colt revolving rifle, because just then Slash heard the dynamite-like explosion of his partner's sawed-off twelve-gauge, followed by the agonized wail of the gut-shredder's victim. Slash glanced to his right in time to see Pecos walking out away from him, to the east, toward where one of the few surviving hunters was running toward the trees ringing the clearing and snapping off shots at Pecos with a revolver.

The revolver leaped and smoked in the running man's hand.

Pecos stopped, crouched over his short, stout barn-blaster.

Pumpkin-sized flames blossomed from the maws of the small cannon, and the running man gave a chortling cry as the double-ought buckshot tore into him, hurling him into the trees where he dropped and rolled, screaming.

Pecos tossed the shotgun around behind his back, where it dangled from his neck and shoulder by its wide leather lanyard. The big outlaw drew his big, silver-chased Russian as he strode with grim purpose toward the place in the trees where his quarry had fallen, intending to finish the wailing man with a .44 round to the head.

"Stay down, you hear?" Slash told Jay, who gave a contrite nod beneath him.

Slash rose and looked around. Only one of the several bounty hunters lying in bloody heaps was moving. Quickly wrapping a handkerchief around the bullet burn across his right arm, Slash drew his Colt, and a second later the last moving bounty hunter in the near vicinity was no longer moving.

Slash gazed off to the west. He could no longer see the man who'd fled, but he could hear his running foot thuds dwindling gradually in the trees that dropped down a gradual slope.

"Is that all of 'em?" Pecos asked, walking up behind Slash now. He'd broken open his shotgun and was replacing the spent wads with fresh ones from his cartridge belt.

"One of 'em is makin' a run for it," Slash said. "You stay here with Jay. I'll finish him."

Pecos nodded at the blood showing on the handkerchief on Slash's upper left arm. "You hit?"

Slash glanced at his arm. "I been cut worse trimming my fingernails."

He shoved his Colt into its holster. Pulling a large hanky out of his rear pants pocket and wrapping it around the bloody burn, he broke into a run to the west. When he gained the forest on that side of the yard, he knotted the hanky, cursing the bite of pain surging up and down that arm, then slowed his pace as he strode into the forest.

The man who'd fled might be lying in wait.

When Slash had moved ten yards slowly, he heard the running foot thuds again. He spied movement ahead. The man who'd fled the dustup was running up a low, forested hill about fifty yards beyond. The man was breathing hard, grunting and groaning anxiously. He'd lost his hat, and he cast frequent, wide-eyed glances back over his left shoulder.

"Coward!" Slash raised his Colt and triggered a shot.

The bullet plumed forest duff well short of the fleeing man's boots.

The man glanced again over his left shoulder. He gave a mocking smile just before he crested the hill and dropped down the opposite side.

Again, Slash broke into a run. When he gained the bottom of the hill he scrambled up the next rise, where he'd last seen the fleeing ambusher. As he crested that hill, he stopped beside a large cedar. He heard the thuds of galloping horses. Now he saw the riders on the next ridge beyond—two horse-and-rider-shaped silhouettes galloping along the crest of that western ridge, angling away from Slash.

The man Slash was pursuing just then gained the crest of that ridge, catching up to the lead rider. He clawed at the man's saddle, yelling, "Pull me up, Jack!"

"Get away, Haskell, you fool!"

Haskell leaped along behind the lead rider's horse, trying in vain to leap onto the horse's back. "Dammit, Jack, pull me up!"

"Let go or I'll gun ya!" The big lead rider bashed his pistol butt against Haskell's head.

Haskell fell and rolled.

The second rider, a smaller man wearing a bright red

neckerchief, reined his calico to a prancing halt, drew his own pistol, and aimed down at where Haskell was rolling up onto his hip and shoulder in a cloud of dust and pine needles. The pistol bucked and roared.

Haskell screamed, dropped, and rolled down the hill through the trees.

"There—I gunned him!" said the second rider with an anxious laugh, holstering his six-shooter and ramming his spurred boots into the calico's flanks.

Slash gazed in bald fury at the two fleeing riders.

The lead man was Jack Penny himself. Slash thought he recognized the second, smaller man as Penny's first lieutenant, Bart Antrim. Somehow, they must have realized even before the shooting had started that Slash and Pecos had the drop on them, and they decided to live to fight another day. They'd hightailed it like the cowards both men were known to be and circled back to their horses.

Slash hadn't noticed because he'd been preoccupied with trying to keep Jay from getting her head blown off.

He dropped to one knee now and, even knowing the Colt was well out of range, triggered three shots toward the two fleeing riders. Both bounty hunters glanced over their shoulders in Slash's direction. Then they jounced off into the trees and out of sight.

Slash stood, cupped a hand to his mouth, and yelled, "Some other time, Jack!"

His voice had just stopped echoing when Penny responded with: "Some other time, Slash!"

Slash muttered a curse and then, fury still roaring in him, he flicked open the smoking Colt's loading gate and plucked out the spent shells. He replaced them with fresh ones from his cartridge belt, closed the loading gate, spun the cylinder, and dropped the piece smoothly into the cross-draw holster on his left hip, snapping the keeper thong into place over the hammer.

Still grumbling about Penny and Antrim getting away but assuring himself he and Pecos would run into them again soon—and that the bounty hunters wouldn't be nearly as lucky next time—he walked back in the direction of the cabin. As he crested the last hill, Pecos stepped out of the clearing and into the trees to meet him.

"Penny and Antrim?"

"Yeah."

"I figured. I didn't see either man's body, and I looked at all of 'em. Dang!"

"We'll get 'em. Eventually."

"What a damn mess, Slash," Pecos lamented, turning back to gaze into the smoky, sunlit clearing. Eleven bounty hunters lay dead around the still-burning cabin. "Look what those devils done to the hideout."

"We'll rebuild the place. For Jay." Slash looked around, then frowned and turned to Pecos. "Speaking of her, where is she, anyways?"

A horse whinnied. Hooves thudded.

Slash and Pecos turned to peer off across the smoky clearing, toward where a small log stable and corral sat back in the brush a good distance from the cabin. A horse and rider bounded out of the trees to the stable's left and galloped west. Jay straddled her steeldust gelding, which she called Good South, the direction the horse always faced when grazing. Her red hair bouncing on her shoulders, hunkered low over the steeldust's dark, billowing mane, Jay galloped into the trees and out of sight, hoof thuds dwindling gradually in her wake.

Pecos turned to Slash. "What in tarnation?"

"Yeah." Slash stared off in the direction she'd disappeared. "Where's she goin' like a bat out of hell?"

Jay galloped Good South down a long, sloping hill northwest of the clearing in which her cabin was still burning and around which the bounty hunters lay strewn as though they'd been dropped from the sky.

Not only the cabin was burning. Everything Jaycee Breckenridge owned—except the clothes she wore and Pistol Pete's two conversion pistols holstered on her lean hips and the Spencer repeater he'd wielded during all his years riding the long coulees of the western frontier—was turning to ashes inside the burning cabin.

All gone.

You might say Jay's very life had burned up in that cabin, along with everything she owned. At the moment she was too enraged to feel grateful that she had escaped with her life, at least. And that her two old friends, Slash and Pecos, had escaped as well.

She'd been betrayed by the only man she'd allowed to get close to her in the five years since Pete's death. Betrayed for money.

Ahead of her, at the foot of a hulking, forested ridge, lay a small ranch headquarters—a long, low, shake-shingled log cabin and a barn, stable, blacksmith shop, and several corrals. A small log bunkhouse flanked the main house, partly concealed by the pines that climbed the northern ridge.

Jay galloped under the ranch portal in whose overarching crossbar was burned the turkey track brand to each side of the name RITTER.

CHAPTER 8

Ed Ritter, owner of the Turkey Track Ranch, had visited Jay's cabin quite a few times over the past year. And he'd always left with a smile on his face.

He wasn't smiling now, Jay noticed, as he stood staring at her from the corral near the rancher's cabin. He stood near the corral's front gate with another, shorter, older man wearing a battered, funnel-brimmed Stetson. He was likely Ritter's hired hand, Howard Long. Ritter himself, in his mid-forties, was a tall, slightly stoop-shouldered man in baggy denims, suspenders, and a light blue work shirt that showed a long, dark patch of sweat down the front.

He was scowling out from beneath the floppy brim of his shapeless, dark felt hat. He was raising one hand, shielding his eyes from the sun. He stood very still, staring without expression, though as Jay drew the steeldust nearer the rancher and the older man, she thought she saw shock in the rancher's dark blue eyes. He was tall and slender, appealing of body if not of face due to his small chin and a callow dullness in his eyes that she probably would have recognized as an indication of a weak character if she'd taken the time to be more discerning.

But there weren't many men out here. Besides, she'd

enjoyed talking with Ed and cooking for him and just having a man about the house from time to time. To spend the occasional night with and to cook breakfast for in the morning.

Now, however, as he stood staring at her dully, she saw in his face all that she hadn't taken adequate note of before.

As he stood staring at her near the gate he and the other man were repairing, one hand holding a hammer, the other hand shielding his eyes, a nail drooping from between his lips, his sunburned cheeks turned a darker red. His rounded shoulders, from which overlong, apelike arms drooped, sagged beneath the weight of his guilt. His eyes slowly widened, accentuating their shallowness and animal stupidity.

As Jay sat the steeldust sideways to him, thirty yards away from the corral, the man she now saw as an apelike dimwit drew a slow, deep breath that made his shoulders and long arms rise slowly.

"Did you take money from Jack Penny?" Jay asked in a low, even voice that did not betray the anger roiling inside her. She could not stop her bottom lip from quivering, however. Nor a single tear from dribbling down her cheek.

"H-hold on," Ritter said, turning the hand he'd been shading his eyes with palm outward. He dropped the hammer as well as the nail from between his lips and stepped sideways, away from the gate. "Hold on, now . . ."

"Did you take money from Jack Penny?" Jay asked again, louder, more firmly.

The old man who'd been crouching over the other end of the gate straightened slowly and gave a foxy grin as he turned toward Ritter and said, "What'd you do?"

"Hold on, now," Ritter said to Jay, tripping over his own big feet as he sidled in the direction of his cabin.

Slowly, hardening her jaws and ignoring more tears dribbling stubbornly out of her eyes, Jay unsnapped the keeper thong from over one of Pistol Pete's two Colt Navys bristling on her hips and slid the bulky piece from its holster.

"Now, just hold on!" Ritter yelled as he sidestepped more quickly toward the safety of the cabin.

Jay raised the Colt, clicked the hammer back, and aimed down the barrel. She triggered a bullet into the ground six inches left of Ed Ritter's sidestepping feet.

"Hey!" Ritter barked, eyes suddenly glassy with terror. "You stop now! Get off my land! You're trespassin' on—!"

"You told Penny where I lived!" Jay triggered another round into the dirt near Ritter's boots.

The rancher held both his large, gloved hands up, palms out. "No! No! No, I didn't!"

Jay swung smoothly down from the steeldust's back. "You did!"

"Hold on, now . . . I never . . . I didn't know . . ."

"That he'd burn me out?" Jay glanced over her shoulder. Dark smoke from her burning cabin uncurled in a thinning column from behind several eastern ridges. Turning back to Ritter, she said, "You had to know he was a bounty hunter. What'd you think he was going to do—ask me to a barn dance?"

Ritter continued to sidle toward his cabin, hemming and hawing, eyes wide in terror beneath his shapeless hat. "I . . . I . . . I didn't . . . I didn't . . . !"

He looked at Jay narrowing one eye down the barrel of her Colt at him, and his eyes snapped even wider in terror. He wheeled and bolted into a shambling run toward the cabin, his hat blowing off his head and dropping into the dirt behind him.

Jay triggered another shot into the dirt just behind his boot.

Ritter screamed as he tripped over his own feet and dropped to his knees.

Walking slowly toward the fleeing rancher, Jay fired again into the dirt just behind Ritter, who gave a frightened grunt, then scrambled to his feet once more and continued running toward the cabin, bellowing, "Crazy bitch—you're on private land!"

Again, Jay fired into the dirt around his running feet.

Ritter leaped up onto the porch rail. He scrambled over it wildly, like a dog trying to climb a tree after a squirrel. As Jay drilled a round into the porch rail near his head, Ritter threw himself over the rail to the porch floor with a heavy thud and a groan. He stared in horror between the rails, saw Jay striding toward him, her upper lip curled, and he scrambled once more to his feet.

Ritter ran to the door, fumbled it open, and disappeared inside.

As Jay walked toward the porch steps, she glanced at the old man staring at her skeptically from the corral. He was holding a hammer in one hand, a board in the other hand.

"You stay out of this, old-timer," Jay warned.

The old man gave a crooked, chip-toothed smile and chuckled. "Hell, I'm enjoyin' the show!"

As Jay mounted the porch's first step, shambling boot thuds sounded inside the cabin. Ritter appeared in the open doorway, cocking a carbine. "Get out! Get outta here, you crazy bitch, or I'll—"

Jay raised the Colt and fired.

Ritter grimaced, eyes snapping wide in shock. He stumbled backward, cursing, dropping his rifle and looking at the ragged hole in his right shirtsleeve. Blood bubbled out of the hole.

"You shot me!" Ritter bellowed, stumbling farther backward into the cabin.

Jay calmly, resolutely climbed the porch steps.

"You shot me!" the rancher bellowed again, staring aghast as Jay crossed the porch and stepped through the cabin's open doorway.

He stumbled over his boots and dropped to his butt about ten feet inside the cabin, between the living area and the kitchen area, to the right of a long eating table. Clutching his arm, he gritted teeth and glared up at Jay, who dropped her empty Colt into its holster. She pulled the second Colt from the other holster, clicked the hammer back, and narrowed one hazel eye as she aimed down the barrel at Ritter's lightly freckled forehead.

"No!" the rancher cried, wincing and turning his head away, dreadfully awaiting the kill shot.

"You knew who I was," Jay said. "You knew I was Pete Johnson's woman. But you never let on."

"Hell, everyone knows!"

Jay frowned, puzzled. "Everyone?"

"Hell, you been in these mountains years now! Don't you think a few folks might've figured it out by now? You don't have any cattle on your place. Only a few horses. Strange men come and go from the cabin once in a while . . . but mostly you're alone. Hell, I recognized Pistol Pete when he was leavin' your place a long time ago. I seen Slash Braddock and the Pecos River Kid, too!"

The rancher gave a caustic laugh. "Hell, I knew who you were. I knew what kinda woman you were—don't think I didn't!"

"Oh?" Jay arched a brow, trying to keep her emotion on a short leash. "You knew what kind of woman I was, eh? What kind of woman was that?"

She paused, awaiting an answer.

Breathing hard, keeping his right hand clutched to his bloody left arm, Ritter moved his lips but didn't say anything. His dull gaze acquired a hesitant, uncertain cast as he looked around the cabin as though hoping for the right response to the question.

"What kind of a woman do you think I am?" Jay asked tightly.

"A, uh . . ." Ritter licked his lips, then shot Jay a fiery look once more. "You get the hell outta here! You're trespassin' on—!"

Jay drilled a bullet into the rug six inches left of Ritter.

The rancher jerked with a start and yelped, "Hey!"

"I asked you a question, Ed," Jay said, taking one step forward, clicking back the hammer of her smoking Colt once more. "What kind of woman do you think I am? One low enough for you to spend the night with, to allow to cook for you. But one so low that you wouldn't invite her over to your own cabin. One so low you didn't want her around to soil your high and mighty reputation?"

Jay tried to hold the Colt steady in her right fist, but her fury made it shake.

She choked back an angry sob and said through gritted teeth, her voice rising bitterly, "A woman you can use for your pleasure and also one you could so easily betray to *bounty hunters for money?*"

"Oh, Jesus!" Ritter still had his head turned to one side, and he was shielding his face with his right hand, nearly sobbing. "Don't do it! Don't kill me!"

"Prepare to meet your maker, you gutless son of a bitch!"

"No!" The rancher scuttled backward across the floor, leaving a long, slender wet stain on the rug before him. "Don't kill me!"

Jay looked down at the urine dribbling down out of his right pants leg, splashing onto his boot and then staining the floor.

"No! Stop!"

Jay smiled as she lifted the Colt barrel up and depressed the hammer.

Ritter looked up at her, wrinkling his brows curiously, hopefully.

"I don't need to kill you," Jay said tightly, glancing at the wet stain on the rug. "I've revealed you for the gutless cur you are."

Ritter looked down at the rug. His face mottled ashen in shame.

Jay chuckled, swung around, and strode back outside. She stopped on the porch and stared out into the yard.

Evidently, Slash and Pecos had ridden into the yard when she'd been preoccupied with Ritter. They sat their horses—an Appaloosa and a big buckskin strong enough to hold Pecos's considerable bulk—where she'd left Good South. Pecos was holding the steeldust's reins as he and Slash sat slouched in their saddles, regarding Jay skeptically.

Jay moved down off the porch steps and turned to where the old man sat atop the corral, near where the broken gate leaned against it. He had a small flask in his hand, resting on his skinny right thigh clad in badly worn denim.

"You leave him alive?" he asked.

"He's alive," Jay said. "For what it's worth."

The old man smiled and lifted the flask in salute. "I got the afternoon off, I reckon!" He winked at Jay and drank.

Jay walked over to Slash and Pecos.

"You all right?" Slash asked her.

"Never better." She held out her hand, and Pecos tossed her the steeldust's reins. When she'd gotten seated in her saddle, she glanced at where the smoke from her cabin was thinning out against the southeastern sky, barely discernible now.

Turning to Slash and Pecos, she drew her mouth corners down and said, "Where to?"

Slash nodded toward purple-gray storm clouds building

in the north. "I don't know. But somewhere out of the weather."

He reined the Appaloosa around and touched spurs to its flanks. Pecos and Jay followed suit, and the three outlaws filed out under the ranch portal and galloped toward a notch in the next ridge to the east.

CHAPTER 9

"Make it hurt, Jay," Pecos said. "Make it hurt real bad. I wanna see ole Slash cry for once in his life!"

"Shut up, you corkheaded lummox!" Slash said through gritted teeth. "I don't cry over a pain. Only women." He grinned at Jay, who returned the smile in kind.

"You never cried over no woman in your whole life, Slash, you lyin' old coot! A poor poker hand, maybe. A woman—never!" Pecos laughed where he lay back against a wall of the cave in which they'd sought shelter, in a deep canyon several miles from their burned hideout. "Make it hurt real bad, Jay!"

Out in the well-dark night, thunder rumbled.

A slowly churning storm had been threatening rain for a couple of hours, but so far all it had managed was some kettledrum thunder and witches' fingers of blue-white lightning flashing over a near ridge.

Inside the cave, a smoky fire crackled and popped, shifting shadows along the cave's walls.

Slash, who had taken off his shirt and peeled his long-handle top down to his waist, laying his chest bare, sat back against his own saddle while Jaycee Breckenridge hunkered close against him, pinched up the skin around the bullet burn in his upper right arm, and poked her sewing needle through each side of the wound.

Slash gritted his teeth and took a pull from the bottle they'd found in the bounty hunters' saddlebags, after they'd unsaddled all the horses and turned them loose to forage on their own before some rancher from the area picked them up and accepted them into his own remuda.

"Does it hurt, Slash?" Pecos asked, grinning hopefully from the other side of the fire.

Slash took another pull from the bottle, shook his head, and swallowed. "Nope," he raked out, gritting his teeth again as Jay drew the thread through the skin, drawing the two flaps up snug against each other.

Pecos gazed on in shock as Jay pulled the thread taut. "You telling me that didn't hurt?"

"Nope," Slash said, taking another deep pull from the bottle. "Not a bit."

"Oh, come on!" Pecos lamented. "You could at least groan a little. You always try to act so tough. Like you're too good to show pain like everyone else."

"I think it's unseemly for grown men to caterwaul an' carry on an' such, the way you do over stubbing your toe." Slash chuckled.

Jay glanced from Slash to Pecos and asked, "Oh, come on, Pecos—you didn't really cry over a stubbed toe, did you?"

Pecos turned a little red and glanced away, embarrassed. "Well . . . dammit . . . it hurt."

"He's always cloudin' up and rainin'," Slash said, as thunder rumbled outside the cave and the air turned colder. "His horse steps on his foot and he tears up. You know how he's always fallin' in love? I mean, fallin' *hard*?"

"Yes, I know," Jay said, again poking the needle through Slash's pinched up skin. "I've heard both you an' Pete tell all about Pecos's romantic entanglements. Most of which," she added, pulling the thread through the wound and glancing again at the bigger of the two outlaws, "ended rather badly."

"Usually ended with him cryin'," Slash said, chuckling and tipping back the bottle once more.

"Well, I get attached, dammit," Pecos said, his big, broad face coloring with anger. "Some men actually fall in love, Slash. I'm one o' them. I got a big heart, and when I tumble for a girl, I tumble all the way down the stairs, across the parlor floor, and out onto the porch. Why, you've never tumbled in your life, have you?"

It was Slash's turn to flush with embarrassment.

Jay canted her head toward him, gazing into his face, plumbing his eyes as though to his soul. "How 'bout it, Slash? You know—I don't ever remember you talking about a woman."

He felt even more warmth under the pretty woman's gaze. It was as though her large, hazel eyes were glowing coals.

"Christ Almighty," Pecos said. "You turn any redder, I'm gonna start to think . . ." He stopped there, glancing from Slash's flushed face to Jay's, then back again. He sagged back in his saddle, chuckled as though to himself, then picked up his bottle again. He stared at Slash across the fire, shaping a knowing smile. "Never mind."

He chuckled again.

Slash quickly glanced at Jay, who continued to stare at him curiously.

"Do you mind if we get on with it?" he said with a grunt. "I'm gettin' right sleepy." He feigned a yawn. "Been a long day."

Jay's mouth corners rose faintly and then she nodded and continued sewing. "Right." She smiled, flushing a little now herself, and said, with too much cheer as though to conceal her own discomfort, "I'll have you all sewn up in three jangles of a doxie's bell. That was one of Pete's favorite expressions, if you remember."

"Oh, we remember," Slash said, snorting, but still feeling as though two hot irons were being held to his face. Wanting to change the subject, he turned to Jay once more and said gently, "Awful sorry about . . . well, about that fella. The rancher you took a shine to."

Pecos snickered. "But you sure handled him!"

"Yeah," Jay said, "I doubt very much that Mr. Ritter will be so quick to take for granted . . . or take advantage of . . . the next woman he meets."

"Don't doubt it a bit," Slash said, laughing. "I don't doubt he won't be so quick to take the next woman he meets for anything!"

They all chuckled.

As Jay drew the catgut through his wound once more, Slash said, "I just want you to know that me an' Pecos are going to stay here and help you rebuild. We're gonna stay for as long as it takes."

Jay poked the needle through Slash's skin once more, drew the thread taut, and cut it with a small folding knife. "That won't be necessary."

"What're you talkin' about?" Slash said after a quick, conferring look at Pecos. "Why won't it be necessary?"

"I don't intend to rebuild. It's high time I leave these mountains. It occurred to me while we were riding out here this afternoon that I've been holed up in that hideout, waiting for Pete to return these five long years that he's been buried in that grave, beneath all that dirt and rock."

Jay held Slash's arm out and poured whiskey from his bottle over the freshly sutured wound. Slash ground his teeth against the burn as he stared at the woman skeptically.

Jay looked at him and then at Pecos. "But he's never coming back. I think I finally realize that. And, with you two getting out of the bank-robbing business, you won't need the cabin anymore." She shrugged as she dabbed at Slash's wound with a soft cloth. "So I'm gonna pull my picket pin, boys. Pete left me with a stake. Almost a thousand dollars. I have it buried near the cabin. It's time I dug it up and used it just the way Pete wanted me to—to start a new life for myself in the event of his never coming back."

Slash whistled softly.

Pecos was sitting up now, arms locked around his upraised knee, his bottle in his hand. "What're you gonna do, Jay? Where you gonna go?"

Jay sighed as she wrapped a long strip of flannel around Slash's sutured arm. "That remains to be seen. Who knows? I might move to a little town and buy a saloon." She smiled as she finished wrapping Slash's arm, knotting the flannel gently over the wound. "Or maybe I'll open my own freighting business and give you boys some competition."

"Or you could throw in with us . . ." Slash suggested, leaning back against his saddle, raising one knee and resting his wounded arm across it.

As she stuffed her sewing kit back into her saddlebags, Jay turned to the dark-haired outlaw. "Is that a real invitation, Slash?"

Slash flushed a little again, averting his gaze and hiking a shoulder.

"Let's not get ahead of ourselves," Pecos said, tipping back his bottle. He pulled the whiskey down and brushed a sleeve of his long, black suit coat across his mouth. "We're gonna need us a stake of our own. An' we best do it quick before Becker sells his business out from under us."

"Pecos is right," Slash said as Jay stirred the pot of pinto beans and bacon she'd been cooking slowly on an iron spider mounted over the fire. "We're gonna need a job. One last takedown. A sizable one, too."

"Don't get your neck in a hump again, Pecos," Jay said with a wry smile, "but you two old cutthroats really could get jobs, build up your stake honestly."

"Ah, Jesus," lamented Pecos, rolling his head on his shoulders.

Slash chuckled and sipped his own whiskey.

Setting the bottle down beside him and pulling up his longhandle top against the growing chill of the mountain night, he said, "That ain't our way. We been cutthroats for too damn long. We're impatient, me an' that big blond-headed lummox over there. Besides, we're old. By the time we built a stake big enough to buy that freight company, Becker would have sold it to someone else, and we'd be too old to run it."

Shrugging into his blue chambray shirt around the collar of which hung his black ribbon tie, Slash winced as he glanced out into the stormy night where another fork of lightning flashed, silhouetting a jagged, black ridge against it. "We're gonna have to come up with a job. One more job. An easy one, since there's only the two of us. But a good-sized one for that . . ."

"I might know of one," Jay said, spooning beans onto a tin plate she'd found in Slash and Pecos's war bags, which they always kept well stocked with trail supplies.

"What's that?" Slash said.

Jay handed the plate of smoking beans and bacon over to Pecos with a three-tined, wooden-handled fork. "I might just know of a job. *Possibly* an easy one. Definitely a *sizable* one."

"Really, Jay?" Pecos said, taking the plate and exchanging a quick look with his partner.

Jay spooned beans and bacon onto another plate and handed it over to Slash, who stared at her expectantly.

"There's a ranch near here," Jay said. "A large one. Foreign owned. It's called the Crosshatch. Ritter told me about it. The owners brought in a bunch of white-faced cattle, and they mixed in some seed bulls that came all the way from England. Gold was discovered on the place, so they have a small mine, as well."

Jay spooned up a plate of beans and bacon for herself and sat back against her saddle, between Slash and Pecos. She grabbed Slash's bottle, took a pull of the whiskey, and ran the back of her hand across her mouth.

Handing the bottle back to Slash, she said, "As you can imagine, with a large spread like that as well as a mine, they have a good-sized payroll. I've stumbled across that payroll being transported through the mountains from the railroad in Saguache. They pass through a canyon maybe five miles from here."

"How'd you know it was payroll they were hauling?" Slash asked.

"Well, the combination had a Wells Fargo express car attached to it." Jay spooned beans into her mouth, chewed, and swallowed. "I've run with outlaws long enough to know what a train carrying payroll looks like."

She raised Slash's bottle in salute and took another pull.

"Hmmm," Slash said, pondering. "How much you think they're carryin'?"

"With the money they make in cattle and horse sales—not to mention bullion sales—and with the amount of men they probably need to pay, I'd say they're carrying anywhere from five to ten thousand dollars on any given run. Probably paper money and coins. I can't guarantee that, of course, since I know so little about their operation. But if they were carrying less, they'd probably just send a couple of riders with saddlebags."

Pecos dropped his fork onto his empty plate and

looked at Slash. "Damn, it's so close, it'd be a shame not to try for it."

Slash set down his own empty plate. "We'd need to know more about it," he said. "We'd need to make sure it'd be worth the risk, and we'd need to know when their next run is scheduled."

"Why don't I look into it?" Jay said, and forked more beans into her mouth.

Slash glanced at her skeptically. "What're you talkin' about?"

Jay swallowed and said, "We women are better equipped to plumb for sensitive information than men are." She reached for the bottle. "I'll dig up the stake Pete left me, head on down to Saguache, which is where the deliveries originate. Under the guise of a poor, grieving rancher's widow, I'll rent a room in a rooming house down there and indulge myself with a fancy set of duds. I've been right curious for years about the latest female fashions. Then I'll moon around town, maybe join a church, and quite possibly befriend some important male amongst the citizenry. An important businessman, say. Maybe even a banker. Some man who might know more than a little about the Crosshatch's money runs."

"Why, she's a devil!" Pecos said, his eager, wide-open blue eyes glistening in the leaping firelight. "I like that plan, sure enough!"

Slash let his gaze roam across Jay's succulent frame. She wore a wool-lined, doeskin jacket against the cold, but it did little to conceal her feminine wares. He shook his head slowly in amazement at the redhead's hazel-eyed, buxom beauty. "If anyone could pull it off, you could, Jay."

She returned his admiring gaze with a warm smile, her cheeks turning a little pink at their nubs. "Thanks, Slash."

"Could be dangerous," he warned her.

"No more dangerous than what we went through today."
"Fair point."

She stared at him, her own eyes deep and soft and also bright with reflected firelight. He found himself holding her gaze, not turning away like he usually did when her eyes found his. It was as though she were mesmerizing him. Slash felt warm and . . . well . . . odd.

He wasn't sure how to describe it. He'd be damned if he didn't want to look away from the redheaded beauty before him—the widow of one of his two very best friends in all the world. They shared way too much complicated history for him to be feeling this way, gazing back at her like this.

But he couldn't turn away.

He barely heard Pecos clear his throat and say, rising from his seat on the cave's floor, "I, uh . . . I'm gonna check on the horses. With all this weather, they might've pulled free of their picket line."

When Pecos was gone, Slash and Jay stared at each other for another three or four heartbeats, then each blinked, as though waking from the same dream, and turned away.

Slash rested back against his saddle. Jay rested back against hers. She crossed her legs Indian style, lowered her head, ran her hands through her thick red hair as though in frustration.

"Men," she said distastefully. Slash knew she was referring to Ed Ritter.

"Yeah," Slash said. "Tell me about 'em."

He held the bottle out to her, around the side of the fire. "Drink?"

Jay looked at him. She smiled then, too, her lips drawing gradually farther back from her perfect white teeth.

"Thanks."

They both laughed.

Jay lifted the bottle to her lips and drank. Pulling it back down, she studied him gravely, almost sadly, then asked, "How come you've never fallen in love, Slash?"

The old outlaw shrugged and looked down at his hands. "Oh . . . I don't know. I reckon the right woman just never came along," he lied.

CHAPTER 10

A fork of blue-white lightning streaked out of the murky black sky from which rain fell nearly sideways, tossed by a wicked wind, and struck a tree just right of the muddy trail. The tree fairly exploded, making a loud *pop*!

The cottonwood broke in two, the top jackknifing and crashing to the ground and again exploding with the impact, branches flying in all directions.

The smell of brimstone and charred wood peppered Jack Penny's nose as his horse lurched away from the burning tree, giving a shrill whinny. Penny, wearing a long yellow slicker against the downpour, rain funneling off the brim of his tan hat, yelled, "Christ Almighty! I don't think the gods is lookin' at us too favorably today!"

"I think they're tryin' to do us in!" yelled Bart Antrim, trying to settle down his own frightened mount beside Penny. "That's what I think!"

"Let's get in out of the storm!"

Penny touched spurs to his mount's flanks and galloped on down the trail, the horse's hooves splashing in the veritable muddy stream the trail had become between two high, rocky escarpments. Another lightning flash revealed the old cottonwood ranch portal he was looking for, dead ahead along the twisting trail. Penny galloped under the portal and reined up in the yard of what had once been a prosperous ranch but was now a remote, San Juan Mountain Valley watering hole that catered mostly to the outlaw breed of clientele.

Ahead and on the bounty hunter's right was the sprawling former ranch house, built of native timber and sporting a wide, wraparound veranda. Under a low-hanging, gently pitched roof, the saloon's windows shone red with lamplight burning within the place. Another flash of lightning briefly silhouetted a man-shaped figure sitting on the veranda, looking toward Penny and Bart Antrim, who just now galloped under the portal and into the yard.

At least, Penny *thought* he'd seen someone sitting out there, staring in his and Antrim's direction from beneath a bullet-crowned, broad-brimmed hat. After the brief lightning flash, the stormy night seemed even darker than before. The big, bearded bounty hunter brushed mud from the corner of his lazy left eye, gigged the buckskin over to a barn on his left, and dismounted. Two young Mexican hostlers in long canvas coats ran out from the barn's open doors, where they'd been smoking, perfuming the air with the peppery smell of Mexican tobacco.

The hostlers grabbed the reins of Penny's and Antrim's horses and led the storm-fidgety mounts into the barn.

Penny raised the collar of his rain slicker and, bowing his head against the stormy onslaught, began running toward the ranch house-turned-saloon but stopped when Antrim tapped his shoulder.

A small man with a hawkish face and thick mustache and goatee, Bart Antrim nodded toward the open barn doors. Another lightning flash briefly illuminated a fancy, enclosed buggy—a custom-built affair resembling a cross between a chaise and a hansom cab—sitting just inside the barn, its tongue drooping toward the hay- and straw-strewn floor.

Penny cursed.

"Out of the fryin' pan and into the fire!" Antrim yelled above the storm.

"We'll see about that!" Penny yelled back, wheeling and stretching out his long, thin legs in a goosey, awkward jog, breathing hard after only three or four strides, his years of hard-drinking and smoking catching up to him yet again.

By the time he'd gained the top of the veranda, Penny's lungs felt no larger than raisins. Raisins filled with sand. He stopped, leaned forward, hands on knees, then hacked a large gob of phlegm from his chest and spat it over the porch rail.

Antrim chuckled. "You feeble old devil!"

The younger bounty hunter ran across the porch and pushed through the storm door, laughing.

Raking air in and out of his lungs, Penny scowled at him. "You'll be old one day!"

He followed Antrim inside and closed the storm door behind him, having to kick it closed at the bottom to get the swollen wood to latch. He turned to look around the low-ceilinged room filled with as much shadow as light. Sooty gas lamps smoked from low rafters, where they hung by rusty chains.

The bar ran along part of the back wall. Mercantile supplies were haphazardly arranged on shelves and bins to the left. There were tables straight ahead, fronting the bar and across the rest of the broad room.

Only one of the dozen or so tables was occupied—one against the far wall to the bounty hunter's right. Penny couldn't see the faces of the three men sitting over there, on the table's far side, their backs to that wall as they faced the room. A lamp hung between him and the three men, lighting mainly their table on which three shot glasses and one whiskey bottle stood. A long, black cheroot smoldered in a stone ashtray.

The wan lamplight glinted dully off the moon-and-star badges pinned to the three men's dark wool coats. All three wore high-crowned black Stetsons.

That was about all Penny could see of them.

He also saw that there were four other men in the room. These men were dead. Two lay on the floor about ten feet from the badge-toting men sitting in silhouette against the far wall. One dead man slumped belly down across a chair, a gun in his hand.

Another dead man lay belly up on the table, atop playing cards and scattered shot glasses and an overturned bottle and ashtray. He stared up at the ceiling, the nearby lamp revealing him in garish brilliance, reflecting off his wide-open, sightlessly staring eyes. Blood trickled from a corner of his mustache-mantled mouth.

Penny gave a caustic chuff, then cursed as he brushed his fist across his nose. He glanced once more at the three badge-toting silhouettes, then squawked in his wet boots to the bar at the room's rear.

Rain drummed on the roof.

It *plop-plop-plopped* from a hole in the roof into a tin bucket to the left of the bar. Thunder rumbled, making the floor quiver beneath the bounty hunter's boots.

Lightning flashed in the windows, intermittently filling the room with a spectral blue light that touched the hard-planed, ghoulish faces of the badge-toting men sitting against the far wall. They sat so still, they might have been mere suit-wearing skeletons over there.

Penny bellied up to the bar beside Antrim. A little old lady behind the bar had just set a shot glass before Antrim and was filling it from an unlabeled bottle. She plucked a glass off a shelf beneath the bar, set it down in front of Penny, and slopped the unlabeled whiskey into it.

She didn't say anything. She merely stared up at the two bounty hunters blandly through her coal-black eyes beneath which dark pockets of flesh sagged against her wizened, coffee-brown face. She was so small that only her head shone above the bar, her coal-black hair pulled severely back against her egg-shaped head.

"Thanks, Ma," Penny said, tossing a couple of coins onto the scarred, varnished pine planks. "Leave the bottle, will ya?"

The little woman, Ma Rondo, owned the place. Or, at least, she tended it. That's all Penny and anyone else knew about her. She seemed to have been here forever, as fixed as the place itself, and would be here forevermore. It was just her and the two Mexicans who lived in the barn.

Ma lifted a rusty, dented coffee tin from under the bar and swept Penny's coins into it with a jangling clatter, then, leaving the bottle on the bar, returned the tin to its shelf, swung around, and disappeared through a curtained doorway.

Penny sagged tiredly forward over the bar and threw back his entire whiskey shot, as did Antrim. Penny picked up the bottle and was refilling Antrim's glass when lightning flashed, and for a second the bounty hunter thought it had struck the building itself, lancing through the roof and into the drinking hall.

A bright, blue-white light lit up the entire room. It flickered, brightened, then dissolved, and again the room was all dull spheres of lantern light and thick, hard-edged shadows. Thunder wailed like a tormented dragon.

"Christ!" the bounty hunter exclaimed, jerking with a start and splashing whiskey onto the bar around Antrim's glass.

Antrim also leaped with a start and looked around, as

though he, too, thought the lightning had penetrated the building. He turned to Penny, laughed edgily, then leaned forward and sucked the spilled tangleleg from the bar around his overfilled glass. He lapped at it like a dog.

He laughed. "Good stuff. Can't waste a drop. Ma brews it herself, ya know!"

Just then there was the *scrape-bark-squawk* of a door opening.

It was followed by another squeaking sound, almost like the faint chirp of distant birds. That sound was accompanied by the dull *zing* of rolling wheels.

"Here we go," Penny said through a fateful sigh, and turned to where two figures moved out of the shadows on the far side of the room, to the left of the three specter-like deputy U.S. marshals.

The two figures moved into a broad, dim sphere of flickering lantern light and stopped about fifteen feet from Penny and Antrim, both of whom had turned to face the newcomers. One of the figures was a tall, severely featured blond woman wearing a spruce-green cape over a blood-red, velveteen gown, the hood of the cape drawn up over her thick, golden curls. The other figure was a man in a stylish, tailor-made, three-piece suit sitting in a wooden wheelchair, which the young woman had pushed into the room.

Chief Marshal Luther "Bleed-'Em-So" Bledsoe was in his mid-sixties, distinctly skeletal in appearance, long and lanky, with very pale skin, cobalt-blue eyes residing in deep sockets, and a tumbleweed of coarse silver hair poking out around his head. Some of the man's hair stood straight up from the roots, as thin as cotton.

A walnut shotgun stock poked up from a leather scabbard strapped to the chair's right side, over the chief marshal's scrawny right thigh.

Bledsoe grinned, showing a set of very large false teeth—

teeth that would have looked more at home in a horse's mouth. "There's nothing like a lightning storm! God, how I love to watch mother nature wreak her wrath. Look at this." He pointed at his head. "My hair's sticking straight up from that last charge. I can feel the electricity hop-scotching around in my bones, in my nerves." He hopped around in his chair to regard the specter-like deputies. "You feel it, boys?"

None of the deputies said a word.

The one who was smoking lifted his cheroot to his lips and took a deep drag, exhaling the smoke toward the ceiling through his nostrils.

"Ah, hell," said the chief marshal, turning back to Penny, "they don't feel nothin'. Even a lightnin' storm can't impress them. The wonders of mother nature. You feel it, Miss Langdon?"

"I do feel it," the statuesque blonde said coolly, standing behind the old man, keeping her flat green eyes on the men at the bar. In her early to mid-twenties, she stood a good six feet tall, and she was pretty in a severe Nordic way, as though she'd been chiseled out of ice.

"See?" Bledsoe said, turning to Penny and Antrim again. "My assistant, Miss Abigail Langdon, feels it."

The tall young woman slowly dipped her deeply clefted chin as though in acknowledgment of her introduction to Penny and Antrim.

Thunder clapped again over the roadhouse, causing the whole room to shudder. Lightning flashed brightly in the windows, eerily illuminating the dead men on the floor and on the table.

When the din had shaken down to only the rain beating on the saloon's roof, the old man's face as well as his tone hardened, and he said, "I'm going to assume the rest of your men are taking their time in the barn, and that they have the heads of Slash Braddock and the Pecos River Kid out there in croaker sacks."

Penny and Antrim shared a dark glance.

Penny picked up his refilled shot glass and strode toward Bledsoe, stepping around the dead men lying on and around the table. He glanced at the dead man on the table, then frowned and gestured at the body with his hand holding the drink, and said, "Say, ain't that Melvin Soledad?"

"Yeah," the chief marshal said. "Imagine runnin' into him way out here. Him and Henry Searls and Scratch Underhill." He smiled, blue eyes glittering delightedly. "They resisted arrest."

CHAPTER 11

Penny walked up to within seven feet of Bledsoe and stopped, looking down at the wheelchair-bound lawman. "We ran into unexpected trouble."

"I paid you to expect anything."

"You didn't pay us to expect an escape tunnel."

Bledsoe scowled. "An escape tunnel?"

"That's right," Antrim said from the bar. "That cabin was outfitted with an escape tunnel. When we set the place on fire, they musta crawled out through the tunnel and snuck around us."

"They cut us down like ducks on a millpond," said Penny, and sipped his whiskey.

"Us?" Bledsoe grunted. He smiled. "I see that you and your little friend managed to get away unscathed."

Antrim bristled at being called little. Penny sensed the smaller man seething behind him. As Antrim lurched away from the bar, setting down his drink, Penny stopped him with an upraised arm.

"We both dropped into some brush when the shootin' started," he said tightly, defensively. "Otherwise, they woulda cut us down with the others. The odds were against us, so we lit out of there. Live to fight another day, is what

I say. We'll have another chance at 'em. One with the odds in our favor. I got no doubt about that. None whatsoever."

Bledsoe was grinning so broadly that anyone watching might have thought he was in danger of losing his teeth. "An escape tunnel?" He chuckled. "Of course. Why not? Pistol Pete probably thought of that, the old devil!" He chuckled some more. "And them two cutthroats an' Pete's woman took full advantage. Circled behind thirteen of supposedly the nastiest bounty hunters on the frontier, and laid waste to all but two!"

Bledsoe laughed again, clapped his big hands together, and glanced over his shoulder at the three deputies concealed in the shadows behind him.

To a man, they were as sober as judges. The one with the cheroot took another long pull on the cigar once more.

Bledsoe looked up at Abigail Langdon, who only quirked her broad mouth a little, keeping her eyes on Penny.

"You gotta love those two, don't you?" said the chief marshal.

"What two?" asked Penny, incredulous.

"Slash Braddock an' the Pecos River Kid. The woman, too—Jaycee Breckenridge. Hell, you gotta love all three." Still chuckling with boyish delight, Bledsoe shook his head and wrung his hands together.

Penny glowered at him, one nostril flaring. "If you love 'em so damn much, why'd you sic us on 'em?"

Instantly, the smile left the chief marshal's long, angular face with its deep-set, cobalt eyes. "I meant it figuratively."

"You meant it . . . what?" Antrim asked skeptically. He glanced at Penny, then back to Bledsoe. "What'd he say?"

"I didn't mean it literally," Bledsoe said.

"I don't care how you meant it," Antrim said, stepping forward, his face red, his little eyes pinched with anger. "And I don't see why you can't talk in a way that—"

"Shut up, you little fool!" Bledsoe bellowed, lifting an arm to point his long, bony finger.

Antrim stopped and hardened his jaws, his little, pinched-up eyes spitting fire. He made a deep, breathy chortling sound in his chest and his feet moved in place, as though he were grinding bugs into the floor. His chest rose and fell sharply. He flexed his gloved right hand over the handle of the .44 jutting from the holster on that thigh, under the pulled back flap of his rain slicker.

"Go ahead," Bledsoe said, leaning forward in his chair, his own face mottled with fury now. "Pull that smoke wagon, you little termite!"

The sounds Antrim was making deep in his chest grew louder. He looked at the three deputies sitting behind the table on the far side of the room, their faces in shadow, smoke from the one deputy's cigar webbing in the guttering lantern light. Antrim shuttled his gaze from the deputies to the three dead men before him.

Penny smiled as he glanced over his shoulder at the smaller man. "Stand down, Bart." His smile grew as he returned his gaze to the gray-haired cripple in the wheelchair. "Stand down, stand down," he added drolly.

Antrim relaxed his hand. The noises stopped issuing from his chest but he held his acrimonious stare on the wheelchair-bound chief marshal.

Bledsoe sat back in his chair. To Penny he said, "You let two of the most elusive cutthroats on the western frontier get away from you, after you had 'em both and that outlaw woman, Breckenridge, corralled in their outlaw cabin. You know how long I've been after those two—Braddock and the Pecos River Kid?"

"A long time, I'd imagine," Penny said, playing along with the strange man's game. "They been at it a long time."

"I've been after them for nigh on twenty years now. Ever since I was a deputy ridin' for ole Cleve Butterworth, who held the position I hold now, in the Denver Federal Building. I almost had 'em once. We thought we had 'em corralled in Abilene, Kansas—eleven of us deputy U.S. marshals and three Pinkertons—when the Snake River Marauders were robbing the Stockman's State Bank on Front Street."

Bledsoe grimaced, shook his head slowly, fatefully. "Somehow, they slipped away. Slick as dog dung on a doorknob on the Fourth of July!"

He shook his head again and added in a low, throaty voice, "That was the day I got the bullet in my back. From Braddock himself when he was comin' out of the bank, both pistols blazing, laying down cover for the Pecos Kid, whose hands were full of money. I caught a ricochet off the sandstone wall behind me."

Penny doffed his still-dripping hat and held it down before him in both hands, and dropped his chin gravely, looking at Bledsoe from beneath his shaggy brows. "I do apologize for your misfortune, Marshal Bledsoe. I didn't know that bullet came from Braddock."

"No," Bledsoe said. "You wouldn't."

"Again," Penny said. "I can't imagine a worse thing than bein' confined to a—"

"Shut up!" the old marshal bellowed.

Penny felt his gut tighten under the crazy old lawman's onslaught. He slid his eyes to one side, glancing at Antrim behind him. Bart slid his own tense, angry gaze to Penny, then to the fiery chief marshal before them, flanked by the severely beautiful blonde in the spruce-green cape, who might have been carved out of alabaster, complete with her coolly mysterious smile.

"The only thing you two corkheads need to be sorry for is letting yourselves get outsmarted by those two cutthroats and that outlaw woman, Breckenridge. You got that close"— Bledsoe raised his hand, holding his thumb and index finger an inch apart—"and let 'em get away. Get outta here! You're fired!"

"You can't fire us!" Antrim shot back, raising his arm and pointing an angry finger.

"You gave us contracts!" Penny added, also pointing an accusing finger at the old marshal. "You agreed to pay us like deputy marshals as long as we tracked Slash 'n' Pecos *and only Slash 'n' Pecos* till we ran 'em down and killed 'em an' brought you back their heads! Then we'd both get the reward money on their heads—*doubled!*—and the rest of our men would get a thousand dollars from Uncle Sam. That was the deal!"

"It ain't our fault they had an escape tunnel," Antrim argued, leaning forward at the waist, glaring at Bledsoe. "So, they pulled one over on us? They pulled one over on you in Abilene!"

He straightened, beaming victoriously.

Bledsoe glared back at the shorter bounty hunter. His eyes were bright with fury though the rest of his face appeared passive except for a nerve that was twitching in his left cheek, just beneath that deep-set, cobalt eye.

The room was silent. The only sounds were the din kicked up by the storm outside. Lightning sparked in the windows, at times filling the entire room with those eerie, blue-white flashes.

Finally, Penny gave a nervous chuckle and, grinning at the ominously silent Bledsoe, holding out his right hand to calm his enraged partner, he said, "Now, now, now. Pshaw! No point in callin' out everbody's mistakes. So, we let them two owlhoots slip out on us here today, just like you did way back in Abilene."

He threw out his arms, shrugging. "None o' that means a damn thing right here an' now, does it? Me an' Bart here will go after them two as soon as the storm clears out. We'll track 'em from the cabin an' finish 'em right an' proper. We'll cut their heads off, cart 'em back to your office in Denver, and collect the money we'll have comin' to us."

He added with a wry chuckle, "Of course we'll forget the money you owe the rest of the bunch, since they're dead an' all. You just keep that money in ole Uncle Sam's bank. That's a savings for you. As soon as Bart and me have collected the reward money . . . along with our retainer fees . . . you and us will fork trails, Chief Marshal Bledsoe. You'll never have to lay your eyes on our ugly faces again."

Penny chuckled again nervously, shifting his eyes from the three deputies sitting silently in the shadows to the right of the chief marshal sitting in his wheelchair, his eyes still blazing at Bart Antrim.

For nearly another full minute, Bledsoe remained silent.

Then he lifted his big, horny hands, opened his coat, and reached into a pocket. He pulled out two sheets of cream paper, which were folded lengthwise. He opened both pages, turned them so that they faced the room, and ripped them along the crease.

Bledsoe's face suddenly brightened in a mocking grin.

"Here are your contracts!" He placed his hands on the arms of his chair and leaned forward over his knees, pointing his chin like a pistol barrel at the two men before him. "Now get your cowardly asses the hell out of my sight!"

Antrim gave a mewling cry of outrage. He bounded forward, reaching for the pistol thonged on his right thigh. "Why, you crippled old son of—"

He didn't get the rest out.

Or if he did, it was drowned by the sudden concussion of Bledsoe's sawed-off shotgun, which the old marshal had drawn with lightning speed from its greased scabbard and held straight out before him in both hands, thumbing the left hammer back and squeezing the trigger.

Antrim was picked up and flung straight back, triggering his Colt into the ceiling just before he hit the floor on his back and lay writhing like a bug on a pin.

Penny stared down at his partner in shock. Antrim stared up at him, the light quickly leaving his eyes as he held both his gloved hands to what remained of his belly. Bart tried to speak but he managed only a few strangled gurgling sounds. His eyes rolled back in their sockets, his bloody hands dropped to the floor, and he lay still.

Penny turned to the chief marshal. Bledsoe gazed back at him, eyes bright with anticipation. Smoke curled from the maw of the shotgun's right barrel. Both barrels were aimed at the bounty hunter's chest.

Bledsoe curled his upper lip. "Want some?"

Penny raised his hands, palms out, and shook his head. He glanced at the three deputies. They hadn't moved. They sat as before, the one with the cheroot just now stubbing out the cigar in the ashtray and exhaling smoke through his nostrils.

Abigail Langdon stood behind and above the little, crippled chief marshal, gazing coolly at Penny. She might have been watching some mildly entertaining theatrical play in a frontier opera house.

Penny's heart thudded heavily, painfully.

"I reckon I'll, uh . . . I reckon I'll just take a bottle and go to bed." He began backing toward the bar where he intended to secure a room for the night.

"The place is done filled up," Bledsoe growled, sliding his shotgun toward the door. "Take the barn."

Penny compressed his lips. Fury was a living thing inside him, trying to claw its way out. He looked at the smoking shotgun before him, then at the three deputies and the cool eyes of Bledsoe's ethereally beautiful assistant gazing at him blandly.

There would be another time, another place for Bledsoe.

Just as there would be another opportunity for the bounty

hunter to take down Slash Braddock and the Pecos River Kid.

Penny sidled over to the door, shrugged deeper into his rain slicker, and left.

Bledsoe sheathed his shotgun and sat staring at the closed door, slowly shaking his head and chuckling.

"What's funny, Chief?" asked Abigail Langdon, gazing down at him. Her voice sounded like the keys of the most finely tuned piano in the world.

"Braddock and Pecos," Bledsoe said, shaking his head as he stared at the door. "Those two old cutthroats got no quit in 'em—I'll give 'em that."

He threw his head back, laughing.

"But I got one more big surprise for 'em!"

The old chief marshal laughed harder.

Outside thunder roared.

Lightning lit up the entire room.

CHAPTER 12

Three weeks later, Slash leaned his Winchester against his knee and plucked his old, dented and tarnished railroad watch from a pocket of his black leather vest. He checked the time, snapped the lid closed, returned the timepiece to its pocket, then pulled his field glasses from their leather, baize-lined case.

As he squatted in the rocks of an aspen-stippled mountainside high in the southern Rockies, he raised the binoculars to his eyes and aimed them along the twin rails of a narrow-gauge spur line snaking down a steep mountain grade to his left.

He adjusted the focus.

Soon, telltale puffs of black smoke appeared down that narrow chasm between towering aspen- and pine-studded cliffs.

"Right on time," the outlaw muttered to himself as he stared through the single sphere of magnified vision.

A few seconds later, as Slash began to hear the *chuffah-chuffah-chuffah* of the locomotive laboring toward him up the mountain, he saw the coal-black stack. A couple of seconds after that, the locomotive itself, its bullet-shaped, black snout fronted by the copper-plated number 31, lurched into view.

Slash's heart quickened anxiously, thrillingly. Maybe that sense of excitement and that alone was what had kept him riding the long coulees all these years since the war. It was nearly as fine a feeling as that of a rip-roaring bender in some wild frontier city—Dodge City, say, or New Orleans.

No, it was better than being drunk, for it didn't dull the experience of living the way spirits did. It washed the mind as clear as a window scoured on a spring morning after a rain, giving it a diamond-edged lucidity as it erased all the demons otherwise on the lurk in a man's consciousness. It expunged all the tedious sundry cares, desires, needling responsibilities, mild annoyances, and lingering angers.

This was life or death, freedom or jail. This was living in its purest, rawest form.

Soon, if the information Jay had gathered over the past three weeks in Saguache was correct—and there was no reason for Slash to think it wasn't—he and Pecos would be nearly ten thousand dollars richer and well on their way to owning their own freighting company in Camp Collins, a quiet little town nestled on the eastern edge of the Front Range between Denver and Cheyenne.

Soon, they'd retire from the long coulees and begin the second half of their lives as respectable businessmen.

Soon.

Chuffah-chuffah-chuffah . . .

Slash lowered the glasses and turned to where Pecos was just then kicking rocks over the dynamite he'd arranged with caps and fuses between the ties at the base of the slope, fifty yards to Slash's right, where the grade leveled out and a sparkling, gurgling creek swung toward the rails from a ravine on the other side of the tracks.

"It's comin', partner," Slash called, keeping his voice down though no one on the train could have heard above the continuing *chuffah-chuffah-chuffah*, which grew steadily louder as the narrow-gauge locomotive kept climbing the hill.

Pecos kicked a few more rocks over his buried dynamite, making sure it was well concealed but careful to make sure it was *subtly* concealed, and that he left no tracks.

He and Slash had acquired the explosive sticks from a long-trusted source in Durango who sold arms, ammo, and remounts to the army. The two cutthroats had been using dynamite to blow train rails for nearly as long as they'd been in the West. Pecos reflected that he'd miss the danger of the dynamite, of its smell that lingered on a man's hands—the mixed tang of pepper and kerosene— and he'd miss the sudden roar of the tracks being blown, the screech of the locomotive's brakes applied in panic by the engineer.

He'd miss the huffing and puffing of the dragon-like locomotives, and maybe even the quick thudding of his heart, the slick sweat popping out on his hands, as it did now, beneath his gloves, as either freedom or jail, riches or poverty, life or death approached along a steep mountain incline, under a faultless bowl of blue western sky.

Slash might miss all of those things and more about the outlaw life, he reflected. But the years were growing long. Trails had dimmed. Gray streaked his hair. He and Pecos weren't getting any younger. Staying in the business any longer, with their skills on the wane, would be suicide. And neither Slash nor Pecos was suicidal.

Glancing down the grade toward the approaching train, Pecos tipped his hat down low over his eyes and wheeled, the flaps of his long, black duster winging out around his high-topped, stovepipe boots as he mounted the rocky slope. He traced a meandering course through the aspens, pines, rocks, and boulders, sometimes scrambling on his hands and knees.

Slash could hear his partner's labored breathing. By the time Pecos reached Slash's position, the bigger of the two cutthroats was wheezing like an overburdened bellows, his fair-skinned, sun-mottled face flushed and sweating.

"Oh, Lordy," Pecos said, dropping to a knee in the rock nest beside Slash. "I think I'm gonna have a heart stroke!" He rammed a gloved fist against his chest as he sagged back against a tree bole and doffed his hat. He chuckled dryly as he raked air in and out of his tired lungs.

"Age is a terrible thing—ain't it, partner?" Slash plucked his small, flat, hide-wrapped traveling flask from inside his broadcloth suit coat and held it out. "Have you a shot o' that. Best heart tonic known to medicine."

"What is it?"

"Tequila."

Pecos gave an ironic chuff. He uncapped the flask, tipped it back, and took a long pull. As he returned the "medicine" to Slash, smacking his lips, he shook his head in relief. "Gracias, amigo. Think you mighta just saved my life."

Slash sipped from the flask, then returned the cap to its mouth. He glanced down the grade, toward where the train was approaching. As a fading memory slithered back into his brain—more and more were doing that lately, filling him with a bittersweet feel—he turned to Pecos and said with a grin, "Wouldn't be the first time one of us saved the other's life—would it, partner?"

Pecos's gaze deepened as he, too, remembered their shared history, over thirty years' worth. He gave a dry chuckle and shook his head. "No, it sure wouldn't. . . ."

"You ready?"

Pecos glanced at the plunger to which he'd already connected the dynamite's fuse. He grinned at Pecos as he leaned forward to place his right hand on the plunger handle. "Partner, I was born ready!"

"Wait for my signal," Slash said, taking his rifle in his right hand and holding up his left hand, palm out, casting a cautious gaze through the rocks.

The train approached, huffing and puffing along the narrow-gauge rails. The locomotive slid up into full view now, about forty feet to the left of Slash's and Pecos's positions. Slash could see the engineer poking his head out the near side window, gazing ahead along the rails. He wore a red wool cap, and a corncob pipe drooped from between his mustached lips. Behind him, the fireman had the firebox door open, and he was busily shoving wood from the tender car into the raging furnace, trying to keep the boiler's temperature up.

As Slash slid his gaze farther back along the train, behind the tender car heaped with split wood, cool fingers of apprehension brushed the back of his neck.

He turned to Pecos, who was hunkered on his left, his hand on the plunger handle, waiting for Slash's signal.

Slash said, "I thought Jay said there would only be the express car and caboose."

Pecos canted his head so he could see between the rocks in front of him. He looked up at Slash. "So, there's one more car." He grinned, blue eyes wide and round with eager anticipation. "Maybe they're haulin' more loot than expected."

Slash's heartbeat quickened, his anxiety growing more keen and uncomfortable. He ran his gaze across the handsome red passenger car with brass window fittings and brass handrails on its forward and back vestibules. It sat in front of the plain yellow car marked WELLS, FARGO & COMPANY EXPRESS and the caboose trailing behind the express car, at the combination's end. It appeared to be a private passenger car boasting four small windows behind which Slash could see no one.

"They're haulin' some mucky-muck, looks like," Slash said.

"Maybe the ranch's superintendent rode down to sell hosses or somethin' down in Saguache, and he's headed back to the spread. Jay said he did that from time to time, but that he usually only took one other man with him—his foreman. We can take 'em both."

"She didn't mention nothin' about the superintendent havin' his own private rail car."

"You got your drawers in a twist again. Over nothin', most likely."

"Uh-huh." Slash's heart raced. He had to make up his mind to go ahead with the job or to let it go. He couldn't bring himself to pull out. He wanted the money in the express car too badly. He wanted to quit the long coulees and buy the freighting business too badly.

He and Pecos weren't getting any younger.

"Go!" He snapped his left hand down.

Pecos shoved the plunger into the box.

The dynamite detonated with a thundering wail, blowing up a great, pyramid-shaped cloud of sand, gravel, and track rail roughly a hundred feet in front of the still-chugging locomotive. Slash felt the ground shudder beneath his knees. He'd poked his gloved fingers into his ears to soften the explosion—he'd finally learned to do that a few years ago, realizing he was growing hard of hearing after taking the full brunt of too many similar detonations over the years—but now he lowered his hands and grabbed his Winchester.

The engineer cursed and pulled his head back into the locomotive's cab, jerking levers to apply the breaks.

"We're on, pard!" Slash yelled, hoping like hell Jay was right about there being only three or four guards in the express car.

It was that extra car, though, that worried him.

He heaved himself to his feet and ran out from between the rocks, starting down the slope. Pecos grabbed his own Colt rifle and slung his sawed-off coach gun behind his back, where it hung by its leather lanyard, and broke into a run behind Slash. A third of the way down the slope, the two cutthroats separated and took two different routes down the steep mountain grade made perilous by low shrubs and large patches of slide rock.

It was on one of these patches that Slash lost his footing, his left boot slipping out from beneath him. He hit the ground, rolled once, and, cursing under his breath and spitting grit from between his lips, lurched back to his feet and continued running at an angle down the slope.

"I saw that!" Pecos said, voice pitched with wry amusement.

Slash told him to do something physically impossible to himself.

He gained the base of the slope and ran up the tracks toward where the locomotive was just then screeching to a shuddering halt about a hundred feet beyond. While Pecos stopped beside the express car, Slash ran back up the grade to the right of the locomotive, and, about fifteen feet up from the bottom of the slope, hunkered behind a rock.

He loudly rammed a cartridge into the Winchester's breech and aimed at the two men cursing and lurching around inside the cab.

"Climb down out of there, you two, and do it fast or I'll fill you so full of lead you'll rattle when you walk!"

It was the cutthroat's customary overblown admonition for the simple reason it usually did the trick, resulting in only infrequent exchanges of lead. Engineers and firemen were not usually armed for prolonged lead swaps, and they didn't usually have much stomach for them, either, since they were getting paid only to drive and fuel the train, not to defend it from owlhoots.

These two were faster than most at climbing down out of the locomotive, leaping from the bottom rung of the iron ladder to the cinder-paved rail bed, turning toward Slash, and throwing their hands high in the air. The engineer was a full head taller than the fireman, who was twice as wide and wore a full white beard and black watch cap pulled low on his freckled forehead.

They both stared wide-eyed up at Slash aiming his rifle at them from behind the rock. The engineer continued puffing the pipe jutting straight out from a corner of his mouth, the smoke wafting around his head.

Neither man said anything. They just stood staring up the slope at Slash, hands raised high.

Slash stared back at them, scowling. He canted his head to one side, studying their expressions.

There they were again—those cold witches' fingers raking the back of his neck. This time the nails were fully extended, tearing at the tender flesh under his collar.

There was something about this setup he didn't like. It wasn't only the extra car, but these two men hadn't needed any convincing to scramble down out of the locomotive. It was almost as though they'd been coached through the entire scenario, told to do exactly what Slash told them to do.

Neither appeared to be wearing so much as a derringer, whereas most of the engineers he'd shaken down had worn a .45 or a .44 somewhere on their persons, and they'd at least made a show of being willing to use it before tossing it somewhat sheepishly down from the engine.

"Belly down!" Slash ordered, gesturing with his rifle barrel.

They did that, too, as though they'd been awaiting the order.

"Stay right there and don't move. You so much as lift your heads an inch, I'll shoot 'em off!"

"Yes, sir," said the engineer.

"You got it, sir," said the fireman, nodding his head against the ground.

Pecos walked on down past the tender car and the mysterious coach car to the Wells Fargo car, outside of which Pecos stood, holding his Colt rifle up high across his chest as he scrutinized the car before him.

He glanced at Slash, then frowned curiously and said, "What's got your tail a-draggin'? Dang, this is turnin' out easy as pie coolin' on a window ledge! I don't hear no one movin' around inside here, neither."

He canted his head toward the Wells Fargo car before him and grinned. "I'm thinkin' Jay was right about there bein' few guards if any at all. Maybe there's just a safe!"

"Don't get your hopes up. There'll be guards. If there's any money at all, men will be guarding it. You should know that by now, you dunderheaded nincompoop."

Pecos widened his eyes and lowered his jaw in exasperated indignation. "Dunderheaded nin—? Jesus! Somethin' really is crawlin' up your behind. Or maybe you hit your head in that fall comin' down the mountain, ya clumsy old fool!"

Slash was studying the train, stretching his gaze from the locomotive to the caboose bringing up the rear, then back to the Wells Fargo car before him. He raked a consternated thumb along his jaw. "I don't like it."

"Don't like what?"

"It's too easy."

"You don't like easy jobs anymore?" Pecos whistled and shook his head. "Boy, it is time for you to retire. Why don't we just order that door open, whistle for hosses, and hightail it out of this racket you've grown too old and scaredy-cat for?"

"I think we should just whistle for our hosses."

"Oh, you do, do you?" Pecos chuckled dryly. "Not me, partner. I still got all my marbles in their rightful pockets. I ain't lost my nerve. Not yet. I ain't goin' nowhere without my saddlebags filled with cash."

Slash raked his gaze along the train again, then narrowed an eye at his partner. "You don't sense anything out of whack here?"

Pecos usually had as keen a sixth sense as Slash did. Since he didn't sense trouble here, maybe Slash really was being an old schoolmarm about the whole thing. Maybe age had, indeed, caused him to lose his nerve.

"All I sense here is a safe brimming with cash. I hear it calling out to us, in fact." Pecos cupped a hand to his ear and leaned toward the train car. "Hear it? I do, sure enough. It's sayin', 'Come an' get me, Pecos! Come an' get me, Slash! It's dark in here all by my lonesome! Come and free me from this dark place and I'll make you two old raggedy-heeled cutthroats rich enough to buy your own business and a girl or two on weekends!'"

He wheezed a laugh.

"All right, all right," Slash said, feeling foolish. He stepped back and raised his Winchester, levering a live round into the action. "Let's get to it."

"That's more like it." Pecos backed up a step and curled back the hammer of his Colt rifle. Pitching his voice with menace, he yelled, "Open up that door or we're gonna blast ya outta there and skin what's left of ya!"

Nothing.

Slash and Pecos shared a skeptical glance.

Pecos cleared his throat and raised his voice louder. "For the last time, open up that damn door or die like a rat in a church privy!"

"All right, all right," said a needling male voice from inside the car. "Hold your horses!"

Pecos glanced at Slash and grinned.

Slash wrinkled his nose at him.

There was some scuffing and grunting from inside the Wells Fargo car. Then the door opened, sliding along its rails from Slash's and Pecos's right to their left. When the door was open a few feet, a little man with close-cropped gray-blond hair wearing a green eyeshade and sleeve garters poked his head out.

"All the way!" Slash yelled at him. "And be quick about it!"

"All right, all right," said the little express agent.

He got in front of the end of the door and grunted as he pushed it along its rail. The door lurched along the rail as it opened, revealing your usual, run-of-the-mill express car complete with a small desk covered with ledger books, a large black safe against the back wall, and an old bull's-eye lantern hanging from the ceiling by a wire. The door opened still farther to reveal a brass-canistered Gatling gun perched in the car's open doorway, around which three severe-looking men wearing deputy U.S. marshal's badges crouched.

One of the marshals had a long, black cheroot dangling from between his mustached lips. Crouching over the nasty-looking weapon, he smiled around the cheroot, exhaling cigar smoke and then hardening his jaws as he turned the Gatling gun's wooden-handled crank.

The big gun roared like a baby dragon, spitting flames as well as .45-caliber chunks of hot lead toward the two cutthroats standing just outside the car with their mouths hanging open in shock.

CHAPTER 13

When he first saw the sun shining off the brass maw of that Gatling gun perched in the car's open doorway, flanked by three black-clad federals, Slash's heart bucked like a wild bronc in his chest.

"Holy cow!" Pecos bellowed.

He and Slash hit the ground as though their legs suddenly evaporated.

At the same time, the Gatling gun roared with a caterwauling cry of *RAT-A-TAT-TAT-TAT-TAT-TAT-TAT-TAT!*

The .45-caliber bullets screamed over the two cowering cutthroats' heads, drumming into the slope behind them, a few screaming even louder as they glanced off rocks. Lying belly down against the ground, his cheek grinding on a knobby rock, Slash glared at Pecos, who lay staring back at him, gritting his teeth as the hot lead stormed over their heads, a few cratering the ground just off the heels of their toe-down boots.

When the gun's witchlike cries died, Slash said, "You plug-headed polecat!"

He lifted his head but slammed it back down again when he heard the Gatling gun's birdlike chirp as it dropped on its swivel, and then another deafening caterwauling broke out.

Ten or so more rounds drilled into the ground in front of Slash's and Pecos's heads, between them and the Wells Fargo car.

When the gun's screech died again suddenly, leaving only a high-pitched ringing in Slash's ears, he looked over to see Pecos's lips move. He couldn't hear what his partner said above the ringing in his own ears, but he could read Pecos's lips. What he said wasn't something Slash would repeat to his grandchildren, if he lived to have grandchildren one day, which at the moment seemed doubtful.

Slash kept his cheek down against the knobby rock, but when the Gatling did not speak again and no bullets tore into his flesh, he lifted his head and cast a dubious glance into the express car where the three federals crouched, grinning through the wafting powder smoke. The deputy who'd been firing the Gatling gun straightened slightly, removed the long black cigar from between his teeth, and added a long plume to the powder smoke.

"Toss away your weapons!" he barked, flexing his black-gloved right hand threateningly around the Gatling's wooden handle.

Slash looked at the man's dark eyes. He looked at the Gatling gun from the maw of which thick smoke curled. The other two federals had raised rifles, and they cocked them loudly now, raised them to their shoulders, and angled the barrels down toward the prone cutthroats.

Slash could feel at least one bead being drawn on his forehead.

He looked at Pecos, who returned the look with a constipated one of his own.

"Ah, hell!" Defeat burned inside Slash. He reflected briefly on growing old in the federal pen but was mildly comforted by the notion he'd probably hang. He just hoped they calculated the drop right, so he didn't dangle too long, dancing while the crowd roared, the dogs barked, and the children beat his legs with sticks.

He considered drawing his Colt, ending it all right here. But that was too much like suicide. Suicide was a coward's way out. Slash was no coward. He'd face what he had to face, a necktie party if that's what was in the cards he'd been dealt, and shake hands with that fork-tailed old demon, Scratch, afterward . . .

Giving a ragged sigh, he unsnapped the keeper thong from over his right-side Colt, shucked the weapon, and tossed it out away from him. When he'd tossed away his second Colt and his bowie knife, and Pecos had tossed away his Russian .44, his sawed-off shotgun, and Colt revolving rifle, the cigar-smoking federal said, "The rest!"

Slash and Pecos shared another dark glance, rolling their eyes. They sat up and dug into their boot wells for their hideout pistols, and tossed those away, as well.

"That it?" asked the cigar-smoking federal.

"Yep," said Slash.

"Don't worry—we'll be checking every nook and cranny," the federal barked back at him.

"I don't know, partner," Pecos said. "He sounds awfully eager to check our nooks and crannies."

"Shut up!" the federal admonished above the chuckles of the two other deputies. "You'll get a rifle butt to the head for every other hideout we find!"

"Oh, go to hell!" Slash said.

Apparently finding the tolerance to ignore the admonition, the federal said, "Get up! Try to run, and I'll cut you in two!"

Grunting and cursing and spitting sand and weed seeds from his lips, Slash heaved himself to his feet. Pecos must have bruised his knee when he'd hit the ground; he was having trouble getting up. Slash gave him a hand, and the two stood facing the three federals—the two with rifles, the cigar-smoking devil on one knee behind the Gatling gun, daintily flicking ashes from his cigar.

All three were chuckling in delight at the two middle-aged cutthroats before them—two rarely seen wildcats they and many others had been hunting for years with no success.

Here they were before them now.

Slash felt like a caged circus animal, and he wasn't even in a cage yet.

He gazed back at the three deputy U.S. marshals and shook his head in deep befuddlement. "How . . . ?" he tried. "How in the hell did you know . . . ?"

He let the question dissolve on his lips when he heard a *click* and turned to see the rear door of the coach car open onto its brass-railed vestibule. A nattily attired, grinning man in a wheelchair was rolled out through the open door and onto the car's outer platform. He was pale and clean-shaven, vaguely skeletal in appearance, with cobalt eyes set in deep sockets. Cottony hair poked out from beneath the brim of his bullet-crowned black hat.

Slash heard Pecos draw air sharply through his teeth. Or maybe it was his own startled intake he'd heard above the bells of disbelief tolling in his ears. Again, his own heart kicked him, like a young colt's hoof, as he saw that the person rolling Chief Marshal Luther T. "Bleed-'Em-So" Bledsoe out onto the vestibule was none other than Jaycee Breckenridge.

"Jay?" Pecos grunted, jerking his head back with a start.

He glanced at Slash, who blinked his eyes as if to clear them. When that didn't work, he used his thumb and index finger.

Still, it was Jay standing there behind Chief Marshal Bledsoe, standing out on the vestibule now, the sunlight glowing richly in her copper hair that hung to her shoulders in thick, curly waves. She wore a rich green traveling gown, low-cut and trimmed with white lace at the full bodice and sleeves. Her cleavage was shaded, like the mouth of a deep canyon at dusk. Around her neck was a double strand of luminous white pearls.

Christ, even pearl earrings dangled from her ears!

Slash could smell the intoxicating fragrance she wore—the sweet scent of ripe raspberries cut with sage.

"Hidy, boys!" Bledsoe called, spreading his thin lips in a grin that revealed nearly all of his oversized, false teeth. He held a sawed-off, double-barreled greener across the arms of his chair. His right thumb was caressing one of the rabbit-ear hammers. "Been a long time! I don't know that we've ever been formally introduced. But I'm sure we all know who each other is, don't we? Oh, and I reckon Miss Breckenridge here needs no introduction—does she, boys?"

He looked over his left shoulder at Jaycee standing over him, behind him, then turned forward to see the expressions on Slash's and Pecos's faces. Suddenly, he broke into hysterical laughter.

Pecos was almost unable to get the words out. "J-Jay? Jay . . . wh-what the *hell*?"

"Why, Jay?" Slash said, shaking his head with a keen incomprehension.

Jay gazed back at them through tear-glazed eyes. Her upper lip quivered.

Pecos stepped forward, thrusting his arm up and pointing an accusing finger at her. "You double-crossed us, Jay!" he bellowed. "*Why?*"

Bledsoe slapped his thigh and rocked with laughter.

Jay lowered her gaze to her tightly entwined fingers, tears streaming down her cheeks. She lifted her gaze again to Slash and Pecos.

"I'm sorry, Slash," she said, sobbing, her face a mask of grief and bitter regret. "Pecos, I'm sorry!"

She wheeled, her hair and her long skirt flying, and ran back into the private car.

Slash and Pecos shared another befuddled look.

"I don't get it," Pecos said, shaking his head. "I just don't get it."

"Me, neither," Slash said, and turned his enraged gaze to Bledsoe, who sat laughing in his chair on the private car's fancy vestibule.

Through his laughter he managed to order his deputies to cuff and shackle their prisoners, adding to Slash and Pecos after he'd sobered somewhat, "We'll be heading on down to Saguache, boys. Got a little party for you. One of the necktie variety. Oh, of course there'll be a trial an' all beforehand. A fair one, of course. A federal judge is on his way down here from Denver even as we speak."

The chief marshal widened his eyes demonically and jutted his chin like a cocked .45. "Then we're gonna hang you on the main drag, in front of the whole town. In fact, the good citizens of Saguache are already preparing for the festivities!"

That made him rock back in his chair and howl once more, slapping the arms of his chair.

As two deputies dropped down out of the express car, each with a pair of handcuffs and spancels, the cigar-smoking deputy remained behind the Gatling gun, narrowing one eye as he aimed down the brass canister at the two cutthroats, grinning as though daring them to resist arrest.

Slash returned his incredulous gaze to the broadly, victoriously grinning Bledsoe. He'd never seen a man look so pleased with himself. The crippled old marshal appeared about to leap up out of his chair, jump down from the train car, and hop around his two, long-sought prisoners, yowling like a crazed Injun on the night before a battle.

"How'd you do it?" Slash spit out at the old lawman.

"How'd you get her to double-cross us? How'd you do it, Bledsoe?"

"Oh, it wasn't so hard," Bledsoe said, shrugging a shoulder. "She's a woman, isn't she?"

"Not just any woman," Pecos said as his arms were jerked around behind his back and cuffs were closed over his wrists. "What'd you do? How'd you threaten her?"

Bledsoe merely sat back in his chair, smiling and taking the sun. "Load 'em up, boys," he said, plucking a gold timepiece from a pocket of his brocade vest. "If we leave now we should be back to Saguache in time for a late lunch." He returned the watch to its pocket and winked at Slash and Pecos. "The special over at the Colorado House is the prime rib sandwich and a boiler maker," he said. "Not that that means anything to you two. You'll be dinin' on burned beans, moldy bread, and stale water till you're dancin' the midair two-step!"

He closed a knobby hand around his neck and stuck out his tongue, feigning strangulation.

Then he slapped his leg and howled again.

"Hurry up, dammit, boys!" he urged the two deputies. "Get 'em aboard and let's get this heap back to civilization. Success of this caliber makes the chief marshal *hungry!*"

CHAPTER 14

"Guilty!" the federal judge bellowed three days later, rapping his gavel atop the bar behind which he sat on a high wooden stool. "Guilty! Guilty! Guilty!" Even louder, he shouted for emphasis above the cheering court watchers in the Busted Bum Saloon and Parlor House on First Avenue in the little Colorado mountain town of Saguache: "GUILTY AS HELLLLL!"

Sitting at a round saloon table with their "attorney," flanked by all three of Bledsoe's rifle-wielding deputies, Slash turned to Pecos. "Well, that was a real surprise."

"Yeah," Pecos said grimly, beneath the cheering of the townsfolk who'd filled the saloon till the place was busting at its seams. "Pardon me while I pick myself up off the floor in shock."

"Sorry, fellas," yelled one of the girls who'd been watching from the balcony over the saloon, above the mahogany bar where Judge Angus McClelland was gathering his papers. "If you're allowed, me an' Betsy'll give ya both a free one before they drop ya!"

The pretty blonde clad in colorful under frillies and with pink night ribbons in her hair elbowed the half-clad brunette beside her, who leaned forward over the porch rail to blow the two doomed cutthroats a kiss.

"Thanks, girl!" Pecos yelled back as one of the deputies pulled him to his feet from behind. "We'll put in a request with ole Bleed-'Em-So Bledsoe, but I got a suspicion he ain't gonna allow us no slap'n'tickle before we saddle our golden clouds and float off to that great express car in the sky!"

"We'll be out in the street cheerin' for your souls to make it to heaven!" yelled the blonde, leaning forward and kicking a slim, pale leg out behind her.

Slash grinned back at the pretty doxie, who was young enough to be his granddaughter, but said to Pecos out the side of his mouth, "She'll be out in the street, all right, but she won't be cheerin' for our souls so much as she'll be tryin' to drum up business. I bet that'll be the biggest day for all the business folks in this part of the territory."

"Ah, don't be so tough on the girl," Pecos said as the three deputies conferred behind them, watching the milling crowd for a break through which they could haze their prisoners back out onto the street and over to the courthouse in which the jail was tucked. "She's gotta make a livin' like everyone else!"

Slash turned to his and Pecos's attorney sitting to Slash's right. The young little lad, who wore a carnation in the lapel of his shabby brown suit coat, was sound asleep, his chin dipped toward his left shoulder. Slash could hear the young man snoring beneath the crowd's din.

He nudged the young man's arm. "Hey, Lester, wake up!"

Lester Hyman jerked his head up with a start, looking around wide-eyed, as though slow to remember where he was and what he was doing here—defending two of the West's most notorious outlaws against a surefire hanging, which he'd lost. He wasn't really an attorney, anyway, though Bledsoe and his close friend Judge McClelland had deemed him so. Lester was just reading for the law; he had no experience in the federal courts at all. His resume included a couple of divorces, a man charged with stealing hay from a neighbor, an elderly teetotaling lady accused of killing her husband by dumping strychnine in his home-brewed forty-rod, and a doxie accused of robbing her jake while he slept upstairs in this very saloon.

"It's all over, Lester," Slash told the young man still blinking as he looked around the room, slowly coming out of his alcohol-induced stupor. He'd been so nervous through the entire trial that he'd drained his little pocket flask over the course of the three-hour proceeding, furtively adding the rye to his coffee beneath the table while the federal prosecutor was regaling the cutthroats and judge as well as the six-person jury with Slash and Pecos's past exploits. "All over except the hangin'," Slash added.

"Ah," Lester said, fighting a yawn and running a grimy sleeve across his mouth, over which he was trying to grow a mustache. "Ah . . . oh . . . golly, I'm really, really sorry, fellas. . . ."

"Don't worry about it, Lester," Pecos said. "You didn't have a chance."

"Bledsoe and McClelland had decided they was gonna hang us long before we even arrived in town," Slash said, remembering the large banner draped across the town's main street, and which he'd first seen when he and Pecos had pulled into town on Bledsoe's dime.

In large, ornate red letters, it read:

NECKTIE PARTY NECKS SATURDAY!

He hadn't been sure, and he still wasn't, if the misspelling had been unintentional or a reflection of the banner maker's wry humor.

"They didn't even allow me to provide any witnesses

who might've testified in your defense!" Lester said, fumbling a second silver flask from his coat pocket.

"That's all right, too, Lester," Slash said.

"Yeah," Pecos said, smiling grimly and adding, "You wouldn't have found any even if you'd gone lookin'."

He and Slash snorted a bleak laugh.

"All right, fellas, let's go!" the perpetually cigar-smoking deputy ordered, ramming his rifle butt against Slash's back. "Get movin', an' no lollygaggin'!"

As Slash and Pecos were hazed toward the batwing doors through the rapidly thinning crowd, Lester hurried to keep up with them, saying, "If they would only wait until I could file an appeal with the appellate courts, I'm sure I could at least get you a stay and a new trial!"

Lester tipped the flask back once more as he and Slash and Pecos stepped out onto Saguache's broad, dusty main street, flanked by the three, grim-faced, Winchester-wielding deputies donning mustaches on their severely chiseled faces, and low-crowned, black brimmed hats.

"Don't waste your ink," Slash said. "You'd only be prolonging the inevitable."

"Ah, Jesus," Lester said, jogging to keep up with the taller men. "I just feel . . . well, I just feel . . ."

"Forget it, Lester," Slash said. "Go home and sleep it off, son."

The young man slowed his pace until he'd fallen well behind Slash and Pecos and their three flanking guards. Slash glanced over his shoulder to see Lester stopping, throwing his arms out in defeat, and taking another deep pull from his flask.

"Poor fella," Slash said to Pecos, striding beside him with his hands cuffed behind his back. "He tried his best."

"Yeah, it ain't his fault we'll be the guests of honor at the necktie party tomorrow." Pecos cast a grim glance at the gallows, still under construction a block ahead. Two men were putting the finishing touches on it, one oiling the trapdoor hinges while the other adjusted the two ropes atop the platform and to which two sandbags had been tied to gauge the drop. He toiled under the tutelage of a tall, gray-haired man in a stovepipe hat and long black, claw hammer coat and whom Slash knew was the hangman, Adolph Grimes.

"No, it wasn't Lester's fault," Slash agreed, adding, through gritted teeth, spitting out her name like a bitter pill he just couldn't swallow: "*Jay!* That's whose fault it is. Jaycee Breckenridge!"

"Why do you think she did it, anyways?" Pecos asked, both men ignoring the three sun-darkened little boys who'd just run out of the gap between a barbershop and a millinery, firing their tree branch rifles at the two doomed men and yelling, "*Bang-bang*—you two cutthroats is wolf bait!"

"*Bang-bang-bang!*" yelled another—the smallest of the bunch, hopping around as though he were galloping hell for leather on a wild stallion. "Consider yourselves planted!"

"Go away, you boys," reprimanded one of the marshals. "You get too close to these polecats, they're liable to jump you and bite your ears off. Now, git!"

Chuckling, Slash turned to Pecos in answer to his partner's question about Jay. "Maybe it's like ole Bleed-'Em-So said. Maybe the marshal plied her with nice dresses and fine jewelry. Most women will do a lot for that sorta thing. I never would have figured Jay for one o' them, but I reckon I had her wrong."

"I reckon we both had her wrong."

"Well, she's a woman. You gotta figure you've figured 'em wrong just when you start to believe you've finally figured 'em out!"

Pecos stared at his partner in wide-eyed admiration.

"I'll be hanged, Slash, if you ain't the wisest man I ever known!"

"I've been tryin' to tell you that for years now."

"Maybe it finally done sunk in."

"Here on the eve of our necktie party."

"Life is odd, ain't it, Slash?"

"That it is, partner," Slash lamented, slowly wagging his head as he drew up to the side of the courthouse, near the two barred cellar doors leading to the basement cell block. "That it sure as hell is."

"You two are real philosophers," said the deputy, Vern Gables, who had the perpetual Mexican cheroot in his hand. They'd all stopped in front of the cellar doors, and the deputy named Vince Tabor crouched to poke a key in the lock.

"You know what my philosophy about you is, Gables?" asked Pecos, staring belligerently down at the slightly shorter, dark-haired deputy U.S. marshal.

"No, what's that?"

"You smoke too much an' you smell bad!"

Gables grinned darkly as he took one step back. He'd just started to raise his rifle to tattoo Pecos's forehead with the brass butt plate when Slash sidled between the two men. "Now, now, now," Slash said, facing Gables. "If that's all it takes to get your dander up, then I, sir, am sorry to inform you that you are sorely lacking in maturity."

"That a fact?" Gables said. "Well, let me tell you something, Slash Braddock, that might make you feel just a tad immature."

Slash grinned defiantly. "Fish or cut bait!"

Gables took a deep drag off his cigar, blew the smoke at Slash, then, leaning forward and grinning like the cat that ate the canary, said, "Guess who I seen comin' out of ole Bleed-'Em-So's room over at the Colorado House this morning, lookin' a little, uh, *disheveled*, shall we say?"

The grin left Slash's face. His eyes grew flat and dark. "Who?"

"That whore who double-crossed you two old mossy-horns—Miss Jaycee Breckenridge!"

Slash glared at him, his face swelling and flushing. "You're lyin'!"

"You'll never know." Gables grinned more broadly, then poked the cheroot into his mouth once more.

Slash slammed his forehead against the man's mouth, smashing the cigar against his lips and throwing Gables straight backward with an indignant scream. Gables nearly went down and would have if the deputy behind him hadn't grabbed him and propped him back up.

"You win," Slash said, his grin in place once more. "That does make me feel a tad immature."

Pecos chuckled.

Gables brushed hot ashes from his mouth. His lower lip was split. "Why, you son of a bitch!"

He rushed at Slash but the deputy behind him grabbed him.

"Hold on, Vern, hold on! Don't mess 'im up—you know . . . before . . . ?" The third deputy, whose name was Tyson Waite, spread a shrewd grin of his own.

That seemed to take some of the hump out of Gables's neck. He lowered his clenched fist, then smiled and released his held breath. Waite released him.

"Oh, yeah." Gables smiled mockingly at Slash and Pecos, smoothing his rumpled jacket. "Right, right."

"I don't get it," Pecos said. "Before what?"

"You'll see," Gables said, raising his rifle and using its butt to nudge Slash toward the open cellar doors. "Get back in your hidy-hole. We'll drag you back out . . . and 'drag' is likely the word for it, too . . . when it's time to stretch some hemp."

"I don't get it," Pecos said to Slash as the two outlaws

walked down the steps and into the cool, dark cell block. "Why are they gonna have to drag us out?"

"Here you go," Gables said when they were roughly halfway down the cell block. "Home sweet home, fellas!"

Pecos and Slash glanced into their respective cells. Pecos's cell was on the left side of the stone-floored corridor between the two walls of strap-iron cages. Slash's was on the right side. Each cell had a prisoner in it.

Before the trial, Slash and Pecos and one other man had been the only prisoners in the cell block. The third prisoner, hauled in last night for getting drunk and tearing up a hurdy-gurdy house, was gone—likely freed after his fine had been paid.

Now there were two other prisoners. One was in Pecos's cell, lying sacked out on one of the two cell cots that folded down from the barred walls on stout chains. The other was in Slash's cell, also sacked out on a thinly padded, iron-framed cot.

Both were big men. Bigger than Pecos, even. They were both snoring loudly.

"I don't get it," Slash said, glancing around the otherwise empty cell block. "Why are they in our cells? Hell, there's plenty of other cells for 'em."

"We were afraid you boys might get lonely," Gables said.

Slash shrugged and said, "I got an idea. Why don't you stick us into another pair of cages?" He smiled mockingly at Gables. "If we get lonely, we'll call for you to read us a good-night story, Vern."

"Nah, nah," Gables said, giving Slash a hard shove into his old, newly occupied cell, through the door that deputy Tabor had opened with a key from his ring of cell block keys. "This is home sweet-home-home for you, my friend, Slash. Till Adolph Grimes plays cat's cradle with your head, anyways."

He laughed.

Tabor shoved Pecos through his own cell's open door and into his own, freshly occupied cell.

When the deputies had removed Slash's and Pecos's handcuffs, closed and locked their cell doors, and clacked off down the cell block, chuckling, Slash massaged his chafed wrists and stared down at the big man sprawled belly up across the cell's second cot.

"Good Lord—this here is one big SOB!" he told Pecos.

"Yeah," Pecos said, staring down at his own bulky cell mate. "This one, too."

The two cutthroats shared dark looks through their cell doors.

CHAPTER 15

"Why do you suppose we got us a coupla cell mates, Slash?" Pecos asked from the cell across the corridor.

Slash looked up from the big, bald-headed hombre sacked out belly down on the cot in Slash's cell and said, "I don't know. Maybe Gables figures they need father figures. You know—two good, upstandin', older citizens to counsel them in the ways of the straight 'n' narrow."

Slash smiled.

Pecos chuckled and shook his head, staring down at his cell mate. "I got a feelin' that ain't so. Just a hunch, though. I might be wrong." He wrinkled his nose and stepped back away from his loudly snoring cell mate. "Pee-*you*! This fella stinks like a whiskey barrel that done drowned a polecat!"

He ran a thick forearm across his nose.

"Yeah, this one, too."

Slash stared down at his own cell mate. The man was maybe six feet, six inches tall, though it was hard to tell with him lying down. He was thick through the chest and neck. Very thick. Thick as a Brahma bull. On the side of his neck was the tattoo of a naked woman.

A gold stud pierced his left earlobe. Another tattoo marked his forehead. It was a circle with a figure eight inside it. Slash had seen such markings before and knew that these, like those, were probably the signature of some coastal city gang. This fella was likely from the Barbary Coast or New Orleans. He and his partner were likely hiding out in the Colorado mountains, on the dodge from a possible murder charge. Probably several murder charges. They had the look of freight-hauling mule skinners. This one's ham-sized hands were badly scarred and thickly callused. Scars across his knuckles marked him as a bare-knuckle fighter. They told of smashed faces, broken jaws, and eyes swollen to the sizes of horseshoes.

He must have gotten into another fight last night, for some of those scars had opened up and shone brightly with fresh blood.

His face was broad and ugly. His thick nose had several knots. It had obviously been broken several times and not been set right. A dollop of blood was crusted beneath his left nostril.

The big man before Slash indeed looked like a merciless, tough nut, as someone here in Saguache had likely learned last night or early this morning the hard way.

The man sucked in a long, deep breath, roaring like a slumbering dragon. When he let out the breath, the snore rose a couple of octaves, and the man's thick, chapped lips fluttered. They were also flecked with blood. He winced a little, shaking his head and frowning.

Likely suffering one hell of a hangover.

"All I got to say," Pecos said, walking up to his cell door and leaning forward, squeezing the iron bands in his hands and regarding Slash gravely, "is when these fellas wake up, I doubt they're gonna be feelin' any too friendly."

"Yeah," Slash said, walking over to his own cell door,

stepping lightly on the balls of his boots so as not to wake his big, mean-looking companion. "Let's just hope they sleep good an' sound till . . . well, till tomorrow, at least."

He leaned forward against his own cell door, pressing his forehead to the iron bands.

"You gotta hand it to ole Bleed-'Em-So," Pecos drawled. "He sure knows how to make a pair of old cutthroats suffer. He's prob'ly hopin' these two wake up an' beat us to greasy pulps."

"Yeah, well, he's been after us for a long time. And I'm the one who put him in that wheelchair." Slash sighed, lifted his head, and scratched the beard stubble on his neck. "I reckon he's gonna wring every bit of pleasure he can out of us before we drop through that gallows floor tomorrow." He glanced over his shoulder at the stout man still snoring behind him.

"I reckon," Pecos said, toeing a crack in the stone floor. He looked up at Slash suddenly, frowning. "Say, Slash . . ."

"Uh-huh?"

"You, uh . . . you afraid?"

"Of what? Dyin'?"

"Of course dyin'!"

Slash pondered the subject, frowning down at the cell block's chipped and dusty stone floor. His frown deepened and then he lifted his gaze to his partner's blue-eyed gaze holding steady on him from the opposite cell.

"Yeah," Slash said, nodding slowly. "Yeah . . . I reckon I am. I reckon we both faced death so much—every time we went out on a job, as a matter of fact—that you'd think I'd have got used to the notion. But . . . now, havin' that gallows staring me in the face . . ."

Slash nodded again, chuckled. "Yeah . . . I reckon I am feelin' a might squishy in the belly about it."

"Me, too," Pecos admitted. Suddenly, he grinned, blue

eyes glowing as they caught the light angling through the high, barred window flanking Slash. "But we had us a good run, didn't we, partner?"

Slash returned the smile. "We did at that, partner."

"Not too many men can say they got through this life without callin' no other men their boss."

"They sure can't!"

"You an' me was never no other man's hammer an' that's a fact. Leastways, not since we was seventeen, eighteen years old. After that, we went into business for ourselves, stealin' other men's money!"

"That's what we did, all right. And we did it in about as honest and upright a way as two cutthroats could do it, too!"

"We sure as hell did!" Pecos agreed, lifting his head suddenly and loosing a victorious, coyote-like whoop.

"Oh-oh," Slash said, stretching his gaze beyond Pecos.

The big man on the cot behind Pecos had stirred, snorting and grumbling. He lifted his big, flat face suddenly, framed by greasy, brown, gray-flecked hair, and glowered toward Slash and Pecos, wrinkling up his broad, doughy nose from which sprouted a wart the size of the tip of Slash's little finger. "Will you two peckerwoods shut the hell up? Can't you see a man's tryin' to get some shut-eye over here?"

His voice was deep and grumbling, like the voice of a grizzly bear—a severely piss-burned one—if a grizzly bear could talk, that was.

Half turned to his cell mate, Pecos said, "Uh . . . yes, sir. Sorry, sir!"

He glanced at Slash, wincing.

"There," grumbled the big man, dropping his head back down to the thinly padded cot, making the chains squawk and groan. "Tha's more . . . like . . . it. . . ."

He was sawing logs once more.

Slash pressed his lips together, biting back a laugh.

Pecos glanced behind him again, then turned to Slash in relief. "Whew! Did you see the size of his head?"

"Looks solid, too."

"And I doubt there's a thing in it," Pecos said, lifting a big forearm to muffle his snorting laughter.

"Shhh!" Slash said from across the stone corridor. "We wake him again, I got a feelin' you're gonna suffer somethin' awful." He fought back his own snorts and yowls, tears of laughter running down his cheeks. "No, I don't think it'll go well for you at all, Pecos! Why, he'll pull you inside out an' stomp on your stuffin' till there won't be nothin' left for ole Bleed-'Em-So to hang but a bag of broken bones!"

Both men slid down the bars of their respective cell doors, howling into their shirtsleeves. They sat on their butts, shouldered up to their cell doors, snorting and grunting for nearly two entire minutes. Glancing at each other through the bars and at the big snoring brutes flanking each of them only made them howl harder.

"Ah, crap," Pecos said finally, when their laughter was dwindling and they were both wrung out, tears bathing their rugged faces.

They let a few minutes pass, just sitting there. They listened to the occasional hammering from outside, which they knew belonged to the final adjustments being made to the instrument of their annihilation—the gallows. There was also the barking of a distant dog, the chirping of birds, and the clomping and clattering of occasional horseback riders and wagons passing the jailhouse.

Men shouted, laughed.

A baby cried.

"Hey, Slash?"

"Yep?"

"What're you gonna miss the most? You know—about livin'?"

"What am I gonna miss the most? Hmmm." Slash looked up at the cobwebbed wooden rafters, pondering. "You know what I'm gonna miss?" he said finally. "I'm gonna miss good bourbon whiskey, that first smoke of the day . . . along with a cup of good, hot mud, of course . . . and the expertise of a good workin' girl. That's what I'm gonna miss. In that order. In my younger days, that order woulda been a whole lot different."

He chuckled as he pressed the back of his head against the cell door. "But now in my later years—there ya have it. Good whiskey, the first smoke, and a talented whore that knows when to get up and haul her freight."

Pecos pursed his lips, nodding. "All right, all right," he said. "That's a good list, I reckon."

Slash glanced through the bars at him. "What're you gonna miss?"

"Me?" Pecos frowned as he stared into space, reflecting. "I'm gonna miss the smell of desert sage and burning piñon pine, an' spring wildflowers. Especially them purty bright yellow and red and purple flowers that paint spring meadows up high in the Rockies. I'm gonna miss the taste of a trout caught fresh in one o' them Rocky Mountain lakes—like that lake where we camped on the shore of a couple summers back with that old rascal Brent Huntley. Remember him?"

"Hell, how could I forget that old scalawag? The stories he told!"

"Remember how he always called Kansas City by its original name—Westport Landing? That old coot!" Pecos shook his head, smiling. Gradually, his expression grew serious once more. "You know what I'm gonna miss more than anything, Slash?"

"What?"

"Don't laugh at me."

"All right, I won't laugh."

"Forget it. You're gonna laugh."

Slash scowled through the bars at his partner, who sat on his butt on the other side of the corridor, his long, thin, blond hair flowing down over his shoulders. Pecos was frowning and pulling at his blond chin whiskers.

"I ain't gonna laugh. I promise."

Pecos considered Slash through the bars, then slowly shaped a dreamy, faintly sheepish smile. "I'm gonna miss fallin' in love." He draped an arm over an upraised knee. "Yessir. That's what I'm gonna miss the most. That kind of achy feelin' you get in your chest and belly when you're tumblin' for a woman."

Slash glanced at him skeptically. "No kiddin'?"

"Damn straight." Pecos glared at him, accusing. "You said you wouldn't laugh!"

Slash threw up a hand. "I ain't laughin'!" He paused. When Jay crept into his mind, he quickly shoved her away, turning to Pecos and saying, "I don't reckon it's any wonder you'd miss that, since you've always tumbled for one woman or another so damn often!"

He chuckled, and Pecos did, as well, likely remembering with no little fondness all of the pretty women he'd been attached to over the years. Most for only a few weeks or months at a time. The briefness of said unions hadn't made them any less poignant for the big, romantic galoot. And it hadn't made the tenderhearted Pecos River Kid hurt any less when those unions had run their courses and he and the ladies had forked trails.

As far as Slash was concerned, women always made him feel fidgety when they were around too long. For more than a few hours, even. They made him feel tight and hemmed in. Downright owly.

Most had, anyway . . .

Thinking of feeling hemmed in, he glanced around the cell block, feeling as hemmed in as he'd ever felt in his life. He and Pecos had been riding roughshod and tail-up around the frontier for a long time, but neither one had spent more than a night or two at any one time in a jail, and those jailings had been merely for getting into drunken dustups in saloons or sporting houses. They'd been here in this county lockup for nigh on a week, and Slash was starting to feel as though he'd been buried alive.

"You don't suppose there's any way out of here—do you, Pecos?" he said, studying the bars of his cell's small window through which bright midday light angled onto the high, lace-up boots of his slumbering cell mate.

"Do you know how many times you've asked me that since we been in here?"

"Twenty, at least." Slash pressed his back against the cell door and rose to his feet, rising from his heels.

"Yeah, I'd say around twenty."

Slash winced as he walked on the balls of his boots past his loudly snoring cell mate and over to the window mounted in the cell block wall. Roughly two feet by three feet, with four bars embedded deeply in the stone casing, the window was about six and a half feet off the floor.

"I just keep wondering if I couldn't loosen up one or two of these bars." Slash leaped up off his heels and grabbed two of the bars in his hands, sort of chinning himself to see out.

As he grunted and groaned, squeezing the bars, testing their strength, he saw none other than Luther T. "Bleed-'Em-So" Bledsoe being wheeled past the jailhouse, not twenty feet beyond Slash, by none other than Slash and Pecos's young, so-called attorney, Lester Hyman. Judge Angus McClelland strolled along behind Bledsoe and Hyman. Included in the four-man group was the prosecuting attorney, George Hill, a sour-looking little man in an opera hat and with thick, curly, red muttonchops.

"Well, well, well—what do we have here? Y'all headin' off to the Colorado House for a prime rib sandwich and a boiler maker to start the celebration? You, too, Lester—our own *loyal* attorney? Shame on you, son!"

Lester stopped pushing Bledsoe's chair. He and the rest of the men all swung around to regard Slash staring at them through the barred, ground-level window.

"Ah, hell, Slash!" Lester said, tossing his head miserably. "I said I was sorry. Now, I don't know what more I can do!"

"Well, you could run off an' have a good cry instead of rushing off to stomp with these corrupt politicians!"

"*Cry?* Over you two scalawags?" intoned Judge Angus McClelland, standing beside the short, fat prosecutor, who wore a rust-red clawhammer coat inside the lapel of which he'd thrust his black-gloved right hand, as though he were waiting to have his picture taken.

The judge pointed his own black-gloved finger at Slash. "Believe you me, no one's gonna cry over the hanging of Slash Braddock and the Pecos River Kid—and that's includin' the poor man who was given the cruel, inhuman, as well as impossible task of trying to defend your depredations against humanity!"

"Don't worry, Slash," said Bledsoe, squinting and wincing against the bright, high-country sunshine, "we'll all be there tomorrow, enjoying the festivities. And you're right—we are about to start the celebration."

"You know, Bleed-'Em-So, the only thing I regret about my ricochet finding its way into your back is it didn't have a twin."

"That so?"

"That's so, sir!"

"Well, under the circumstances, seein' as how I'm gonna

watch you two dribble down your legs tomorrow," Bledsoe said, "no hard feelin's! In fact, why don't I have the barman over at the Colorado House deliver you and Pecos your favorite skull pop, just to ease your misery a little in this great time of sorrow for you both, seein' as how you're about to have your necks stretched. Okay? Can I do that for you?"

Slash turned his head partly to one side, frowning skeptically yet hopefully, imagining bathing his tonsils in one more bottle of his favorite Kentucky bourbon.

"Really?" he said, pulse quickening in anticipation of such a treat. "You'd do that?"

Bledsoe grinned and shook his head. "No," he said dryly. "I wouldn't do that!" He threw his head back, laughing. "Did you hear that, fellas? He really thought I was gonna send a bottle of his favorite forty-rod over to the jail? Hah! Hah! Hah!"

"Yeah," laughed the prosecutor, Hill, "as if a U.S. marshal known as 'Bleed-'Em-So' would ever do such a thing!"

Hill's jowls shook as he roared, leaning over to slap his thigh.

The judge and even Lester Hyman laughed.

Slash released the bars and dropped back down to the stone floor of his cell. "Crap!"

He leaned forward against the wall.

"Hey, Slash!" Pecos called.

"What?"

"Turn around."

Slash turned. "What fo—"

He cut himself off. Directly in front of him was the broad chest of his cell mate, clad in sweat-stained wool spotted with blood from last night's fight. The man smelled like a bear fresh from hibernation. One who'd gone to sleep drunk.

"You really Slash Braddock?" the big man said, painfully poking Slash's chest with his banana-sized index finger.

"Uh," Slash said, tentatively. "What if I was?"

"Why, you don't look like so doggone much!" The big man poked his big finger into Slash's chest once more, shoving Slash back up against the cell's stone wall. "Why, I bet I could break you over my knee like kindlin'!"

CHAPTER 16

"I bet you could," Slash told his tattooed, muscle-bound cell mate towering over him. "But why on earth would you want to do such a thing, pray tell?"

"Marshal Bleed-'Em-So done told us what you two said about us. How you two was *laughin'* at us!"

Slash glanced around the big man before him at Pecos, who was facing down his own cell mate. The big brute had also risen from his bunk and was backing Pecos, who at six-foot-four stood a good four inches shorter than his cell mate, with long dark-brown hair, against the back wall of their cell.

"Bleed-'Em-So said we said what about you?" Pecos asked, staring warily up at his own opponent.

"That crippled-up old fox was on the street last night when the town marshal's deputies was haulin' us over here. He told us we might like to know that you two seen us out on the street the other day and you called us a couple of overgrown bunghole pirates."

"We're mighty tired o' them rumors bein' spread about us!" said Pecos's cell mate, shoving Pecos back hard against the cell's rear wall. "Mighty tired!"

"'Cause it ain't one bit true!" professed Slash's ape. He glanced quickly over his left shoulder. "Is it, Tiny?"

"It sure ain't, Buck!" Tiny shot back, glaring down at Pecos.

"Gentlemen, please believe me," Slash said, holding up his hands in supplication "Pecos and I never saw you before in our lives."

"We wouldn't know neither one o' you fellas from Adam's off-ox!" agreed Pecos.

"And even if we had—and even if we'd been privy to the rumors being so maliciously spread about you two fellas, who obviously never played grabby-pants a single night around the old campfire in your lives!—we'd certainly never spread such lies ourselves. Would we, Pecos?"

Pecos choked on a dry laugh, then quickly recovered to shout, "Hell, no!"

Buck glared down at Slash, wrinkling up his massive, broken nose. "Slash Braddock, huh?" He raked his gaze from Slash's face to his boot toes, then back up to his face again. "You don't look like so damn much!"

"Neither does the Pecos River Kid," agreed Tiny, staring down at Pecos. "They don't look nothin' like the newspapers are always tootin' about 'em!"

"And you know what, Tiny?" asked Buck.

"What's that, Buck?"

"I think they're funnin' with us!"

Slash had stepped away from Buck, moving to the side of his cell, backing away from the large, unwieldy, and red-faced giant who kept pace before him, glaring down threateningly, ham-sized fists bunched at his sides.

"Now . . . take it easy, Buck!" Slash said, backing toward his cell door, holding his open hands farther out from his chest as Buck decreased the space between them.

"What you two do in the privacy of your own campfires ain't no one's business but your own!"

"You know what I'm gonna do to this one here?" Tiny asked Buck, following Pecos around their own cell.

"What's that, Tiny?"

"I'm gonna tear his head plum off his shoulders!"

"That's a good idea," Buck said. "I'm gonna tear this one's off, too, and I'm gonna paint the walls with his brains!"

Buck lunged for Slash, raising his arms as though to wrap them around Slash's head. Slash ducked out from under the man's arms, then scrambled around behind Buck, who was lumbering and slow, wheezing like an ancient bellows, spreading the fumes of the whiskey oozing from his sweaty pores.

When Buck turned, Slash yelled, "Stand down, Buck, or this ain't gonna go well for you!"

"I doubt that, you little dung pile!"

Again, Buck lunged for Slash.

As he did, Slash pulled his right foot back, then launched that boot straight forward and up, burying the toe high between the raging Buck's stout legs. He felt the soft, pillowy flesh yield and give a soft cracking sound.

Buck loosed a high-pitched, wailing, effeminate-sounding scream and, closing his knees inward, jackknifed forward and closed his massive hands over his ailing crotch. His head swelled up to nearly twice its normal size, and his face turned first flour white, then fire red, his eyes flashing like diamonds in their doughy sockets.

"Buck!" Tiny yelled, swinging around and bounding away from Pecos and toward his cell door. "Buck! My God—Buck, honey, you okay over there?"

He canted his head to see through the bars, and when his eyes found Buck dropping to his knees, wailing, he switched his gaze to Slash and bellowed, "What did you do to Buck, you crazy polecat!"

Pecos strode up behind Tiny. He picked up the empty white enamel thunder mug from beneath his cell mate's cot. He raised it high by its metal bail, then gritted his teeth as he swung it down hard against the back of Tiny's pumpkin-sized, long-haired head.

Bang! went the bucket against Tiny's stout skull.

Tiny appeared to hardly notice. He merely stopped, blinked, then slowly turned around to face Pecos, whose wide blue eyes betrayed his fear. Pecos raised the bucket high again and then swung it forward and down against Tiny's skull once more.

Bang! went the bucket against Tiny's stout skull again.

Tiny had his back to Slash now. Slash didn't think the giant flinched against the assault this time, either. He just stood facing Pecos—nearly a whole head taller than the blond-headed cutthroat, who cowered back away from the bigger man, staring up at him in wide-eyed trepidation.

For several seconds, Tiny stood facing Pecos without moving. The giant gave a ragged sigh and fell straight forward, like a tree shorn off near the ground by a two-man ripsaw. Pecos gave a startled grunt and scrambled to one side, away from the big man, who dropped like that cutdown tree in the woods, and smashed face first and belly down against the stone floor of the cell.

Tiny lay unmoving.

Pecos looked through the bars at Slash and shrugged.

Slash looked down at Buck, whose face was still bright red. Buck glared up at his cell mate, clamping his hands between his legs.

"You injured me, you crazy devil!" Buck croaked, a forked blue vein throbbing in his tattooed forehead. "You injured me real bad. I . . . I think you . . . broke me somethin' *awful* down there!"

"Better than you breakin' me something awful up here," Slash said, pointing at his head.

Following Pecos's lead, Slash picked up his own cell's slop bucket, which he was glad to find empty. The deputies must have emptied the buckets.

"Here ya go, Buck," Slash said, raising the bucket by its bail. "I'll put you outta your misery."

"D-don't you dare!" Buck raged.

He'd started to raise his arms but didn't get them even to his chin before Slash slammed the bucket down against his head with a wicked-sounding crash.

Buck's big head wobbled on his thick shoulders.

His eyes rolled up in their sockets.

He sagged back against the cell wall, dipped his chin to his shoulder, wagged his head, gave a long ragged sigh, and fell fast asleep.

"You boys ready for that long, last walk?" asked Deputy U.S. Marshal Vern Gables late the next morning, another long, black Mexican cigar poking out from between his swollen and scabbed lips that looked more than a mite sore.

Despite his painful mouth, he appeared in a good mood, all smiles and glittering blue eyes. His black hat was set at a rakish angle upon his dark head. His cheeks were cleanly shaved, his thick dragoon-style mustache freshly clipped. He smelled like peppermint pomade and Ogallala Bay Rum & Sandalwood Skin Toner. He winked through the bars as Deputy Vince Tabor unlocked the door of the cell that housed both Slash and Pecos together now.

Late yesterday afternoon, the town marshal's deputies had hauled Buck and Tiny off to the local sawbones for tending. The local lawmen had had to carry the ailing brutes out on stretchers. Tiny had been curled in the fetal position, thumb in his mouth. The sizes of both patients had evoked quite a bit of grunting and cursing, and more than a few incredulous gazes had been directed toward the two middle-aged cutthroats whose clocks the two giants were apparently supposed to have cleaned, and who'd stood smiling and waving as their cell mates were evacuated.

The cell block still stunk with the fetor the two had carried in here, however. It would likely linger well into next week.

"No, I ain't ready for that walk," Pecos said, scowling at Gables as Tabor opened the door, which grated loudly on its dry hinges. "But if you think I'm gonna dribble down my leg and sob for mercy, you got another think comin', you lawdog son of a weasel!"

"There's the spirit!" Gables said, holding his cigar out and gingerly tapping ashes from the coal. "The two old catamounts are gonna go out cussin' blue streaks!"

"Not me," Slash said, holding out his wrists as the third deputy, Tyson Waite, clicked handcuffs around them.

Tabor applied the spancels to the prisoners' ankles. Two deputy town marshals stood at the end of the cell block, near the outside doors, both big men cradling long-barreled, double-bore shotguns in their thick arms, all-business expressions on their mustached faces, beneath the brims of their pulled-down Stetsons.

"I'm not gonna cuss none," Slash continued. "There's likely young children and old ladies on the street. I wouldn't want to be a bad influence. If I dribble down my leg while I'm doin' the midair two-step, though, Vern, I'll be sure to dance in your direction. You'd best stand upwind."

He winked at the sore-mouthed federal.

"Thanks for the advice," Gables said, taking a long pull off the cigar and blowing the plume directly at Slash.

When the cuffs and spancels were secured to both prisoners, preventing them from throwing any punches or running, Gables stepped back, drawing the cell door wide.

Waite and Tabor shoved the prisoners out into the corridor, and Slash and Pecos started that long, last walk, having to shuffle awkwardly along due to the two-foot length of chains securing their ankles. Ahead were the two stout, oak, iron-banded doors. Beyond those doors were the stone steps rising to the barred cellar doors.

Beyond lay the crowd that Slash and Pecos had heard gathering for the past hour or so, milling in eager anticipation of the necktie party. For the past twenty minutes or so the crowd as well as the two condemned prisoners had listened to the spiel of a traveling snake oil salesman, using the opportunity to hock his Doctor Roman's Liver Purifier as well as his sure-fire cure for the chilblains and occasional pleurisy—Mrs. Parker's Lung Tonic.

Through the barred outside window, smoke from several cook fires had slithered into the cell, rife with the tantalizing aromas of roasting meat. The lingering smell was still making Slash's mouth water, though his throat was dry and his neck ached in anticipation of the rope and the sudden drop through the trapdoor. His and Pecos's last meal, which had been this morning's breakfast, had consisted of what all their meals had consisted of so far— beans cooked with very little bacon, and a tin cup of water.

Just as there'd been no last bottle of good Kentucky bourbon, there'd been no lavish last meal for the condemned men, either. Chief Marshal Luther T. "Bleed-'Em-So" Bledsoe was going to laugh the two former heads of the Snake River Marauders all the way to the gallows and beyond. . . .

The two deputy town marshals unlocked and opened the stout oak doors. They climbed the stone steps, unlocked the cellar doors, then pushed them wide, ordering the crowd that had gathered around the cell block entrance to stand back. Bright, high-country sunlight poured down over the steps and into the faces of the condemned men, who hadn't seen direct sunlight in nearly a week.

The bright light was like a million tiny javelins stabbing Slash's and Pecos's eyes and causing both outlaws to jerk back on their heels.

"Get out there!" Gables barked, ramming his rifle butt against Slash's back, shoving the old outlaw on up the steps and out into the street.

Tyson Waite gave Pecos similar treatment, and suddenly both outlaws were stumbling forward, a small crowd of gawkers converging on them. There were old and young, men and women, crying babies and barking dogs. A particularly tall elderly man in a black suit and with a Bible in his hand jutted his hawk face toward Slash and Pecos, wailing, "Repent sinners! Repent! Rejoice in the word of your Lord and Savior, or have thee sins drowned in the fires of *eternal hell and damnation!*"

"Speaking of hell, old man," Pecos barked back at him. "Hop back into it and get the *hell* out of my face!"

A little towheaded boy pushed through the crowd to stare up in delighted horror at Slash and Pecos before glancing over his shoulder at several other little boys pushing up close behind him. He pointed a dirty finger at the two cutthroats and bellowed, "That's them! That's them! It's Slash Braddock an' the Pecos River Kid their own selves!"

A fat little boy with mean, little, close-set eyes, and holding a thick pork roast sandwich in his fat little fist, bulled in close to shout up at Slash and Pecos, "My ma says no two badder cutthroats have ever fogged the western trails! She says hangin's too good for ya!"

"My pa says you're both meaner'n rabid wolves!" chimed in another little boy, a small sack of rock candy in his hand. "That true?"

Slash chuckled, then leaned down and shoved his face up close to all three little boys, snarling, "Come here, you little devils—I'm gonna chew your ears off and eat 'em while ya watch!"

The three boys screamed, wheeled, and ran, one crying loudly for his mother.

"For shame, Slash," Pecos reprimanded his partner. "You like to have taken several years off those poor children's lives!"

"Ah, hell," Slash said, chuckling as he and Pecos were shoved on ahead, the lawmen batting their rifle butts at the clambering crowd, "they'll delight their grandchildren with that tale!"

He laughed.

He sobered up right quick, however, as he stared at the gallows looming ahead, a block away now and standing in the middle of the main street, out in front of the Colorado House Hotel with its broad front veranda. The gallows looked like an especially wicked thing, looming there with the two nooses drooping from the wooden frame mounted on a plank board platform only a little larger than a boat dock, five or six steps running up one side.

Slash had seen gallows before, but he'd never paid them much mind.

He paid this one plenty of mind, however. The instrument of his own annihilation.

Oh, well. No point in thinking about it. He supposed he had it coming. What had he thought all those years running hog-wild down the long coulees—robbing banks and trains and even saloons and parlor houses at times—would add up to if not a stretched neck?

He'd never killed anyone who hadn't tried to kill him first. He'd never crippled anyone who hadn't been trying to do the same to him, or worse, as Bledsoe had been trying to do when Slash's bullet had chewed into Bleed-'Em-

So's back. Tell that to the good marshal, he thought with a clipped, dry chuckle.

Tell it to Judge McClelland.

Tell it to the hangman, Grimes, resembling a withered old crow where he stood atop the gallows in his black suit and black hat, his gaunt, pale face as grim as a deacon's. The swallowtail of his coat fluttered in the hot, dry mountain breeze that kicked up the dust being churned by the crowd, salting Slash's eyes. Despite the dust, Slash saw the old executioner's face clearly. He thought he detected the first quirk of an eager smile on the man's lipless mouth.

This was Grimes's payday. He'd eat well and sleep under a roof for the next few weeks.

As he and Pecos approached the gallows, the crowd cheering or cajoling, salesmen and newspaper boys hawking their wares, Slash found his eyes scanning the crowd and the buildings and boardwalks along both sides of the street for one familiar face out of all the eager faces of the strangers surrounding him.

Jay.

CHAPTER 17

Slash had tried to put her out of his mind, and he'd thought he'd been successful, but apparently he hadn't. For some reason, he found himself yearning for one more look at her, however brief. It was only a half-conscious desire, and it was followed close on its heels by the sharp bite of her having double-crossed both himself and Pecos, two of her closest friends. Two of her very few friends in all the world.

Why, Jay?

If one merciful saint had suddenly swooped down from heaven just then on the pale wings of a dove and granted him one wish—anything at all in heaven or on earth—he'd have asked to have that one last question answered.

Why did you do it, Jay?

Slash's gaze swept the broad veranda fronting the Colorado House.

A dozen or so men milled there. He spied McClelland and the prosecutor, George Hill, both holding soapy beer mugs in their fists while chatting and smiling, occasionally laughing. There was Lester Hyman, as well, also with a beer and talking to two men who were probably town council members or the like. The rest appeared wealthy ranchers judging by their natty Stetsons and tailored suits.

But then Slash's eyes picked out the small, wiry, cotton-headed, big-toothed visage of old Bleed-'Em-So sitting huddled in his wheelchair and flanked by the remote, beautiful, statuesque blonde, Abigail Langdon, clad in a frilly black gown and veiled black picture hat, gold-blond hair tumbling in ravishing ringlets to her shoulders. Bledsoe's eyes had already found Slash, and now, as Slash's gaze met his, he raised a whiskey goblet high in his clawlike right hand in mock salute to the doomed outlaws.

He threw his head back, laughing.

Abigail Langdon smiled coolly.

Ignoring them both, Slash swept his gaze across the veranda, to the right and left of the chief marshal as well as behind him, looking for Jay. He'd half expected to see her at Bleed-'Em-So's side, since, if what Gables had told Slash was true, they were spending time together. Or had that one night in the Colorado House been all that the chief marshal had required of her? That and double-crossing Slash and Pecos, of course. Maybe Bledsoe had paid her off and she'd lit a shuck for New Orleans or San Francisco. A woman with Jay's devious, manipulative mind would do well in either place.

Apparently she wasn't anywhere out here. If she wasn't altogether shameless, shame would no doubt keep her away from witnessing the fruits of the whipsaw she'd put Slash and Pecos in.

"Welcome, gentlemen!"

Adolph Grimes stood atop the steps leading up to the gallows, smiling almost mockingly down at the two condemned men staring up at him. He had bulbous eyes and a mouth that sort of stuck out, as well, bulging out over a mere nub of chin. Gray muttonchops ran clear down to his doughy jawline.

"Are you prepared for your reckoning?" Grimes inquired through a broad smile, showing very small, yellow-brown teeth.

Slash mounted the steps, tripping a little on his spancel chain. "Don't just stand there chinning. Let's get on with it, hangman!" The outlaw mounted the platform and shambled over to one of the two ropes awaiting him.

"Yeah, let's get this show on the road!" Pecos agreed, dragging his own chain across the platform and standing behind his own noose, to Slash's left. "I got me a purty Mexican angel awaiting me in heaven with a bucket of fresh sangria and a bag of Mexican tobacky. She's a purty one with ruby lips and long, jet-black hair. She came to me in a dream last night. So come on—tie them nooses tight and drop these doors." Chuckling, he danced a little jig on the trapdoor he was standing on, and elbowed Slash in the side.

But when Slash glanced at his partner, he saw that the man's humor hadn't made it to his eyes. The bigger man's smile was more than a little stiff, and his cheeks were sweaty and pasty. That's when Slash realized his own face felt a little warm and damp, as well. His hands, cuffed behind his back, were slick with sweat.

Slash tried to return his partner's smile, but he could tell that it barely made his mouth corners rise.

He gave up and turned his head forward.

Grimes dropped the noose into place over Pecos's head, then did the same thing to Slash. Deputy Tabor removed the spancels from the men's ankles, making sure the two cutthroats could dance unimpeded for the crowd, while Vern Gables and Tyson Waite flanked the outlaws, aiming their rifles at their heads as though daring them to try to run.

The town marshal himself and his three deputies as well as the sheriff's deputy, who'd been sent to oversee the hanging here in Saguache, stood to each side of the gallows, holding either rifles or shotguns up high across their chests. To a man, they were grinning mockingly up at the two doomed cutthroats, looking almighty pleased with themselves and their good fortune of having the privilege of watching two such notorious criminals stretch some hemp on the main street of their fair town.

Near the town marshal, a man in a shabby suit and bowler hat was scribbling into a small notebook. He was likely the local newspaper scribe taking detailed notes on this momentous day, anticipating a big sale, no doubt, to the eastern rags as well as Denver's *Rocky Mountain News*. The trial had been scheduled and held so quickly—giving the cutthroats no time to slither out of Bleed-'Em-So's clutches—that no newsman from Denver had probably had time to travel here to the southern Rockies, so this local reporter likely had the scoop of his career.

The sun was nearly straight up in the sky, its brassy light bathing the crowd that was a large, milling mass forming a ragged semicircle out front of the gallows. Ladies gussied up as though for church twirled their bright parasols and conversed with others similarly attired. Many of the townsmen had also raided deep into their closets and bureaus for the occasion, clad as they were in suits complete with foulard ties and derby or bowler hats. The bulk of the men were holding either beer schooners or whiskey glasses—sometimes both and some even with fat stogies drooping from between their mustached lips.

Several boys of various sizes ran wild amongst the crowd, two appearing to pretend they were the notorious cutthroats Slash and Pecos while four others were the posse giving chase and snapping off shots with their crude treebranch rifles. Two dogs barked and nipped at their heels.

Men cursed the rowdy horde, kicking at the dogs, while the jostled women berated them less saltily.

Ranch hands in dusty range garb including chaps and billowy neckerchiefs watched from the brush ramadas fronting saloons while painted "ladies" in all the colors of the rainbow and more lounged, laughing, drinking, and smoking, from second-floor parlor house balconies and occasionally lifting their camisoles to flash the young men ogling them from the street.

A few salesmen were weaving their ways through the crowd with their display kits, occasionally holding their wares up high above their heads and shouting sales pitches.

When the nooses were drawn almost painfully taut around the men's necks, the crowd began to quiet down, men and women hushing each other and directing one another's attention toward the gallows where the grand finale was about to commence.

A knot nearly as big and bulky as the coils on the noose drew taut in Slash's stomach.

The executioner stepped up in front of the two doomed men and looked down at a short, big-bellied man in a bullet-crowned black hat and clerical collar and holding a Bible. Slash had seen him pacing around in front of the gallows for some time now, gesticulating as though quietly practicing his sermon.

"Ready to give 'em the final send-off, Preacher Donleavy?"

The preacher looked up, but before he could open his mouth to speak, Slash said, "Skip it. Pull that consarned lever!"

"Now, just hold on a minute, Slash," Pecos said, glancing sidelong at his partner, his voice a little pinched because of the hangman's noose around his neck. "I'm startin' to think I might want a little extra . . ."

"All right, then!" said the executioner. He turned to one of the deputies manning the wooden lever bristling out the left end of the gallows and which when thrown would open the trapdoors. "Get ready, Deputy Samuelson!"

"Oh, hell," Pecos said quietly, so the now-silent crowd couldn't hear him. "Slash?"

"What?"

"I got a confession."

"I don't think there's a priest on the premises. The preacher looks Lutheran to me. They don't believe in confessin' their sins, the Lutherans don't. They just believe in payin' for 'em."

"Will you please shut up, fer cryin' in the king's ale? Our time is short!"

"All right—what is it?"

"I know . . ." Pecos hesitated. "I know about how you . . ."

Again, he let his voice trail off but not because he was hesitating. A drumming sound rose from somewhere Slash couldn't distinguish. The crowd seemed to hear it, too, because the men and women and even the children were looking around, frowning curiously and muttering.

"What?" Grimes said, also looking around and frowning. "What on earth . . . ?"

"Want me to throw the lever?" asked Deputy Samuelson eagerly, grimacing up against the sun at the executioner.

Grimes held up a hand. "Hold on just a min—"

He cut himself off when a pistol popped beneath the drumming of what now sounded like a good dozen galloping horses.

Another pistol popped. Another. And another . . .

The crowd looked this way and that, men calling out inquiringly, women gasping and drawing babies and young children protectively against them.

The shooting and drumming grew quickly louder until the sounds fairly exploded as a gang of riders broke into view a block straight up the street from the gallows, turning sharply onto the main street from a cross street, triggering pistols and rifles into the air. The riders appeared to be wearing masks and long dusters that streamed out behind them on the wind.

They continued triggering their weapons as they crouched low over their horses' wildly jostling manes, making a beeline for the gallows. The crowd lurched as one, then suddenly began scattering, men cursing sharply and yelling, women screaming and lifting the hems of their gowns above their ankles as they ran, one awkwardly pushing a whicker stroller.

"Good Lord!" intoned Grimes.

"What in Christ's name?" shouted Vern Gables, stepping up in front of the two prisoners and loudly pumping a cartridge into his Winchester's action.

A man in the quickly approaching group of horsebackers triggered his pistol toward the gallows.

Gables grunted and cursed as he lurched backward before dropping his rifle, then tumbling over the front of the gallows to the ground.

More of the horsemen's fire was directed at the gallows and in seconds both Deputies Tyson Waite and Vince Tabor were down on the gallows floor, howling and writhing.

Slash and Pecos exchanged exasperated looks, both men's lips moving but no words making it out of their mouths. They didn't really have to speak, because they knew they were both thinking the same thing.

Are those hell-for-leather riders here for *us*?

If so, who in the hell *were* they?

A couple of the marshal's deputies including Deputy Samuelson returned fire. As bullets stitched the air around their heads and popped into the dirt around their boots, they cut and ran, one man screaming, "Pull out, fellas! We're outnumbered! Pull out! Take cover!"

Slash cut a glance toward the Colorado House Hotel. As most of the crowd beat a hasty retreat toward the doors, the men shouting anxiously, a couple dropping their beer glasses with the sounds of shattering glass, old Bleed-'Em-So himself shucked his shotgun from the leather scabbard strapped to his chair. Raging wildly, though Slash couldn't hear what he was saying against the thunder of the gang's horses and the caterwauling of their guns, he extended the big popper straight out over the veranda and added the thunder of his twelve-gauge to the rising cacophony.

As he reared back his shotgun's second hammer, Abigail Langdon backed him toward the hotel's front door, running up against several men beating a hasty retreat behind her and too frightened to stop and help with the old cripple. The judge, prosecutor, and even Lester Hyman were nowhere to be seen, likely cowering under a table in the hotel saloon.

Old Bleed-'Em-So was raging like an angry lion, showing all those false teeth as he flopped furiously around in his chair. He stabbed another bayonet of flames into the crowd of galloping riders, though if his buckshot struck any of the gang members, Slash didn't see which one it was.

Suddenly, as the street cleared, one of the riders leaped from his bay horse onto the gallows platform. He was a tall man in a snuff-brown Stetson with an Indian-beaded band around the tall crown. The mask hiding his face was a flour sack with the eyes and mouth cut out. It drew back against his lean face as he breathed. He faced Slash, both blue eyes glinting sharply inside the off-white mask.

He drew a big hogleg from a holster tied low on his right

thigh and clicked the hammer back. He stepped around behind Slash and pressed the pistol's barrel against the chain between the two cuffs binding Slash's hands behind his back.

Bang!

The chain broke.

Bang!

The chain between Pecos's wrists broke.

Their savior holstered his smoking pistol and drew a big bowie knife from a sheath on his right hip. He thrust the knife up quickly, holding the razor-edged blade up close to Slash's face, smiling menacingly.

"Slash Braddock!" he said with a sneer.

Slash winced, gut tightening, beginning to wonder if he hadn't leaped out of the frying pan and into the fire.

Vigilantes out for the cutthroats' blood?

"You got me at a severe disadvantage, friend," Slash croaked out.

"Just know I'd as soon gut you as free you, but them's the cards!"

The masked stranger raised the knife and swept it through the rope above Slash's noose, freeing Slash from the rail above his head. He did the same to Pecos's rope, and suddenly both cutthroats were freed, though the locked bracelets remained on their wrists.

Slash and Pecos shared a dubious look.

"Mount up!" their savior yelled as he leaped off the gallows.

"Who are you fellas?" Slash called.

"Mount the hell up!" their savior yelled again as he mounted his bay.

Slash looked into the street.

His own Appy and Pecos's buckskin stood before the

gallows, their reins being held by a second masked rider who swung his head this way and that, watching for enemy fire though it appeared the marshal's deputies had run for their lives. The only shooting was coming from the masked riders, the other ten of which were circling the gallows and triggering their pistols and rifles warningly into the air, like Indians circling a wagon train.

The three federals lay in the street around the gallows, twisted in death.

As Slash and Pecos leaped down off the gallows platform, Slash cut a glance at Vern Gables, his gaze lingering curiously.

"Hurry up, Slash!" Pecos said, grabbing his buckskin's reins and fleetly swinging his big body into the saddle. "This ain't no time to be lookin' a gift horse in the mouth!"

"Right," Slash said, grabbing his own reins and leaping onto the Appy's back. "I'm with you, partner!"

He quickly set himself in the saddle, and soon both he and Pecos were galloping hell-for-leather behind their gang of galloping saviors, heading south out of Saguache. The buildings and stock corrals dropped away behind them, and then they were out in the open country, fogging the sage for the high-and-rocky.

Slash had no idea who had freed them.

But they were free, by God. He could feel the thrill in his belly. His heart was singing. The San Juans loomed before them, severe and blue and beautiful, mantled by high, billowy, white clouds. Slash wanted to laugh and spread his arms.

Instead, he hunkered low over his familiar horse's fluttering mane and squinted his eyes against the dust being kicked up ahead of him, by his and Pecos's angels of mercy.

Soon, he found himself frowning. As good as he felt, there

was a needling apprehension. It was like a fly buzzing in his ears.

Something told him that his initial feeling of having leaped out of the frying pan and into the fire hadn't been entirely unfounded, and that his avenging angels might have black wings.

CHAPTER 18

Slash and Pecos followed their rescuers at a dead run straight south of Saguache, following a two-track stage road that cleaved a long, broad valley that appeared to end at the San Juan Mountains looming darkly ahead.

Crouched low over their horses' polls, the two aging outlaws shared an incredulous look, then turned their heads back forward. Again, they were both asking the same silent questions.

Who were these men?

Why had they rescued the two cutthroats?

Where were they going?

All were questions Slash hoped he and Pecos would have answers for soon.

Soon it didn't look likely. Roughly two miles from town, the gang halted near a large cottonwood where the fork suddenly grew two single-track tines, one tine angling southwest, one angling east. The gang members were still wearing their masks, as though they didn't want even Slash and Pecos to know who they were.

The one who'd freed the two outlaws from the gallows rode back to where Slash and Pecos had stopped their mounts. He jerked his head to indicate the southwestern-angling horse trail, which dropped down into an arroyo sheathed in cedars and thick brush.

"Take that trail. After three miles, you'll meet up with the old Gunnison Stage Road. Take it straight south for six or seven miles. You know Sam Scudder's old station?"

"What about it?" Slash said, frowning curiously at the masked rider before him.

"Ride there. Stay there. Someone will come for you."

The stranger started to turn his bay, but stopped when Slash said, "Who?"

"Someone!"

Pecos said, "You fellas wouldn't happen to have our guns, would you? I feel a little naked without my weapons. I mean, if it wouldn't be too much to ask . . ."

The leader of the masked riders just stared at him blankly, as though he wouldn't lower himself to answer such a stupid question.

One of the other eleven masked riders behind him chuckled softly, dryly.

Pecos flushed, sheepish, and hiked a shoulder. "I was just askin'."

"Who are you fellas?" Slash asked the mysterious stranger. "Why did you pull us out of that necktie party?"

But the mysterious riders, led by the tall man, had already swung their horses onto the northeastern-angling horse trail, in the shade of the sprawling cottonwood. Touching steel to their mounts' flanks, they lunged off into another hard gallop, dust lifting behind them.

They galloped off around a low spur ridge and were gone, the thuds of their horses' hooves dwindling gradually.

"I'll be damned," Slash said, staring after them curiously.

"I thought it was a fair question," Pecos said. "I mean,

what's an outlaw without his guns? Especially one who likely has a posse foggin' his trail."

He turned a look over his left shoulder, to stare back toward Saguache, adding, "I bet that town marshal's got one after us by now." He turned to Slash again. "Didn't you think it was a fair question?"

"It was fair."

"Did you see the look that masked hombre gave me? Made me feel little more than change for a penny."

Slash looked off down the trail he and Pecos had been directed to take. "I reckon we'll have to make do without our weapons."

"I didn't mean to sound ungrateful," Pecos said, still injured by the masked rider's mocking stare. "I mean, whoever they are, I couldn't appreciate them rescuin' us from that gallows any more than I do. My God, I've never felt so grateful to be alive in all my days! But, still . . . I'd like to have my guns."

He glanced at the silver bracelets still adorning his wrists. "They mighta had a key for these cuffs, too. I wouldn't mind bein' rid of them, either. They'll mark us as prisoners wherever we go."

"I'd just like to know who in the hell they were. They sure didn't seem friendly. Aside from keepin' that hangman from playin' cat's cradle with our heads, that is."

"That's a fair bit!" Pecos threw his head back and laughed. He laughed a good long time, obviously thoroughly feeling the exhilaration of having been spared from certain death. After a time, he shook his head. "Whew! Look around, Slash! We're alive!"

"Feels good, don't it?" Slash took a deep breath. He felt a little dizzy, like a kid after his first few sips of his old man's home-brewed wine.

He swung his head to stare after the masked riders

again, frowning into their dust still sifting in the shade of the sprawling cottonwood. "Still, I'd like to know who they were . . . what this is all about."

"Like I said," Pecos said, turning his horse onto the trail they'd been directed to follow. "Don't look a gift horse in the mouth, mi amigo. Let's just do as he says, head to Sam Scudder's old station. Wait for whoever is supposed to come for us."

As Slash turned his Appy onto the single-track trail, following Pecos down the gradual grade toward the arroyo, Pecos shot him a wide-eyed, eager look. "Hey, what if it's Jay?"

Slash looked at his partner, his own expression hopeful, and said, "Could it be, you think?"

"Who else?"

"You think Jay organized that posse?"

"I didn't see her nowhere in town, did you? Maybe she's waiting for us at Sam Scudder's old place!"

"Christ Almighty," Slash said, scratching his chin. "Maybe it's true!"

Just as suddenly, he frowned again as he and Pecos stopped to let their horses drink from a spring-fed freshet that threaded the middle of the otherwise dry arroyo.

"But why would she send them riders to free us after she double-crossed us with ole Bleed-'Em-So?" he asked. "Don't make sense."

He looked at Pecos, hoping maybe his partner had a convincing explanation.

Pecos didn't seem to, however. The bigger man stared down at the dark, meandering stream at which both tired horses drew eagerly, then shook his head and turned to Slash again. "I don't know, partner. But it's got to be her. I think she'll have an explanation for what she done. I mean, it's *gotta* be her. Who else would have sprung us from that gallows? I mean, besides Jay, we don't have another friend on God's green earth!"

Again, Slash silently chewed on the possibility, nodding slowly.

Pecos was right. Who else could have sprung them?

Jay would have an explanation for being on the train with Bleed-'Em-So. She'd explain everything. Damn soon, the three of them—him, Pecos, and Jaycee Breckenridge—would be heading back down to Mexico together as the first snows powdered the Rockies.

That thought made him even happier to still be dancing on this side of the sod.

"Did you see the look on Bleed-'Em-So's face?" he asked Pecos, grinning broadly, the possibility that he'd see Jay again soon improving his mood even more. "When he seen them masked riders swarming in around us?"

Pecos threw his head back and laughed.

Slash laughed, too, thoroughly enjoying the remembered image of the chief marshal's incensed, horrified, and exasperated face as Bledsoe cut loose with his double-bore greener.

After they'd shared a good long guffaw, he and Pecos pulled up their horses' heads and continued on down the trail. They crossed the arroyo, climbed the opposite bank, left the cedars, and trotted off across a prairie carpeted in purple sage.

"Hey," Slash said, turning to his partner trotting his buckskin off his own left stirrup. "What was that confession you were about to make to me on the gallows? You know—just before our angels swooped down to save our asses, er . . . leastways, give us a reprieve from eternal damnation?"

Pecos looked at him, slack-jawed. "Huh?"

"You were gonna tell me you know how I felt about somethin'."

"I was?"

"I could have sworn you were!"

"Hmm." Pecos frowned and studied his saddle horn a little too closely and thoroughly. "Boy, I just don't recollect, Slash. I reckon in all the commotion it slipped my mind."

"Come on," Slash said, prodding his partner. "You know what I'm talkin' about."

"Golly, I don't, Slash." Shaking his head, Pecos batted his heels against his buckskin's flanks, urging the horse into a rocking lope. "Looks like we got another one o' them bad summer storms rollin' down from the Sawatch behind us. We'd best haul our freight!"

Slash scowled after him, frustrated. He glanced over his shoulder.

Sure enough, another gully-washer was on its way. High, gunmetal clouds were sliding toward them, grumbling with distant thunder and stitched with lightning.

Slash lowered his hatless head, shivered against a rising wind, and booted his Appy down the trail after Pecos.

The storm was like a hapless posse.

Twice it almost caught up to the two southward-heading cutthroats, spit a little rain and shot a little lightning at them, then, as though taking the bait of a false trail, it veered off to the east or the west. Ever persistent, however, like a posse made up of riders who'd had money in the bank the two cutthroats had robbed, it veered back after them.

It caught up to them when they were dropping into the broad swale in which the late Sam Scudder's relay station on the old Gunnison Stage Road hunkered low amidst brush and sage. It was positioned across the stage road from a low-slung adobe brick barn and several other now-dilapidated outbuildings as well as a cedar rail corral and a windmill jutting above a broad stone stock trough.

The place had become tumbledown in the wake of Sam's passing, Slash saw. He didn't know who owned it now. It had been years since he and Pecos had stopped here for a hot meal and strong drink.

The rain came in a thick curtain from the northwest. In seconds, both riders were drenched from their heads to their boot toes, the downpour matting their hair to their heads and streaming down their faces.

Slash and Pecos stabled their mounts in the barn, re- moving their saddles, rubbing the horses down with scraps of burlap provided for the job, and giving them water and a pail of oats. Pecos stopped in the barn's open door, star- ing toward the brush-roofed former station house that now served as a backcountry watering hole.

Three horses stood beneath the brush arbor fronting the place, hanging their heads and tails against the sharp bite of the wet wind. The rain ran off the ends of the arbor poles to patter into the mud behind them, forming a broad pool.

Slash moved up to stand beside his partner. He looked at the saloon and the horses, then turned to Pecos. "What're you waiting for?"

"I don't like it."

"Like what?"

"Goin' in there without my guns."

"Well, what're you plannin' on doin'—cowering out here like a dog without your guns?"

"Yeah, I just might." Pecos turned to Slash. "What're you gonna do? Just walk in there with those cuffs on your wrists and no guns at your side?"

"This is an old outlaw camp," Slash said with an amused grunt. "I'm sure the patrons are probably very accustomed to seein' fellas sporting handcuffs. Besides, we might know someone in there. Hell, Jay might be in there!"

"The cuffs will draw attention to us. And I don't like havin' fellas payin' attention to me without havin' access to my guns, which are probably still locked up in that town marshal's office in Saguache, consarn it anyways!"

Pecos brushed his wet coat sleeve across his wet nose and mouth.

"Look," Slash said, "those horses might belong to whoever we're supposed to meet here. I say we go in and have a look around."

"You're right," Pecos said. "We might know someone in there. Someone whose fur we mighta rubbed in the wrong direction. You know how folks is sayin' there's no honor amongst thieves? We're livin' proof, Slash!"

"Ah, crap," Slash said, throwing an arm out in disgust. "I'm goin' in. You hide an' watch!"

CHAPTER 19

Leaving the barn, Slash strode back out into the rain that was coming down at a forty-five-degree angle. What the hell? He couldn't get any wetter than he already was. After he'd taken a few steps, he said over his shoulder: "I can already taste that ale and whiskey! *Mmm-Mmmmm!*"

He turned his head forward, grinning. He knew that would get Pecos's goat, and it did. Wet footsteps sounded behind him and then Pecos was falling into step beside him. "You devil!"

"Chicken liver."

"I just don't like pokin' my head into a known wolf den without my guns." Wolf dens were what the outlaw breed called watering holes and other such places that relied mainly on their own breed of law-dodging clientele. "Besides, you know how these places attract bounty hunters."

"Like I said, chicken liver."

"Better a chicken liver than wolf bait!"

Slash moved past the three horses tied to the hitch rack on his right and mounted the wooden boardwalk from which a clay olla pot hung from the rafters. He steeled himself a little as he pushed through the batwings. Pecos had been right about the foolhardiness of entering such a place unarmed, but under the circumstances, he didn't see what choice they had.

The masked stranger had said someone would meet them here. Jay might be that person.

Instinctively and automatically, Slash stepped to the left of the batwings, and Pecos stepped to the right, so that any lead that might be directed at them would fly on out the doors and also so that they wouldn't be outlined against the light behind them, murky as it was. Just as instinctively and automatically, Slash's hands moved to where he normally wore his guns—for the cross-draw on his left hip and thonged low, butt back, on his right thigh.

Of course the guns weren't there. He'd been all too aware of the absence of his weapons for nearly an entire week.

He felt a little foolish for having reached for them, though he doubted anyone inside the place had seen his hands move. The saloon was awash in dark shadows relieved only by the dull gray light pushing feebly around the batwings now slapping into place behind him and Pecos, and through the rain-washed windows.

As his eyes adjusted to the room's twilight, Slash saw that there were four other people inside the place. Two men stood at the crude plank bar that ran along the rear wall. A girl who appeared at least part Mexican stood behind the bar. A fourth man sat at a table ahead of Slash and to his and Pecos's right, near a wood stove that issued fragrant smoke from the cracks around its ill-fitting doors.

The man at the table was a Mexican around Slash's and Pecos's age—mid- to late fifties. He was playing a mandolin and smoking a loosely rolled cornhusk cigarette. At least, he'd been playing the mandolin and singing softly, mournfully when Slash and Pecos had first entered. Now he was staring incredulously at the two soaking wet newcomers, narrowing one eye and peering through the smoke wafting around his head, on which he wore a ragged straw sombrero.

He'd removed his right hand from the mandolin's strings and placed it on the Colt Navy resting on the table before him, near a glass and a tequila bottle.

The other two men at the bar, also Mexican, had closed their hands over the grips of their own holstered pistols.

"Hola, amigos," Slash said affably, showing his empty hands to set them at ease, then striding forward, Pecos falling into step behind him.

They bellied up to the bar, to the right of the two Mexicans, both of whom were younger men. All three wore the garb of ranch hands. Slash couldn't help feeling a poignant pang of disappointment at not seeing Jay here. But, then, maybe she was still on her way. If it was she they were going to meet, that was. He wasn't going to let go of that hope just yet.

He turned to the dark-eyed Mexican girl standing behind the bar, facing the two young Mexican men, and said, "How about a pair of ales, little miss? And whiskey?"

She was a pretty, frail girl with long, dark-brown hair falling straight down her slender back. She wore a calico blouse, sleeves rolled to her elbows, and denim trousers with a hemp belt trimmed with a round brass buckle.

She shook her head quickly, glancing at the silver bracelets on Slash's and Pecos's wrists. "No ale. No whiskey. Tequila only, amigos."

Slash glanced at Pecos, who shrugged. Slash turned to the girl and smiled, saying, "Tequila it is, senorita."

While the girl prepared the drinks, Slash could see out of the corner of his left eye the two young Mexicans taking his and Slash's measure, no doubt noting the handcuffs and the lack of weapons. Slash didn't look at the young men directly but only ran his hands back through his longish hair, pressing out the excess rainwater and brushing it off on his damp trousers.

When the girl had poured two shots of tequila, Slash and Pecos leaned forward against the bar, nursing their drinks, each holding his own quiet counsel, wondering who they were waiting for, waiting . . .

Meanwhile, one of the young Mexican men resumed a conversation he'd apparently been having with the senorita before Slash and Pecos had entered. The young man and the girl were speaking Spanish, which Slash, having spent a good bit of time hiding out on the other side of the border, spoke nearly fluently, as did Pecos, to the point where they could distinguish regional accents.

Slash wasn't purposely trying to eavesdrop, but as the young man's and the girl's voices grew gradually in volume, both also acquiring a nasty edge, Slash couldn't help overhearing. Apparently, the young man had been sparking the girl for a time, taking her to dances. They'd even talked of marriage. But then the girl had caught the young man with another girl, several times, and . . .

"That was the last time, Tio," the girl said in Spanish, backing away from the bar and crossing her arms on her chest. "I told you I wanted never to see you again, so go now. You must leave!"

The young man cursed, slammed his shot glass down, and leaned over the bar, his face red with anger. He threw out an arm to grab her but she lurched back out of his reach.

"Blast it, Justianna!"

Slash emptied his glass and slammed it down on the bar, frowning at the young man standing six feet away on his left. "Listen, sonny—you heard the girl. Time to pull your picket pin!"

Pecos elbowed Slash, saying tightly, "What the hell you doin', partner?"

The young man—he had a long, narrow face with a slender, slightly crooked nose and two molasses-dark, close-set eyes—turned to scowl at Slash and say in heavily accented English, "Shut the hell up and drink your tequila, old gringo!"

He swept a flap of his buckskin jacket back away from the Remington riding high on his left hip, in front of a large Green River knife, and nodded pointedly, threateningly at Slash. "Comprende?"

Slash's cheeks flushed slightly. He'd forgotten himself, reacted automatically. Reminding himself where he was and of the unarmed condition he was in, he gave a weak, sheepish smile and turned his head to stare back down at the bar. He glanced at Pecos, who stood glaring admonishingly at him, and then grabbed the bottle the girl had left on the bar and refilled both his and Pecos's glasses.

"What do you say we sit down and behave ourselves?" Pecos said, keeping his voice low and tight with admonishment.

He grabbed the bottle and his glass, swung around, and headed for a table near where the third, older Mexican had once again kicked back in his chair, quietly strumming his mandolin and singing very softly and gently in Spanish about a young man and a girl who met along a shady creek:

"*Cuando las rosas silvestres estaban,*
En flor y el aire de la primavera olía a manzanas . . ."
(When the wild roses were in full bloom
And the spring air smelled like apples . . .)

"Yeah, yeah—I'll be right behind ya," Slash said, glowering down at his tequila.

He wanted to sit down, but he felt compelled to stay where he was, for the young man was fuming at the girl now, jutting his head belligerently across the bar and threatening to skin her alive if she didn't listen to reason. The second young man stood on Tio's far side, chuckling softly through his teeth.

The girl stood back against the shelves of the back bar, arms crossed on her chest. She shook her head slowly, defiantly, quietly sobbing, her heart broken.

"No, Tio, I am done with you. You must go now. If Papa comes back and finds you here . . ."

"Mierda!" Tio yelled, slamming his right open palm down on the bar, making a sound like that of a pistol going off.

The girl jerked with a violent start, gasping.

"I have had enough of your insolence, Justianna!"

The young man stepped around his partner and moved through a break in the bar, tramping around behind it toward the girl.

"Hey, now!" Slash said.

Tio's amigo turned to face Slash, grinning and tucking his coat back behind the low-slung Colt thonged on his left thigh. It was just then, seeing that the two young men were so well-armed, that he realized they weren't ranch hands but cutthroats not all that unlike himself and Pecos.

The only difference was that these two were younger.

And Mexican, of course.

They were likely hiding out up here from the law in their own country, whiling away their time sparking the *norteamericana* girls like Justianna. Breaking their hearts. Slash once did the same thing in these two young desperados' native land, but he'd never threatened nor frightened any girl on either side of the border like this *hombre* was threatening and frightening this girl here.

"Stay out of it, partner," Pecos warned as he eased himself into a chair at the table he'd taken.

Slash drew a sharp breath through his teeth in frustration. He threw back half of his tequila shot, set down the glass, then grabbed the edge of the bar, leaning forward, trying to keep his wolf on its leash. But when the young man stalking the girl down the bar toward Slash suddenly lunged forward, grabbed her arm, and slapped her savagely across her right cheek with the back of his right hand, Slash's wolf ran to the end of its chain.

He slammed the top of the bar and lunged forward, his fingers digging into the edge of the bar's crude planks. "Now, boy—that ain't how you treat a—"

Before he could get another word out, the kid pulled his Remington and thrust it across the bar toward Slash, clicking back the hammer with an angry snarl. "What I tell you, old gringo?"

His close-set eyes bored into Slash. The kid's eyes were dark and flat, like a panther's eyes.

Slash stared at the dark, .44-caliber maw yawning at him two feet from his face, the barrel aimed at his left eye. The kid's hand didn't shake a bit. He'd killed before, and he'd kill again without hesitation.

Slash heard Pecos give a bereaved groan behind him.

The man to Slash's left, shorter and softer than Tio but roughly the same age, smiled broadly, cheeks dimpling behind three or four days' growth of beard stubble. The older man had stopped playing the mandolin. He was chuckling very softly and darkly behind Slash, about ten feet away.

The girl stared at Slash from across the bar. Her mussed hair hung in tangles around her face. Her right cheek was welting up from the force of her suitor's blow. Her dark eyes were round and fearful. She'd been through such a dustup with this firebrand before. She knew how it went. She knew Tio's black heart. She was scared.

Slash cursed under his breath and heeled his wolf. He wasn't going to do the girl any good deed. Despite the fury raging behind his breastbone, he raised his hands, palms out, and turned his head to one side in resignation.

Tio grinned at him mockingly. He depressed his Remington's hammer, but before he could pull the gun back, Slash's left arm shot out across the bar. That hand closed around the kid's gun. As Slash ripped the gun back toward him, out of Tio's grip, Slash grabbed the kid's head by his hair and slammed his face down atop the bar.

Tio screamed. There was a wet crunching sound as his nose broke against the bar's surface. Blood sprayed, staining the scarred wood.

As Slash flipped the Remington around, grabbing its handle, he saw in the corner of his left eye the shorter kid claw one of his Colts out of its holster. As he cocked the gun, aiming it straight out toward Slash's head, Pecos bellowed, "Hold on, sonny! I got a twelve-gauge cannon ready to blast a tunnel in your belly big enough to drive a freight train through!"

That was enough to make the kid hesitate, jerking his pistol toward Pecos.

"No, no, lo hace!" shouted the older man, tossing the mandolin onto his table and reaching for the Colt Navy. "No, he doesn't!"

The kid to Slash's left cursed loudly in Spanish as he triggered a round toward Pecos, who threw his big bulk out of his chair and hit the floor with a heavy thud. The kid's bullet slammed into the back of the chair in which the big outlaw had been sitting. As he swung the pistol toward Slash, the Remy in Slash's left hand bucked and roared.

The kid stumbled backward, screaming and triggering his Colt into the ceiling.

Slash wheeled toward Tio behind the bar. The kid was bellowing Spanish curses at Slash, spewing blood out his smashed nose and cut lips as he raised his second Remington.

Again, Slash's newly acquired hogleg spoke once, twice, three times, flames stabbing across the bar.

Tio triggered his second Remy into the top of the bar as he flew back against the shelves behind him, wailing and dislodging several bottles. Dying fast, he fell to the floor, his long, dark-brown hair buffeting like a muddy tumbleweed around his long face and startled eyes.

As the older Mexican bolted up out of his chair, Pecos threw a chair at him with a bellowing wail. The chair smashed into the older man's right shoulder, nudging wide the bullet he'd just hurled toward Slash. Slash whipped around, crouching and firing, punching two bullets into the man's chest and belly and throwing him backward across his table.

The older Mexican threw his pistol wide as he rolled off the table's far side and piled up on the floor near the batwings before which Slash just now saw a man sitting . . . in a wheelchair.

A tall blond woman, a Nordic statue in a dark wool cape, stood behind the man in the wheelchair.

Three tall, ramrod-straight younger men stood side by side on the other side of the batwings, looking into the saloon, their faces expressionless. One just then drew a long, slim, black cheroot to his mustached mouth, drew on it, then blew the smoke over the louvred doors, making the tip glow orange.

Chief Marshal Luther T. "Bleed-'Em-So" Bledsoe looked up from the man who'd just died on the floor before his chair, and smiled broadly, showing all those oversized false teeth as he grinned. He clapped his gloved hands together and roared, "By God, you two old cutthroats still got it. I won't give ya much but I'll give ya that!"

Bleed-'Em-So threw his head back, gazing up at Abigail Langdon, and roared.

CHAPTER 20

Slash stared in hang-jawed shock at the crippled old roarer sitting there with his shotgun resting across his knees. So did Pecos.

The two cutthroats exchanged disbelieving glances, and then Slash sidestepped cautiously to where the young Mexican lay sprawled at the base of the bar. Quickly, Slash crouched, scooped up one of the kid's Colts from off the floor near the growing blood pool. He tossed the pistol across the room to Pecos, who caught it one handed, cocked it, and leveled it at Bledsoe.

Slash plucked the second Colt from the kid's holster and snapped it up quickly to hold it straight out at the chief marshal and his three-man and one-woman armada. Bledsoe was still smiling delightedly.

"Yep," the chief marshal said, nodding slowly, approvingly. "You might be a little long in the tooth . . . and you might get careless from time to time . . . *overconfident,* probably after all these years of unfettered success . . . but you still got some bottom left—don't ya, boys?"

Slash didn't say anything. He just stared at the five unlikely newcomers in total disbelief, his mind reeling. He could tell from his partner's silence that Pecos was in the same immensely puzzled condition.

"You don't get it?" Bledsoe shook his head wonderingly. "It ain't clear to you by now?"

"Is what clear?" Pecos said tightly, keeping the Colt's sights on the old man's spindly chest behind a fancy, flowered, pink and gold brocade vest and white silk shirt with ruffled cuffs poking out of the sleeves of a black frock coat that owned a layer of beaded moisture from the rain.

"He sprung us," Slash said, glancing at Vern Gables smoking his ubiquitous cigar behind the batwings, his eyes smugly condescending. "I thought somethin' looked off, him layin' in the street without any blood showin'. He wasn't shot. He was only fakin' it." He glanced at the other two deputies, Waite and Tabor. "You were all fakin' it."

He frowned at Bledsoe, who sat in his chair, thoroughly enjoying himself, like a wizened old man watching half-naked girls dance in some remote mining camp opera house. "You were fakin' it, too, when you fired your greener over the rail. I noticed you didn't seem to hit any of those angels ridin' in to save our hides. You fired wide."

Deep lines of incredulity cutting across his forehead, still staring over the Colt at the chief marshal, Slash shook his head slowly. "Why?"

"Wait," Pecos said. "I don't understand."

"A setup," Slash told him.

Pecos glanced at him skeptically, then returned his befuddled gaze to Bledsoe. "No. The train. That was the setup. The train . . . with Jay . . ."

"Gentlemen, gentlemen," Bledsoe said, raising a gloved hand from his shotgun as though he were blessing the room. "It's been a long pull down from Saguache and the weather is horrid. What do you say we stoke the stove"— he gave a little shudder in his chair, as though demonstrating the chill the storm had pushed into the near-dark watering hole—"and have a few drinks? Then I shall explain everything."

Gables and the other two deputies pushed through the batwings, stepped around Bledsoe and Abigail Langdon, and stood facing Slash and Pecos, thrusting their chests out bullishly but keeping their revolvers in their holsters. The three lawmen wore rain slickers beaded with moisture. Rain was pooled on their hat brims, dribbling onto the floor in front of their boots.

"Lower the hoglegs, fellas," Gables said commandingly. "Put 'em away. You've got no more use for 'em here."

"That's yet to be proven," Slash said.

"It'll be proven soon enough."

Pecos and Slash shared another conferring glance.

Pecos lowered his Colt, depressing the hammer, and shoved it down behind the waistband of his pants. "I'll be holdin' on to mine. I been unarmed long enough."

Slash did the same with his own weapon. "Me, too."

He glimpsed the girl, Justianna, standing behind the bar, looking around bewilderedly. "You all right, darlin'?"

She slid her gaze from Slash to the floor behind the bar, where Tio lay sprawled in death. She didn't say anything but only stared down at the dead Mexican. Her cheeks were flushed with terror, damp with tears.

As Abigail Langdon wheeled Bledsoe over to the table at which the older Mex had been sitting, near the potbelly stove, the chief marshal glanced at Waite and Tabor, and said, "Drag the bodies out of here for that poor child. Good grief!"

He shoved his shotgun into the leather scabbard strapped to the right arm of his chair. He glanced with mock reproof at Slash and Pecos still standing where they'd been standing when they'd first spied Bledsoe's party. "Such a mess you cutthroats have made!"

The chief marshal turned to the girl behind the bar and

said in fluent Spanish with a distinctly Sonoran inflection, "Senorita, I've often discovered the best medicine for anxiety is good, old-fashioned work. So, if you will, roll up your shirtsleeves, in a manner of speaking. We'll have drinks all around!"

"Sí," Justianna said quietly, then brushed the tears from her cheeks and sprang into action. As she carried a tray with a bottle and several glasses on it out from behind the bar, Slash touched her arm and said, "I apologize for the trouble, senorita."

She smiled up at him sweetly, then rose onto her toes and planted a tender kiss on his cheek. "Gracias, amigo, uh . . ."

The old cutthroat returned her smile. "Slash."

She drew a deep breath. "My father is out hunting. I fear that if it hadn't been for you, Papa would have returned tomorrow to find me lying where Tio lies now, with my throat cut."

"Let me give you a word of advice I feel uniquely qualified to make."

The girl arched a brow over a lustrous brown eye.

Slash crouched to whisper into her ear. "Stay away from cutthroats. Purty we may be, but looks ain't everything." He squeezed her arm and winked.

She gave a knowing smile, glancing at the cuffs on his wrists, then carried the tray over to the table at which Bledsoe sat with Abigail Langdon, who had set a leather valise on the table before her. She'd also stoked the potbelly stove, which pushed an inviting warmth into the room. Pecos stood where he'd been standing before, the Colt shoved down in his pants. He was staring skeptically at Slash, still unable to wrap his mind around the confusion of recent events.

He had that in common with his partner.

Gables stood near the batwings, smoking, one hand on one of his Colts, his wet yellow slicker folded back behind the walnut handle. He seemed to be on guard duty. Meanwhile, Waite and Tabor had dragged the older Mexican out onto the boardwalk fronting the place and were on their way back into the saloon, heading to where Tio's amigo lay on his back near the bar, one leg curled beneath the other one.

As Tabor grabbed the dead Mex's arms and Waite grabbed his ankles, dragging him toward the batwings, Justianna moved around the table at which Bledsoe was sitting, pouring tequila into the glasses. Abigail Langdon slid the filled glasses to various points around the table while old Bleed-'Em-So toyed with the older Mexican's mandolin, holding it high, strumming it softly, shifting his gaze between Slash and Pecos, still grinning that annoying, ever-present grin, as though he was always on the verge of telling a joke he thought was hilarious—a joke about the person he was telling it to.

An annoying habit.

Maddening.

Slash had a feeling the next joke Bledsoe would tell was going to be a doozey. And that he and Pecos would be the butt of it. Even though they'd escaped the gallows and so far remained upright, Slash had a feeling that they'd already been the butt of some supreme joke of the old marshal's. Slash was waiting to learn what it was.

And Jay's part in it. That part was of particular interest to him for some reason he couldn't explain to himself.

"Please, gentlemen, come," Bledsoe said, beckoning. "Sit down with me and my lovely assistant. Have a drink. I will explain everything. Soon, it will all be as clear as that lovely rain falling out there. Isn't it lovely? I do so love a summer storm!"

Again, Slash and Pecos shared a skeptical glance.

Remaining defiantly in place, Slash said, "Where's Jay?"

Bledsoe stared at him. He seemed to be studying him, a

shrewd cast gradually entering his gaze. It was as though he were deciphering letters from far away. The longer he stared, the clearer the letters became.

Slash felt uncomfortable under the old man's perceptive, penetrating gaze.

"Ah, yes," Bledsoe said at last. "Of course, you mean Jaycee Breckenridge."

Slash moved slowly to the table. He felt like a wild dog being baited into a trap, but he walked to the table anyway. So did Pecos.

Both men pulled out chairs across from the chief marshal and the strikingly beautiful Abigail Langdon. Slash had heard of the woman's beauty, as well as the mystery surrounding her and Bledsoe's relationship—was it strictly professional?—but he'd never seen her until the other day in Saguache, and he'd never seen her up close until now.

With thick, rich, red-gold hair coiled stylishly atop her head, her wide cheekbones that tapered severely down to a fine chin and regal jaw, and her crystalline, lake-green eyes, long and slanted, like a cat's eyes, she looked like some long-dead Viking warrior's lurid dream. Big, too, but as stalwart as a warrior queen. Slash thought she was maybe in her late twenties, early thirties but, despite a raw carnality about her, there remained an innocence, a purity about the woman you normally only found in young virgins or nuns.

However, as though to contradict the cutthroat's estimation of her saintliness, she just then plucked her tequila shot off the table before her, between her thumb and index finger, and, sticking out her little finger, tossed the entire shot straight back and swallowed it as though it were no stronger than tea.

Miss Langdon set the glass down and looked across the table at Slash, as though letting him know she'd been reading his mind, and then resumed writing in the cloth-covered notebook she'd been writing in for the past several minutes, her head canted to one side, tongue pressed against the inside of her left cheek. She seemed somehow removed from the proceedings while being very much integral to them, a shadowy figure even when she was present.

Slash kicked his chair around and sat with his arms crossed on its back.

"Where is she?" he prodded Bledsoe.

Again, that shrewd look, the old marshal's eyes squinting just a little, then his lips spreading slightly with a self-satisfied smile of understanding. Slash's cheeks warmed.

"Oh, that whole thing," said Bledsoe, kneading his chin between thumb and index finger.

"Yeah, that whole thing."

"It's a tad on the cheap side, I'll admit."

"What happened?"

"What can I tell you?" Bledsoe said, hiking his shoulder. "She's a woman." He glanced at Miss Langdon, still scribbling in her book to his left. "Uh . . . no offense, dear Abigail."

"None taken." Idling her pen, Abigail Langdon looked across the table at Slash. Her green, gold-flecked eyes were ever so vaguely crossed, which added to her aura of mystery and forbidden charm. "Yes, she's a woman, some of whom are easily swayed, Mr. Braddock." Slash wasn't surprised that she spoke with a lilting Irish burr. "*Some*, but not *all*, I assure you," she added, punctuating the statement with a raised brow before returning to her writing in a large, flowing, feminine hand.

"I don't think you've ever been properly introduced," Bledsoe said, glancing from Miss Langdon to the two outlaws. "This is my assistant, Miss Abigail Langdon. Miss Langdon, Slash Braddock and the Pecos River Kid."

Miss Langdon set down her pen to shake Slash's hand, a cordial nod included. She slid her hand over to where

Pecos had extended his. When her gaze met that of the blond-haired, blue-eyed cutthroat, Slash couldn't help noticing the slight flush that rose in the woman's fair, beautifully if severely sculpted cheeks.

Glancing at Pecos, Slash noticed the same thing—a brief but definite flush of emotion in his partner's face. These two were like a boy and a girl exchanging honey eyes across a schoolhouse floor!

When Pecos glanced at his partner, Slash raised a brow. Pecos's face tightened with embarrassment. He looked away quickly, scowling.

"Let's get on with this thing about Jay," the blond cutthroat said after clearing his throat, fidgeting uncomfortably around in his chair. "You expect us to believe you merely paid her off to double-cross us like that? I don't believe it!"

CHAPTER 21

"Come now, fellas," Bledsoe said. "Don't be too hard on the poor woman. Imagine what it was like—all those years in that mountain hideout, for the most part alone. With very little in the way of creature comforts." He glanced pointedly at Slash. "Without a man . . ."

Old Bleed-'Em-So looked at Abigail Langdon, who'd finished writing to lean forward, elbows on the table, her chin in her hands, a thoughtful expression pooching her lips out slightly. The pen dangled from between the first two fingers of her right hand.

"Could you endure that kind of loneliness, Miss Langdon?"

She glanced at Pecos, then quickly flicked her eyes to the table. There was that flush again. Slash knew that if he looked at his partner, he'd see a similar pinkening of the big devil's cheeks, a tense tightening of his mouth. He chuckled ironically to himself.

"Just like every man," said the jade-eyed Nordic queen in her lilting accent, "there is only so much every woman is willing to endure. When a better offer comes along . . ." She looked at Slash now, keeping her eyes away from Pecos, and shrugged.

"Tell me she didn't go to you, at least," Slash said to Bledsoe.

"No, no." The chief marshal shook his head. "The sheriff down there thought he recognized her. He wired me, informing me of the beautiful redhead who'd just come to town, claiming to be a rancher's widow. He'd seen her dining out a few times with the owner of the Saguache Bank and Trust, the man who handles the Crosshatch accounts and arranges the cash shipments to the Crosshatch headquarters via the ranch's own private spur line. I sent a Pinkerton down there to investigate. When her story about being a widow of some rancher didn't check out, and the operative suspected she was, indeed, Jaycee Breckenridge, Miss Langdon and I called on her one night in her hotel room. That was when I made my offer."

"Of what?"

Bledsoe sighed as he refilled Miss Langdon's glass from the tequila bottle. He waved the bottle toward Slash and Pecos, but seeing that neither outlaw had touched their own shots, he splashed the liquor into his own empty glass, then returned the bottle to the table.

"A few nice dresses . . . some jewelry, including a string of pearls that Miss Langdon personally picked out. Two thousand dollars . . ."

"Full amnesty and a train ticket to San Francisco," Miss Langdon added.

Bledsoe frowned at the ceiling, tapping his index finger against his chin. "Let's see—what day is it? August fourteenth. Hmmm . . . She's likely arrived on the Barbary Coast by now, starting a new life for herself."

He saw the constipated looks on both Slash's and Pecos's faces and turned his mouth corners down. "Like I said, fellas, don't judge her too harshly. It was not an easy thing for her to do. She felt guilty as hell. I mean, she's known you both a long time."

"But she still did it," Slash said tightly.

Pecos turned to him, frowning angrily. "She double-crossed us." He shook his head. "I never would have figured her for doin' somethin' like that. Never in a million years."

Slash cursed under his breath and threw his entire shot of tequila back.

Miss Langdon reached across the table to refill the shot glass.

She held the bottle out to Pecos, who quickly threw his shot back, as well. Bledsoe's beguiling assistant refilled the big outlaw's glass and then topped off the chief marshal's glass, as well.

Slash sat fuming for a while, his belly aching.

Jay.

It wasn't so much anger as the pain of being betrayed by someone he trusted almost as much as he trusted Pecos.

He turned his shot glass between his thumb and index finger, then shoved Jay from his mind and looked across the table at Bledsoe sitting back smugly in his chair, the grin of a Cheshire cat on his sagging, pallid face beneath his tumbleweed of cottony gray hair.

"So why didn't you hang us?"

"You had us on the gallows, nooses around our necks," Pecos said, scowling his befuddlement. "And who were the fellas who rode in to save us?"

"Pinkertons," Bledsoe said. "Undercover operatives. They didn't want to show their faces. I chose them because they're professionals. They knew how to ride in shooting and making it look like they were killing but without actually harming anyone. I'm glad my men here were good enough actors to sell the whole charade with no one getting hurt."

He smiled over at Gables, Waite, and Tabor, all three now sitting at a table near the batwings beyond which the rain was lightening, the mountain storm grumbling quietly as it moved on. Justianna had delivered a bottle and glasses to their table, as well.

"Who all knew about the fiasco?" Slash asked Bledsoe.

"My men, the Pinkertons, and Nelson's men."

"The Saguache town marshal," Slash said.

"That's right."

"What about Grimes?" Pecos said.

"No, no. I couldn't risk it. Doubted he'd be able to act his part. On the other hand, I was worried he might have a heart stroke." Bledsoe sipped his tequila and chuckled as he set the glass back down. "He's all right. Just a little shaken. I sent him a bottle of Spanish brandy and, uh, the best parlor girl in town."

He glanced over at Abigail Langdon, who smiled shrewdly, her cool gaze flicking toward Pecos once more before returning to the table. Again, Slash glanced at his partner. Pecos scowled at him, curling a nostril.

Slash shook his head.

"Let's get down to brass tacks—shall we, gentlemen?" Bledsoe said.

"Let's do that," Slash said. "Why in the hell did you go to all the work of setting that trap Jay helped you bait, arranging that necktie party for us in Saguache, and then at the last minute sending in that posse of Pinkertons to cut us down?" He chuckled drolly. "I swear you got you a future in Old West shows, Bleed-'Em-So!"

"You'd be worthless to me dead," Bledsoe said. "But I wanted to give you both a good scare. To show you what I *could* have done . . . and still *could* do . . . if you don't accept my offer."

"What offer?" Pecos asked.

"I want you to work for me."

Slash and Pecos just stared at him, another wave of befuddlement washing over them both.

"Not in an official capacity," said the chief marshal. "In an *unofficial* capacity, I want you to hunt down and kill the worst of your own lot. You see, you two know how your ilk thinks, how they move, *where* they move. What drives them. What they're capable of. The worst of you are too elusive for my men. Too dangerous."

He glanced over at the three deputy U.S. marshals, all three of whom colored a little at the chief marshal's antagonizing remark. Gables brought the cheroot to his lips and drew on it deeply.

"You're insane," Slash said.

Bledsoe grinned his toothy grin. "Be that as it may, I think it's a prime idea. It even has the sanction of the president of the United States, who has allowed me to offer you both clemency if you accept employment under me as—"

"Regulators," Pecos finished for him.

"Government assassins," Slash said.

"Yes, yes," said Bledsoe, frowning as though with annoyance. "Call it what you want. There's no official job description because there's no contract, because *officially* you won't even exist. At least, *officially*, neither the government nor I will know you . . . or acknowledge you as working for us." He looked at each directly in turn. "But—if you do come to work for me, *unofficially* hunting down and killing the worst of your ilk, you yourselves will no longer be hunted men."

Slash and Pecos shared a skeptical glance.

"That's all?" Pecos asked. "That's your whole offer?"

"Not by a long shot." Bledsoe smiled broadly again, fishy blue eyes glittering. "I will give you enough money for that freight company you've been ogling up in Camp Collins. Between jobs you do for me—two, possibly three a year—you can live like civilized men. *Work* like civilized men. Live quiet lives."

"If a leopard can change its spots." Vern Gables smiled smugly as he blew out another long plume of cigar smoke.

The other two men at his table smiled mockingly.

"Understandably," Bledsoe said, "my men's pride has taken a hit, this plan being based, of course, on the proven fact of the limitations of their own abilities."

Bledsoe smiled condescendingly but did not look toward his deputies' table.

The deputies' faces grew taut. Gables glared at Slash, who'd turned to look at him over his right shoulder. Slash smiled.

Bledsoe returned his gaze to Slash and Pecos. "There will be no retainer between jobs. Between jobs you do for me, you'll have to make your own living. However, for the jobs you do for me, you will be well paid."

"How much?" Pecos said.

"A thousand dollars."

"Apiece?" Slash asked.

"Of course."

Again, Slash glanced at Pecos, who pooched out his lips and raised his brows.

Slash threw back his tequila, then refilled the glass himself. He folded his hands on the table and stared down at them, pondering.

Finally, he sucked his upper lip and shook his head.

"What is it?" Bledsoe asked.

Slash sagged back in his chair with a sigh. "First off, you got us painted wrong. We ain't killers. Robbers, thieves—yeah. But not killers."

"What are you talking about?" Bledsoe said, chuckling under his breath. "You've each killed your share and more. In fact"—he leaned forward, wincing and reaching around his skinny body with one clawlike hand—"I'm wearing your bullet in my back even as I sit here, Braddock!"

"You know that wasn't intentional," Slash said. Then he smiled. "I was tryin' to blow your head off."

"Ah-hah!" the chief marshal snarled.

"But only because you was tryin' to kill us!" Pecos said.

"Aside from the fact that we ain't killers," Slash said, "is the fact that . . . that, well . . . we're gettin' on in years, and . . . well . . ." He raked a hand across the back of his neck in chagrin. "We lost our edge. There, I said it. But it ain't somethin' we both don't know and haven't already owned up to. That's why we decided to retire from the long coulees."

"Yes, from the vantage of the train's express car, it looked like you were retiring," Bledsoe said ironically.

The three deputies snorted with amusement.

Miss Langdon didn't really smile but her cheeks dimpled.

"That was gonna be our last job," Pecos said, squeezing his empty shot glass in his hand. "With the money we intended to take out of that car, we was gonna buy that freighting company." He frowned suddenly at the chief marshal. "Say, how did you know about that?"

"I have my ways," Bledsoe said self-importantly.

Slash hardened his jaws. "Jay."

"Christ!" Pecos said.

"Oh, what are you talking about?" said Bledsoe, his eyes brightening again, again shaping that toothy smile. "You two might have lost a step or two, but you still got an edge. Look how you cleaned up in here! When you entered this place, you weren't armed—am I right?"

He looked at the Colts that Slash and Pecos had set on the table, near their right elbows.

"That was luck," Slash said, shifting around in his chair.

"No, it wasn't." Bledsoe shook his head. "You still have most of the physical abilities you had twenty years ago.

What you lost physically you've made up for in smarts, cunning, and clear-eyed knowledge of your own strengths and weaknesses. And of the ways of the world, particularly the frontier West. True, you've gotten careless, which is obvious by the somewhat more than embarrassing fact that you allowed Loco Sanchez and Arnell Squires and the rest of your gang to leave you behind at Doña Flores's place down by the Arkansas River, the day they robbed the bank in La Junta."

Pecos bolted half out of his chair, stretching his bull neck and his big head across the table at the chief marshal. "Who told you that?"

Bledsoe only smiled.

"Jay," Slash said, spitting out the name like a bad chunk of apple.

"Damn her!" Pecos sagged back down in his chair. Turning to Slash, he said, "I'll never trust another woman again!" He glanced quickly at Miss Langdon, blushing like that schoolboy again. "Uh . . . no offense, Miss, uh . . . Miss Langdon."

"None taken, Mr. Baker. Don't worry, I wouldn't trust you any farther than I could throw your big, smelly carcass uphill against a stiff wind." She smiled devilishly and winked.

Pecos's blush deepened. Slash saw him lift his left arm a little and turn to that side to give his armpit a furtive sniff.

Slash and Bledsoe chuckled. Pecos looked like he wished the floor would open up and swallow him.

"You two are the right men for the job I need filled," Bledsoe said after the moment of levity had passed. He was caressing the shotgun jutting straight up above the right arm of his chair. "You see, I thought Jack Penny's gang could do it. Obviously, they couldn't."

Slash studied him closely, suspiciously.

"Penny?" Pecos said.

"You devil," Slash said, glaring at the chief marshal now. "You sent Penny."

Bledsoe smiled pridefully and lifted a shoulder.

"You old devil," Slash said again.

Bledsoe's grin broadened.

"You sent Penny to kill us?" Pecos said.

"If that's how you want to look at it," said old Bleed-'Em-So. "I'd prefer to see it as I was pitting Penny's skills against yours."

"Whoever came out on top got the job," Slash said. "That it?"

"No, I sent them to kill you, all right." Bledsoe laughed, slapping the table and laughing even louder. "But when you turned the tables on them, even after you were badly outgunned, I decided I'd been looking in the wrong direction. It was you two I should have gone after in the first place. Hell, you two are as good or better than Penny's entire gang . . . may the good Lord have mercy on their souls!"

He slapped the table and laughed again.

When he finally sobered, he looked at each outlaw directly and said, "So . . . will you accept the job as well as the freight company you've been wanting?" He lifted his shot glass and smiled over the rim. "Or hang. It's up to you."

Abigail Langdon reached into her valise and withdrew a fat manila envelope on which was penciled: "$3,000 CASH."

Slash looked at the envelope. His heart quickened. His head grew a little light. He lifted his gaze to old Bleed-'Em-So, looked the old devil straight in the eye, and said, "You SOB!"

"You should be more grateful," Miss Langdon chas-

tised him gently, sliding the envelope of money a little farther across the table. "You're getting everything you've
wanted, Mr. Braddock. And your lives in the bargain."

"Bullcrap. Uh . . . pardon the French," Slash quickly
added for the young woman's benefit.

Miss Langdon sat back in her chair.

To Bledsoe, Slash said, "We wanted to leave the long
coulees. For good. Now you wanna keep us in 'em. Ridin',
shootin' an such, likely gettin' shot our ownselves. Only,
we'll be doing it for you this time. Just when we wanted to
get clear of the flames, you wanna throw us back into the
fire."

"And he really ain't givin' us much choice," added Pecos,
glancing at the enticing envelope, then sitting back in his
chair and crossing his big arms on his chest.

Bledsoe gave a sardonic grunt. "Who do you two old
cutthroats think you are fooling?"

Slash scowled at him, indignant.

"You'd never be able to ride clear of those coulees. Not
for good. Sure, if you had your way, you'd probably ride
up to Camp Collins and buy that freight outfit. And you
might even make a good show of living a peaceful, upstanding, hardworking life—for a year. No, maybe nine
months. You might even join a church, heaven help us all!
But then you'd both start to feel the itch. You know what
I'm talking about. The itch of the career cutthroat.

"You'd bust your asses delivering a few goods to some
mining camps here and there in the mountains, getting
paid peanuts compared to what you used to make for far
easier work, and not having to negotiate those tight mountain roads with six-mule hitches. Then you'd start to get
tired of doctoring those galls those hard wooden wagon
seats flame up on your asses, and you'd eye the stage-

coaches loaded with bullion being driven down out of those mountains, heading for Denver.

"At some point, you'd look at each other and you'd say, 'Hey, pardner, whadoyasay we give 'er one more go-'round, take down one o' them stagecoaches, pop the strongbox, and head for Mexico for just one more winter entangled in them warm senoritas young enough to be our granddaughters!'"

Miss Langdon fired another quick glance toward Pecos, sitting to Slash's left, then lifted her shot glass, her hand shaking ever so slightly, and threw back the shot.

Pecos grunted and shifted around, making his chair creak.

Slash's ears warmed. He lowered his gaze to the table in chagrin.

The old cripple was right. He and Pecos would miss their old life, their outlaw ways. He hadn't realized it before, but when he'd thought about how his next life would be—his next life as an upright businessman and productive member of the Camp Collins community—he'd felt a very small but tight knot in his belly. A knot of restlessness. The way an adventurous young boy feels in church.

Fed by the tedium of an ordinary life, that knot would grow into a cancer until something very much like the picture old Bleed-'Em-So had just painted would come to pass.

Slash looked at Pecos. The big cutthroat shrugged a shoulder.

Slash scooped the envelope off the table, opened it, and quickly counted the bank notes. He set the envelope down between him and Pecos, near the edge of the table, and threw back the shot glass that Miss Langdon had just refilled for him.

"You'll each get another thousand when your first job is complete," said Bledsoe.

"What's the job?" Pecos asked him.

Bledsoe wrapped his right hand around his sheathed shotgun, squeezing. He slammed his left fist onto the table, causing the glasses and the tequila bottle to jump. "Hunt down and kill every man in your old gang—the Snake River Marauders!"

CHAPTER 22

Slash and Pecos shook their heads, jaws hard with defiance.

"Uh-uh," they said in unison. "No way."

Bledsoe leaned forward in his chair, keeping one fist clenched atop the table, the other hand wrapped tightly around his shotgun. "I want them hunted down and murdered. Killed in cold blood. Each and every one of them. And you two are the only two for the job!"

Slash widened his eyes in shock at the old man's murderous fury. Raising his hands, palms out, he said, "Hold on there, Bleed-'Em-So! Hold on! What in the hell have the Snake River Marauders done to get your neck in such a hump? Hell, we never was nothin' but bank, train, and stage robbers. The occasional moneyed hotel . . ."

"That's true," Bledsoe said. "When you two were leading up that bunch, you mostly plundered. You killed . . . or crippled . . . very few and usually only those you were defending yourselves from. Including me, unfortunately." His cheeks colored with fleeting anger. "But that isn't how the Snake River Marauders are anymore. It seems when they turned out the two old bull-buff herd leaders, they turned their wolves loose. I know that personally."

"Personally?" Slash glanced at Pecos, then back at the crippled chief marshal. "How?"

His right hand shaking as though with a palsy, Bledsoe lifted his shot glass over toward Miss Langdon. She replaced the tequila that Bledsoe had splashed out of the glass when he'd assaulted the table, and the chief marshal threw back half. With exaggerated gentleness, he set down the glass, glaring at it as though it had offended him in some way. He seemed to be suppressing an enormous rage.

"When they left you that day . . . the morning in the whorehouse by the Arkansas River," he said slowly, his voice occasionally trembling with emotion, "they robbed the bank in La Junta."

"We figured that's where they were headed, all right," Pecos said. "That was the job we had planned."

Bledsoe stared hard-eyed at the big cutthroat. "Do you know they murdered three tellers in cold blood that day?"

"No," Slash said, shaking his head defiantly. "That ain't true. It can't be true. We were never cold-blooded killers."

"It's true," said Bledsoe. He ground his back teeth as he glared down at the glass in his hand. "They shot the tellers for fun. They shot up the place for fun, and set fire to it, and left the bank laughing. As they rode out of town, they killed two more people on the street. Innocent bystanders. And then they plucked a girl, only fourteen years old, from her father's buckboard wagon in front of the La Junta Mercantile."

Bledsoe squeezed his eyes shut as though clearing a vexing vision from his retinas. When he opened them again, he threw back the rest of his tequila, then stared with even more piercing intensity at his empty glass.

Miss Langdon glanced at her boss and then, as though sensing he couldn't continue, said, "They took that poor child off on the trail with them. The posse found her later." She placed a comforting hand on the chief marshal's shoulder. "Her clothes had been ripped off. She'd been savaged. Multiple times. And she'd been badly beaten."

"She lived for three days," Bledsoe said, "though she never regained consciousness. She died in her mother's arms."

Slash sat ramrod straight in his chair, staring at the chief marshal in disbelief. At the same time, he did believe it. He'd suspected that something similar might happen if Loco Sanchez and Arnell Squires ever took the gang's reins, as both he and Pecos had sensed they'd been planning to do for a couple of years, believing the wolf pack might do better—or at least have more fun—with their muzzles off.

Slash had suspected the gang would grow more savage. But not so soon.

Not *this* soon.

Killing in cold blood had been the best way for any gang member to get themselves kicked out of the gang and kicked out with a cold shovel—dead.

Slash and Pecos had taken that extreme measure a few times. Now, it appears, they should have taken it at least two more times. . . .

"I'll be damned," Pecos said, half to himself. "Sanchez an' Squires."

"Wait," Slash said to Bledsoe. "You said it was personal."

"Oh, it is." Bledsoe lifted his gaze to Slash's. The old marshal's eyes were gimlet-hard but his voice was low and soft. "That poor raped and murdered child was Grace Vanderhall, my granddaughter."

Later that night, Pecos strummed the mandolin that the oldest of the three dead Mexicans had unwittingly bequeathed him, while Slash and Justianna danced closely, hand in hand, turning slow circles in the near-dark saloon.

A fire cracked and popped in the potbelly stove, holding the chilly night at bay. The storm had returned as storms often did in the late summer mountains, but not with as much vigor as before. Rain drummed a steady, even rhythm on the roof. The thunder rumbled softly, as though from far away, and lightning flashed occasionally from behind distant peaks.

It was a quiet, moody night. A lonely night. The story of Bledsoe's dead granddaughter remained in the shadowy room as though the ghost of the poor raped and murdered girl haunted the place.

Slash and Pecos had watched from the saloon's front veranda as the old chief marshal and Miss Langdon had rattled off in the marshal's fancy carriage, wheels splashing in the puddles pocking the muddy yard. They'd been accompanied by the three deputy U.S. marshals who'd cast Slash and Pecos incredulous, vaguely sneering glances over their shoulders as they'd trotted onto the trail heading north toward Saguache, following the marshal's carriage driven by a large, mustached Chinaman in a three-piece suit and a top hat, who'd apparently remained outside with the horses, sheltered by the covered buggy.

When the visitors were gone, Justianna served Slash and Pecos heaping plates of beans and steak from what remained of a butchered cow hanging in her father's keeper shed behind the saloon. The girl seemed relieved to have the two older men remain with her at this lonely place in the mountains, after the terrifying dustup that had left Tio and the other Mexicans dead. Her father and brother would not return from their hunting trip until the next day. Tio and the other two pistoleros lay at the bottom of a nearby ravine to which the deputies had dragged them, kicking dirt and rocks over their bodies.

Occasionally, Slash could hear the snarls and angry yips of wolves fighting over the carcasses now as the rain continued. He heard the savage skirmishes over the soft, inelegant strumming of his partner's big, untutored fingers manipulating the mandolin strings.

Pecos sat tipped back in his chair, holding the instrument up high across his chest, boots crossed on the table before him and on which Bledsoe's men had piled the cutthroats' weapons—Slash's prized Colt .44s, bowie knife, and Winchester Yellowboy repeater. Pecos's big Russian was snugged down in its holster around which the shell belt was coiled. It lay between the blond outlaw's twelve-gauge Richards coach gun and his Colt revolving rifle. Both men's hideout weapons were there, as well—everything piled like armaments gleaned from a bloody field of battle, which Slash supposed they were in a way.

That battlefield was about to get bloodier. . . .

He closed his eyes now as he held Justianna close against him, trying to stop thinking about the large task he and Pecos faced. Tonight, he just wanted to rest and enjoy the rain and this pretty senorita in his arms, and the dissonant strumming of Pecos's fingers on the mandolin. There would be time, starting tomorrow, when he could think of the distasteful duty that lay before them—the stalking and killing of every man in their old gang.

Of course, they'd accepted the job. They'd been given their freedom in exchange for it. They'd been paid to do it. But beyond that, they felt obligated to do it. The gang—*their* gang, the Snake River Marauders—had gone bad. They were running like a plague on the land. They were a pack of rabid wolves, and they needed to be run down and killed before any more innocents, like Bledsoe's granddaughter, fell victim to their fangs and claws.

According to a report in Miss Langdon's valise, only a couple of days ago Sanchez and Squires had shot two deputy U.S. marshals up near the mountain town of Morrisville. So it was toward the southwestern San Juans that Slash Braddock and the Pecos River Kid would head tomorrow at first light, their guns cleaned and loaded and ready to kill.

Tonight, however, there was only the rain, the distant thunder, the pretty, frightened, young, heartbroken senorita in Slash's arms. . . .

When Pecos's fingers chomped down too hard on a string, making the instrument squeal, Slash chuckled and stopped. He looked down at Justianna, who stood with her cheek pressed against his chest, her bare feet planted atop his boots. He pecked the girl's cheek, slid a lock of hair back away from her left eye, and brushed his thumb across her dimpled chin.

"I do believe I'm gonna sit down, young one," he said. "I'm beat. Think I'll have one more drink and a smoke, listen to the rain for a while, and head on up to bed. We'll be pulling out early, Pecos an' me."

"You are going after your old gang?" the girl asked in her Spanish-accented voice.

"Sí."

"The men who killed the old gringo's granddaughter?" She'd heard everything from behind the bar.

"That's right."

"I wish you well, Slash." Justianna reached up and placed a hand against his cheek. "If you wish . . ." She slid her eyes to a curtained doorway flanking the bar and which likely led to a few small, crudely appointed bedrooms, including her own.

Slash chuckled quietly, smiling down at the pretty senorita with the large, round, dark eyes. "I'd take you up on that offer—if I could shave off about twenty-five years or you could pack that many on."

"I am done with young men," the girl said in a quiet snit. "I prefer the older, more mature ones."

"Well, while I might be older, I'm not sure how mature I am. Besides, didn't I tell you to stay away from cutthroats?"

Slash brushed his thumb across her cheek, marveling at the smoothness of her warm, supple skin.

She smiled prettily, cheeks dimpling. "Think of the stories I could tell my grandchildren. Uh . . . when they were older, of course!" The girl chuckled, showing a rare, earthy character. "Besides, lying with you tonight," she added, her eyes beseeching, "I would sleep better."

"Yeah, well, I'll take that as a compliment," Slash added with a snort. He shook his head. "You go on back, get a good night's sleep. Pecos and I'll sleep in the barn with our horses. We're used to it."

"You can sleep in here. Papa's room is free. He won't be back till late tomorrow. He and my brother rode high into the mountains on an elk hunt."

Slash shook his head. "Wouldn't be proper."

Justianna looked up at him, frowning and pooching out her lips.

Slash kissed her cheek again. "Thanks for putting an arch in this old stallion's tail, though you've probably guaranteed me a restless sleep to boot."

"Good!" Smiling, she squeezed his hand and turned toward the curtained doorway. "In case you change your mind, I will leave a lamp burning on the bar." She glanced at where Pecos had quit torturing the mandolin and was taking apart his rifle to clean it, setting each piece on a white handkerchief. "Good night, Pecos!"

"Good night, darlin'!" the blond outlaw said around the quirley sagging from between his lips.

Slash walked over to the table, kicked out a chair across from his partner, and sat down. He splashed tequila into his empty shot glass and began building a quirley from the bag of makings Bledsoe had left them, an added benefit of their agreement to work as hired killers for the old renegade marshal.

As he sprinkled the Durham into the wheat paper

troughed between the first two fingers of his right hand, he caught Pecos grinning across the table at him.

"What?" Slash asked, frowning.

"That pretty li'l senorita done tumbled for ole Slash!"

"Of course she did. It's about time one tumbles for me instead of you."

"They all tumble for you, you handsome old catamount," Pecos said, carefully oiling his rifle's cylinder. "It's that dark hair and dark eyes. And your ornery disposition. They make you seem *dangerous*. Women—they like a man with a little danger in him. The problem with you is you don't reciprocate the feelin'."

"'Reciprocate'?" Slash said, scowling. "What the hell is 'reciprocate'?"

"I got it from a book that schoolteacher read to me last winter down in Phoenix. It means to return the favor. You'd know that if you'd spark a book-readin' woman once in a while instead of just bouncin' from parlor girl to parlor girl."

"I got better things to do than to spend the winter chasin' old-maid schoolteachers." Slash grinned suddenly. "Or the chief marshal's purty Viking secretary . . ."

Pecos flushed. "Ah, hell."

"I thought I was gonna have to restrain that gal, keep her from crawlin' over the table right into your lap! There was somethin' goin' on between you two. I seen it right off, an' so did she!"

Slash laughed.

Pecos brushed a fist across his nose in embarrassment. Then he looked at his partner. "What you got to do that's better than chasing a good lady around of a winter, Slash?"

"Oh, shut up, will you!" Slash scratched a lucifer to life on the table, touched the flame to the cigarette, and drew the rich smoke deep into his lungs. He didn't want to think about women tonight.

Blowing out a lungful of the invigorating smoke, he set to work taking apart his own weapons and placing each piece carefully onto neckerchiefs he'd spread out upon the table. Soon, he was lost in the task and feeling good again after all that had happened over the past several days.

He'd just taken all his weapons apart and had started cleaning them and lubricating each part carefully from a tin of bear grease, when Pecos shot a startled look across the table at him.

Slash frowned. "What is—?"

Then he heard it beneath the steady drumming of the rain on the roof—hoofbeats.

Two or three horses entered the yard at fast trots.

Slash looked down at his .44s, the Yellowboy, and his .41-caliber pocket gun spread out in pieces before him. He looked over at Pecos's weapons. All of his were in pieces, as well. Between the two of them they did not have a single working weapon—aside from Slash's bowie knife, of course, but the blade was of little use against men wielding cold steel.

And whoever was riding into the yard sounded in a hurry—maybe to get out of the rain, maybe for a more nefarious reason.

Both cutthroats cursed at the same time and immediately went to work assembling one gun apiece—Slash, one of his .44s, and Pecos, his big Russian.

Meanwhile, the hoof thuds grew louder just outside the batwings. A horse blew and shook its head, rattling the bit in its teeth. A man said something in a deep, raspy voice. Another answered, though Slash couldn't hear what either man said because of the rain's steady drumming.

Boots made sucking sounds in the mud.

Slash worked quickly, furiously snapping the parts of his pistol back into place.

"Damn!" Pecos said when, working too quickly, he

dropped his Russian's cylinder onto the table. It rolled. Slash caught it and flipped it to him. Pecos caught it and quickly snapped it into place.

Spurs rang on the wooden steps and boots thumped on the veranda.

A man's large, hatted head appeared over the batwings, silhouetted against the stormy night. The batwings parted, and the man stepped into the room. He was followed by two others, the batwings squawking on their unoiled springs, then clattering back into place behind the three.

The trio spread out in a line fronting the door, the rain showing silver in the dark, stormy night behind them.

All three wore rain slickers, the rainwater streaming off them to the floor. They were an unwashed, raggedy-heeled lot—all three bearded, two enormously fat, one skinny and a full head taller than the two fat ones. Two held carbines. The third held a long-barreled, double-bore shotgun. The saloon's wan lamplight touched the nubs of their cheeks beneath their dripping hat brims, leaving their eyes in darkness.

The larger of the two fat men, standing in the middle of the trio, held his shotgun up high across his thick chest. "You two Slash Braddock and the Pecos River Kid?"

His voice sounded like low thunder.

"Who wants to know?" asked Pecos tentatively.

The fat man in the middle of the group pulled down his shotgun, bellowing, "Tiny Wade and Buck Dawson—that's who!"

Slash and Pecos both grabbed the pistols they'd barely gotten put back together and loaded before the three newcomers had pushed in out of the storm. But they wouldn't get the pistols raised and cocked before Fat Man went to work with his gut-shredder.

They both recognized that grim fact at the same time.

"Holy crap—look at the size of that barn-blaster, Slash!"

Pecos bellowed as he bounded straight up out of his chair and launched himself over a table straight ahead of him.

"I seen it!" Slash returned, leaping up out of his own chair, twisting around sharply to his right, and bounding off his boot heels.

At the same time, Fat Man's shotgun thundered, turning the seat of the chair Slash had just vacated not a full second before to little more than feather sticks and splinters. Slash dove over a table to his right, dropping his shoulder into the edge of it so that as he hit the floor on the other side of it, it crashed down at an angle and jutted up before him like a shield.

An inadequate shield, however.

As the two other men went to work with their carbines, two bullets . . . then three . . . then four bullets plowed quarter-sized holes through the table, thumping into the floor on either side of where Slash crouched, cocking back his Colt's hammer.

The shotgun roared again, but that second barrel must have been meant for Pecos, because it was two more rifle rounds that crashed through Slash's table, one chunk of hot lead carving a stinging line across the outside of the cutthroat's neck.

"Damn!" Pecos yowled above the cacophony. "These fellers mean business, Slash!"

"Tell me somethin' I don't know, you dunderhead!" Slash returned, wincing as yet another blue whistler sizzled the air a cat's whisker to the right of his right ear.

"No reason for insults!" Pecos shouted.

"Hah! Hah!" bellowed one of Slash's and Pecos's would-be executioners. "Like shootin' rats in a privy, boys!"

Slash had a feeling the voice had belonged to Fat Man. As Slash edged a look with one eye around the side of his overturned table, he saw the two others firing their carbines toward him and Pecos. Fat Man tossed his barn-blaster onto a nearby table, shoved the flaps of his oiled leather coat back behind his womanishly stout hips, and clawed two hoglegs from their holsters.

Slash knew he couldn't let Fat Man join the fray with those six-shooters. Slash and Pecos had merely been lucky that they hadn't yet caught a bad case of lead poisoning. If Fat Man started in with his two smoke wagons, the odds against the two middle-aged cutthroats would be way too tall.

As another bullet tore through Slash's table, closely joining three other tightly patterned holes, Slash loosed an exasperated roar and punched his .44 barrel first through the ruined table, glad the bullet-pocked wood gave as easily as he'd expected. He crouched to peer over the .44's barrel through the hole that was about twice as large as his fist, and began shooting.

As the .44 bucked, leaped, and roared, stabbing flames toward the two fat men and the string bean, Pecos joined the dustup from about ten feet straight out away from Slash, extending his Russian from over the top of his own shielding table.

Both cutthroats' pistols roared, smoke and flames streaking toward where the three newcomers stood, two shooting while Fat Man brought his own six-guns to bear. He didn't get off a single shot before Slash and Pecos's bullets chewed into him. More rounds found the flesh of the other two men, twisting one completely around and throwing him back out through the batwings, screaming.

The third man dropped his rifle as one bullet punched a hole in his chest while another one shattered his cheekbone, making him look like he'd taken a tomato to the face. He flew backward, bounced off the wall, then dropped to his knees, screaming, while Slash finished him with a bullet to his forehead.

He fell facedown to the floor and lay quivering.

Fat Man had dropped to his knees, throwing his head back and yelling shrilly as blood pumped from two holes in his chest. He triggered one of his two pistols into the floor while raising the other one.

"You devils!" he roared.

Slash triggered his last round into Fat Man's forehead. Pecos did the same thing, he and Slash giving the man two new eyes, though he'd have had a damned hard time seeing out of either one if he'd lived.

Which he didn't.

He dropped forward with a loud death rattle and hit the floor with a heavy thud.

Smoke wafted in the dull light and swaying shadows.

Silence save for the rain once more descended upon the saloon.

Slash lifted his head to peer over his shielding table. "You okay, Pecos?"

"Fine as frog hair." Lifting his head over his own table, Pecos turned toward Slash. "You?"

"Fine as frog hair split four ways."

"They musta followed us out of Saguache," Pecos said. "Buck an' Tiny musta been mighty piss-burned when, layin' up at the doctor's place, they heard we'd cheated the hangman and split tail for the tall an' uncut."

"Yeah. These was friends of theirs, apparently."

"Yeah," Pecos said, grinning meaningfully. "*Friends.*"

Slash snorted a laugh.

Someone gasped.

Slash and Pecos jerked their heads toward the back of the room. Justianna stood behind the bar wearing a wash-worn cotton nightgown and cream dusting cap. She held her hand over her mouth as she stared through the still-smoky air toward the two dead men lying near the bat-wings, the boots of the third dead man showing under the doors, toes pointed skyward.

Lowering her hand from her mouth, the pretty senorita glanced from Pecos to Slash, and hissed, "Cutthroats—mierda!"

She threw up an exasperated arm, wheeled, and disappeared through the curtained doorway behind the bar.

Slowly, wincing at the creaks in their bruised old bones, Slash and Pecos gained their feet.

Pecos turned to Slash and said, "She's got that right."

CHAPTER 23

One week later, Slash and Pecos reined up in the pines at the edge of the little mining camp of Paris, Colorado Territory, which lay ten miles beyond the even smaller camp of Morrisville, high up in a mountain valley at nearly the rim of the Sawatch Range.

It was in this direction that Slash and Pecos had been told by a couple of Morrisville residents that the Snake River Marauders had headed after shooting two U.S. marshals in a Morrisville saloon.

In cold blood.

The marshals had only been playing poker with several men from the gang, including Loco Sanchez and Arnell Squires. When the game had ended, Sanchez and Squires and two others whom the onlookers hadn't been able to identify stood up and casually shot the marshals where they sat, laughing and howling like coyotes congregating on a moonlit ridge. The camp's constable had been sitting at the same table, but he'd been so rattled by the sudden savagery of the killings that he'd frozen in his chair, unable to intervene.

Which was probably just as well. If he had, he'd likely

be lying six feet under the same boot hill cemetery as the two federals.

In the wake of the killings, the gang had simply mounted up and rode off as though they were riding off to a church picnic on Sunday afternoon.

Now Slash doffed his hat and ran a gloved hand through his sweaty, longish hair and took a good, long look at the main street of Paris stretching out before him—two blocks long and abutted on each side by log shacks and business establishments of various sizes. Smoke from noon cook fires unfurled from tin chimney pipes to billow out over the street, tanging the air with the smell of burning pine and cooked meat.

"How do you wanna play this one, Slash?" Pecos said.

Frowning curiously, Slash turned to his partner, who was staring at a humble log building sitting a hundred feet away, on the street's right side, and which a hand-lettered shingle identified simply as BANK.

"What're you talkin' about?" Slash said.

Pecos cast him an annoyed look. He held his right hand over the grips of the Russian holstered over his belly, butt angled toward his right hip. "How you wanna play—"

Pecos cut himself off. Removing his hand from his pistol's butt, he flushed with chagrin. "Crap!"

"That's the second time you done that," Slash told him.

"I'll be damned if old habits don't die hard!" Still flushed with embarrassment, Pecos shook his head. But then he looked at the bank again. "I got me a feelin', though, Slash, that that little bank is chock-full of gold bars. Filled to burstin'! Why, there's probably enough gold locked up in there to . . ."

He'd looked at his partner again, saw the disapproving cast to Slash's dark-eyed gaze.

"All right, all right. We're here to track the Marauders. Okay. I get that." Pecos grinned suddenly, the high-country sunlight dancing merrily in his blue eyes. "But, dammit all—don't it tempt you just a little?"

Slash looked at the bank. He felt the tingle in his fingers, heard the hum in his ears.

Chuckling dryly, he gigged the Appy forward. "Come on!"

He rode on past the bank, ignoring the prospect of those glittering ingots likely piled in a barred cage or a stout safe, awaiting shipment to the U.S. Mint in San Francisco, and reined up in front of a livery barn just beyond the bank. The barn's doors were thrown open and a beefy, bearded gent in overalls was filing the left rear hoof of a sorrel gelding just inside.

The sorrel whinnied a greeting at the newcomers.

Slash's Appy shook its head in kind, twitching its ears warmly and snorting.

Horses were the most social of animals, including humans. At least, they were more social than Slash Braddock was, though that wasn't saying much. They were probably more sentimental to boot. Slash hadn't even given his horse a name, believing that only debutantes and fools named horses, whereas Pecos, the gentle giant, had given his buckskin the unimaginative handle of Buck.

But it was a name, at least.

"Hidy, old-timer," Slash said, pinching his hat brim at the oldster, whose tangled gray beard hung nearly to his waist. A fly had gotten entangled inside the nasty mess, as though in a spiderweb, and appeared to have exhausted itself trying to find its way out. Apparently, the old-timer hadn't noticed. But, then, he probably hadn't noticed the eggs and chili staining the ancient bib beard, either—and several other foods Slash couldn't identify.

The old man looked up from his work, then dropped the horse's hoof, which he'd been sandwiching between his knobby knees.

"Happy midday to ya, gents!" he said, eyes sparkling at

the prospect of business. He hooked a thumb to the shingles tacked to the second story of his barn. "The name's Leif Olmstead, and I'm the proud owner of this heap."

He dipped his chin cordially, chuckling. "As you can see from the signs I painted my ownself, boarding is seventy-five cents a hoss, ten cents extry if you want your animals grained, another five if you want 'em rubbed down. I'll perform the task myself with fresh burlap"—he gave a dreamy smile—"and oh, I've got a sweet 'n' gentle hand, I do. I can calm the most contrary of beasts—exceptin' women of course. I don't know any man alive who can calm a contrary woman! No, sir, don't stable your woman with ole Leif Olmstead!"

He laughed loudly, showing a mouthful of brown, cracked, or missing teeth.

"Boy, ain't that the truth?" Slash said, leaning forward against his saddle horn.

"You can say that again," Pecos chimed in, chuckling and shaking his head. "There sure ain't no calmin' a contrary woman, an' there's plenty o' them to go around!"

All three men had a good laugh over that, and then Slash said, "We'd take you up on the offer, Mr. Olmstead, but you see we ain't here to stable our hosses. At least not yet. We might be pullin' our picket pins in just a few minutes, if need be."

Olmstead frowned in disappointment, looking a little peeved that he'd been wasting time chinning with prospective customers when they weren't prospective at all. "What you takin' me away from my work for, then, if you don't wanna stable your hosses? Like I said, I run this here *livery barn*, fer cryin' on Calvary Hill! I don't serve drinks an' I ain't a whorehouse!"

"Easy, old-timer," said Pecos, holding up a placating hand. "We was just wonderin' if the Snake River Marauders rode through town in the past day or two, that's all."

"We figure if anyone had seen 'em, you would, bein' right here on the main drag, an' all," Slash added. "They mighta even stabled their hosses here . . . let you rub 'em down real gentle-like. . . ." He added that last with a smile meant to be endearing.

The oldster was having none of it.

His face clouded up like a stormy sky, turning white above his beard. He crouched to lift the gelding's hoof and pin it between his knees. "Go 'way, now—I got work to do. Don't got no time for palaverin' about other folks' business!"

He resumed filing the hoof, the shavings joining the others strewn like tiny curled worms in the hay-strewn dirt of the open barn doors.

Slash looked at Pecos, who returned the glance, arching a curious brow.

The cutthroats reined their horses away from the barn and booted them on up the street, Pecos saying off Slash's right stirrup, "Am I imaginin' things, or did that gent get a little off his feed as soon as I mentioned the Marauders?"

"Looked like he'd just taken a bite out of a wormy apple."

"Hmm."

"Here we go," Slash said, his expression brightening.

"What?"

"If anyone'll know about the Marauders passin' through town, it'll be these pretty young ladies of the line."

Slash angled his Appy over to the left side of the street, which was ankle-deep mud from the frequent afternoon downpours, toward where two young women, doubtless of the working variety, dolled up and as scantily clad as they were, milled on the timber-railed balcony of a two-story log cabin that boasted two red oil lamps mounted to either side of its halved-log, Z-frame front door, directly below the low-hanging balcony.

"Slash, now, we got work to do, you randy ol' mossy-horn!" Pecos cajoled his partner.

"An' workin' is just what I'm doin', partner!"

One of the girls was a willowy redhead with curly hair and the other was a fleshy-bodied, flaxen blonde. The redhead was smoking a quirley and the blonde was caressing the liver-colored cat lounging on the balcony rail between the two girls, slowly curling and uncurling its tail and blinking luxuriously, enjoying both the attention and the warm beams of the high-noon sun bathing the high-mountain mining camp.

As Slash and Pecos approached the parlor house, the redhead yelled to a dapper gent in a natty suit and bowler hat just then passing on the boardwalk beneath the balcony, a leather valise tucked under one arm, heading away from Slash and Pecos. "Hey, Wally!" the redhead called. "How come you ain't been over to see me in a month of Sundays?"

The dapper gent stopped and turned around, raising a hand to shield his eyes from the sun as he gazed up at the two doxies. He flushed a little, and said, "Why, Miss Grace— you know I done got married to June Carpenter last month!"

"Oh, that's right," Grace said in a somber tone. "I reckon I done heard about that an' just plain forgot. The banker's daughter, huh? You have my condolences."

The dapper gent smiled weakly.

The flaxen blonde leaned over the balcony rail, snorting with ribald laughter.

Grace said, "In that case, you'll be needing me more than ever in about two months, so you just remember where I am, Wally!"

Wally's blush deepened, and his smile grew strained. He pinched his hat brim to the two nymphs du pavé, then wheeled and continued on his way, quickening his step and holding his head down in shame while a nearby shop-keeper watched, grinning from his open front door.

"The first one after ya come back'll be on the house, Wally!" the redhead called, then shared a raucous laugh with the blonde before sticking her quirley between her lips and taking a deep drag.

Stopping his horse beneath the balcony, Slash doffed his black hat and cast a broad smile up at the two girls leaning forward over the balcony rail. "Happy midday to you, ladies!"

Both looked down at the two newcomers. The blonde kicked a bare foot out behind her while the redhead said, "Hey, look at these two, Shyla. Why, ain't they handsome!"

"Pshaw!" Pecos said, blushing. He might have been a hard-bitten outlaw, but there wasn't a woman alive who couldn't make him blush like a ten-year-old with his first crush.

"Come on up," said the blonde, Shyla. "Me an' Grace'll curl your toes for yas!"

She turned toward the two strangers, grinning broadly and planting a fist on her full, matronly hip.

"Now, ladies," Slash said. "I am shocked! Truly, I am. How do you know that, not unlike your pal Wally, we ain't married?"

"You two ain't under a yoke," said Shyla. "I can tell. When you're in our line of work, you can tell right off the difference between a man who's married and one who ain't."

"Oh?" said Pecos. "Pray tell!"

"It's easy. Married men have bowed shoulders. You know, like they're under yoke. You fine-lookin' gentlemen are sit-tin' them nice ponies straight in the saddle."

"No, sir," Grace said, shaking her head slowly and beam-ing down becomingly at the two cutthroats smiling back up at them. "You two don't have no harpies or wailin' babes

back home in the cabin. You're both free as the moon!"
She stepped, beckoning. "Come on up. Me an' Shyla play
ya a little slap 'n' tickle, though we promise there'll be a
whole lot more ticklin' than slappin'!"

She and Shyla snickered.

The cat sat up and stretched.

"Now, ladies," Slash said, again feigning shock. "Can't
you see me an' my partner here are old enough to be
your . . . your, er . . . well, your slightly older brothers?"

He glanced at Pecos, snickering.

The doxie laughed, then Shyla sobered up and nodded,
saying with mock seriousness, "We can indeed see that you're
both mature, upstandin' adults. Me an' Grace, though—
we been *baaad*."

"Very bad!" said Grace.

"Say it ain't so!" returned Slash.

"You know what I think?" said Shyla. "I think our two
older brothers better come up here an' take us over their
knees!"

"It's no worse than what we deserve!" Grace added,
turning to Shyla soberly.

The two girls nodded in solemn agreement, then broke
down in laughter.

Pecos slapped his thigh and threw his head back, roaring.

Slash laughed and shook his head.

The two doxies leaned far out over the rail, tittering,
giving their prospective customers a brazen display of their
low-cut, well-filled, lace-edged bodices.

"What do you say, fellas?" Grace urged.

"Now, now, ladies," Slash said, still chuckling, "while
you are both provoking my partner and I to indulge in unclean thoughts, we're gonna have to save that slap 'n'
tickle for another time."

"Yeah, another time," said Pecos. "Today, we just got a question for you."

"A question?" Shyla asked, frowning curiously. "A question about what? Grace an' myself don't know much about nothin' . . . other than . . . well, other than the most important stuff in the whole wide world!"

The doxies looked at each other and laughed again, raucously.

Slash shared a dubious glance with Pecos. The dark-haired cutthroat was beginning to wonder if these two doves hadn't been sucking on opium pipes.

Slash waited for the doves to pipe down again before he said, "We was wonderin' if you two seen or heard about . . . or maybe *entertained* . . . any of the Snake River Marauders who might've passed through town in the past day or two."

If only a few seconds ago the two girls had looked as though they'd been indulging in the midnight oil, it now appeared they'd been doused with buckets of cold water.

Grace's gaze grew hard, downright unfriendly. "You . . . friends . . . of . . . theirs . . . ?"

"Friends?" Slash glanced at Pecos and shook his head. "Nope."

"Lawmen?" Shyla asked, arching her brows hopefully.

"In a manner of speaking," said Pecos.

"Let's just say, we're hunting the gang," Slash said. "They passed through here, then, I take it?"

Slash hadn't realized until now that a third girl had been on the balcony. This one had been sitting in a chair behind Grace and Shyla. At first mention of the Marauders, she'd risen slowly from her chair and strode just as slowly over to the railing to stand beside Grace and scowl down at Slash and Pecos. She was a mulatto with short hair and striking green eyes.

Slash's gut tightened when, raising a hand to shield his eyes from the sun, he got a good look at the girl's face. One eye was badly swollen and a long, scabbing cut ran at an angle down and across her lips. The knife slash started an inch from the corner of her left nostril and ended on the right side of her chin.

"Yeah, they passed through here," the girl said in a heavy Cajun accent. "The whole gang. Only"—her jaws hardened and quivered with emotion, one nostril swelling— "two are still here in town."

Again, Slash and Pecos exchanged a quick glance.

"Still here?" Slash asked.

"Tha's right. Two of 'em."

"Which ones?" Pecos asked the disfigured doxie.

"The leaders," the mulatto said, her jaws still iron-hard, her enraged gaze shifting quickly from Slash to Pecos, then back again.

Slash's heart quickened. Could he and his partner have gotten this lucky?

"Loco Sanchez and Arnell Squires?" he asked.

The mulatto shook her head. "No. That weren't them." She continued shaking her head as she glared darkly down at Slash. "Slash Braddock an' the Pecos River Kid." She pointed at her ruined lips. "The Kid held me down while Slash, true to his name, gave me this!"

CHAPTER 24

Slash and Pecos sat frozen in their saddles, shocked. Enraged.

They glanced at each other, darkly.

Composing himself, Pecos turned back to the three girls glaring down at him and Slash and said, "Sure never hear of ole Slash an' Pecos mistreating women like that. No, sir. Slash Braddock an' the Pecos River Kid, you say? Hmmm." He thoughtfully scratched his chin. "They're here in Morrisville, you say?"

"They sure are," Grace told him. Neither she nor Shyla appeared nearly as friendly as they'd seemed before the Snake River Marauders had been mentioned.

Slash said haltingly, "Where, uh . . . where do you suppose we might be able to find Slash Braddock and the Pecos River Kid?"

"Only place you could find 'em," said Grace, "since they been gamblin' for the past three days, ever since they left here." She glanced quickly, sympathetically at the mulatto girl. "There's only one gamblin' house in town."

The redhead stretched her droll gaze toward where a two-story log saloon with a large front veranda sat on the main street's right side, about a block beyond the parlor house. A large sign over the high, false facade announced THE LUCKY LADY. The saloon/gambling house was situated on the corner of a cross street and the camp's main drag. Several men dressed in miners' garb stood out on the veranda, talking, laughing, and swigging heavy schooners of soapy ale.

Pecos pinched his hat brim to the doxies staring coldly back at him. "Much obliged, ladies." He slid his eyes to Slash, and the two cutthroats touched spurs to their horses' flanks, moving on up the muddy street, weaving through the heavy, midday traffic.

"Slash Braddock and the Pecos River Kid, eh?" Slash said, raking a speculative finger down his neck.

"Sounds like," Pecos said. "Me? I'm lookin' forward to meetin' those two notorious old owlhoots."

"Me, too," Slash said as he and Pecos drew their horses up to one of several hitch racks fronting the saloon. "Me, too . . ."

Roughly a dozen horses were tied at the hitch rails, indicating the Lucky Lady was doing a fair business at midday. Slash and Pecos added their own mounts to the tally. Pecos removed his sawed-off Richards ten-gauge from where it hung from his saddle horn by its leather lanyard. He draped the lanyard over his head and right shoulder.

Turning to Slash and shoving the formidable-looking popper behind his back, he said, "A feller can never be too careful."

"Nope," his partner said, unsnapping the keeper thong from over the hammer of the .44 holstered for the cross-draw on his left hip. "Especially when them two devils Slash Braddock and the Pecos River Kid are in town."

"Ain't that the truth, though?" Pecos chuckled dryly as he and Slash climbed the veranda steps, their spurs *ching-ing* softly on the risers.

They edged around the small crowd of men drinking

suds and sipping whiskey on the veranda—mostly a stout, bearded lot of Germans and Scandinavians clad in the dungarees, wool shirts, suspenders, and high, cork-soled, lace-up boots that marked them as prospectors. They were conversing in either their own mother tongues or in heavily accented English or combinations of both—a jovial but sun-seasoned, work-hardened breed taking a midday break from their toils.

Side by side, Slash and Pecos pushed through the batwings. As usual, they separated quickly on the other side of the threshold, Slash stepping to the left, Pecos to the right.

Slash's gaze swept the room in which a good two-dozen men sat at tables or stood at the large bar at the back. The crowd in here appeared very much like the one on the veranda. Sprinkled in small clusters about the room were men in the chaps, high-crowned hats, and bright, billowy neckerchiefs of cowpunchers. The air was so smoky, and the bright light angling through a handful of windows contrasted so sharply with the shadows, that Slash doubted he'd be able to recognize any of his old gang if he'd been staring right at them.

Raising his voice to be heard above the low roar that echoed loudly in the cave-like room, Slash canted his head toward Pecos, standing on the other side of the batwings, and said, "Why don't we get us a drink, so we don't look too conspicuous, and walk around?"

Pecos started to nod but then he glanced to his right, froze, and walked over to Slash, canting his head and saying quietly into Slash's right ear, "I think I just spotted Sanchez."

Slash started to turn his head toward the far side of the room, but Pecos placed a hand on his partner's shoulder, stopping him. "Don't look. Let's get us a table, have a drink, and work out a plan."

Slash moved toward an open table ahead and to the left, which had just been vacated by three black-bearded men speaking in heavy Russian accents. At least, they sounded Russian to Slash, who'd encountered such men and their heavy language here and there about the West, mostly where mines were dug and tracks were laid.

Slash sank into a chair. Pecos did, as well, across from Slash, and swept several empty beer mugs and a whiskey bottle to one side. Folding his arms on the table, he looked at Slash and said, "To your right. Under the grizzly head."

Slash feigned a yawn, running a gloved hand down his face, and glanced as inconspicuously as possible to his right.

The grizzly head was mounted on the far wall, which was covered in red paper patterned with gold diamonds. Several other game trophies decorated the four walls of the place, but under the grizzly head sat Loco Sanchez—at a table with six or seven other men, most of them dressed like cowpunchers.

One of those others, however, was definitely not a cowpuncher.

The little, wiry man decked out in a black hat, green silk neckerchief, and black shirt under a pinto vest was Arnell Squires.

Squires wore black gloves on his hands and, just as he always did, he wore a gold-banded diamond ring on his right hand, over the glove. Squires had been very proud of that ring ever since he'd won it down in Mexico playing poker with a famous Sonoran border bandito.

Squires sported the ring everywhere he went, usually wearing it outside the black glove to better show it off. Now he had poker cards fanned out in the hand trimmed with the ring, and he was smoking a fat stogie and talking as he played, snorting and snarling and scowling menacingly, placing bets and calling.

He sat beside Loco Sanchez, a beefy half-Mexican whose black sombrero hung down his back by its horsehair thong. Sanchez had a broad, Indian-featured face but with long mare's tail whiskers and thick, black chin whiskers.

He had a nasty scar across his coffee-colored forehead. He'd acquired the scar long ago, he claimed, by the stiletto heel of a former, jealous Mexican wife—one of many he'd claimed over the years. All, of course, had been beautiful and jealous of his frequent bouts of cheating with other beautiful women.

However, Slash had known the man long enough—for ten years and more, in fact—to know that Sanchez had never actually been married and had only ever lain with whores. The cutthroat had acquired the scar from a drunken tumble out of a haymow one night while answering the call of nature, after the gang had robbed a bank in Bullhook Bottoms up in the Montana Territory.

Slash's heart surged.

He glanced at Pecos and gave a cunning smile. "You see . . . ?"

"Arnell? Yeah. Just seen him."

"Which one do you suppose is you and which one is me?"

"I don't know, but it galls me somethin' painful that those two hydrophobic polecats are raping, pillaging, and plundering their way through the territory, calling themselves Slash Braddock and the Pecos River Kid."

"Yeah," Slash said, nodding slowly, cutting his eyes toward the pair. "Disfiguring doxies, too."

"What you two see over there?" The girl had just walked up to them, an empty tray in her hands. She was a pretty saloon girl, maybe twenty years old, with creamy, pale skin and wearing a corset and bustier, black fishnet stockings, and high-heeled red shoes. Painted ribbons poked out of her piled-up hair. For all the garishness of her attire, there was a midwestern innocence about her. In her high-heel shoes, she looked like a newborn colt trying to stand on its new legs.

"Oh, nothin'," Slash said quickly, inwardly wincing, hoping the girl hadn't drawn Sanchez's and Squires's attention.

She turned toward Slash and Pecos and said, "Those two friends of yours—are they? Slash Braddock and the Pecos River Kid? I'll let 'em know you're here if—"

"No, no friends of ours," Pecos interrupted her quickly. "Why don't you bring us a couple of beers—won't you, little sister?"

"Yeah, make it fast—will you, honey?" Slash said. "We're powerful thirsty!"

"Everybody in Morrisville is powerful thirsty!" the girl grouched as she hurried to the bar, stumbling in her shoes.

When she'd set down two frothy dark ales in front of Slash and Pecos and scooped the coins off the table, she headed off to answer the shouted orders of a stout German at the back of the room, near the stairs that rose to the second floor.

Slash glanced toward the table at which Sanchez and Squires were playing poker, Squires just then laughing his belligerent laugh as he raked the pot into the already sizable pile of scrip and specie before him. Slash licked some of the cream-colored foam off the top of his beer and looked at Pecos.

"What do you say we walk over and shoot that son of a bitch? Shoot 'em both."

"They'll see us before we get there. They'll open up on us, and innocent folks'll get shot."

Slash sipped his beer, thought it over.

He glanced at the poker players once more, then said, "Wait till they leave? Shoot 'em on the street or out on the trail?"

"Might be best," Pecos said. "Out on the trail. Yeah, that'd work."

"Sure would be nice to know where the rest of the gang is," Slash said. "Maybe wing one of 'em, make the other one ta—. Wait, hold on."

"What is it?"

Slash had just then seen the saloon girl deliver a tray of beers to the poker table. As she'd tried to turn away and head back to the bar, Loco Sanchez had grabbed her arm and pulled her down on his lap. Sanchez was saying something into the girl's ear. Slash couldn't hear what the cutthroat said, but he could tell the girl didn't like it. She was frowning and shaking her head, trying to climb off Sanchez's lap.

Loco held her down firmly, and his hands were straying.

Slash looked at Pecos, who had followed Slash's gaze to Sanchez and the girl. Pecos turned to Slash and pursed his lips, jaws hard. "He's sure got a way with women, Loco does. I see that ain't changed."

"What's changed," Slash said, "is he thinks there's no one around to make him keep his wolf on its leash." Slash took a quick sip of his beer, then kicked his chair back, rose, and closed his right hand over the grips of his cross-draw .44. "But there is, by God. Me!"

He froze as Sanchez laughed loudly and rose from the chair, heaving the girl up before him and then crouching and pulling her up over his right shoulder.

"No!" the girl squealed. "I told you, damn you—I don't work the line! I just serve drinks!"

Sanchez laughed louder and, making his way toward the stairs with the girl draped over his shoulder like a sack of grain, yelled, "Well, you work it now, girl. Don't worry— I'll give you top dollar!"

The other poker players, including Arnell Squires, whooped and laughed.

"Give her hell, Slash!" Squires bellowed, cupping his hands around his mouth.

Sanchez turned to yell back over his shoulder at Squires, "Watch my winnin's, Pecos. Anybody tries to rob me, shoot 'im!"

Squires clapped his hands and laughed. The other poker players looked a little less delighted than Arnell did at that last comment.

"That tears it!" Slash stepped out around the table and slid his .44 from its holster, turning toward the stairs.

"Slash, sit down!" Pecos hissed up at him, pulling Slash's gun hand down. "Sit down, dammit. You're liable to hit the girl!"

Slash glared toward where Loco Sanchez was climbing the stairs, laughing while the blond saloon girl pounded his back and kicked her legs, though her struggles were in vain. Sanchez was three times her size, and five times as strong. He had her clamped hard against his shoulder.

Most of the men in the room were laughing.

The two bartenders, however, stared after "Slash Braddock" and the innocent saloon girl, darkly shaking their heads. They appeared unwilling to do anything about the girl's violation. Too frightened to interfere.

The reputations of Slash Braddock and the Pecos River Kid, adorned with legend, had preceded them. . . .

Slash released the breath he hadn't realized he'd been holding, then holstered his pistol and sat back down in his chair. "Dammit all!" he raked out, keeping his voice down.

Pecos was looking toward the poker table. "Dammit, Slash—I think Squires mighta seen you."

"Good!"

"Slash, dammit—for the last time, stand down. We don't need lead flying through here like rain in a mountain storm. The room's got too many innocent folks in it!"

Slash glanced toward the poker table. Squires and the other gamblers had resumed their game. Slash kept his eyes on Squires, looking around several men sitting between them. Squires didn't glance toward Slash even once.

Slash turned to Pecos, shaking his head. "I don't think so, pard. I think we're all right."

"Whew!"

"Yeah."

"How should we play it?"

"Well," Slash said, glancing at the ceiling. "One of us better get upstairs and trim Loco's wick before he gives that girl what he gave the mulatto or better. You best do it. In the state I'm in, I might not have too steady a hand. I don't want to get that poor girl killed. Did you see her? She could barely stand up in them shoes."

"Yeah, I saw." Pecos cast a quick, furtive glance toward where Arnell Squires, alias the Pecos River Kid, was back playing poker with the cowpunchers, raising and calling, cajoling and threatening, bluffing and mocking. "Ole Pecos over there looks purty preoccupied. I think I can make it upstairs without him spottin' me."

"I'll wait to hear your shot before I go to work on Arnell. He'll likely rush to the stairs. I'll wait for a clear shot and take it." Slash hardened his jaws as he glanced toward the poker table. "Even if I have to back shoot the crazy devil."

Pecos rose from his chair, shoving his shotgun back behind him. Drawing his hat brim low over his eyes and keeping his head down, he strode back toward the bar and the stairs flanking it, on the room's left side. He walked past a table of Germans also playing cards, conversing loudly in their own tongue, and swilling small tin buckets of suds, their beards and mustaches frothy with the stuff.

Pecos climbed the stairs, trying to look as casual as possible. At the top, he turned and walked down the hall

220 William W. Johnstone and J.A. Johnstone

opening on his right. The hall was dimly lit by a fly-specked, dirt-streaked window at the far end, and by a single bracket lamp with a badly soot-stained mantle.

Pecos thought he was going to have trouble locating the serving girl and Loco Sanchez, but he hadn't taken more than four steps along the hall, padded by a musty runner, before he heard a girl give an anguished cry behind a door just ahead of him, on his left. What sounded like a water pitcher crashed into a wall, breaking and dropping to the floor.

Sanchez thundered a laugh. "You like it rough—do you, sweetheart? Ain't that a coincidence? I do, too!"

CHAPTER 25

The half-Mex cutthroat laughed again. Boots thumped behind the door ten feet from Pecos now. The girl gave another cry, this one more pinched.

A door latch clicked to Pecos's right. He paused mid-stride as a door opened on that side of the hall, and a man with mussed hair and a thick mustache peered out from behind small, round spectacles. He wore only white cotton longhandles and black socks. One of the socks was half off. He was likely a traveling drummer who'd rented a room to sleep off a drunk but had been rudely awakened by Loco Sanchez.

He peered toward the door behind which the girl just then gave a wail, and said, "What in God's name is—"

Pecos pressed two fingers to his lips, stopping the man midsentence.

The man scowled up at him, indignant. He opened his mouth to speak but Pecos dropped a shoulder so that his savage-looking shotgun swung around in front of him. He held up the twelve-gauge in both hands, giving the sleepy drummer a good look at the savage weapon. The drummer gasped, stumbled back into his room, and quickly but quietly closed the door and locked it.

Pecos continued walking forward, hearing more commotion behind the door on his left. He'd nearly reached the door before a bellowing wail rose from below, and a man's lunatic voice—which he recognized as belonging to Arnell Squires—shouted, "Die, you old devil!"

Bang!

"Die!"

Bang!

"Die!"

Bang! Bang!

Pecos froze in his tracks. His heart leaped into his throat.

"Ah, crap," he said aloud to himself. "Slash!"

He swung around and started running back toward the stairs. A door opened behind him.

A familiar voice said, "Howdy, Pecos—how you doin', old pard?"

Again, Pecos froze in his tracks.

The shooting continued from below. One floor down, men shouted and cursed as they scrambled to avoid the lead storm.

"What's wrong, brother?" Sanchez said behind Pecos in a hard, cold, Spanish-accented voice. "Don you wanna come in for a dreenk?"

"Sure, sure," Pecos said, his heart battering the backside of his sternum. "Let's do that. Why don't I come in an' we'll have—"

Pecos started to wheel, but knowing what was coming, he hurled his big two-hundred-plus-pound bulk against the wall beside him. Before him, Sanchez fired two quick rounds, both stitching the air where Pecos had been standing a half a second before, and hammering the stair rail twenty feet behind Pecos now.

Sanchez swung his six-shooter toward where Pecos crouched low against the wall and snarled through gritted teeth as he hurled another round, this one tearing into the wall six inches in front of Pecos's broad nose. As Sanchez clicked his six-gun's hammer back, he saw the two large, round, black maws of Pecos's cannon level on him, and yelled, "No—wait!" knowing he'd be just a hair too late with his own next bullet.

He was right.

Pecos tripped one of the sawed-off's rabbit ear triggers and watched as the long-haired, scar-faced Sanchez was picked up off his feet and hurled out the window behind him, his high, caroming wail dwindling quickly as he flew down, down, down toward the cross street, glass raining along behind him.

"Jesus Christ!" a man shouted in the cross street below.

Pecos slid his gaze toward the left. The girl stood in the open doorway of the room Sanchez had hustled her into. She stared at Pecos wide-eyed, then turned to look at the blown-out window. Some of the glass remaining in the frame was speckled with dark-red blood. Some of the blood dripped from the shards to the floor.

The girl clamped a hand over her wide-open mouth in shock.

She looked all right. Just frightened. She was still wearing her dress, which meant the goatish Sanchez hadn't gotten too far along with her.

Suddenly, Pecos realized that the shooting had stopped in the saloon below.

He swung around and ran toward the stairs, yelling, "Slash!"

Five minutes earlier, Slash had sat watching Pecos climb the stairs at the back of the saloon. As the big cutthroat turned at the top of the stairs, disappearing into the hall, Slash took a sip of his beer, which he found uncommonly malty and delicious for this neck of the high and rocky.

Wiping the foam from his mouth with the back of his hand, he cast another furtive glance toward the poker players.

Arnell Squires, alias the Pecos River Kid, was just then slamming his cards down with an angry scowl and saying something to a man sitting across the table from him and to his right. Slash couldn't hear what Squires said, but he could tell by the angry look on the outlaw's face, it wasn't pleasant.

Just then a big, barrel-shaped figure stepped between Slash and Squires, obliterating Slash's view of his former cutthroat cohort for a good three or four seconds. The big, barrel-shaped man clad in greasy overalls was not only big, he was extremely slow moving. When he finally passed, Slash saw that Arnell Squires was no longer seated, playing cards.

Squires was now standing and aiming a cocked six-shooter out over the poker table and grinning like a lunatic at Slash. He was also aiming the pistol.

"Die, you old devil!" Squires bellowed from across the room.

Slash threw himself straight back in his chair, he and the chair hitting the floor as Squires's Schofield roared. The crowd parted between Slash and the shooter, not terribly unlike the parting of the Red Sea but probably with even more noise and violence, men hurling themselves to each side, dropping drinks and cigarettes and cigars and turning over chairs and tables in their haste to avoid a bad case of lead poisoning.

"Die!" Squires bellowed as another bullet plunked into the floor about six inches from Slash's body, which he was rolling feverishly to avoid being turned into a sieve.

"Die!" Squires bellowed again, as another bullet smashed into the top of the table Slash had just rolled under.

"Die!" Another round chewed through the table to graze Slash's left hand and the outside of that shoulder.

He rolled out from beneath the table, both fists filled with iron.

He didn't know how he managed to do it, for he never could have performed such a nimble, effortless maneuver had he not been drunk, showing off for a girl, or had his life not been imperiled and electricity fairly popping and snapping in his blood. No, he didn't know how he did it, but he rolled up smoothly onto his knees, snapping his boot heels down under his butt and hoisting himself to a half crouch, shooting, both Colts bucking in his hands.

Squires loosed a womanish scream as he stood in place, dropping his Colt on the poker table and jerking as though struck by the same lightning bolt that was sparking fire in Slash's blood.

As Slash stopped shooting, Arnell Squires continued to jerk, blood gushing out of him, head thrown far back on his shoulders, a death snarl stretching his lips and causing the chords of sinew to stand out like ropes from his neck.

Finally, he dropped his chin. He leveled his face at Slash. He looked drunk as he stared almost blandly at his killer. A weird light of merriment flashed in his eyes, and then he gave a girlish giggle, twirled around as though he were performing a pirouette, and dropped to his knees.

He knelt there for about five seconds.

He said, "Oh, damn—I'm dead, aren't I?" and fell face first to the floor.

The room was suddenly as quiet as an empty cave.

Half the men in the room were on the floor, cowering under tables or against walls.

Slowly, one of the bartenders lifted his head above the bar and turned his wide eyes to stare in shock at the dead man lying belly down on the floor. One of the cowpunch-

ers who'd been playing poker with Squires crawled out
from beneath the table he'd been cowering under to stare
in disbelief at the dead outlaw. He held his high-crowned
hat in his hands as, kneeling there beside Squires, he said
to no one in particular: "Jee-Jeepers—the Pecos River Kid
is . . . is . . . *dead*!"

He glanced around the room, chuckling nervously, eyes
wide and filled with disbelief.

"Dead, all right," said a little man who'd been playing
poker with "Pecos." He moved out away from the wall to
stare down at Squires. He appeared strangely boyish but
with a broad-brimmed black hat and a clean-shaven face
aside from a thick black mustache. "The Pecos River Kid
is dead."

There was something odd about his voice, as well. But,
then, the West was populated with human oddities.

A stocky, gray-haired man in a three-piece business suit
said, "Are you sure it's the Kid? I heard the Pecos River
Kid was a big, beefy gent." He looked around, frowning.
"With long blond hair and blue eyes."

"Nope," said the little man who'd been playing poker
with Squires. "That's the Pecos River Kid, all right. I'd recognize him anywhere." He turned his vaguely familiar eyes
toward Slash. "You killed the Pecos River Kid, mister. Con-
gratulations!"

Slash frowned at the little man, wondering where he'd
seen him before. Distracted by sudden thunder at the back
of the room, he turned to see the actual Pecos running
down the stairs from the second floor, yelling, "Slash!"

Pecos stopped when he picked his partner out of the
crowd.

"He dead?" asked one of the two bartenders, turning
toward Pecos standing on the stairs, midway between the
first and second floors.

Frowning uncertainly, Pecos turned toward the barman. He hesitated for a second, then, remembering the aliases, said, "Yeah. Yeah . . . Slash Braddock is dead. He's, uh . . ." The big cutthroat continued dropping slowly down the stairs. "He's lyin' dead in the street."

As he strode across the floor toward Slash, he looked toward where Arnell Squires lay dead under the mounted grizzly head. Haltingly, he asked, "The Pecos River Kid—he dead, too?"

"Deader'n hell," Slash said, stifling a dry chuckle.

Just then the crowd, recovering from the shock of the lead swap, lifted a low roar as the men in the room began exclaiming as they converged on the body of the "Pecos River Kid" lying dead under the grizzly head.

"I want his boots!" yelled one man, crouching over Squires's body.

"I got his hat! I got the Kid's hat!" shouted another, smiling like a happy boy around a Christmas tree as he held Squires's hat aloft. "Look here, Davey," he yelled to another man on the far side of the room. "I got the Pecos River Kid's felt topper!"

"Get out of the way—I want that damn ring on his finger!" cried another gent, one of many now dropping like vultures over the fresh carrion of Arnell Squires.

"I git dibs on that ring, dammit!" retorted another man. "He done cheated me out of a hundred and twenty dollars! *Give me that goddamn ring!*"

As Pecos approached Slash, a foxy smile twisting his mouth, Slash looked around for the little man who'd appeared so familiar but whose face the outlaw could not place, try as he might. His eyes sweeping the raucous crowd fighting over Arnell Squires, Slash spotted the little man, clad in wool trousers, plaid wool shirt, and suspenders just then pushing out through the batwings.

"Hey," Slash called, and started toward the doors.

Just then someone shouted, "Slash Braddock! That's whose guns *I* want!"

And then a good half dozen men or more dashed toward the batwings, blocking Slash's way.

When Slash finally made it out the doors, the little man was gone.

"Who you lookin' for?" Pecos asked, moving up behind his partner.

Frowning, Slash shook his head. "I'll be damned if I know."

CHAPTER 26

"What's got your neck in a hump?" Pecos asked Slash later, after the two cutthroats had ridden out of Morrisville as their dead counterparts were still being pillaged and plundered and stripped as naked as proverbial jaybirds. "We done just escaped eternity one more time, my friend."

The big blond scowled and shook his head. "I wonder who got Arnell's boots. As I remember, he had one hell of a nice pair of boots—with fine red stitching all over 'em." He glanced at Slash. "Didn't he get those boots down in Mexico a couple of years ago?"

Pecos gazed at Slash riding just off his left stirrup.

"Yeah, yeah, I think so," Slash said, distracted. He'd only half heard the question.

"I wish I'd gotten my hands on those boots," Pecos said, riding easily in his saddle. "I doubt they would have fit me. I think Arnell had little feet. Wasn't Roy always teasin' him, sayin' Arnell had little-girl's feet. Purty, too. Hah!" Pecos chuckled, then grew thoughtful, speculative once more. "Still, that was some fine footwear!"

He turned to Slash. "Don't you think, partner?"

Slash looked at him. "Don't I think what?"

"All right," Pecos said in frustration. "I'll ask it again. What's got your neck in such a hump? You ain't been listenin' to a word I been sayin'. Not that that's all that unusual, but . . ."

Slash glanced back along the trail they'd been following southwest through the San Juan Mountains. Having climbed a low divide, they were now dropping down into the broad valley on the other side and through which the Animas River twisted and turned, lifting a low, steady roar in the pines to their left. Towering stone ridges, like gothic cathedrals and English castles, and scalloped with tufts of spruce, firs, and tamaracks, jutted high over both sides of the valley, which was fragrant with the piney, winey smell of the high mountains and whose air was refreshingly cool even now in the midafternoon.

Slash wasn't thinking about the peaceful, picturesque surroundings, however. Pecos was right. He had his neck in a hump. It had been that way ever since they'd dropped over the first ridge out of Morrisville.

Now he turned to his partner and said, "You know that itchy feeling I get down my right leg? The one that usually means we're bein' shadowed?"

"Yeah, I remember you fussin' about it."

"Well, my right leg is itchin' somethin' awful right now. If I didn't know better, I'd swear I had a whole nest of chiggers chewin' away at me under my trousers and inside my longhandles."

Pecos glanced behind him, scowling toward the top of the last hill. "That's good to know."

"Why?"

"You know that low buzzing I get in my ears whenever I think someone's slogging along our back trail?"

"Yeah."

"If I was wearin' a bonnet, there'd have to be a bee in it for all the caterwaulin' inside my head!"

"That tears it," Slash said, pulling back on his Appy's reins and turning sideways to the trail. Gazing back toward that last hill, which was stippled with rocks and tall firs, he said, "I think someone's been shadowin' us ever since we left Morrisville."

"I done looked behind us several times," Pecos said, deep lines cutting across his forehead, "and I ain't seen a thing. I thought it was just my imagination even though, as you know, I ain't never had much of one."

"Yeah, I was thinkin' the same thing."

"About my imagination?"

"No, about us bein' shadowed, you dunderhead!" Slash swung down from his saddle, tossed Pecos the reins, and shucked his Yellowboy repeater from his saddle boot. "Wait here with the horses. If someone is behind us and we ain't both just all too ready for the Sisters of Christian Charity Home for the Old and Feeble, I'll spot the son of a buck!"

Slash pumped a cartridge into the Yellowboy's breech, off-cocked the hammer, and strode back up the hill along the narrow, meandering, rock-pocked horse trail he and Pecos had been following. When he was near the top, he doffed his hat and rose up onto the toes of his boots, gazing back down the hill's other side, toward the long, broad, open valley they'd just traversed.

Seeing nothing, he got down on hands and knees, crawled a little closer to the top of the hill, then stopped and took a long, sweeping gaze out across the valley.

It was all open ground before him for a good four, five hundred yards. There was little to no cover. About the only thing that grew out there, between low, fir-clad mountain ridges to either side, was short grass and low-growing mountain sage.

Slash took another long, slow look, sweeping his gaze from the far northern ridge on his left to the southern ridge on his right, separated by at least two miles. Between those ridges was only the sage. Slash's eyes were still keen. At least, he thought they were; he had to admit he'd never had them checked by a professional. All he knew was that he could still bring down a deer with his Yellowboy from a good hundred to a hundred and fifty yards without any problem, and hit the beast where he intended.

You didn't get any more professional than that.

If someone were out there, he'd have seen him. But he didn't see a damn thing except a hawk riding the thermals high over the valley, a ragged-edged speck against the faultless arch of cobalt sky. The hawk was likely hunting for mice or jackrabbits.

Slash crawled backward several yards down the slope, then rose, grunting his grievances against the aches and pains his roll across the saloon floor had inflicted on his joints. Fleet he might have been, but he'd be paying for that brisk maneuver for several days, likely waking up in the dark of night for sips of whiskey to ease his discomfort.

Old age wasn't for sissies. . . .

He set his hat on his head and walked down to where Pecos sat his buckskin, frowning curiously toward him.

"Nothin', huh?"

"Nope."

"Shoulda taken your spyglass."

Slash pointed at his eyes. "You know I got a hawk's peepers."

Pecos gave a snort and tossed the Appy's reins to Slash, who toed a stirrup. "Maybe we're ready for that charity home, after all."

"Hmmm," Pecos said, casting another frustrated scowl along their back trail. "Damn peculiar."

When they were riding again, angling close to the splashing river on their left, Slash turned to Pecos. "Did you see that little, peculiar-lookin' fella in the Lucky Lady?

He was playin' poker with Sanchez and Squires, and he seemed really damn sure—I mean, *bonded* sure—that Arnell Squires was you. He also seemed determined to convince the others he was you."

Pecos shook his head. He'd pulled his makings out of his shirt pocket and was building a smoke as they rode. "Didn't see him. What was peculiar about him?"

Slash winced, unable to put his finger on what had made the little man stick out in his mind—beyond the fact the little man had seemed so determined that Squires was Pecos. "Hell if I know!"

They rode a few more paces and then Slash looked at Pecos again. "Hey," he said.

Pecos ceased rolling his quirley closed to cast a skeptical glance at Slash. "Hey, what?"

Slash checked his Appy down again and scowled over at his partner. "What in the hell are we doing out here, Pecos?"

Pecos finished closing the cigarette, then stopped his own mount, turning it to face Slash and the Appy. "I get your drift," he said, turning his mouth corners down. "We done killed Sanchez and Squires. They're the ones who took over the gang after they pulled that stunt on us back at Doña Flores's place."

"We cut the head off the snake," Slash said. "The Snake River Marauders don't have a leader no more. Who'd take over for Loco and Arnell? Snook Dodge? Billy Pinto? Kansas City Dave?"

"Hah!" Pecos said. "Kansas City Dave can't find his butt with both hands most days of the week. Too much of the . . ." He hooked his thumb to his mouth, pantomiming a pull from a bottle.

"Used to be a good man," Slash said. "But, yeah, the drink got him."

"Cal Thornton?"

"Nah."

"There's the Johnson brothers—Goose and C.J."

"Neither one of them two could command the respect of the rest of the boys."

Pecos took a deep, thoughtful drag off his quirley, then, blowing the smoke into the wind, he turned to Slash. "What're we gonna do—hunt all them fellas down an' kill 'em? It was most likely Sanchez and Squires who abused old Bleed-'Em-So's granddaughter."

"Possibly the Johnson brothers."

"Yeah." Pecos lifted his chin and scratched his neck, pensive. "I reckon Kansas City Dave might've taken a turn. Thornton, too. Prob'ly the half-breed."

"Floyd Three Eagles?"

"Yeah. We've both had to pull him off more than one doxie, or he woulda cut their throats. When he was smokin' that wild tobacco from Mexico, you remember. But neither him nor most of the others would've initiated none of that with Bledsoe's granddaughter. I s'pect they was just followin' Sanchez's and Squires's lead."

Slash stared down at his saddle horn. "No way young Billy woulda had anything to do with any of that."

"Billy Pinto?" Pecos said. "Oh, hell no! Yeah—think about him, Slash. Young Billy. He's part of the gang. What're we gonna do—hunt down young Billy and shoot him, too? Hell, you was like a father to Billy!"

"Older brother."

"Whatever," Pecos said. "That's what Bledsoe wants us to do."

"Yep." Slash reached back to pat the saddlebags in which his half of the three thousand dollars was riding. "Paid us good money to do it. If we don't do it—we'll be wanted men again. He'll run us down and give us another necktie party. A real one this time!"

"Crap," Pecos said. "I don't want to talk about that.

That was a nasty experience. One I don't ever care to have again!"

"Me, neither."

The men thought it over.

Finally, Pecos looked at Slash, narrowing one eye. "What're we gonna tell Bleed-'Em-So?"

"Nothin'. Maybe we oughta just head on down to Mexico. Hole up there till they plant us."

"What're we gonna live on?"

Slash grinned as he leaned back and patted his saddlebags again. "We got us a three-thousand-dollar head start on a new life!" He chuckled.

"That won't get us far. Not the way we go through it. Sooner or later, we'll have to get jobs."

"Crap," Slash said.

"Yeah."

"You were right. That's a nasty word."

"Ain't it, though?" Pecos looked around and sighed. "I reckon we could buy a freighting business down there as easy as up here," he said speculatively. "If we make it that far. If we light out with that three thousand dollars, Bledsoe's likely gonna send a posse for us. U.S. marshals and Pinkertons, most like. He'll wire sheriffs and bounty hunters between here an' the border."

"Yeah," Slash said, spatting into the dust of the narrow trail. "They'll likely cut us off well north of the border."

They paused, thinking again.

"Crap," Pecos said.

"Yeah," agreed Slash. "Maybe we oughta just keep ridin' up toward Ouray or Silverton. I know some parlor houses up there, some purty doxies. We can get us a coupla bottles, a coupla women, maybe play a little poker and think about our futures."

"Yeah, there's nothin' like drinkin' an' whorin' to figure

things out," Pecos agreed, nodding. He reined his horse back up the trail. "All right, let's mosey. Gonna be dark soon. We'd best find a place to camp. Should pull into one o' them towns on up the Animas by—"

He stopped and looked at Slash.

"What was that?"

Slash stared into the forest off the trail's right side. "A girl's scream?"

"Out here?" Pecos scoffed. "Musta been a trick of the river."

But then it came again—the agonized cry of a female in distress.

CHAPTER 27

Slash and Pecos galloped off the trail and into the brush north of the Animas.

The girl's cry had come from the forest about a hundred yards off the trail, from the slope aproning up toward the towering northern crags. The forest was too thick to ride through any faster than a slow, careful walk, so Slash and Pecos checked their mounts down at the edge of the trees and swung down from their saddles.

Slash shucked his Yellowboy from his rifle boot.

Pecos slid his sawed-off twelve again around to his chest, taking the shotgun in both hands.

Slash moved slowly into the forest, holding the Yellowboy up high against his chest, wary of a trap. More than one bounty hunter had tried luring him and his partner into a trail baited with women. This wasn't the cutthroats' first rodeo.

Pecos moved along slowly to Slash's right, both men stepping over deadfall trees and large, fallen branches. The forest was thick and filled with shadows angling down from the northern crags. It may have been only three in the afternoon or so, but in here it was near dusk. The tangy air had a knife edge chill to it.

The men stopped, looked around.

"You see anything?" Pecos whispered.

Slash shook his head.

He continued moving forward but had taken only one step when he heard a girl's voice say, "Oh, damn!" A slight pause, then: "Damn, damn, dammit all, anyway!"

The cursing was followed by a guttural groan of deep frustration.

Slash and Pecos looked at each other.

The girl seemed to be just ahead, on the other side of a low knoll. Slash motioned with his hand and then he and Pecos split up, Slash moving around the knoll's left side, Pecos moving around its right side. As the knoll slipped away, giving Slash a view of what lay on the other side of it, he stopped.

He drew a breath and held it. The girl sat on a log about twenty feet before him now, near a saddled calico mare that stood grazing just beyond her.

She appeared a pretty little thing, maybe eighteen or nineteen, with a thick head of curly auburn hair to which pine needles and bits of dead leaves clung. She sat on a log, facing away toward Slash's left. Pecos would be flanking her on her own left. She was leaning forward, grunting her discontentment as she unlaced the ankle-high work boot on her left foot.

She wore baggy dungarees with rope suspenders, and a baggy gray plaid shirt that was ripped partway down the middle. Slash could easily see that she wasn't wearing anything at all beneath the shirt. Even without really wanting to, he could see deep into it—what with her bent so far forward like that.

Chagrin warmed Slash's cheeks. The girl was obviously in distress, and here this old cutthroat stood, ogling her.

He turned to his right. Pecos had stepped out around the far side of the knoll, flanking the girl. He gave Slash a slantwise look of admonishment, as though he realized where Slash's gaze had been feasting itself. Cheeks turning even warmer, Slash stepped forward, setting his rifle on his shoulder and saying, "Hello, there, little girl. Looks like you're in need of a little—"

"Oh, crap!" the girl cried, grabbing a pistol that had been resting atop the log beside her. She jerked to her feet with a terrified start and raised the old-model hogleg.

"Hold on! Hold on!" Slash and Pecos cried in unison.

She triggered a shot toward Slash, who threw himself straight back and to his right as the bullet plunked into the spongy forest duff behind him. As he hit the ground on his chest and belly, the girl screamed.

Slash whipped around to see that she'd fallen back over the log and lay writhing and cursing. She'd dropped the pistol. It lay in front of the log, several feet away from her now. A relatively safe distance, Slash opined. He just hoped she didn't have another one.

Slash heaved himself to his feet, cursing at the pain the tumble had aggravated in his back and neck after his circus-act in the saloon only a few hours earlier. Retrieving his rifle from the ground, he glanced at Pecos, who looked at him wide-eyed and shrugged. The big man was unsure how to proceed.

Slash hurried forward, holding his rifle out in one hand, barrel up, and holding his left hand wide to his other side. "It's all right, miss. We're not gonna hurt you. We just heard you scream is all, and came to investigate."

He crouched to scoop the girl's pistol, an old rusted Remington conversion, out of the dead leaves and dirt. Straightening, he looked down at her.

She was in a half-sitting position on her rump, writhing in pain. She'd gotten the boot and sock off her left foot, and she held it up now, her face swollen and red with fear and misery, her light-brown eyes switching from Slash to

Pecos and back again, saying, "Leave me alone, you rapscallions! Oh, please leave me alone! I don't have anything of value except my hoss, an' she's lame! That there pistol's my dead pappy's, and it misfires more times than it shoots, but it's the only protection I got from wolves like you—preying on injured girls!"

She glared at each man, regaling them with, "Don't you have anything better to do than stalk the forest for innocent young ladies!"

Pecos looked exasperated. "We wasn't stalkin' the forest for no innocent young ladies!"

The girl flopped back against the ground, writhing, her torn shirt showing way too much of her for the cutthroats' comfort. "Oh, just go ahead and rape me and kill me and get it over with. Go ahead. My life has gone to hell, anyways, since Daddy died!"

She flung her arm over her eyes and bawled.

Slash set the girl's old hogleg on the log and dropped to a knee beside her. He wiped his hands on the thighs of his corduroy trousers, glanced tentatively up at Pecos hovering over the girl now, as well, and poked her arm very softly.

"Miss . . . ?"

"Oh, just rape me and get it over with!" she sobbed.

Again, Slash poked her very gently. "Miss . . . ?"

She jerked her arm away from her eyes and glared up at him. "Oh, what is it, fer chrissakes!"

"We ain't gonna rape you," Slash said.

"We ain't gonna kill you," Pecos added.

She blinked up at Slash. Then she blinked up at Pecos. "You ain't?"

"Nah," Slash said. "We done grown weary of stalkin' the forest for purty girls to rape and murder. That's work for younger men."

She stared up at him uncertainly through a sheen of wa-

CUTTHROATS 241

vering tears. She sat up and rested against the heels of her hands, shuttling her gaze between the two men before her. "Is this some kind of trick to get me to let my guard down?"

"No, it ain't no trick," Pecos said.

She frowned skeptically. "You two look like cutthroats to me!"

Slash and Pecos shared a guilty glance.

"Th-that we were, little lady," Pecos said, slowly easing his own bulk down to a knee on the other side of the girl from Slash. "But we cashed in our chips. We're gonna be good now."

"No more stalkin' the forest for purty girls, though if we was, I doubt we could've found a purtier one than the one we found here." Slash smiled affably down at the frightened child, then glanced at Pecos. "Ain't that right, Pec . . . I mean, *Melvin*?"

"That sure is right, uh . . . James. You're purtier'n pump-kin pie, miss, but we swear we're only here to help you. We heard you scream an' all, and couldn't very well just ride off and leave you alone way out here. It's a good half a day's ride to Silverton."

Slash said, "What's your name, honey?"

She was still frowning warily at both men, as though they were coyotes milling around her chicken coop and she didn't have a rifle handy. She sniffed and swiped a hand across her cheeks, brushing away the tears.

"Myra Thompson," she said softly, and sniffed again.

"Right purty name," Pecos opined.

"You from around here, Myra?"

The girl nodded. "Leastways, I was. Pa died a few days back. I was making my way to Silverton to look for work. Pa was a prospector. His mule kicked him in the head last week. Killed him. Not outright. I doctored him for a week. I went into his room one morning, and he was dead. Just starin' at me. He didn't leave much but he did leave me a fair-sized poke."

Realizing she'd said too much, she gasped and clapped a hand over her mouth. "Oh, crap!"

"We ain't after your poke, Myra," Slash said gently.

"You ain't?"

"Nope," Pecos said, shaking his head certainly.

"You ain't after my poke and you ain't after my body," Myra said, beetling her thin, light-brown brows over those pretty tan eyes. "What kind of men are you, then?"

She'd meant it as a serious question.

"Good, honorable, upstandin' citizens," Slash said.

"Even way out here?" Myra just didn't seem able to wrap her mind around such a thing.

"Even way out here," Pecos said. "Now, what happened? What'd you do to your foot, Miss Myra?"

"Well, first the mare threw a shoe about a mile back. I just couldn't bring myself to back trail myself to that lonely old cabin, so I thought I'd lead her until I found someone who could nail the shoe back on. There's a fella who travels through here often, shoeing horses for the prospectors. But now I think Elvira—I named her after my dear old grams—has gone lame, to boot. I was leading her through these trees, looking for the main trail, when I tripped over that cotton-pickin' log. I think I broke my ankle!"

The girl scrunched up her face, gritting her teeth, and punched the ground. "Oh, misery—thy name is Myra Thompson!"

"Oh, now, I don't think it's all that bad," Pecos said.

Slash gestured at her ankle. "Can I take a look?"

Myra shrugged and rolled her head. "I guess if you're not gonna rape and kill me, you might as well stay an' help."

"I'll take a look at the mare," Pecos said. "I'm right handy with a shoein' hammer."

While the big man walked over to where the mare now stood eyeing both strangers warily, Slash removed his gloves and took the girl's foot in his hand. It was an uncommonly pretty, delicate appendage, with cute little feminine toes, each one resembling a tiny baby's nose. He tried not to entertain any unclean thoughts about this girl, who was young enough to be his—well, young enough to be his oldest daughter if he'd fathered the child when he was still a boy himself.

"What're you chuckling about?" Myra said, frowning suspiciously at him, as he gently probed her bare foot with his fingers.

Slash's cheeks warmed slightly. "Was I chuckling? I didn't realize. Just the uncommonly odd turnings of my mind, girl. Nothing to worry about. We older fellas get a little soft in our thinker boxes. I think it's due to an overabundance of memories. Every damn thing we see reminds us of something else we saw. And by my age, we've seen a few things!"

"Really?" the girl said, staring up at him while he continued to probe her foot, turning it gently this way and that while carefully prodding the ankle, feeling around for swelling. "What does my foot remind you of?"

"Youth," Slash said, smiling at her fondly.

"I suppose you had your pick of the girls at one time. You're kinda handsome for an old fella. I bet you were uncommonly wicked to heat up a girl's bloomers back when you were my age." For the first time since he'd met her, Myra Thompson smiled.

Slash hiked a shoulder and looked away, embarrassed. "Hell."

"Hell," Myra said, playfully mocking him.

"Hell," Slash said, chuckling.

"You're shy, ain't ya, James?"

"Me? Hell, no!"

Slash released Myra's foot, though it had felt pleasingly warm and supple in his hands. He hadn't touched a foot of a girl Myra's age in many a year, and he hadn't realized it till now how much he'd missed it. Nor how much he'd missed being young enough again for such occurrences to be somewhat commonplace.

Maybe as the years pass, it's best if we forget what we long for, he vaguely, silently opined.

"Hell," Slash said. "That ankle's just fine, Miss Myra. You might've twisted it some, made it ache. But it sure ain't broke and I don't think it's even sprained. I couldn't feel any swelling, and believe me if it was broke or sprained, it be swelling like a balloon by now."

"Really?" the girl said hopefully, looking at her foot, which she waggled around, flexing her cute little toes. "You know, I think you're right. It doesn't hurt half as much as it did before you two came."

"I think you were mainly just scared," Slash said.

"Yeah," Myra said. "I think you're right. Hey—what did you say your names were?"

CHAPTER 28

Slash rose, doffed his hat, and held it over his chest. "Miss Myra Thompson, I am James Braddock. Please call me Jimmy."

He glanced over to where Pecos was down on one knee, examining the calico mare's left rear hoof. "That big drink o' water over there is ... is, uh ... Melvin Baker." He knew Pecos's given name well enough. It was just that he hadn't called him or even thought of him as anything but the Pecos River Kid for so long that "Melvin Baker" felt funny coming off his tongue.

Pecos looked over toward Slash and Myra and pinched his hat brim to the girl. Flashing a smile, he said, "Call me Melvin."

Myra canted her head to one side and narrowed an eye at Slash. "Melvin Baker, eh? Have you always called him Melvin Baker, Jimmy?"

Again, Slash colored up like a summer sunset. He gave a nervous laugh. "Of course I have! Of course I have! What else would I call him—besides 'Big 'n' Stupid,' of course?"

Pecos scowled at him.

Slash laughed again and called, "How's Myra's mare look, *Melvin*?"

"The frog might be a little tender, but not too bad . . . *Jimmy*. I'll smear a little salve on it, then tap the shoe back on the hoof. She'll be good to go in no time. I got some nails in my saddlebags." Pecos dropped the mare's hoof and started walking back in the direction from which he and Slash had come. "I'll fetch the hosses."

Sitting on the log she'd tripped over, Myra started pulling her sock back on her foot. She shifted her concerned gaze from Pecos back to Slash and said, "You two gonna pull out, then? As soon as Mr. Baker . . . I mean, *Melvin* . . . has set the shoe?"

She glanced around as though looking for some nightmare creature that might be lurking in the forest around them.

Slash studied the obviously frightened, lonely gal for a time and then glanced at the sky. He turned to where Pecos was walking back through the trees toward the horses, and called, "Hey, uh, Melvin?"

Pecos stopped and looked back.

"It's gettin' purty late in the day. We'll no sooner get started back up the trail before it'll be time to camp. Why don't we sink a picket pin right here for the night? I see a nice little clearing over there by that stream yonder."

Pecos stared back toward Slash and the girl. He gave a knowing nod and a shrug, and said, "I don't see why not. Like you said, it's getting late, and this canyon'll be good dark in an hour, I s'pect."

He turned and continued striding back toward the horses.

Slash turned to Myra and said, "I do apologize, Myra, but it looks like you got a couple of old devils as camp mates for the night."

"Oh, that's all right," Myra said, smiling cheerfully up at Slash as she pulled on her boot. "I got some jerked rabbit meat in my saddlebags—enough for all three of us. And I ain't a half-bad cook, neither!"

* * *

"Well, if you fellas will excuse me," Myra said an hour later, as she set the lid on the tin pot in which she'd just prepared a hearty stew. "While that simmers nice and slow, I'm gonna hobble over yonder and have a swim."

"A swim?" Slash said in exasperation, holding his cup of fresh, piping hot coffee against his chest. "Why, it's gettin' right cold out here, girl. The sun's been down behind yonder peak for nigh on a half hour!"

"Gettin' colder by the minute," Pecos added from where he sat across the cook fire from Slash, propping his own coffee on an upraised knee.

"Don't you worry about me," Myra said, reaching into a war sack for a towel and a cake of soap wrapped in burlap. "I was raised in these mountains. Compared to the long winters up here, this cold ain't nothin'. Hell, up where Pa and I lived since only a few weeks after I was born, we often saw snow on the Fourth of July! I find swimming in a good, cold stream right healthy and invigorating. Makes me sleep real peaceful like.

"This stream here is the one that runs past our cabin. I followed it down here to this valley. It's a tributary of the Animas. Pa once told me a Spanish explorer gave the Animas its full name—Rio de las Animas, which means 'River of Souls.' Pretty, ain't it?"

"Couldn't be purtier," Pecos said, smiling at the girl.

Myra glanced at her war bag, which sat on the ground with her saddlebags. "I bet I know what you two might find even purtier."

"What's that, darlin'?" Slash asked her.

Myra reached into the canvas sack and withdrew a package wrapped in wool and burlap. "I don't imbibe myself, but I grabbed this bottle off a shelf before I left the cabin. Not sure why. It's Pa's own brew. Last bottle. He tended a still out back of our cabin. Men from all around these mountains used to come and buy jugs from him, real often. They said they couldn't get whiskey as good as Pa's even down South in Tennessee and Kentucky, where some of them hailed from, as did Pa."

Myra handed the corked, brown bottle to Slash. "Here you go. Drink up. Take the chill off."

She winked coquettishly, tossed the towel over her shoulder, then tramped off toward the stream gurgling and splashing about forty yards northwest of the camp.

When she'd taken half a dozen steps, Myra stopped and flashed another coquettish smile over her shoulder. "No peekin' now, boys. I swim in my birthday suit, don't ya know."

She chuckled, then drifted off through the trees toward the stream.

Slash looked at Pecos, who stared after the girl, frowning. "Whew!" he said.

"Uh-huh," Slash said. "Hey, stop lookin'. You're old enough to be her—"

"Slightly more mature brother," Pecos said, grinning.

Slash laughed as he uncorked the bottle and laced his coffee liberally with Myra's old man's whiskey. He corked the bottle, then handed it over to Pecos, who laced his own mud with the brew. Both men sank back against their saddles, relaxing after a long day of shooting and riding.

Pecos sipped his coffee, then cast a puzzled look over to Slash. "Did you notice she wasn't even limping on that injured foot?"

"Yeah, I did notice," Slash said. "Like I said, I think she was frightened more than anything. Fearful of being alone out here." He sipped his own spiced mud, swallowed, then turned to Pecos. "How's her hoss?"

"Just fine. The frog might've been a little swollen, but I think the main problem was the missing shoe."

"Yeah. She was just frightened," Slash said. "Scared and alone and making mountains out of molehills."

"For sure." Pecos took another sip of his coffee.

A splash sounded from the direction of the stream. It was followed by a raucous whoop, then delighted laughter.

"Oh, Lordy, that feels good!" Myra cried, splashing around in the stream.

Slash glanced toward the stream. The forest was all hazy shadows, but there was still enough light in the sky that he could see the silvery water and the silhouette of the girl kicking about between the low banks.

"Damn," Slash said.

"Yeah," Pecos said. "Damn is right. The years ain't been kind to us, Slash."

"The years are kind to no one, mi amigo."

"Not all that long ago, you an' me would've been over there, swimmin' and frolickin' with a girl who looked like that."

"Yeah, and likely comin' to blows over her."

Pecos chuckled. "Yeah, that, too."

"Besides," Slash said, "it was a long time ago, you old geezer. It just don't seem like it. But if you look back, it was a long time ago, all right."

"A man still has thoughts, though. Urges."

The girl gave another low whoop as she splashed in the stream. She shivered audibly but delightedly, chuckling to herself, cooing luxuriously as the cold stream wrapped itself around her supple, young flesh.

"Hey, you told me not to look," Pecos scolded Slash. "That means you can't look, neither, you old goat!"

Slash hadn't realized he'd been staring through the trees toward the stream again. He looked away now, and took another sip and then several more sips of his whiskey-laced mud.

"I wasn't lookin'," he said, squirming around uncomfortably.

"Yes, you were."

"Well, I didn't see anything."

"Yeah, but you were tryin'!"

"Oh, shut up." Slash set his coffee down. "Hand me that damn bottle!"

"Ohhhh," Myra cooed, splashing. "Feels . . . sooo . . . goooooodddddd!"

Slash and Pecos both turned to stare toward the stream through the trees. Myra was standing up in the knee-deep water, standing sideways toward the camp, her female body silhouetted against the soft salmon light bleeding out of the sky beyond.

"Crap," Pecos said dreamily.

"Holy moly."

Pecos tossed the coffee from his cup, uncorked the bottle, and filled the cup three-quarters full of straight whiskey. Corking the bottle again, he handed it back to Slash. "There you go. Hellfire!"

Slash tossed out his own coffee and replaced it with straight whiskey.

He leaned far back against his saddle, took several deep sips of the whiskey, and sighed. "There," he said, crossing his ankles. "That's better."

"You fellas oughta join me," Myra called. "It feels soooo good!"

"So we hear," Slash grumbled in frustration, taking another deep pull from his cup.

"No thanks, honey," Pecos called. "We'll just sit here and let this fire seep into our old bones."

"Thanks for the invite, though," Slash said, pouring more whiskey into his cup.

"Scaredy cats!" the girl returned, chuckling.

As she continued splashing around in the stream, groaning and grunting and making several other provocative sounds, Pecos looked over his cup of whiskey at his partner and said, "I think she's intentionally torturing us, Slash!"

"What was your first clue?" Slash chuckled. "It's women's way of getting back at men in general for all our scoundrel-like ways."

Pecos chuckled and wagged his head. "Women." He reached forward. "Stop hoggin' the bottle."

"Hold on." Slash refilled his own cup before he handed the bottle back to his partner. Leaning back against his saddle, he suddenly grew light-headed. He looked at the fire. There appeared to be several fires now, one overlying the other. He felt a little queasy.

"Damn," he said, shaking his head to try to clear his vision. "That lightnin' has some kick to it!"

"I just noticed that myself."

Slash looked across the fire at Pecos, who sat six feet away, arms draped over his raised knees. His head was hanging, as though it had suddenly doubled or tripled in weight. His eyes looked bleary, out of focus, the pupils enormous. Or so Slash thought. He couldn't be sure, though, because his own vision was swimming even more than it had been before.

He looked around.

The camp with the piled gear and the three horses tied to a picket rope to his right spun around him. It was as though he were on a merry-go-round. He dropped the cup. It clinked to the ground. He dropped a hand to the ground beside him, trying to steady himself, to slow the merry-go-round.

It didn't work.

"Hold on," Slash said, heart quickening, fear racing through him. "Some . . . somethin' ain't . . . right here . . . partner."

"I'll say it ain't!" Pecos shook his head. He dropped his

own cup and sagged back against his saddle, knocking his hat off his head. "I think . . . I think I'm . . . gonna . . . take . . . a little . . . nap. . . ."

Slash leaned forward, both hands on the ground. He tried to get his feet beneath him. He'd suddenly felt the overwhelming urge to stand. "I don't think . . . that's a good idea . . . partner!"

His blurred vision darkened. Liquid lead seemed to fill his veins, his bones, his entire body, making him extremely heavy.

Sleepy.

"Ah, hell!" He flopped back against his saddle.

He heard himself rake out a deep snore and then that was all he was aware of before he sensed a presence in front of him, heard the menacing click of a gun being cocked.

Slash opened his eyes.

Myra stood before him. She was wrapped in a blanket. Her legs and feet were bare. Her wet hair dripped. Flash felt the coldness of some of those drops soak through his pants leg.

Myra raised her old hogleg. She extended it toward Slash, who tried to raise his arms, to reach for her, but it was as though his arms were pinned to the ground by an enormous weight.

"Damn you!" the girl cried, scrunching up her face, gritting her teeth. "You would've made this a whole lot easier if you'd tried to savage me!" she sobbed. Her hand quivered. She narrowed one eye as she aimed down the revolver's barrel at Slash. "I'm sorry!"

Her head jerked sharply.

The gun roared and flashed. Myra swayed, then sagged to one side, knees buckling, falling. . . .

Another person now stood just behind where Myra had been standing. A small, slender man, extremely clean-shaven except for a large mustache—the mustache too large for the strange, effeminate delicateness of the man's face. He lowered the pistol whose butt he'd just rapped against Myra's head.

Staring at Slash, the strange little man drew his mouth corners down and gave his head a disapproving shake.

"Who . . . ? Who . . . ?" Slash tried.

But then the warm darkness of sleep washed over him.

When he opened his eyes again, the copper-haired beauty, Jaycee Breckenridge, was spooning pancake batter into a cast-iron skillet over the fire.

CHAPTER 29

"Wait," Slash said, trying to sit up, staring at Jay but knowing he was only dreaming. "Why, uh . . . why do I . . . ?"

Jay glanced over the fire at him. "Why do you think you see the lovely and sophisticated Jaycee Breckenridge making breakfast this bright and sunny mountain morning?" she asked. "Because you do. She is." She arched a brow and, the batter sputtering in the skillet perched on an iron spider, raised a steaming coffee cup to her lips.

Slash still wasn't convinced he wasn't dreaming. He had to be. Jay had betrayed him and Pecos, taken Bleed-'Em-So's gifts and money, and started a new life for herself in San Francisco.

The Jay in his dream set down her coffee cup. She plucked something out of a saddlebag to her right and lifted it to her lips. It was a thick, black mustache. Holding the mustache above her mouth with one hand, she drew her thick, long, copper hair back behind her neck with her other hand, out of sight.

"Holy . . ." The face Slash was staring at was the face of the mustachioed little man he'd spied first in the Lucky

Lady in Morrisville. The *feminine-looking* little man who'd insisted that Arnell Squires was really the Pecos River Kid.

Jay lowered the fake mustache and drew the thick tresses of her hair forward over her shoulder.

Slash slid his gaze to the right of Jay. Pecos lay on his side beneath a wool blanket, curled slightly, snoring loudly. In the periphery of his still somewhat blurred vision, Slash saw another figure. He shuttled his gaze to his right and drew a sharp, angry breath. Myra Thompson was sitting on the ground, her back against an aspen. Her hands were drawn behind her back. A rope had been coiled three times around her belly and chest, tying her to the tree.

She returned Slash's gaze with a guilty one of her own, then stared down at the ground between her legs. She was dressed in the wool shirt and denims she'd worn the previous evening, before she'd gone swimming.

"You little polecat," Pecos said, having to clear his throat first. Still, he sounded froggy. "You . . ." Gradually, he remembered, but it was like staring back a long ways through time, though it had likely occurred only the night before. In his mind, he saw Myra standing soaking wet before him, clad in only a towel, aiming the old hogleg at him. "You was gonna . . ."

"Blow your head off." Jay had gained her feet. She walked around the fire, holding a fresh cup of hot coffee in her hand. She stopped before Slash, held the coffee down to him.

He gazed at her skeptically, accepting the cup of hot mud.

Jay crossed her arms on her chest, cocked one foot forward. "How's your head?"

"It hurts like hell." In fact, he couldn't remember ever having such a throbbing ache in his head as the one he was currently experiencing. He felt as though a powerful little man were inside his skull, smashing the tender, exposed nerve of his brain with a big hammer.

Over and over and over again . . .

"No," he said. "Hurts worse than hell." He remembered the whiskey, looked around for the bottle, and saw it lying on its side near where Pecos lay beneath the blanket, loudly snoring.

He returned his deeply puzzled gaze to Jay. "What the hell happened?"

Jay canted her head toward Myra. "She drugged both you idiots. She laced the whiskey with raw opium."

Angry and befuddled, Slash scowled at Myra, who continued to stare at the ground between her legs. "Why?"

"She wanted to kill you."

"Why?"

Jay glanced at Myra again. "Would you like to tell him?"

"*Jay?*" Pecos had woken suddenly, with a start, and turned his head to stare up in shock at the copper-haired beauty standing by Slash. "What in God's—*ahhhh!*" he cried, gritting his teeth and clamping a hand to the crown of his skull.

"Yeah, it was quite a party," Slash told him.

Pecos glared up at Jay. "You double-crossed us! Sold us out to Bledsoe!"

"Shut up," Slash said. "We'll get to that."

"Don't tell me to shut up," Pecos said, indignant. "I want to get to it right now."

"Shut up!"

Pecos just groaned against the pain in his head, leaning back on his saddle.

Slash turned to Myra. "Why'd you want to kill us, you little puma? Was you gonna rob us? If so, boy, I sure had you read wrong."

Myra sucked in her cheeks a little but kept her eyes on the ground, not saying anything.

"Rob us?" Pecos said, turning to Myra. "Hey, why is Myra tied up?"

"I told you to shut up," Slash said, wincing against the blows of the little man and his hammer.

"Stop tellin' me to shut up, Slash!"

"Shut up! She was about to kill us both last night. She *would* have killed us both if . . . well, if Jay hadn't stepped in and brained her."

"*Brained* her?"

"You were asleep," Slash said. "Passed out. That wasn't just whiskey in the bottle. It was opium, Jay thinks."

"Oh, I know," Jay said. "I found the little blue bottle of the deadly stuff in her saddlebags."

Slash glared at the shame-faced Myra. "I'd still like to know why she drugged us and was gonna kill us." He glanced at Jay. "Then we'll get to you."

Jay drew a deep breath. Her own cheeks were touched with the soft blush of shame. Glancing at Myra again, she said, "The girl was working for the Snake River Marauders."

"What?" Pecos and Slash said at the same time.

"That ain't possible," Pecos said.

"Why?" Jay asked him. "Because she's young and pretty?"

Pecos flushed and glanced at Slash.

Slash said, "It can't be. We killed Loco and Arnell in Saguache. You know. You were there."

"Who was there?" Pecos said, gritting his teeth again and groaning at the battering his own head was taking.

"I was," Jay said.

"She was the funny-lookin' little man with the big hat and the big black mustache," Pecos said.

Pecos glowered up at Jay. "You was?"

"Yes. I bought the hat and the mustache from a traveling theatrical troupe out of Denver."

"Why?"

"I was shadowing you two. I didn't want to be recognized until I was ready. I also didn't want to be pestered by other men. Thus the costume."

"Wait, wait, wait," Slash said. "This would be way too complicated for me even if my head didn't feel like it had been run over by a runaway train. Let's take it one step at a time. First, how do you know Myra was gonna kill us for the Marauders even though the gang's two leaders are as dead as last year's Christmas goose?"

"I saw her in Silverton with the gang."

"What were you doing in Silverton?" Pecos asked her.

Jay had returned to the fire and poured another cup of coffee. She gave the cup to Pecos, saying, "Drink that. It'll make you feel better."

Pecos looked skeptically down at it. "You sure it ain't spiked?" He grimaced and glanced at Slash. "Does your head hurt as bad as mine?"

"If your head hurts like holy hell, then twice as bad."

Jay sat down on a rock by the fire and flipped the pancake. "I've been tracking the gang since you two scalawags got run down by Bledsoe."

"With your help!" Pecos lashed out at her, then sucked another pained breath through gritted teeth.

"I'll get to that," Jay said, removing the pancake and adding it to the five she'd already cooked, on a plate over which she draped a cloth to keep them warm. "I learned of the gang's whereabouts from friends of mine peppered throughout the mountains. Old friends. They're in the *old* business—saloon business and parlor houses."

"Oh, those businesses," Pecos said knowingly.

"Yes, *those* businesses. They're loyal women. Some were once like mothers and sisters to me. I've kept in touch with a few of them over the years. A woman never knows when she's going to need the help of other women."

Jay prodded the fire with a stick. "I sent telegrams out, and one of my friends wired me back, telling me the gang was in Saguache. By the time I got to Saguache, most of the gang, except for Loco Sanchez and Arnell Squires, had left for Silverton. I headed for Silverton, then, as well, knowing that Sanchez and Squires were deeply involved in their poker game and also knowing, from my friend, that the gang was planning a job soon. A big one.

"My friend has a friend who entertained one of the gang, and he'd bragged to her about their plan to kill Sanchez and Squires, thus ridding themselves of all the old men who they equated to 'dead wood' merely holding the gang back from the greatness they thought was their destiny."

"Who said that?" Slash and Pecos said at the same time, angrily.

"Billy Pinto."

"Billy?" Slash and Pecos both intoned at the same time.

Slash shook his head. "No way. Billy wouldn't say nothin' like that. He was a good kid. Quiet and respectful of his elders."

"Or so he let on," Jay said.

Sitting tied to the aspen, Myra snorted a caustic laugh. "Or so he let on!"

"How would you know?" Pecos asked her.

"When I first met him, he was nice. Then, suddenly he wasn't so nice. But he got me out of a—well, we'll just call it a bad situation in Silverton. He shot a man for me. A man who thought he owned me. Billy took me under his wing, so to speak. He said he'd let me run with him and his gang, and protect me. Give me a cut of what they robbed."

Slash and Pecos shared another dubious glance. They couldn't wrap their minds around the kid they knew as the quiet, respectful, even bashful Billy Pinto shooting anyone. He'd always acted as though a pistol were pure poison in his hands. A stick of dynamite with its fuse lit.

Could both aging cutthroats have been so wrong?

Myra must have been reading their minds. "He was going to shoot you, too."

Slash and Pecos cut her a shocked look.

Myra nodded. "Since he first joined the gang, he told me he'd been maneuvering to take it over. He was just learning from you older owlhoots how to do things, then he was going to shoot you and anyone else who stood in his way, and take the reins. He said the others—mostly younger men—were in on it with him. Pretty much all of them, anyways. They were ready to cut you out.

"Billy didn't like it when Sanchez and Squires left you, drunk and sound asleep, in that saloon, an' rode off without you. They were content with shaming the old dogs, as Billy called you, but he knew you'd be trouble. He figured he was proven right when one of the spies he left behind in Saguache cabled him in Silverton, informing him that you two had killed Sanchez and Squires. He made me ride back this way to set a trap for you and kill you. He said by doing so I'd earn a place in the gang."

"I followed her," Jay said. "Lost her for a time. I got waylaid, you might say, by a gentleman who followed you out of Saguache. A friend of yours."

"That would be the man—Goose Johnson—that Billy left behind to keep an eye out for you . . . and to ambush Sanchez and Squires before they could get to Silverton. He didn't want them taking part in the next job he had planned."

Slash glanced at Pecos. "I reckon that explains them chiggers down my pants."

Pecos nodded. "An' that buzzin' in my ears."

"I ran into Johnson when I was looking for you three,"

Jay said. "I glassed him from a distance with my spyglass and recognized him. I'd met him one time in Denver, with the rest of you Marauders. When he'd stopped to fill his canteen, I fired a shot to frighten his horse off. Couldn't bring myself to kill him in cold blood. Which means he's likely out there . . . somewhere."

"Maybe he rode on to Silverton," Myra opined.

Jay sipped her coffee. To Slash and Pecos, she said, "When I finally saw your fire late last night, I was *almost* too late to keep you from acquiring third eyes." She slid her dark gaze to Myra, who looked down again in shame.

Slash studied the girl, who appeared nearly as miserable as he felt. "Was there anything true about anything you told us about yourself?"

She nodded dully and said to the ground, "It was all true. Except . . . Pa died a year ago. I left the cabin last year. Went to town. Not much a girl can do in a town, except . . ." She gave a little sob and continued staring at the ground, then looked up at Slash, tears glazing her eyes. "It wasn't an easy year for me in that mining camp!"

"So you took up assassination for a livin'," Pecos growled.

"So you got us drunk to make us pass out, eh?" Slash asked. "So you could shoot us while we slept."

"It would've been a whole lot easier if you'd come after me while I was swimming. You could have done that at least!"

"So the swimming was to bait us into your trap," Pecos said, and glanced angrily over at Slash.

Jay chuckled as she took another sip of her coffee.

"What's funny?" Pecos asked her.

"You two were low-hanging fruit for that conniving child." Jay laughed again without mirth. "Billy Pinto sure did know who best to send for the job. You two old cutthroats would never suspect a pretty girl. She set the most obvious trap in the world!"

262 *William W. Johnstone and J.A. Johnstone*

Slash ground his molars, the heat of embarrassment rising in his cheeks. He glanced at Pecos, who was also flushing, scowling over at Myra.

"I'm sorry," the girl said, sobbing, chin down against her chest.

"Where'd you get the raw opium?" Slash asked her.

"Chinaman in town." She looked over at Slash, tears running down her cheeks. "It really was my pa's whiskey! I'd saved a bottle from home!"

"Oh, well," Pecos said ironically. "It's nice to know you didn't lie about everything!" He laughed, then groaned through gritted teeth as the little man in his head bashed his brain extra hard with his not-so-little hammer.

"It's our own damn fault," Slash said to his partner guiltily. "There wasn't anything swollen about her ankle."

"Yeah," Pecos said. "And the mare's hoof was fine." He glanced at Myra. "She must've removed the shoe herself."

They looked over at the girl sobbing with her head down.

"Eat the pancakes before they get cold, boys," Jay said, rising from her rock. "I'm gonna take a little stroll."

"Hey, wait a minute!" Pecos called after her.

Jay glanced over her shoulder. "All in good time."

She walked off through trees, heading in the direction of the stream.

Slash tossed away the blanket that Jay must have covered him with. "I'll talk to her."

He'd tried getting up too fast. He sank back down to his butt, pressing the heel of his hand against his throbbing temple. "Damn, girl," he hissed. "You sure got us good."

Myra looked up at him. "I know there's no reason for you to believe me, but I wasn't going to go through with it. I was about to lower Pa's old Remington, but then Miss Breckenridge laid me out with her pistol butt."

"No," Slash said, rising more slowly, tenderly, to his feet. He turned to look at the girl. "I don't believe you."

She nodded weakly, understandingly.

"Ah, don't be so hard on the child, Slash," Pecos said. "You were right. It's our own damn fault we walked into that trap without sniffin' the bait. All the signs were there."

Slash glared at him. "Well, don't walk into it again, you damn fool!"

"Stop callin' me names!"

"Oh, shut up!"

Slash set his hat very gently on his tender head and followed Jay toward the stream.

CHAPTER 30

Slash found Jay strolling pensively along the water, arms folded across her chest.

He moved up behind her. Hearing his footsteps, she turned toward him, one brow arched over a pretty hazel eye. The morning sun danced in her copper hair spilling down over her shoulders. Clad in a gray plaid shirt tucked into her form-fitting denim trousers, the cuffs of which were tucked into the tops of her high-heeled black boots, she had one of Pistol Pete's old Colt Navy pistols stuffed into a back pocket.

"Are you going after them?" she asked.

"That can wait."

"Can it?" Apparently noticing the anger burning in his eyes, Jay turned to face the stream, and said, "Don't be angry with me, Slash."

He closed his hand around her arm, turned her toward him. "Don't be angry? You sold us out, Jay!"

She drew her head back in shock. "Sold you out? I saved your life, you idiot!"

"Yeah, okay, you got me there. Thanks for keeping that girl from drilling our fool hides last night. Much appreciated. Still, I'd like to know—"

"Wait," Jay said, interrupting him, frowning at him curiously. "I wasn't talking about last night. At least, not *only* last night. I was talking about *selling you out*, as you so inappropriately called it, to Chief Marshal Bledsoe. I did that because he promised to spare you, you utter fool!"

"Oh, come on," Slash said. "What about the things he gave you? The jewelry! The new wardrobe! Enough money to start a new life in San Francisco?"

Jay stared at him as though in total befuddlement, her eyes large and round, lower jaw hanging. Suddenly, anger sparked in her eyes. She slapped him hard across his right cheek. He felt the full burn of her anger as the blow aggravated the pounding in his head.

He bunched his lips defiantly against it. The slap enflamed his own anger and he had to restrain himself from slapping her back.

Jay said, "Thank you for proving just how right I was to call you a fool! You an' Pecos both. Fools!" She gave a frustrated groan and turned away, again crossing her arms on her chest.

Gritting his teeth, Slash said, "Are you denying he gave you those things in return for betraying us? Hell, Jay, for all you knew, me an' Pecos might've really hanged!" He paused, thoughtful. For a few seconds he stared off over the water, then turned back to her and said, "Hey, wait a minute—how did you know where to find us, anyways? Why were you so sure me an' Pecos were going after the Marauders?"

"He told me!" Jay said, curling her upper lip back from her gritted teeth. "He told me all about the whole hanging ruse. He told me he was going to spare your lives in return for you two going to work for him."

She balled her fists at her sides and leaned forward at the waist, her face brick red with rage. "That's why I *sold you out*! It had nothing to do with any *gifts*, because—lis-

ten, you idiot, and listen hard!—Bledsoe didn't give me one goddamn thing except your lives in exchange for me telling him about that narrow-gauge train you were going to rob! I bought that dress and those fake pearls with the money Pete left me. If that crazy old marshal had given me enough money to start a new life for myself in San Francisco—believe me, I'd be drinking fancy drinks on the Barbary Coast right now!"

Not only the woman's fury, but the information she'd just imparted, almost literally rocked Slash back on his heels.

Haltingly, incredulously, he said, "Bledsoe . . . he said that . . . he said he gave you—"

"He lied, Slash," Jay said, enunciating her words clearly, as though talking to a simpleton. "Obviously, he lied!"

"Why would he . . . why would he do that?"

"I don't know. Maybe just for the fun of it. You saw how eccentric he is. Maybe he . . ." Jay shrugged, looked off again, her cheeks coloring again slightly, this time with embarrassment. "Maybe he wanted you to forget about me. Just focus on the task he gave you—of running down . . . and killing . . . the Marauders."

Slash thought it through, the heat of his anger changing to a burning shame.

"Jesus," he said.

"Yeah."

Slash looked at her. "What are you doing out here? Why didn't you take the stake Pete left you and . . ."

"Go to Mexico?" Jay shrugged again. "I don't know. I guess I'd never been in Mexico alone. It didn't seem all that appealing. And . . . well, I thought maybe you two could use a hand bringing down the Marauders. If what Bledsoe . . . and Miss Thompson . . . said is true, they're not your old gang. They're far different. Far more savage than the men you once rode with.

"Not that I'd be much good against them directly, but I'm right good at getting information between shoot-outs." She smiled, adding wistfully, "Like finding out when that ranch train was going to pull through the mountains, and how much money was aboard. I mean, of course it all went for nothing . . . after Bledsoe's operative recognized me . . . but I did quite well up to that point—wouldn't you say?"

Slash smiled, nodded. "You sure did." He paused. "Even afterwards you did just fine."

"Thank you."

"I'm sorry, Jay. I never should've doubted you. You didn't deserve that."

"No, I didn't," she said with a wry smile.

Slash hadn't realized how heavy his heart had been, believing that Jay had double-crossed him and Pecos to Bledsoe. Believing that she'd literally sold their lives to the half-crazy chief marshal. He realized it now, however. Now, suddenly, his ticker felt as light as a newborn bird.

He found himself reaching out, taking her hand, squeezing it. He stared at her, his soul opening like the wings of that baby bird. Jay gazed back at him, her eyes soft, lips slightly parted. Slash leaned toward her. He began to slide his mouth toward hers.

He stopped, hesitating. Jay gazed back at him, her eyes vaguely curious. She'd parted her lips slightly farther, as though ready to accept his mouth with her own. Seeing him hesitate, she drew her lips together and turned away.

The breeze tussled her hair, blew several locks across her cheek, obscuring her expression.

"I reckon we'd better get back to the camp," Slash said, his heart suddenly feeling heavy again, a vague frustration vexing him. "Them pancakes are gettin' cold."

"You go ahead," Jay said. "I'll be along in a bit."

Slash headed back toward where the fire danced and

smoked. He paused to kick a rotten log in frustration. Glancing toward the camp, he saw Pecos standing at the edge of it, holding his coffee cup in his hands, gazing skeptically toward his partner.

"What're you lookin' at?" Slash said testily as he approached.

"You."

"Yeah, well, stop lookin' at me."

He stopped before Pecos, then glanced away as he said, "She didn't double-cross us the way we—"

"I know—I heard."

"All of it?"

"Enough to know we were dunderheads to believe that crazy old man." Slash stepped around Pecos and moved toward the fire. "Enough to know I'm a dunderhead for a totally different reason," he added.

"What's that?"

Slash knelt by the fire and glanced back at Pecos. Beyond Pecos, Jay was crossing the stream via a beaver dam, holding her arms out slightly for balance. Returning his gaze to his partner, Slash said, "Huh?" He hadn't realized he'd spoken that last sentence aloud.

"What else have you been a dunderhead about, Slash?" Pecos glared at him, his voice reproving. He glanced over his shoulder at Jay.

Slash's cheeks warmed as he used a leather swatch to remove the coffeepot from the iron spider. "Nothin'."

"Nothin'," Pecos mocked.

Slash grabbed a pancake off the plate, then sat down again by his saddle. He glanced at the girl, Myra Thompson, who sat as before, her eyes on him now, vaguely speculative.

"What're you looking at?" he asked grumpily, and took a bite of the hotcake.

"She's in love with you." Myra arched her brows, incredulous. "Even I could see it and I don't even know her. You're in love with her back. I can see that, too."

Slash wheeled away from her. "Like you said. You don't know her . . . or me!"

Myra shrugged. "Have it your way." She paused, hesitated. "What . . . what're you gonna do with me?"

"It's a fair question, Slash," Pecos said, leaning against a pine at the camp's far edge. "What are we gonna do with her?"

Chewing, Slash said, "By rights we oughta shoot her."

"You might as well." Myra's voice trembled slightly. "If you don't, Billy will. If he ever sees me again."

Slash narrowed a skeptical eye at her. "Is that really how it is?" He just couldn't wrap himself around this new, black-hearted version of Billy Pinto.

Myra gazed at him directly. "That's really how it is."

Slash glanced at Pecos. He took another bite of hotcake, sipped his coffee, then set the cup down and rose to his feet, wincing against the hammer-wielding little man in his head. He walked over to where Myra was tied to the tree and shucked his bowie knife from the sheath on his right hip, behind the .44 holstered on that side.

Myra looked up at him from beneath her brows, her wide eyes cast with fear.

Slash crouched beside her and cut through the rope tying her to the tree.

"What're you doin'?" Pecos asked.

"Yeah," Myra said. "What're you doing?"

"What's it look like?" Slash cut the girl's hands free. "If Billy really is as evil as you claim, you got more to fear from him than you do us." He pulled her to her feet, canted his head toward the horses. There were now four, including Jay's steeldust, tied to the picket line. "Mount up. Light a shuck out of here."

The girl looked up at him uncertainly, rubbing her wrists.

"Well, now, look at that," Pecos said, smiling over the steaming rim of his cup. "The old cutthroat's heart ain't completely stone, after all."

Slash touched the point of his knife to the underside of the girl's chin. "You'll find out how hard my heart is if I ever see you again, little girl. Go on. Hightail it out of here, and stay out of trouble!"

No sooner had that last word left Slash's lips than he heard Jay yell, "Slash! Pecos!"

The yell was followed by a gunshot. Jay called out again but this time it was more like an agonized grunt.

Slash and Pecos both wheeled to stare off toward the stream. It was from that general direction the shot had come.

"Jay!" Slash cried, breaking into an all-out run. "You see her?" he asked Pecos.

"There!" Pecos said, pointing.

As Slash ran past Pecos, he shucked a Colt .44 and stared off toward the stream. About twenty feet beyond the stream, he saw where Jay lay on the ground. He couldn't see much of her but he thought he saw her moving, extending her Colt Navy straight out in front of her.

Jay turned to yell back over her shoulder, red hair winking in the sunshine, "We got company, boys!"

She swung her head forward again and fired up a low ridge beyond her, and which was probably a former stream bank before the tributary had changed course.

"Hold up!" Pecos shouted. "I'm fetchin' my rifle!"

But Slash didn't slow his pace until more gunfire erupted from the ridge above and beyond Jay. Smoke and flames jetted from a tangle of brush topping the ridge. One bullet screeched over Slash's left shoulder while another curled the air off his right ear and thudded into a tree behind him.

Slash threw himself to the ground and extended his Colt, triggering three rounds toward where the smoke was still billowing atop the ridge. The shooter fired again. Slash couldn't see the shooter himself, only the smoke and flames from his rifle. The bullet plowed into the soft, spongy ground only a few inches in front of Slash, who scrambled to his feet and ran to a tree just ahead and on his right.

The bushwhacker's next bullet hammered the side of the pine just as Slash took cover behind it. Bits of bark sprayed out past Slash's left shoulder.

Slash edged a look around the left side of the tree. Jay lay on the other side of the stream from him, another twenty feet beyond the sliding water that flashed in the intensifying morning sunshine. The forest was thin enough over there that Slash could now see Jay clearly. She lay prone, legs spread, her copper hair fanned out across her shoulders. Her right hand and pistol were still thrust straight out ahead of her, but her head was down. She wasn't moving.

"Jay!" Slash yelled.

No answer.

"Jay!" Slash shouted, his heart pounding fiercely. "Jay, are you hit?"

Running footsteps sounded behind Slash. He glanced behind to see Pecos running through the forest toward him, weaving around trees, holding his Colt revolving rifle nearly straight up and down in his gloved hands.

The ridge-top bushwhacker fired toward Pecos.

Slash cut loose on the shooter, emptying his right-hand Colt, the hammer pinging benignly down against the firing pin. Pecos ran up to a tree about fifteen feet to Slash's left and dropped to a knee. He looked at Slash, red-faced, breathing hard.

"Jay?" he asked.

Slash shook his head. He edged a look around his covering pine and a cold stone dropped in his stomach when he saw Jay's unmoving body, head tipped toward the ground.

"She's still alive!" the shooter called from the ridge. "But she ain't gonna be for much longer unless you two show yourselves!"

CHAPTER 31

"That's Goose Johnson," Pecos said.

"Yeah, I recognized his voice," said Slash.

He edged a look around the side of the tree and yelled up toward the ridge: "Easy, Goose. You shoot her again, I'll kill you so slow you'll think you've been dyin' longer than you been alive!"

"You talk tough, old man!"

Slash gritted his teeth when he saw a rifle barrel angle out of a tangle of brush atop the ridge. The barrel angled down toward Jay.

Flames lapped from the barrel.

The bullet blew up dirt and dead leaves maybe eight inches to the right of Jay's head.

"Goose, dammit!" Pecos bellowed.

"Get over here!" Johnson yelled. "Show yourselves!"

Slash glanced at Pecos.

Pecos shook his head. "He'll just shoot us and then he'll kill Jay."

"I know." Slash was reloading his Colt, quickly plucking out the spent shells and replacing them with fresh ones from his cartridge belt. As he flicked his Colt's loading gate closed and spun the cylinder, he said, "Cover me!"

"Forget it," Pecos said. "It's too much ground to cover. He'll drill you!"

"It's the only way."

Pecos cursed in frustration, then raised his rifle, extending it out around the side of his covering tree. "Go with God, you copper-riveted fool!"

Slash unholstered his second Colt, clicked the hammer back, and bolted out from behind the fir, running hard. "Cover me," he raked out at Pecos. "But don't shoot me, ya peckerwood!"

"You're name-callin' again!"

Pecos opened up with the revolving rifle. As he did, Slash triggered his right-hand Colt, then his left, aiming at the thicket atop the ridge. He leaped up onto the beaver dam and moved forward across the intricately woven branches, looking down at his feet, careful to avoid tripping over up-thrust sticks, looking up every few seconds to trigger another shot at the ridge.

He and Pecos needed to keep Johnson pinned down so he couldn't shoot Jay.

Pecos continued to trigger his rifle as Slash leaped off the dam and bounded up the opposite bank, running hard as he climbed the grassy incline toward the ridge. He ran a weaving course, shooting every three or four steps, dodging behind trees.

"You're not gonna make it!" Johnson howled atop the ridge, laughing as his rifle thundered, flames and smoke jetting toward Slash.

The bullet plunked into the ground just right of Slash's right boot.

Slash cursed and glanced up at the ridge, where Pecos's bullets were ripping leaves and branches from the thicket covering Johnson, keeping the bushwhacker pinned down for the most part. At least, Johnson was having a hard time drawing a bead on Jay, and that was good enough for Slash at the moment.

But in another moment, Slash and Pecos were going to run out of lead, and Johnson would have an opening.

Slash glanced at Jay. She lay as before, prone against the ground, about twenty feet ahead and on his left.

He needed to shoot the jackass atop the ridge.

Slash dropped to a knee. He hadn't been counting his shots, but he knew instinctively that he had one bullet left in his right Colt, two remaining in the second Colt. He aimed carefully, waited until he saw Johnson's rifle barrel show amongst the foliage once more, and then aimed just above it.

He triggered the right Colt.

He whipped up the left Colt and triggered two more shots before, as he'd expected, the hammer dropped with a ping instead of a roar. That was all right. A muffled yelp and a rustling of the brush told him he'd hit his mark. At the very least, he'd probably winged Johnson.

Slash holstered both Colts, sprang to his feet, and ran up and over to where Jay lay against the ground. He placed a hand on her back.

"Jay!"

She groaned. He rolled her onto her back, and she stretched her lips away from her teeth in a grimace.

"Ohh," she said, and groaned again, eyelids fluttering.

Another cold stone dropped in Slash's belly when he saw the blood oozing out a ragged hole in her shirt about six inches down from her right shoulder.

"Oh, Jay."

He glanced into the brush atop the knoll. He could hear the brush rustling up that way. Johnson was moving.

Quickly, Slash slid his hands beneath Jay's body. "Gotta get you to cover, lady."

He rose from his knees, lifting Jay as he did, and ran over to a broad pine. He eased Jay down behind it, resting her back against the tree and tucking her legs up close to her body so she wasn't exposed to another possible rifle shot.

"I'll be right back, honey," he said.

Glancing behind, he saw Pecos now jogging up behind him from the river, reloading his rifle. Slash wanted to reload his Colts, too, but there was no time. Johnson might be composing himself, preparing to start hurling lead down from the top of that ridge.

Slash lunged forward, sprinting as fast as his middle-aged legs could take him, leaping over deadfalls and blown down branches, his breath raking in and out of his lungs. He shucked his bowie knife as he reached the ridge's base. Grinding his boots into the side of the knoll covered with a thin layer of soil peppered with gravel, dead leaves, and pine needles, he grunted as he heaved himself straight up the rise.

His knees ached, his lungs strained, his heart was a sledge hammering his breastbone.

Too much whiskey, too damn many cigarettes . . .

He stared at the moving brush just above him now. Reaching the crest of the rise, he plunged into the thicket, holding the knife, blade forward, in his right hand. Johnson was just then heaving himself up off his knees, raising his rifle.

Slash swung the knife up underhanded. He kept the blade so sharp that there was little resistance when the knife perforated Johnson's belly. It was almost as though the knife wasn't even in Slash's hand but that he was merely punching the man in the gut with his bare, empty fist.

Until the hot blood flowed over Slash's hand.

"*Ohhh!*" Goose Johnson croaked.

He was a lean little dimwit with a long, crooked nose and dull brown eyes. Those eyes snapped wide now as he triggered his rifle into the ground to the right of his and Slash's feet, and he stared at Slash, his face only six inches away from his killer's.

He opened his mouth but only gurgling sounds issued.

"Well, hello, Goose," Slash said, glaring at the startled man slumped toward him, driving the blade up . . . "Fancy meetin' you out here!"

"Sl-Slash," Johnson gasped.

"What's the next job, Goose?" Slash said, so close to Johnson that the stench of the man's unwashed body was heavy in his nose.

"Slash—"

"The next job?"

"T-Tra-Train!" Johnson gasped.

"Where?"

"S-Si-Silverton! Dur . . . Dur-ang-go. Gold!"

"Thank you, Goose," Slash snarled.

Johnson gained a thoughtful, perplexed expression. "Billy . . . Billy was . . . just . . . more fun . . . than you an' Pecos, Slash. . . ." He'd said the words almost sadly, as though he were imparting regrettable news.

"Well, I'm glad you had a good time now at the end," Slash said again, quietly, tightly through gritted teeth. "But it was them good times that just got you killed by me, you cow-brained fool. Good night, Goose!"

Slash delivered the final death blow.

Johnson grunted once more, then stumbled backward, his body sliding off the knife as he fell away down the opposite side of the rise, rolling in the thick brush. Slash gave his knife a cursory cleaning in grass and tangled green branches, then sheathed the bowie and ran back down the front of the rise. As he gained the bottom and began running toward Jay, he saw Pecos on one knee beside her.

Pecos's head was down as though in prayer, one hand on Jay's shoulder. At least, Slash thought his partner's hand was on her shoulder. He couldn't see Jay clearly because of the pine he'd set her down behind.

Slash stopped. He didn't realize he'd stopped, but then suddenly he wasn't running. His knees burned, weakened. His heart banged against his ribs.

He also didn't realize he'd been holding his breath until Pecos glanced over his shoulder at him and said, "She's conscious. I think she's gonna be all right, but we gotta get her to a sawbones pronto!"

Slash heard Jay say something to Pecos, and then Slash released that breath he'd been holding and, relief washing over him, he ran over and dropped to a knee beside Jay and Pecos. Jay grimaced as she looked at Slash, holding her own neckerchief against the wound.

"Did you get that slimy devil?"

"Oh, yeah."

"Good. He potshot me, the coward!"

"How bad you hit?" Slash asked.

"Not bad at all . . . I don't think." She winced sharply.

Pecos looked at Slash. "Bullet's still in her. We gotta get her to a doc."

"We'll take her to Silverton." Slash moved closer to Jay, extending his hand. "Let's get her back to camp. We gotta get that bleeding stopped before we take her anywhere."

Pecos touched Slash's shoulder. "Let me take her. I'm bigger'n you."

"Get away!" Slash slid his arms under Jay and lifted her.

"Boys, boys, don't fight over me, now!" Jay chided them, chuckling, then sucking a pained breath through her teeth.

Pecos jogged back in the direction of the camp. "I'll get the horses ready to go!"

Slash carried Jay toward the beaver dam. She had her

arms wrapped around his neck, and she was gazing up into his eyes, frowning. "You'd best be careful, Slash. If you keep carryin' on like this, someone's gonna think you got a heart, after all."

"Typical woman. Even with a bullet in you, you're still a harpy all the way!"

Jay kissed his cheek. He tried to ignore the inviting sensation of her lips. "Sometime still in this old life of yours, James Braddock, you're gonna make some woman a right honorable husband. If you can find one who can see who you really are, that is. And you don't scare her away first."

"Be quiet, Jay, dammit!" Slash leaped down off the beaver dam and strode quickly toward the fire.

He was surprised to see Myra Thompson lingering around the camp. He'd expected her to have ridden off by now. Myra stood gazing with concern toward Slash and Jay, wringing her hands together, fidgeting.

"How bad's she hit?" she asked.

"Bad enough."

"We gotta get the bleeding stopped," Myra said. "And we have to get a poultice on the wound to keep it stopped and to prevent infection."

"'We'?" Slash asked the girl, brushing past her and carrying Jay into the camp.

He eased the woman down against his own saddle and tossed several branches on the fire, building it up.

"I helped a midwife for a while," Myra said. "She took care of pregnancies and injuries up in the mountains around my and Pa's cabin. She taught me lots of stuff, even about bullet wounds." As the girl poured water from a canteen into a small pot, she said, "I'll get some water boiling, for cleaning the wound, and while it heats, I'll forage for roots for the poultice."

She quickly set the pan on the iron spider, over the fire,

then bounded up and jogged out into the woods. Slash shared a glance with Pecos, who was quickly saddling the horses.

"Well, I'll be damned," Slash said, staring after the girl in surprise. "Maybe she's got some good in her, after all."

"Yeah, well, maybe you do, too." Pecos winked at him. "But don't worry, partner.

Slash turned toward Jay. She'd passed out with her head resting back against his saddle.

Slash placed his hand on one of hers and squeezed. "Just keep fightin', Jay. Just keep fightin'."

CHAPTER 32

"That smells awful," Jay said twenty minutes later as Myra, having cleaned the bullet wound thoroughly, applied a compress. "What's in it?"

"You won't like it."

"Won't I?"

"It's mashed pine needles with aspen leaves, mud, and . . . uh . . . horse urine."

"Horse urine?" Jay arched a brow. "You're not trying to get back at me for that tattoo I gave you, are you?"

"Yeah," Slash said, grabbing the girl's arm. "Maybe you're funnin' with us."

Jay chuckled. "Leave her be, Slash. I trust her." She looked up at Myra speculatively. "I'm not sure why. But I do."

Slash released Myra grudgingly. The girl finished wrapping a bandage around Jay's neck and under her shoulder, securing the poultice to the wound, then finished drawing Jay's shirt up over it.

"You really shouldn't ride," Myra said, leaning back on her heels. "I packed it good, but that wound could open up again." She bit her lower lip in consternation. "I wish I knew how to get the bullet out, but that's one trick I never learned."

"I'll be fine," Jay said.

"We could fetch a sawbones here," Pecos said. He had the horses saddled and ready to go. "I could ride up to Silverton and bring him back." To Myra, he said, "There must be a doctor up that way, isn't there?"

"I can't recollect seein' a shingle for one, but I'm sure there is. Or someone as good as the real thing." Myra looked at Jay. "I'll fetch somebody for you."

Jay shook her head. "No need. I'm tough as sin. I can make the ride." She lifted her hand toward Slash. "Help me into my saddle."

Slash pulled her gently to her feet and then, wrapping one arm around the small of her back, began leading her toward where the four horses stood in a loose clump, ground-tied. "You're not riding alone. I don't think you have the strength to sit a saddle. You'll be ridin' with me."

Jay shook her head. "Too hard on your horse."

"That's one tough hoss. Toughest one I ever owned. Had him a long time. He's got a sound back on him, that horse does."

"He's right," Myra said, walking up behind them with Pecos, who'd kicked dirt on the fire. "You might feel strong now, but I have a feeling that after a few miles up the trail, you're going to weaken. Falling out of your saddle could be bad. Really bad."

She gazed directly at Jay.

Jay looked at Slash and nodded.

Slash helped her up onto the Appy's back. When he had her safely in the saddle, he toed the stirrup and swung up behind her, easing his own weight behind Jay and the saddle's cantle, on his bedroll and saddlebags.

Pecos mounted his own horse. Slash started to rein away from the camp but then he saw Myra standing there at the edge of the camp, holding the reins of her horse but not mounting. She just stood there, looking a little lost and forlorn under the round brim of her battered felt hat.

"Where you headed?" Slash asked her.

The girl hiked a shoulder, gave a weak half smile. "I don't suppose there's any chance I could tag along with you all, is there?"

"To Silverton?"

Again, the girl shrugged.

"Pinto's there," Pecos said. Slash had told him what Goose Johnson had told Slash about the gang's next job.

"I got nowhere else to go," Myra said, fear in her eyes as she slid her gaze from Slash to Pecos and back again. "Nowhere."

Slash and Pecos glanced at each other.

"Never mind," Myra said, swinging up into her saddle and reining the mare away from the three. "I understand. Bad idea."

Jay glanced over her shoulder at Slash, placed a hand on his knee, and gave him a beseeching squeeze.

"Oh, what the hell," Slash said.

Myra looked hopefully over her shoulder at him.

"It ain't every day a man gets to share the trail with the gal that nearly drilled him a third eye!" he said.

Chuckling, he swung the Appy through the forest, heading toward the trail hugging the Animas—the trail that should take them in a couple of hours up to the mountain mining camp of Silverton, where Slash hoped against hope they'd find a doctor.

Slash and Pecos were eager to get on up the trail to Silverton, but they had to keep their speed down to lessen the jarring for Jay. After they'd pushed a little too hard for a two-mile stretch, and then stopped to rest Jay as well as the horses, Myra checked the bandage to find it spotted with fresh blood.

Jay, sitting against a tree, looked pale and worn out. Her eyes were clear, her expression brave, but that didn't change the fact that she still had a bullet inside her. It didn't change the fact that she might very well bleed to death before they reached Silverton.

"We can always stop here, Jay," Slash said. "One of us can ride on ahead for . . ."

Jay shook her head, flung up a hand toward Slash. "Let's ride. The gang's up there. You have to get after them before they kill again."

"Not at the expense of killing you," Pecos said.

"Thanks, boys," she said, laying a hand against the side of the big cutthroat's face. "But, really. I'll be fine. Come on." She strode toward the Appy. "Stop dragging your behinds!"

Slash looked at Pecos. Pecos shrugged. He looked at Myra, who also shrugged.

"Your wish is our command, your highness," Slash said, helping Jay up into the saddle.

"Now, those are the words a gal likes to hear!" Jay glanced back, placed a hand on Slash's cheek, and smiled. "You're learning. Slow but sure . . ."

Chuckling, Slash reined the Appy out onto the trail and touched spurs to its flanks, continuing their meandering trek along the Animas River. It wasn't long before Jay lolled back against Slash, groaning in troubled sleep.

Pecos rode up beside his partner. He looked at Jay slumped back against Slash's chest. He leveled his gaze on Slash and said, "What I was gonna tell you back in Saguache . . . just before them Pinkertons galloped into town . . ."

"Yeah?"

"I was gonna tell you I know how you feel about her." Pecos glanced at Jay. "And I'm gonna tell you now you best tell *her* an' tell her soon. Not that I think she's gonna die but, hell, you never know when any of us is gonna kick off. If you don't tell her, you'll regret it."

"You done with the sermon, Preacher?"

"Yeah, I'm done." Pecos reined away from Slash, putting more distance between them. "That's all I'm gonna say on the subject, you stubborn damn fool. . . ."

By the time they reached Silverton, cradled in a small valley hemmed in by towering, thirteen-thousand-foot-high peaks including Anvil Mountain, which already had a light dusting of snow on it, Jay had been leaning back against Slash, sound asleep, for a good half hour.

She didn't stir even after she and Slash as well as Pecos and Myra Thompson began weaving through the camp's heavy traffic and became ensconced in the loud hubbub issuing from every quarter—sudden bursts of laughter rising from raucous conversations here and there about the street, the barking of dogs, the loud pings of blacksmiths' hammers, and the frenzied pattering of pianos caroming out through the camp's many and sundry saloons and houses of ill repute.

"Pardon me, friend," Slash said, drawing up to a tall, bearded man in buckskins who'd just pulled a freight wagon drawn by a six-mule hitch up before a sprawling mercantile building. "Can you tell me where I'd find a sawbones hereabouts?"

He hadn't finished the question before Myra said, "There!"

Slash followed her pointing finger toward a wooden sign jutting into the street atop two unpeeled pine poles, roughly a block ahead and near where two dogs sat, licking their chops as another man in smoke-stained buckskins butchered a deer hanging upside down from a wooden tripod. As the man carved, he tossed each cur a chunk of the sinewy meat.

"Thanks anyway, pard," Slash said to the burly freighter, and reined the Appy back into the street where he barely avoided a collision with a passing ore dray. He was roundly cussed by the stout black man driving the four-mule team, likely heading for the smelter.

Ignoring the black man's regaling, Slash booted the Appy over to the building—or part of the building—the sign identified as the office of DR. H.T. ROSENCRANTZ, M.D. A painted hand pointed up a rickety stairs toward the second story of the equally rickety-looking building, the bottom half of which a sign identified as HATCH KETTLEMEYER FRESH MEAT & JERKY.

As he drew the Appy up to the two-story building, Slash turned to the man butchering the deer and feeding the dogs and said, "The pill roller in his office?"

"Nope." The deer butcher, also bearded and burly— Slash had so far seen few unshaven men in Silverton— rolled a lucifer match around between his lips and shook his head.

"Where might we find him?" Pecos said. "We got an injured woman."

"I got no damn idea," said the bearded deer butcher, who appeared in his early to mid-thirties. While dressed in bloodstained denim overalls and a ragged, wool plaid shirt and floppy-brimmed leather hat adorned with a lone hawk feather, there appeared a vague air of refinement about the man.

"Take a look at this camp," he said. "It's filled to brimming with men of every stripe, an' they're still comin'. Miners and market hunters, mostly, and when they ain't fightin' with pickaxes and shovels in drunken saloon brawls or shootin' each other over claim disputes"—he did not pause while he tossed each cur a chunk of fatty meat from the half-skinned deer's left ham—"they're blowin' themselves up with dynamite or gettin' their bones crushed to fine powder in mine collapses. The doc left early this mornin' after delivering a baby just after midnight an' I ain't seen him since. Likely won't see him again till midnight tonight, if then."

Slash cursed.

"Is he the only doctor in town?" Myra asked.

The man eyed her suspiciously, pausing for a moment in his work of trimming the skin and sinew away from the deer's hide as he peeled it down the carcass's back. "Don't I know you?"

"No!" Myra said, coloring angrily.

"I think I do."

"Answer the question," Slash said.

"Yes, he's the only sawbones this camp has," the man said, continuing his work of peeling the hide down the deer as though he were peeling a giant banana, grunting with the effort.

"Ah, hell," Pecos said, turning to Slash. "We might just as well have stayed in camp. We came all this way, put Jay through that long ride for nothin'!"

"Oh, don't get your drawers in a twist!" cajoled the butcher.

Slash wrapped his hand around the grips of the .44 holstered for the cross-draw against his left hip, aimed the revolver at the bearded man's head, and clicked the hammer back. "I don't like your tone, mister."

The butcher turned to Slash and held his bloody knife and other hand up in supplication. "Don't you get your drawers in a twist, neither! What I was gonna add, if you'd give me half a chance, is Uncle Henry is the only *bona fide, paper-wieldin'* sawbones here in Silverton. When Uncle Henry's busy, as he is now, I take up the slack for him."

"What?" both Slash and Pecos asked the man skeptically.

"Sure enough," the butcher said. "Name's Hatch Kettle-meyer. H.T. 'Henry' Rosencrantz is my uncle on my mother's side. Henry done taught me near on everything he knows about the cuttin' an' sawin' an' suturin' business. It ain't all that different from what I do for a regular livin'—you know, cuttin' up meat to sell to folks to eat!"

He laughed.

Slash and Pecos shared their deeply skeptical expressions with each other.

Hatch Kettlemeyer stuck his skinning knife into the deer's ribcage, then turned around and dipped his bloody hands and arms into a corrugated tin washtub steaming over a low fire behind him. "Oh, don't worry—I'm just joshin'. I might not have a fancy diploma with gold letters and fancy writin' hangin' on my wall, but"—he held a hand up to the side of his mouth and imparted with a secretive air—"do you know that when Uncle Henry's out of earshot, a lot of folks around town tell me they'd prefer to have me cuttin' on 'em . . . or settin' their broken bones . . . than Uncle Henry his ownself?"

He pressed two still-bloody fingers to his lips, chuckling devilishly, then sunk his hands in the steaming water once more. "Go ahead an' take that purty lady up to Henry's office. Door's open. Take her on into the examining room behind Henry's desk, and don't mind the mess in there. Or Henry's cat, Rufus. That's Henry! Even if he wasn't too busy to straighten up, he wouldn't do it. He'd rather go fishin' up at Crater Lake or in the Animas instead, though he has damn little time for it. Go ahead—take the lady upstairs. I'll be along in a minute."

Slash hesitated. He glanced down at Jay, who had awakened now and was looking around groggily, as though trying to get her bearings.

"It's all right," Myra said. "I've heard about Mr. Kettle-meyer. He's as good as a doctor."

Scrubbing his hands and arms with a sliver of soap, working up a good lather, Kettlemeyer turned to Myra, his eyes wide with sudden recognition. "I *have* seen you before! Where was it now?" He paused, thoughtful, then: "Oh—*whoops!*" he added quickly, flushing and turning back to his scrubbing. Under his breath, he said, "Me an' my big mouth. When do I ever not stick my foot in it?"

Slash glanced at Myra, who had turned bright red and was staring down at her saddle horn.

Quickly and maybe a little too loudly changing the subject, Slash said, "All right, then—I guess we don't have no choice in the matter."

"Don't reckon we do!" Pecos said.

Slash swung down from the Appy's back but quickly reached up to hold Jay upright in the saddle. "Jay, we're gonna take you up to the doctor's office, have this man take a look at you." He drew her gently down to him and took her in his arms. "How you doin'? You all right, darlin'?"

Weakly, Jay nodded and said, "I sure could use a shot of Taos lightnin' . . . dull this pain . . ."

"Comin' right up!" Pecos swung down from his saddle, tossed his reins over a hitch rack at the base of the stairs climbing to the doctor's office, then headed across the busy street toward the nearest saloon—the Silver Lode.

Slash carried Jay up the rickety stairs. Myra hurried ahead to open the office door, and ten minutes later, Slash and Myra stood around the examining table as Hatch Kettlemeyer, now donning steel-framed spectacles, crouched over Jay, slowly removing the bandage and poultice, wrinkling his nose against the stench.

"Despite the stink of that stuff, I commend you, young lady," Kettlemeyer said. "That's a good poultice. Nothin' like mud and horse water to clot the blood and keep out infection. As long as the horse wasn't carryin' infection, of

290 William W. Johnstone and J.A. Johnstone

course," he added with a wry chuckle, which he clipped quickly when he saw that neither Slash nor Myra laughed at the joke.

On the leather-padded table, Jay lay groaning and stretching her lips back from her teeth. She lifted one knee and then the other, and her face was pale. Seeing her like this made Slash feel as though he were sporting a rusty knife in his guts.

He was glad when Pecos showed up with the whiskey.

Slash took the bottle from his partner, popped the cork, and showed the bottle to Kettlemeyer, who was closely examining the exposed wound. "This all right, Doc?"

"Sure, sure." Kettlemeyer looked at Jay. "Drink up. There's laudanum around here somewhere but no tellin' how long it would take me to find it, what with the mess an' all."

A fat, gray, tiger-striped cat lay atop an overstuffed medicine cabinet, licking its front paw and using the paw to scrub its face. Out in the main room, the doctor's desk looked like a small mountain of medicine bottles, medical instruments, note pads, and books spilling pages of scrawled notes. There were also a couple stuffed fish and deer and elk trophies on the walls, caked in dust and spiderwebs. A cabinet clock ticked loudly.

"Here you go, Jay," Slash said, helping Jay sit up just far enough that she could tip the bottle to her lips without spilling.

As Jay took several pulls of the whiskey, Pecos leaned close to Slash and said into his right ear, "I overheard a couple of men over at the Silver Lode. They were bullion guards from the Old Hundred Gold Mine. Sounded like they'd just delivered a goodly amount of gold onto the narrow-gauge leg of the Denver and Rio Grande heading for Durango."

Slash looked at Pecos. "The train still at the station?"

Pecos shook his head. "A fella on the street said it pulled out for Durango less than a half hour ago."

Slash whistled.

Apparently, Jay had overheard the conversation. She just now pulled the bottle down once more and said, "What're you two lugs loitering around here for? You're just getting in the way and stinking the place up."

"No," Slash said, shaking his head. "We'll be right here for you, Jay."

"Yeah, we ain't budging until that bullet's out, Jay."

Jay's eyes nearly crossed in anger. "Will you two cutthroats listen to reason for once in your lives? You go do what you came here to do, and keep yourselves out of jail! Like I said, I'll likely be here for a while." She took another pull of the whiskey, then corked the bottle and laid her head back against the examining table. "You'll know where to find me."

"She'll be here for a while, all right," Kettlemeyer said, dabbing a cloth soaked in carbolic acid around the edges of the puckered, quarter-sized wound in Jay's chest. "That bullet's in there deep. Going to take me a while to get it out. Go do whatever it is you got to do." He added under his breath, "Just for godsakes don't tell me what it is . . ."

"Can't do it," Slash said, stubbornly shaking his head. "I won't leave you alone."

"I'll be here." Myra had spoken from where she stood in a corner near the medicine cabinet atop which the cat now lay sprawled on its back. Myra took a step toward the examining table, entwining her hands before her. "I'll stay with her."

Jay looked at Slash and Pecos. "There you have it. Now, haul your freight!"

Slash sighed. He was still reluctant to leave her, but there was a good chance the Snake River Marauders had that gold-bearing train in their sights.

Better than good, in fact. They were too close for Slash and Pecos to not go after them.

Who knew when they'd get another chance this prime?

"All right," Slash said, nodding. "All right." He looked at Pecos. "You heard the lady. Let's haul our freight!"

They strode out of the examining room, across the cluttered main office, and out the front door.

"Wait," Slash said.

"What is it?"

"Hold on."

Slash walked back into the office and into the examining room. Jay scowled at him, lifting her head from the table. "Slash, dammit, I told you to—"

Slash doffed his hat, placed his hand on the back of her neck, crouched down, and kissed her smack on the lips. He kissed her hard, and he held it. When he pulled away, he narrowed his gaze commandingly and stared into her eyes. "You best be here when I get back or there's gonna be hell to pay, woman!"

Jay just stared at him, eyes wide with shock. So did Myra and Kettlemeyer, though Myra was smiling a little, too.

Slash set his hat back on his head and left.

CHAPTER 33

"What'd you do in there?" Pecos asked as Slash stepped back onto the stairs fronting the doctor's office.

"Nothin'."

Slash stepped around him and strode down the stairs.

"Nothin'?" Pecos exclaimed, following Slash down the steps. "You didn't go back in there just to do *nothin'*. You had to do *somethin'*!"

"Oh, shut up!" Slash carped as he gained the bottom of the steps.

"Stop tellin' me to shut up, dammit." Pecos wagged a finger in Slash's face. "I'm gettin' damn tired o' that."

"Shut up!"

Pecos leaned close to Slash and wagged a finger in the shorter outlaw's face. "You tell me that one more time, I'm gonna beat the snot out of you, and you know I can lick you in a fair fight!"

"Yeah, but you know I wouldn't fight fair." Slash chuckled, then said, "Focus, now, dammit. If the Marauders really did go after the Denver and Rio Grande out of Silverton, where would they hit it?"

Pecos stared thoughtfully across the busy street, thinking. "Wait, wait—didn't we hit that train a time or two?"

Slash frowned at his partner. "Did we?" Then it dawned on him. "Damn, you're right!"

Pecos wagged his head despondently. "Our memories ain't what they used to be, Slash."

"Well, hell, we hit so many trains and stagecoaches over the years, we can't be blamed for forgettin' one or two." Slash gestured with his hand. "I think . . . I think I remember hitting it one time just beneath a high ridge. A ridge with a name . . ."

"Yeah, yeah—Thunder Ridge! And another time we hit it farther down the line, near . . . near a rapids, I think . . ."

"Confederate Rapids! Near the first Confederate Boy Mine!"

"Yeah, yeah, that's it!"

"Some of the older salts in the gang will remember both those places—Dakota Todd, for instance, and Chico Gonzalez."

"All right, then." Slash grabbed his reins off the hitch rack and swung up onto the Appy's back. "Let's head for Thunder Ridge first. We should reach the canyon before the train does. As I remember, it's a slow mover and it follows one hell of a twisting route along the river. There's an old Indian trail above that canyon—on the west side. A shortcut!"

"Let's get on it!" Pecos said, swung up onto his buckskin, and reined it into the street.

The cutthroats put spurs to their horses and lunged down the street at nearly a full gallop, dangerously twisting their way through the heavy pedestrian, wagon, and horseback traffic, evoking more than a few curses, fist pumps, and all-out threats against life and limb.

They headed south from the camp by the main stage

and army trail. When another trail broke from the main one, they took the secondary trail up a steep, bald mountain ridge and out across a treeless bench. The air was cold up here, for they were at nearly ten thousand feet above sea level. The trees were scrubby, the grass almost nonexistent, and frost from a previous night's freeze still furred the ground on the shady sides of boulders.

They climbed a rocky pass and galloped out across another broad bench.

Shortly, they could see the cut of the Animas River Canyon just ahead, appearing first as a slender, dark line against the base of pale, craggy peaks beyond it. Gradually, that dark line widened and gained definition until Slash and Pecos could see into the canyon itself as they rode up on it hard.

They stopped in a fringe of stunted spruce and cedars stippling the rocky ridge, and swung down from their mounts. Slash grabbed a spyglass out of his saddlebags, and then he and Pecos crawled through the prickly brush and rocks until they were belly down along the lip of the ridge, the canyon yawning wide below them.

The river lay at the bottom, a couple of hundred feet below, like a dark green snake with the sun glistening off its scaly hide. Slash could see occasional beaver dams and the white stitches of water tossed up by rocks and boulders. The wind blew up from the canyon, cool and fragrant with the smell of wild water, sage, rock, and pine.

Directly across the canyon from the two men, Thunder Ridge jutted its craggy head straight up to tickle the dark blue belly of the faultless blue sky. From this vantage, there didn't appear any way down that side of the canyon, but Slash knew of a trail that dropped down around the north shoulder of Thunder Ridge. It was a perilous ride, and you had to be young and foolhardy, not to mention dead set on acquiring the gold and/or silver bullion riding the Denver & Rio Grande narrow-gauge flyer from Silverton, to go after it.

From what Slash and Pecos had learned about Billy Pinto, to their astonishment, the kid was foolhardy enough to take that ride. And commanding enough to get the others to take it with him.

Slash raised the glass to his right eye and adjusted the focus, bringing into view the shelf that the Denver & Rio Grande tracks had been laid upon, about halfway up the limestone wall on the canyon's far side, roughly a quarter mile straight out from his and Pecos's position. He closely glassed that shelf, looking for any sign of impediments— rock dynamited out of the side of the canyon, or cut-down trees blocking the tracks, for tall, slender spruces and firs grew out of the rocks of that steep ridge.

"Nothing," Slash said.

"Let me see."

Slash handed the glass to Pecos, who studied the shelf.

"Nothing."

"Told you."

"Maybe it's still to come. No sign of the train yet."

"Unless it's already passed."

"Yeah."

"If it hasn't come yet, I doubt they're planning to hit it here. If they were, they already would have blocked the tracks."

"Yep," Pecos agreed. "I remember—you gotta block the tracks early because the conductor has to see it right when he comes around that bend to the north, or he'll hit it and probably roll right off the shelf and into the canyon. Gone, gold, gone!"

"Yeah," Slash said wryly. "To say nothin' of the passengers."

He patted Pecos's shoulder. "Come on. Let's head for the rapids."

"Hold on."

"What is it?"

"The train."

Slash heard the distant *chuffah-chuffah-chuffah* just before the locomotive poked its blunt snout out from behind a bend on the other side of the canyon and upstream a quarter mile or so, though it was hard to judge distance because of the canyon's meandering nature. The locomotive crawled into fuller view, issuing puffs of black smoke from its stack, dragging the red tender car, with its stacked split firewood.

Behind the tender car clacked several passenger coaches and the little red caboose.

Slash grabbed the spyglass out of Pecos's hands. "Let me take a look."

"Say 'please' next time!"

"Shut up!"

Pecos gritted his teeth and punched Slash's shoulder, like an indignant brother acting up in church. Ignoring him, Slash glassed the train.

Behind the dining car was a sleek black car with only two windows. As the train drew nearer, still curving along the bulging belly of the canyon wall, drawing nearer Slash and Pecos—the *chuffah, chuffah, chuffahs* growing louder with each second—Slash could read the words WELLS, FARGO & COMPANY EXPRESS in large gold letters blazed on the side of the glistening black panel, right of the large, closed door that was likely reinforced and barred from inside with stout iron.

Most of those doors were. That's why the two cutthroats had gotten so friendly with dynamite over the years. . . .

Pecos tapped Slash's shoulder. "Come on. Let's mount up and try to stay ahead of it."

"All right." But just as Slash began to lower the glass, he spied movement out of the corner of his left eye. "Hold on."

He raised the glass to his eye again.

"What is it?"

Slash stared through the sphere of magnified vision, raking the glass across the train, which was maybe a hundred yards upstream now, wending its way along the opposite ridge wall. "I don't know. Thought I saw somethin'."

"What?"

"I said I don't—wait." Slash had just spied movement again—something or someone stepping off the wall just above the train and settling onto the roof of one of the passenger coaches.

Then he saw it again, clearer now.

A man stepped out away from the wall, dropping off a slight ledge maybe fifteen feet above the train. He held a rifle in one hand. He held his hat on his head with his other hand. The flaps of his long duster rose like the wings of a giant bird up around his shoulders. Dropping straight down the wall, he bent his knees and crouched and lighted on the tin roof of the second passenger coach.

Slash's heartbeat quickened. "Holy bullheads in hell!"

"What is it?"

"They're dropping onto the train like buzzards on carrion!"

As Slash watched, another man and then another and still another stepped out from a niche in the canyon wall to drop onto the train. He handed the glasses to Pecos but now the train was directly in front of him, straight out across the canyon, and he saw with his naked eyes two more men step out from the side of the canyon wall and drop, crouching, atop the roof of the express car.

One of those men was carrying what appeared a gunny-sack.

Dynamite.

Pecos lowered the glass and stared wide-eyed up at Slash. "Holy moly, partner. No wonder they wanted us old mossy-horns out. Them fellas under Billy Pinto's command has upped their game!"

Slash lowered the glass. "Come on. Let's get after that train!"

He and Pecos crawled back out of the brush. They mounted their horses and raced off along the lip of the ridge, following the canyon's twisting course generally southwest. As they rode, Slash peered over the canyon lip to see the train still chugging along the shelf halfway down the opposite ridge. The train was to the south of Thunder Ridge now, and several of the men milling atop the train, looking little larger than ants from this distance, dropped down onto the platforms between the cars. Several others converged on the roof of the express car.

As the train turned a bend and swerved away from Slash and Pecos, the two cutthroats got ahead of it.

"Hold up!" Slash said.

He stopped the Appy and reached back into his saddle-bags for his spyglass again.

"What's goin' on?" Pecos asked, stopping his buckskin beside Slash.

Slash raised the glass to his eye and adjusted the focus.

Four men remained atop the train, which was following a shallow inner bend in the canyon wall. Now as the train began angling straight south again, Slash could see that the four men were atop the express car. He could tell that one was Billy Pinto, for he was the shortest and he wore a long, ragged, tan duster and low-crowned black sombrero with a beaded band.

Billy and one other man, who appeared to be the bulky

half-breed Floyd Three Eagles, were kneeling atop the express car, the gunnysack resting on the roof beside Billy. They were fiddling with something atop the car. Slash knew what it was even before the men drew back toward both ends of the car and poked their fingers into their ears.

There was a bright orange flash and a thick puff of roiling, black smoke where they'd been standing a moment before. As the smoke quickly cleared, Slash could see that the dynamite—two or three sticks, probably—had blown a hole roughly the size of a wagon wheel in the center of the shake-shingled roof.

Now all four cutthroats cocked their rifles and converged on the hole. Even from this distance, Slash could hear one of them whooping and hollering like a mooncrazed coyote. Through the glass he could see that the one yelling was Billy Pinto, who pressed the butt of his Henry repeater to his shoulder and angled the barrel down into the car.

The blasts of the rifles reached Slash's ears nearly a full two seconds after he'd seen the flames lick from the barrels of the four robbers' rifles.

"Christ Almighty," Slash said, handing the spyglass over to Pecos. "They're shootin' the express guards like ducks on a millpond!"

"Holy . . ." Pecos said in awe, staring through the glass.

With his naked eyes, Slash saw the express car's door slide open. A man clad in what appeared the blue wool uniform of a Wells Fargo guard tumbled out, his body engulfed in flames from the explosion. Smoke billowed out behind him. Another guard stumbled out, clutching himself, turning a forward somersault, arms and legs akimbo, as he plummeted toward the bottom of the canyon.

Another guard followed. Slash could hear the man's shrill screams as he too dropped toward the river.

A fourth guard fell in the doorway, arms dangling over the edge of the car toward the canyon, his leather-billed cap blowing off his head in the wind to smack against the side of the car following the express car. The cap caromed out over the canyon and hung there, dropping slowly, like a bird riding the thermals.

Pecos turned to Slash, eyes wide in shock. "It's a massacre," he said. "That's all you can call it."

"Come on," Slash said, reining the Appy out away from the canyon wall. "Time to put those rabid dogs down!"

CHAPTER 34

Slash and Pecos cut across a sharp horseshoe curve in the canyon wall.

As they rode, crouched low over the billowing manes of their galloping mounts, they could hear the chugging of the train in the canyon as the Denver & Rio Grande flyer continued to make its way downstream along the Animas, its staid, purposeful *chuffs* likely belying the murderous chaos that was no doubt occurring inside those coaches as the gang plundered the Wells Fargo car and robbed the men and women in the three passenger coaches.

Robbed them and did God only knew what else to them . . .

"What you got in mind, Slash?" Pecos asked, the wind basting the brim of his hat against his forehead.

"I'm open to suggestions!"

"Well, it's a dozen-plus against two!"

"Yeah, an' the odds aren't likely to get any shorter!"

As they fogged the sage and buck brush of the canyon rim, the canyon occasionally edged close enough to the riders that Slash could peer partway into it. The canyon wall was dropping gradually, putting Slash and Pecos closer to the canyon bottom as well as to the train that continued to snake along the cut of the opposite ridge.

As the ridge continued to drop, the two cutthroats now galloping downhill beside it, Slash saw a bridge inside the canyon—a bridge spanning the Animas that would bring the train over to his and Pecos's side of the canyon.

A plan began to solidify and clarify in his racing mind.

He watched the train curve out away from the opposite canyon wall and head for the bridge. The flyer was roughly a hundred yards ahead and left of Slash and Pecos now. As the train crossed the bridge, its rumbling and chugging reverberating off the bridge's stout timbers, Flash looked for a way into the canyon. After a few more of his tiring horse's strides, he saw what appeared a game trail angling down the canyon wall, the rim of which was now only about a hundred feet above the canyon floor.

"This way!" Slash yelled as he reined the Appy sharply left.

He and Pecos dropped down along the narrow, switchbacking game trail littered with deer scat. Fifty feet ahead was a nest of boulders to the right of the trail. The riders stopped in the boulder nest, and Slash swung down from the Appy's back.

He was sweaty, sunburned, and wind-burned, his heart racing.

"What's on your pea-pickin' mind, pard?" Pecos asked.

They could hear the train chugging toward them, from their left, along the same ridge they were on now, but maybe twenty feet below them and around a slight curve in the canyon wall. They couldn't yet see it below the rocky bulge in the ridge's shoulder.

Slash tossed Pecos the reins. "You take the horses. Head for the rapids. That's likely where they intend to get off."

He stared ahead along the canyon. He could see the white of the rapids maybe a mile ahead, where the stony walls on both sides of the canyon jutted skyward once more.

Pecos eyed his partner uneasily. "What the hell are you gonna do?"

The train was huffing and puffing, iron wheels clacking on the rail seams. Slash could feel the reverberations through his boot soles. The big, black locomotive came into view nearly straight down the slope from Slash and Pecos, drawing the tender car behind it. It was moving maybe fifteen, twenty miles per hour, the steam and smoke filling the air with the smell of brimstone.

At his angle, he couldn't see the engineer or the fireman inside the engine's black iron housing. The gang might have already taken them out.

Slash looked at Pecos and grinned. "I'm gonna hitch a ride. Hope the conductor don't mind I didn't buy a ticket!"

"You're loco!"

"Shut up!"

Slash stepped closer to the lip of the ridge they were on. He could see the gray tin roof of the second coach directly beneath him. In one of the cars below, a gun popped. A woman screamed. A man cursed loudly. Another shot followed, and another woman screamed.

"Stop tellin' me to shut up, or I'll pound your scrawny butt!"

"See you at the rapids, partner!" Slash stepped forward off the ridge, into thin air, stretching his Winchester out to one side and his free hand out to the other side for balance.

He bent his legs just before he hit the roof of the third car. He dropped to his knees and rolled backward, almost losing his rifle and clawing wildly at the corrugations in the tin roofing for purchase. His left hand slipped off the ridge he thought he'd had, and he continued rolling to the end of the car—rolling and sliding perilously toward the outside edge of the car, toward the canyon.

He cursed under his breath, heart pounding, as his legs dropped over the end corner of the car, one foot dangling toward the iron vestibule, the other toward the canyon. As he struggled to pull himself up, his hands slipping off the ridges in the corrugated roof, he heard several more gunshots in the very coach he was fighting to stay on.

Men were whooping and hollering. Women were screaming. A baby was crying hysterically.

"Fork-tailed devils," Slash said, gritting his teeth and clawing his way back onto the coach roof. "That . . . ain't . . . the way . . . we do it . . . boys!"

With that, he pulled his legs and feet back onto the roof and clambered up to the peak. He sat there for nearly a minute, catching his breath, the wind and high-altitude sun blasting against him. The Animas slid by on his left now as he faced the rear of the train; the stone wall of the ridge slid by on his right.

He doffed his hat, ran a hand through his thick, salt-and-pepper hair, then snugged the hat down tight on his head so it wouldn't blow off. He considered a plan of attack.

"Think I'll start at the end and make my way up toward the locomo—"

He stopped when he heard a shout from the express car flanking the coach car he was on. Answering shouts came from somewhere else. He glanced to his right. The rock wall had slid back away from the tracks, and now in the brush and rocks lining the canyon between the tracks and the wall he saw a half-dozen men and horses. Slash recognized members of his own gang.

They must have split up. Roughly half had leaped onto the train while the others had stationed themselves here to accept the strongboxes, which could only be opened with dynamite from the train itself, which they must have wanted to keep moving throughout the robbery for some reason.

Sure enough. There was a loud thud followed by another loud thud and then one more.

Slash turned to look toward the express car. Someone had just rolled three iron-banded strongboxes out of the express car's door facing the ridge. The boxes rolled and bounced amidst the rocks, kicking up dust, and the half-dozen gang members ran toward them.

One of those running men recognized Slash riding the crown of the third passenger coach. Donny Landusky pointed toward Slash, yelling, "Hey, it's him! It's him! It's Braddock! That's Braddock up there!"

But then the men running down the strongboxes fell back away behind the ridge wall that had suddenly shoved up to within a few feet of the tracks again.

Had anyone on the train heard him identify Slash?

Slash slowly gained his feet. He'd forgotten how hard it was to maintain your balance on a train car that pitched and rocked like a baby's cradle and continually shuddered as the iron wheels clattered over seams. He got close enough to the rear of the coach that he could see the coach car's front door open. It was the small door opening onto the vestibule between it and the rear of Slash's passenger car.

Slash ducked, dropped to a knee.

He waited. From his recent dangle over the passenger coach's end corner, he knew that a ladder ran up the rear wall, on that side, which was on his left now as he faced the rear.

He pumped a cartridge into his Yellowboy's action, pressed the butt against his shoulder. He aimed toward the rear left side of the car, waiting, staring at where the ladder poked up slightly from the rear wall.

Nothing.

He waited another couple of seconds.

The crown of a brown hat appeared. A bullet had nipped one side of the crown's crease. That would be "Big C" Chuck Dawkins, who had joined the gang only a year ago, when they were down in Arizona. He'd come from another gang that had disbanded when its leadership had succumbed to the bottle and found itself without a rudder.

Not a bad hombre, Big C. At least, Slash remembered him as a good jake.

Slash waited, caressing the hammer of his cocked Winchester with his gloved right thumb.

The brown hat slid upward until a pair of dark-brown eyes set in sunburned sockets rose just above the level of the coach's roof. The eyes snapped sharply to Slash, widened in recognition.

Slash smiled, nodded.

"It's him!" Big C shouted, and raised a cocked Colt over the top of the coach, aimed at Slash.

Or it would have been aimed at Slash if, before he'd gotten it leveled, Slash hadn't drilled a neat round hole through Big C's forehead, just above his left eye. Big C's Colt flared, the slug flying wide of its intended target.

Big C himself sagged backward off the ladder. There was a crunching thud as he fell off the train and apparently was smacked smartly by the front of the express car. The bullet-creased brown hat flew up over the coach car and then was whipped out over the canyon by the wind.

"Oh, boy," Slash said, hearing men frantically shouting in the car beneath him, ejecting the spent cartridge casing and seating a fresh round in the Yellowboy's action. "I do believe this dance is about to begin!"

He was right.

A gun barked behind him. The slug screeched over his right shoulder as he whipped around to face the man,

Snook Dodge, aiming a Winchester over the top of the coach car at him. Slash threw himself flat against the car's roof just in time to avoid another bullet exploding out the flame-lapping muzzle of Dodge's Spencer repeater. As Dodge worked the repeater's trigger guard cocking mechanism, Slash raised his rifle and fired—a hair too late.

Dodge had seen Slash bearing down on him and jerked his head down below the car's roof. Slash cursed and pumped another round into the chamber.

Dodge jerked his head back up, swinging the Spencer around once more. Slash fed the man a pill he couldn't digest, by way of Dodge's mouth, which he'd opened to hurl a curse at Slash at the same time he hurled lead.

Only, he hurled neither.

Dodge's head snapped back, eyes wide in shock at the bullet that had just drilled through the back of his mouth and out the back of his head, painting the panel of the car behind him with dark red blood.

He dropped the Spencer. Then he himself dropped away out of sight.

A gun barked in the coach below Slash, blowing a quarter-sized hole in the tin roof two feet to Slash's right.

"Holy . . . !"

As Slash scrambled to his feet, the gun barked again.

Another hole appeared six inches to his left.

Slash wanted to fire back through the roof at the hombre triggering lead at him from inside the coach, but he could hear the terrified passengers in there, down beneath his boots, and he didn't want to kill any of them by mistake. That wasn't what he was about. Never had been. Under the leadership of Billy Pinto, the Snake River Marauders had become a pack of bloodthirsty wolves.

Slash ran forward, avoiding more bullets hammering up from inside the coach, drilling quarter-sized holes through the corrugated tin roofing just behind his boots.

Slash leaped off the front end of the third passenger coach, hurdling the gap between the cars. He landed atop the end of the second passenger coach and dropped to his knees.

He stood there at the rear of the second coach, waiting, staring toward the grated iron floor of the vestibule below, wondering from where the next threat would come. Only vaguely, he became aware of the train picking up more speed as the front end of the long iron caterpillar began dropping.

Only vaguely, he wondered who, if anyone, was at the controls. . . .

Shouting issued from inside the third passenger coach. Slash stared at the closed door, waiting for one of the Marauders to emerge. Instead, there was a loud explosion. Like the triggering of both barrels of a double-barreled shotgun. A man in a blue wool uniform came plowing through the door, turning the door to splinters and smashing up against the rear wall of the coach Slash was on.

The man, a black man, lost his leather-billed conductor's hat as he sagged to the floor of the vestibule, his entire torso a mass of blood from the buckshot that had torn through him. He groaned and sagged in a lifeless, bloody heap.

A man poked his head out the door and glared up toward Slash.

No, not really a man. A kid. A towheaded kid wearing a low-crowned, black, felt sombrero with a beaded band and holding a sawed-off, double-barrel shotgun in his gloved hands, gray smoke curling from both barrels. The face was lean and clean-shaven but the brown eyes were flat. As flat as a snake's and twice as mean.

Billy Pinto laughed up at Slash, who snapped the Winchester to his shoulder. Billy drew his head back, laughing girlishly. He grabbed someone behind him—a young girl—

and tossed her out onto the vestibule. Slash had been in the process of firing the Winchester at Pinto and couldn't hold the bullet, but he managed to nudge the shot a hair wide so that it only grazed the girl's temple before smashing into the wall of the coach over her right shoulder.

She dropped to the vestibule floor, holding her head in both hands, screaming. She was small and frail. She couldn't have been over fourteen years old, around the same age as Bledsoe's granddaughter.

Inside the coach, Billy Pinto yammered like a wolf on the first night of a blue moon.

CHAPTER 35

"You little coward!" Slash bellowed toward the half-open coach door beyond which Billy Pinto was laughing. "Don't shield yourself with an innocent girl, you gutless heap of trash. Show yourself and fight!"

Just then a familiar voice muffled with distance shouted, "*Slash!*"

Slash glanced to his right. Pecos was sitting his buckskin on a low ridge just beyond the train. He held the reins of Slash's Appy in one hand. He was waving his other hand and pointing up toward the locomotive. His shouts were drowned by the chugging roar of the train and by the wind blowing over Slash's ears. But Slash thought he picked out the words "bridge" and "speed."

Before Slash had time to put the words together, a gun thundered in the car beneath Slash. A bullet tore up through the roof, kissing the outside edge of the sole of his left boot.

"Dang!"

Slash leaped forward, hurdling the gap between the passenger coaches again and landing on the roof of the coach he'd started out on. The wind nearly blew him off the coach and into the canyon. He dropped to the roof and grabbed a tin ridge with his gloved left hand, inadvertently releas-

312 William W. Johnstone and J.A. Johnstone

ing his grip on his Yellowboy, which dropped to the coach roof and slid away before Slash could grab it again. He watched in horror as his prized rifle dropped over the edge of the roof and out of sight.

He cursed roundly, clinging to the ridge for dear life until he got his feet back under him again.

The wind had grown stronger. The train was also rocking more violently.

It was then that Slash realized what Pecos had been trying to tell him.

Somewhere ahead along the severely dropping grade the apparently driverless train was barreling down, a bridge spanned a deep gorge. The train was picking up too much speed to cross the bridge without demolishing the bridge and hurling itself into Wild Horse Gorge, which Slash remembered scouting with Pecos back when they'd robbed the train a few years ago.

If he remembered right, the highest speed the bridge could handle was twenty miles per hour. Any more than that, the rickety wooden structure would rattle and shake and be quickly turned to jackstraws at the bottom of Wild Horse Gorge, making a prickly bed for the train that had destroyed it.

Without a doubt, the train was moving considerably faster than twenty miles an hour, and it was picking up more speed with every *clack* and *chug.*

A large, cold rock dropped in Slash's belly.

He didn't have time to consider the problem further at the moment, however, because just then another hatted head poked up above the opposite end of the passenger coach. Slash pressed his belly flat against the coach roof. The bark of the shooter's gun was muffled by the train's roar and the wind, but the bullet made a grisly screech as it ricocheted off the roof two inches right of Slash's cheek.

Slash clawed both his six-shooters from their holsters,

whipping them up and firing both several times, watching in satisfaction as the shooter's face, poking up just above the ladder, turned red. The man screamed and fell away.

Billy Pinto laughed shrilly beneath Slash. The kid fired through the roof, the bullet punching a hole just ahead of the middle-aged former outlaw.

Slash cursed and leaped to his feet. He ran—if you could call running the stiff-legged death dance he performed—as he headed toward the rear of the violently rocking coach while Pinto howled beneath him and drilled more slugs into the roof, just a few inches behind Slash's hammering boot heels.

The car lurched.

Slash's left boot jolted out beneath him, and he dropped to a knee with a curse. Knowing that Pinto would be honing in on the sound of his footsteps, he lurched to his feet and, sure enough, a bullet was sent hurling straight up through the place where Slash's boot had been planted a half a blink before.

Gaining the end of the car, Slash looked straight down.

As he'd suspected, two men stood there, pistols raised, grinning up at him, waiting. They were Kansas City Dave Schotz and the one-eyed C.J. Johnson.

Slash lurched straight back as the two pistoleers hurled lead at him. At the same time, Billy Pinto, having followed Slash's footsteps to the back of the train, punched another slug at him through the ceiling beneath his boots. Slash sucked a breath as the slug burned a hot line up his right leg and across the outside of his right arm.

Suppressing the galling pain of the burn, Slash stepped forward and fired both his Colts down into the vestibule.

"*Gnahhh!*" Kansas City Dave cried as he flipped backward over the brass handrail, hit the ground, and bounced off the side.

Slash's second shot had taken C.J. Johnson through the

man's chin, jerking his head back. He'd just started cater-wauling and bringing his own pistol back to bear on Slash when Slash drilled two more pills through his chest, making dust puff from the front of his corduroy vest and hickory shirt.

"Say hi to your brother Goose for me, C.J.!" Slash bellowed as the pistoleer did an imitation of Kansas City Dave, rolling backward over the brass rail, dropping to the ground, and quickly bouncing back out of sight.

Slash leaped down onto the ladder as two more slugs were punched up through the roof, again narrowly avoiding making him sing soprano. He slid straight down to the vestibule, kicked open the door, and raised both his cocked Colts straight out in front of him.

"I'll kill her!"

Billy Pinto stood just inside the coach door, grinning, holding a cocked, long-barreled Smith & Wesson to the head of the young blonde he'd shoved out of the front of the car a few minutes ago. The poor girl was bleeding from the gash Slash's bullet had carved across her right temple. Her blue eyes were wide and bright with fear.

"I'll kill her!" Pinto said, backing slowly down the aisle, away from Slash. "You stay right there, or I'll blow a hole right through her purty head, you old catamount!"

Slash followed him slowly down the aisle, stepping over a dead passenger whom Pinto or one of the other savage Marauders had killed—a fat, gray-haired man in a green suit. The dead man jerked from side to side with the violent rocking and swaying of the speeding train, which must have been doing a good forty miles an hour as it dropped down a steep hill. Slash tried to pull the brake through-chain that ran along the right side of the car, up near the ceiling. No good. Someone had rendered the through-chain inoperable, probably so that the brakes could be applied only in the locomotive.

"Don't do it, Billy," Slash warned as he continued moving along the aisle, leaning against the seats to either side of him to keep his balance. "You shoot her, I'll kill you quick as sin on a Saturday night in perdition. You know I will!"

"Stay right there, you old fool!" Billy screamed in a shrill girl's voice.

Slash slowed his pace, not wanting to get the poor blonde hurt any more than he'd already done himself. Around him, the car appeared only about half full, though it was hard to tell. Most of the passengers were hunkered down low or in their seats, mostly out of sight.

Slash could hear a woman sobbing and an injured man grunting. He just then walked past a woman cowering in a seat to Slash's left, crouching over her two children, shielding the boy and girl with her arms. She squeezed her eyes closed, muttering, praying.

"Don't kill me," cried the blonde to whose head Billy's cocked pistol was pressed. "Please don't kill me!"

Following her and Pinto slowly, aiming both his Colts straight out before him, Slash said, "Don't worry—he's not going to kill you, honey. He's not stupid. He doesn't want to die."

"Shut up you old blowhard!" Billy bellowed. "Didn't I tell you to stay where you was!"

He stopped suddenly and aimed his pistol straight out over the girl's right shoulder. Flames licked from the barrel. The bullet tore into Slash's upper left arm, throwing him backward and causing him to inadvertently dodge the next two bullets, which screamed over him to plunk into the coach's rear wall.

Slash hit the floor near the dead man, groaning, the bullet searing his arm, filling him with a white-hot agony and fury. He snapped his guns back up but Pinto had just wheeled, dragging the girl along behind him as he bolted out the front door and onto the vestibule.

Slash clambered his way back to his feet and ran shambling, staggering as though drunk with the coach's violent pitch and sway, to the front door that was swinging loose on its hinges. He bounded out, leaping across the vestibule, then twisting around and slamming his back against the next car's closed door.

Billy Pinto stood with the girl before him, to Slash's left.

"Die, you old devil!" Pinto screamed, triggering his pistol at Slash once more. "Die! Die! Die!"

He'd fired a shot on the heels of each "Die!" but only one hit home.

It was enough.

The bullet plowed into Slash's right side, maybe six inches above his belt and hammering him back against the coach door, grunting. He cursed loudly against the pain exploding inside him, then raised his Colts toward Pinto. But the young firebrand had just then hurled himself and the girl off the vestibule, the firebrand howling like a devil loosed from hell.

The girl screamed shrilly, horrifically.

Slash lunged toward the vestibule step and peered back along the train to see both Pinto and the girl rolling down a steep hill toward the Animas glinting in the canyon below. They rolled . . . rolled . . . and rolled, like rag dolls, dust kicking up around them, until they were gone from Slash's view.

Slash dropped to his knees, groaning.

He rested his back against the front of the coach he'd just emerged from.

He glanced to his right and left. The world passed in a blur as the train, dead-heading on a steep incline, headed toward the gorge and that rickety bridge.

Slash needed to get to the engine and stop the train or in a few minutes he and the rest of the passengers would be nothing more than fresh carrion at the bottom of Wild Horse Gorge. It might even be too late to get the train stopped in time to save it. They must be damned close to the bridge by now.

Still, he had to try.

He cursed loudly as, using every ounce of strength he had left, he heaved himself to his feet.

"Ahh!" he said with relief, having steadied his boots beneath him. "There!" He stepped forward, toward the next car. "Now . . . just . . . have . . . to . . ."

He reached for the knob of the next coach's rear door. He'd nearly grabbed it when a loud *thunk* muffled by the train's roar sounded from somewhere above. It was as though something big and heavy had landed on the roof of the coach ahead of him.

Thunk-thunk-thunk! came the sounds, one after another, each louder than the last.

Slash glowered up at the roof of the coach car ahead of him.

Then something big caromed off the roof and before he knew it, the big, hulking bulk of . . . of what—a *man?*— had smashed into Slash, laying him out on his back on the vestibule floor, head reeling, body feeling as though it had been doused with kerosene and set on fire.

"*Ohhh!*" Slash cried in misery.

He opened his eyes to see Pecos staring down at him, his partner's lips cracked and bleeding, his hair hanging over his face. His hat was gone. His sawed-off coach gun hung down in front of him by the lanyard around his neck and shoulder. Two blue eyes stared out from that tangle of long, gray-blond hair.

Gradually, they focused on Slash.

"Jesus jump!" Pecos exclaimed.

Slash stared at him in shock. "Oh, fer chrissakes! What . . . what the hell are *you* doin' here?"

"Jumpin' jiminy, Slash," Pecos cried, stretching his lips back from his teeth as he clutched his right arm. "I think I dislocated my shoulder!"

"Serves ya right, you corkheaded lummox!"

"What the hell are you so sore about?"

"You damn near killed me!"

"How do you think *I* feel? I misjudged the drop from the ridge! And I didn't realize the train was moving this fast!" Pecos gazed incredulously at Slash. "What the hell you been *doin'*, anyway—playin' poker on a runaway train?"

"What did *I* do? You almost killed me, you privy snipe. I been shot twice. And then you come rollin' down off that roof like a boulder down a mountain!"

"Oh, hell!" Pecos pushed up onto his butt and eased his back against the wall of the forward car. "I'm the injured party here. You been hurt worse fallin' into bed drunk!"

"Once!"

"Stop complainin' is all I'm sayin'."

"You're in better shape than I am, you corkheaded scalawag. Hightail your raggedy butt up to the locomotive. If you don't get this train stopped, we're gonna be spending the night at the bottom of Wild Horse Gorge!"

"What about the through-chain?"

"Disengaged!"

"Damnation!" Pecos leaned forward with a grunt. With a louder grunt, he heaved himself to his feet. Leaning back against the coach wall for purchase, he glanced around. "I lost my hat."

"Get up to the locomotive, you lummox!"

"It was a good hat!"

Slash glared at him.

"All right . . ." Pecos waved him off, then turned and pushed through the door of the forward coach. There were a good dozen people in the car, all cowering in seats. Two men lay dead in the aisle. A young, red-haired woman in a poke bonnet, and sitting on the right side of the middle aisle, turned her head from the blanketed infant she cradled before her in both arms. When her horrified gaze found big Pecos stumbling down the middle of the car, she screamed and lurched back against the wall.

Pecos held a calming hand out to her. "I'm friendly, honey! I'm friendly!"

"Are we a runaway?" yelled a small, gray-haired man in a charcoal suit and string tie, hunkered down against the coach's left wall.

"Yessir, I think so!" Pecos said, continuing on down the aisle.

"We're doomed!" bellowed an elderly lady behind Pecos. "Doomed! Let's all get right with the Lord! Bow your heads in prayer, sinners!"

"She's right," another old man yelled somewhere behind Pecos. "Wild Horse Gorge is likely dead ahead!"

"It is, indeed," Pecos said, aloud but mostly to himself as he shoved out through the coach's front door. "It is, indeed. . . ."

CHAPTER 36

Pecos crossed the vestibule and walked as though badly inebriated through the very first coach in the three-passenger-car string, finding two more dead men, one slumped forward across a seat back, and one dead woman. The other passengers were howling and cowering, a baby screaming shrilly while its very young mother sobbed, tears streaming down her cheeks.

Stepping over the dead woman, who must have objected to being robbed and was thus shot through the dead center of her forehead, Pecos bounded out the coach's front door.

Now he faced the back of the tender car. He climbed the tender car's ladder into the giant, wood-filled bin. He crawled over the neatly stacked wood, dislodging some of it, wincing when slivers bit into his hands and knees and thighs. In the locomotive just ahead, he saw the fireman and the engineer both slumped in death.

The fireman sat back against the firebox that heated the boiler. He stared straight ahead. Blood from a bullet to his left ear dribbled down his neck, beneath his knotted red neckerchief and into the collar of his hickory shirt. Just beyond him, the engineer stood crouching forward, as though looking for something he'd dropped on the hard, grease-stained iron floor. His straw-blond hair slid around in the wind, showing the mat lines made by a hat that was now gone.

Pecos continued crawling, glancing at the engineer and then out beyond the train at the tracks that the big iron horse was chewing up way too fast.

"Hellfire an' damnation!" Pecos bellowed, stopping suddenly, lower jaw dropping. A cold steel rod of trepidation drove itself up against his spine, from his tailbone to the back of his neck.

The bridge stretched a brown line across the deep chasm opening before him maybe a half mile away but coming up fast. Way too fast to get the train stopped in time before it hurled itself out onto the bridge.

Under a train this heavy and moving this fast, the bridge would start losing timbered struts immediately. Long before the locomotive could gain the other side—a hundred yards across the chasm—the bridge would tumble down beneath the iron wheels, like a wind-blown house of cards. The train and all its passengers, young mothers and babies included, would plunge to the bottom of Wild Horse Gorge.

Pecos dropped over the bulkhead and into the locomotive, losing his footing on the floor of the badly swaying engine, and fell over the legs of the dead fireman. He cursed roundly, clambered back to his feet, and drunk-walked over to the engineer.

He pulled the man's head up by his hair and drew back a little when he saw what a bullet had done to the poor cuss's right eye socket, fired from what appeared point-blank range. It had bounced around in his skull and exited the left side of his neck.

Pecos would have bet gold ingots against navy beans that the gang had killed these two first. For some reason, they'd wanted to keep the train moving. No, Pecos knew the reason. They'd intended for all eyewitnesses to end up at the bottom of Wild Horse Gorge.

So they'd killed the engineer and slumped his body over the brakes' dead-release lever that disengaged the through-chain that ran through the other cars.

"Sorry, fella." Pecos shoved the engineer off the long, wooden-handled brake. He dropped with a dull thud to the floor.

Pecos drew back on the brake, grunting, putting all his weight into it. The locomotive trembled beneath his boots, the brake jaws grabbing at the iron wheels of every coach in the combination.

"Oh, hell!" he cried as the brake handle fought against him, wanting to climb back to the left. The combination's forward momentum was just too great for the brakes. They wouldn't grab. Pecos cursed again, grabbing the handle with both hands and shoving his torso against it, heaving it left.

No doing.

The lever picked him up off the floor and then backward as it angled back to the right, the jaws resisting the force of the barreling iron wheels.

"Forget it!"

Pecos whipped his head around to see Slash staggering toward him from the tender car, bleeding from low on his right side and from his upper left arm. He looked as pale as death, his thick, salt-and-pepper hair blowing around his head in the wind.

"We're going too fast!" Slash lifted the firebox's iron door, yanked the door wide. He reached back into the tender car, yelling over his shoulder, "Help me!"

"What the hell you doing, you loco shoat?"

Slash stuffed two sticks of split wood into the firebox.

"Our only chance is to get across fast enough that that

bridge don't even know we're on it till we reach the other side!"

"You're crazier'n a peach orchard sow!"

"Yes, I am, but this is our only chance, partner!"

Slash shoved more wood into the dragon's maw of the firebox. Pecos threw up his hands, fatefully shaking his head, then, knowing his partner was right—gallblast his handsome mug, anyway!—sprang into action.

"Sit down before you bleed dry!" Pecos ordered Slash.

When he had the box roaring, stuffed to brimming with well-seasoned firewood, Slash closed the door and rammed the iron locking bar into place. He stepped over to the side of the housing, poked his head out to stare up the tracks.

He'd already known they were on the bridge, because he'd heard the timbers groaning, felt the locomotive pitching and swaying from side to side—even more than when they'd been barreling over solid ground. He could feel the reverberations run through the bridge beneath him.

"Ah, hell!" Pecos had peered out the locomotive's opposite side. He glanced back over his shoulder at Slash. "That old woman had it right—I think it's time to get right with the Lord, partner!"

"I'm as right as I'm ever gonna get!" Slash bellowed into the wind, grinding his molars when he saw several timbers dislodging from the bridge ahead of the engine.

"Then I reckon you best get ready to shake hands with ole Scratch!" Pecos bellowed back with a nervous laugh.

The timbers peeled away from the bridge, tumbling down . . . down . . . down . . . occasionally slamming into timbers below, dislodging a few of them, too, then spinning and turning end over end, plunging into the Animas running through the gorge two hundred feet below.

Slash could smell the cloying odor of pine tar wafting on the wind.

The timbers splashed into the water far away down there, causing explosions of white around them, like little scalloped stitches on a blue satin gown—one after another, until, as Slash watched, the whole damn bridge appeared to be collapsing before his own eyes as he and Pecos were barreling across it. . . .

The world grew blurry through Slash's eyes as the bridge shuddered, the locomotive shuddering, too, and thus Slash shuddering along with it.

"I think we're gonna die, Slash!" Pecos bellowed, his voice shuddering too because he was shuddering inside the locomotive shuddering atop the shuddering bridge.

Slash had a dizzy, unreal feeling. A giddy feeling. In his mind he already began to drop down through the collapsing bridge toward the blue waters of the gorge. But then, suddenly, the world clarified. He was no longer dropping but caroming forward.

The blurriness went away, and Slash found himself no longer staring at the bridge disintegrating ahead and below him. He was staring at the cinder-paved bed of the rails, at the precious little rocks and pinecones and twigs and fallen leaves . . . at a forested ridge pushing up close on his left.

He turned toward Pecos, who sat facing straight ahead, eyes closed, a weird little smile on his face, as though the big, blond cutthroat were preparing to meet the angels.

Slash heard a laugh lurch up out of his chest.

Pecos opened his eyes. He stared straight ahead, frowning. He turned to Slash, opening his mouth a little with shock and chagrin.

Slash laughed louder.

Pecos turned his head to stare out his side of the locomotive. Over there, a ridge of blue-green pines dropped down toward the rail bed, as well.

Slash swung his head to peer back behind him, along

the train snaking after the locomotive, one car after another trailing off the bridge that continued to quiver and sway, rock violently to and fro as more and more timbers began to tumble away beneath it. Finally, its center bucked up violently, as though a giant, invisible hand chopped up through it from below.

It was like two sheets of ice plunging together on a frozen lake.

Both ends dropped.

Slash sucked his breath, staring at the caboose at the very end of the train.

The back end of the caboose plunged downward as the bridge gave beneath it. There was a vast roar of complaining steel as the underbelly of the caboose, still being pulled by the train ahead of it, slammed into the side of the cliff and ground there, against the cliff itself, the couplings all through the train clanging loudly as the caboose pulled back against the locomotive, in the opposite direction.

The locomotive, which had been slowing quickly as Slash applied the brake and the caboose pulled back from behind, ground to a lurching halt.

A loud groaning and hissing sounded from inside the locomotive.

A fitting popped. Steam exploded out of a blown release valve. It was like the detonation of a Napoleon cannon.

"The boiler's too hot, Slash!" Pecos bellowed, lurching toward the locomotive's steps. "She's gonna blow!"

Slash hurried after him, grunting against the pain of his throbbing wounds. Pecos stopped at the edge of the steps, wrapped Slash's right arm around his neck, snaked his own left arm around his partner's waist, and helped him down the steep iron rungs to the ground.

They headed for the trees as behind them the boiler groaned and chugged like a giant's belly after he'd enjoyed too many chili peppers in his lunchtime meal.

"She's gonna blow, Slash!"

"I know! I know!" Slash was moving stiffly. He'd grown weak from blood loss, and the wounds were biting him deep. He hurried along beside Pecos, sort of skip-hopping on his right foot. As they moved into the trees and brush, climbing the steep ridge, they stopped behind a giant fir and crouched, poking their fingers into their ears.

They'd witnessed boiler explosions before and it was neither pretty nor quiet.

They each edged a look around opposite sides of the tree.

The boiler clanged and wheezed, as though a smithy were inside, banging around with a hammer. A sudden clanging explosion made the ground lurch beneath the cutthroats' knees. The front cap of the locomotive blew out like a giant cannonball fired straight up the tracks. Anyone in its way would have been pulverized.

Several smaller fittings gave way, as well, with the sound of a half-dozen rifles being fired at the same time. One of those fittings, roughly the size of a man's fist, slammed into the backside of the tree Slash and Pecos cowered behind. The fir bucked and trembled. Other fittings blew straight out the back of the locomotive and against the tender car, which reared like a disgruntled stallion.

More fittings blew straight up in the air, releasing the frantic screech of released steam and boiler water.

To top it all off, the locomotive leaped up off the ground, tearing free of its rear coupling. It turned nearly entirely over about fifty feet in the air above the tracks and slammed back down to the ground on the cab's steel canopy, on the far side of the rail bed.

Again, the ground lurched beneath Slash's and Pecos's knees. Pinecones tumbled from branches above their heads.

The engine's front end was angled up the slope, knocking over several pines. It slid slowly and violently back down toward the rail bed, plowing up dirt, grass, and shrubs in the process, groaning loudly to lie idle on the far side of the tracks, wheels in the air, sighing out its last breaths, like a gutted iron dinosaur.

Boiling water bathed it, pie-sized bubbles sputtering.

Slash and Pecos glanced at each other, awestruck.

When the last of the boiling water had rained down, turning to mud the area around the ruined engine, Slash and Pecos heaved themselves to their feet and stepped out from behind the fir. Clutching his wounded right side, gritting his teeth against the pain of both wounds, Slash followed Pecos back down the slope to where the tender car sat back on its haunches, like a well-trained circus horse waiting to be signaled it could stand. The coupling resembled the frayed end of a rope.

Inspecting the wreckage, they walked slowly, like men in a trance, back along the trail toward the chasm. As they passed the three passenger coaches, passengers peered out the open windows, also appearing like people in a trance or maybe sleepwalking. The baby was still wailing. Slash could hear women and children sobbing or crying.

Several men had gathered on the vestibules between the cars, looking around, muttering amongst themselves in the hushed tones of a funeral.

Slash followed Pecos all the way back along the train to stand by the caboose, staring out over the gorge.

Only a very small part of the bridge remained, poking a hundred feet out from the opposite ridge. Even as Slash and Pecos gazed at it, however, it lost more of the timbers comprising it. A few seconds later, it hiccupped, shuddered, broke away from the ridge, and tumbled down into the gorge where the rest of the bridge was being washed downstream by the fickle currents of the Animas.

To the cutthroats' left, the caboose hung down over the side of the gorge.

The coupling attaching it to the express car in front of it groaned against the strain of its weight. The sounds were similar to the sounds that had issued from the overheated locomotive only a few minutes before. It made Slash's and Pecos's hair stand on end.

The caboose lurched violently downward. The groaning grew louder.

The wheels of the express car screeched along the rails as it lurched backward, pulled by the caboose as the couplings on several other cars in front of it banged like drums.

"Oh, hell," Pecos said. "She's gonna go!"

CHAPTER 37

Slash turned to where the passengers were dropping slowly down off the train, looking around like aliens from another planet.

"Everybody off!"

He waved his right arm, wincing against the strain that the gesture grieved his bullet-battered body. To the men regarding him skeptically, he yelled, "Make sure everybody's off the train! Looks like she'll be dropping into the canyon! Get everybody off!"

Several men leaped back into the train, and soon everybody appeared to be off, the women and children sitting down against the pine-carpeted slope, a few of the men walking slowly toward where Slash and Pecos stood dubiously watching the caboose.

It lurched again.

Then again . . . and again.

Slash and the other men who'd walked over to join them stepped back as the coupling jaws tore away from each other with an enormous, thunder-like peel of tearing iron and steel. The brakes gave, as well. They watched in awe as the caboose fell straight down the cliff wall. It fell and fell and fell, occasionally gouging a boulder or a spindly tree or shrub out of the side of the wall.

Then it slowly turned backward, flipping butt over teakettle before quickly growing smaller as it plunged toward the Animas, hammering into the river with a loud thudding and tearing sound, which was the water's distant splash.

"Jeepers, there goes another one!" one of the other men exclaimed as the Wells Fargo express car rolled backward.

Everybody including Slash and Pecos stepped back again as the express car's rear wheels, ripping free of the brake sleeves, rolled backward off the broken rails. The car's rear end plunged violently. The front coupling roared free, and the car did a very good imitation of the caboose—dropping and dropping straight down toward the Animas winking below.

Its rear end smashed into the side of the canyon. After that, it rolled wildly as it dropped, like a tossed craps dice, until it too plunged into the river, driven beneath the surface for a few seconds before floating back upward, then rolling slowly on downstream, dragging against rocks embedded in the stream's bottom.

Having been pulled toward the canyon, all the other cars were rolling backward now, as well—one by one and hand in hand, the couplings holding, dropping over the side of the cliff and plunging into the Animas like one giant caterpillar.

Suddenly, except for the gutted and overturned locomotive, no cars remained on the rails. The passengers stared in hang-jawed shock at where the train had stood only a moment before. Even the baby that had been crying shrilly now stared in silent shock from where its mother held it against her chest, opening and closing its little hand as though doing a silent count of the cars that were no longer there.

A rifle barked once, twice, three times.

Slash, Pecos, and the other men grouped along the lip of the ridge flinched with starts.

The rifle shots echoed hollowly, chasing each other over the canyon.

Pecos raised an arm, pointing. "There!"

Slash stretched his gaze across the chasm. Five or six horseback riders were gathered on the canyon's far side, roughly a quarter mile away, outlined against the blue sky behind them. There appeared to also be two beefy horses, maybe mules, outfitted with packsaddles. They flanked the horsebackers, one of whom carried an extra rider.

Slash recognized Billy Pinto and the blond girl the young killer had taken off the train. Pinto held the girl before him on his saddle. He and the others were facing Slash and Pecos's side of the canyon.

The girl was crouched forward as though trying to put as much distance as possible between herself and the firebrand. It wasn't much.

Pinto yelled something that Slash couldn't hear from this distance. The pitch of his voice, however, was taunting. Billy waved his rifle, jeering, mocking the aging cutthroats.

"That's Elsie!" said a burly, bearded man in overalls, standing to the right of Pecos, pointing across the canyon. "They got my granddaughter! Those dirty polecats!"

Pinto waved his rifle again. Slash could hear him laughing. Then all five of the surviving gang of Marauders reined their mounts away from the canyon and disappeared.

"They got Elsie!" cried the bearded man, who appeared in his mid-sixties. He turned to Slash and Pecos. "They got my granddaughter. Someone's gotta do something!"

Slash dropped his gaze toward the canyon floor. His and Pecos's horses stood on the river's far side, reins tied to their saddle horns. Pecos's buckskin was dipping its head toward the river, drawing water. Slash's Appy stared up toward its rider and the other men on this side of the canyon. The well-trained horses had followed the train, knowing that their riders were aboard.

"Elsie!" the old man bellowed hoarsely in anguish, leaning forward at the waist. "Elsieeeeeee!"

"We'll get her," Slash told the old man. "Don't worry, old-timer. We'll get her back."

Pecos turned to Slash. "How do you propose we do that?" He dropped his gaze to the two wounds oozing blood from his partner's hide. "Even if we didn't have a river between us and our hosses, you're in no shape to do anything except head back to that sawbones in Silverton. You got two bullets in you, partner, an' you're bleedin' bad!"

"We gotta find a way across that stream," Slash said, shrugging out of his suit coat. "There's gotta be a way across."

"There is," another man said—a short, stocky gent in a shabby brown and orange suit. Holding a large leather satchel in one hand, he appeared a drummer of some kind. "I once prospected before I turned to sellin' whiskey. A whole lot easier on an old man's joints, don't ya know."

"What about it?" Slash had removed his vest and now he was unbuttoning his shirt.

"I prospected along the Animas back before the Denver and Rio Grande laid rails an' built that bridge. East along the rim here"—he jerked his head to his right—"the wall drops considerable. It's an easy way down to the water. A little ways farther east, there's a shallow ford. You could get across that river and over to them horses in a half hour or so. Maybe forty-five minutes."

Breaking open his sawed-off barn-blaster to make sure both tubes were loaded, Pecos looked at Slash. "You stay here. I'll get after 'em."

"Not a chance."

"Look at you!"

"Flesh wounds, both. I can ride. I just need to tie these wounds and kill the pain." Slash walked over to the drummer. "What you got in your valise?"

The man frowned down at the satchel, then held it up, protectively, against his chest. "Why, whiskey samples, of course . . ."

"Just what the doctor ordered."

"Wha . . . wha . . . you can't . . . !"

Slash pulled the valise out of the man's hand. He unbuckled the straps and reached inside to see four flat bottles secured by leather loops. "Indeedy," he said, removing two bottles, shoving one into his back pants pocket, then returning the valise to the drummer. "Just what the doctor ordered."

While Pecos and the other men watched him, deeply incredulous, Slash lifted the first bottle to his lips and half emptied it. The busthead was pure rotgut probably brewed in some Denver alley with snake heads and strychnine, and then adorned with a fancy label, but he'd be damned if it didn't set up a burning glow inside his head and belly and file the teeth off the rabid dog tearing into his arm and side.

He ripped a sleeve from his shirt, bathed it in whiskey, then wrapped it securely around his arm.

"You're crazier'n a tree full of owls," Pecos said, walking over to tie off the ends of the shirtsleeve around Slash's arm. "But you still got the hide on—I'll give ya that."

"I'll take it."

Pecos glanced at Slash. "You ready?"

"Do it."

Pecos jerked both ends of the whiskey-damp sleeve taut over the wound and tied it tight.

Slash tipped his head back, growling like that rabid cur with its foot in a trap and casting aspersions upon his partner's lineage.

When he'd taken another couple of painkilling pulls from the bottle, he soaked a portion of the rest of his shirt, then gave it to Pecos, who wrapped it around his waist, covering both ends of the bullet wound that had carved a ragged tunnel through his flesh above his cartridge belt.

"My granny did no such thing," Pecos said with mock indignation. "Besides, she hated coyotes!"

He drew the shirt tight and tied it off behind Slash's back.

Again, Slash ground his molars and roared before draining the bottle, then tossing it into the canyon.

"With that, mi amigo," he said, sliding his Colt from the cross-draw holster on his left hip and twirling it, still gritting his teeth against the bite of both wounds, "let's ride like hell, burn the rest of the Marauders down, and let the devil take the hindmost!"

Pecos shook his head and began walking eastward along the rim of the canyon. "You ain't gonna make it. You *were* just shot. Now, you're shot up an' drunk to boot!"

Slash fell into step behind the big man, leaning forward and placing his hands on his broad shoulders. "You lead the way an' stop chinnin'. I purely can't wait to kill that kid, an' it's gonna be me that gets to do it, by God. He done pulled the sheep over ole Slash's eyes, pretendin' he was sweeter'n fresh-spun honey and as innocent as an Amish bride on the eve of her weddin' night. Instead, he was playin' me!"

"He was playin' us both," Pecos pointed out, seeing the drop in the wall just ahead.

"Yeah, but you're played all the time," Slash said, keeping his hands on Pecos's shoulders, leaning into him hard to keep from falling. "Now, Slash, see? Slash don't *get* played!"

"Oh, shut up!"

"Don't tell me to shut up, you big galoot!"

"Shut up!"

Slash didn't take another drink until they'd descended the canyon by way of that easy drop in the cliff wall and had crossed the stream via a rocky ford, barely getting their boots wet. He was worn out, however, so when he gained his Appy, he fell forward against the saddle and, clinging to the horn by one hand, used the other hand to fumble the whiskey out of his back pocket.

The first sip braced him.

The second sip braced him even more, and leashed that flesh-hungry dog that had started nipping at his arm and side again in earnest when they'd been halfway across the river.

He was so soothed that he felt gracious enough to extend the bottle to Pecos, who'd swung up onto his buckskin's back, from which he regarded Slash as though he were something a bird had left on his own saddle. Pecos waved off the drink.

"Suit yourself," Slash said, grinning, and tossed back another shot. "More for me!"

"If you keep imbibing like that, you're gonna be three sheets to the wind by the time we catch up to Pinto an' them other savages."

"Nah." Slash shoved the bottle back into his pocket. Clumsily, he heaved himself into the saddle, then, getting comfortable, flashed his partner a toothy, drunken grin. "I straighten up at the trigger."

Pecos gave a wry snort as he reined his horse around

and looked for a way up the canyon wall on this side of the Animas.

Slash reached instinctively for his saddle boot. Only, his Yellowboy wasn't there. He remembered watching it bounce off the top of that coach car to fall somewhere either in the canyon or beside the tracks. Likely gone for good.

"Hell's bells," he grouched. "I sure feel naked without my Winchester."

"Yeah, you ain't much good without it, either," Pecos said. "Why don't you do the sensible thing for once in your misguided life and ride on back to Silverton before you die out here and I gotta take the time to plant your sorry butt?"

"You're green with envy." Slash used his teeth to tighten the knot on the bandage around his wounded arm. "You know I'm twice as handy as you ever were with a six-shooter, an' I got these two purty ladies." He glanced down at his Colts.

Pecos rolled his eyes as he booted his horse toward a trail he'd spotted angling up the canyon wall. "Come on then, if you're comin'. If you die, be kind enough to drop in a hole so I don't have to dig you a grave."

"Oh, shut up with all that grave talk!"

Pecos glared over his shoulder at him. "Stop tellin' me to shut up!"

"Shut up!"

"You shut up, or I'll kick your scrawny butt!"

Slash held his tongue. In his raggedy-heeled state, Pecos was right. He could kick Slash's butt up around his shoulders. Slash had witnessed what the big man could do when riled. He'd left more than a few demolished saloons in his wake as well as howling and toothless men.

When they gained the crest of the ridge twenty minutes later, they stopped to rest the horses. Slash didn't dismount because in his weakened condition he didn't want to have to expend the energy to climb back into his saddle again. Pecos kicked around in the short, wiry, brown grass until he'd found Pinto's tracks, and the other Marauders' as well as the pack animals' tracks, along with several fresh horse apples.

Slash took another pull from his bottle, enduring Pecos's reproving scowl. Then they set off once more, following the clearly delineated trail of the men they were after.

CHAPTER 38

It was late in the day, mountain shadows stretching out from the west wall of the narrow valley Slash and Pecos found themselves in, when, smelling wood smoke on the cooling breeze, they stopped and swung down from their saddles.

Ten minutes later, they lay belly down in rocks and boulders, peering toward a small fire in a slight clearing in the aspens before them. Flanking the fire was a chuckling creek, another tributary of the Animas River, which Pinto and the other five riders had been following from Wild Horse Gorge, likely beginning their long southerly trek down toward Mexico where, with all the gold they'd taken from the express car, they could live like kings.

For a few years, at least. Until they'd blown all their plunder.

It was Billy Pinto and five other Marauders, all right. The young girl, as well. Slash could see them all clearly through the spyglass he held up to his right eye, sweeping the camp with his gaze.

Apparently, they'd ordered the girl to cook for them. She knelt by the fire, shoulders slumped, halfheartedly chopping meat for a stew pot beside her. She wore a bandage around the top of her head, likely to doctor the bullet burn Slash had inadvertently given her on the train. Billy Pinto and Cletis Brown were down on one knee, gazing into one of the three strongboxes they'd set out in the trees just left of the fire, near where they'd tied their horses to a picket line tied to two aspens.

Earl Willey and Poncho Davis were just then each hauling armloads of firewood toward the fire. Tex Halstrom stood over the girl, fingering her hair, needling her. Young Elsie was doing her best to ignore the tall, lanky Texan, who wore two pearl-gripped Bisley .44s in shoulder holsters on the outside of his brown leather vest. His rifle leaned against a nearby tree.

The sixth man, Randall "Doc" Peterson, was at that moment standing off to the right of the fire, evacuating his bladder, leaning back slightly, fists on his hips. Gray smoke wafted from the quirley dangling from between his lips. It was so quiet out here that Slash could hear him singing softly to himself above the chuckling of the stream beyond him, as he dribbled into the grass.

They were all here, all right. All six surviving members of the Snake River Marauders. They'd posted no picket. They'd done nothing to cover their tracks from the gorge, and they hadn't picked the most appropriate place to build a cook fire, either. Obviously, they believed Slash and Pecos were still on the opposite side of Wild Horse Gorge, and that no one else was trailing them.

A tinhorn move if there ever was one . . .

Slash gave the spyglass to Pecos, then took another liberal slug from his whiskey bottle, draining it. Pecos gave the camp a long, critical gander, then lowered the glass and turned to his partner. He grinned.

"What's so funny?"

"They got your Yellowboy. Leastways, it looks like yours, and I don't remember any of them carrying a Winchester Yellowboy repeater." Pecos gave the spyglass back to Slash. "Look at the rifle leanin' against the tree near Billy."

Quickly, heart thudding hopefully, Slash peered through the glass. He focused on the rifle—a Winchester with a brass receiver and cocking lever—leaning against the pine near Billy Pinto, Cletis Brown, and the strongboxes.

Slash lowered the glass, smiling. "I'll be damned. Time to thank that little snake for finding it along the tracks! Only, I remember catchin' him eyein' that Winchester a time or two. Probably wondering how he could steal it . . . ."

Pecos said, "How should we play it? Wait till it's a little darker, then come around from behind 'em?"

"Hell, no." Slash pushed up onto his knees, tossed the empty bottle aside, and shucked his Colts. "You know what I always say—there ain't no time like the present. Besides, I'm right lonely without my Yellowboy!"

"Wait—hold on!" Pecos said under his breath. "You're drunk!"

"Maybe so, partner, but I—"

"Yeah, yeah, I know," Pecos said dreadfully. "You straighten up at the trigger."

Grinning, Slash cocked his Colts.

"Wait for me, now!" Pecos stood, slid his shotgun around in front of him, checked to make sure both tubes were deadly. Snapping the Richards closed, he picked up his rifle and looked at Slash, who stood glaring, a muscle in his cheek twitching, toward Billy Pinto.

Pinto had just gotten up from where he'd been kneeling by the open strongbox with Cletis Brown, giggling like a hyena.

"We're so damn rich," he cried, "I feel like dancin'!"

He marched over to the fire and dragged Miss Elsie up off her knees. She gave a little cry of protest, but it did her no good. Pinto immediately took her off dancing a scuffling, bizarre sort of waltz to the left of the fire. Her feet were bare, and she groaned at the pine needles and small, sharp rocks grieving her feet.

Billy hummed loudly to the music, if you could call it that, of his haphazard, manic waltz, his spurs trilling, dust kicking up around his boots. He stepped on the girl's feet several times, and she cried out in pain.

Billy stopped suddenly and slapped her with the back of his hand. "You stop complainin' and dance with me!"

The others laughed. Standing with Tex Halstrom and Poncho Davis by the fire, Earl Willey spit out a mouthful of the whiskey he'd been drinking straight out of the bottle he and the others were passing around.

Sobbing, the girl danced, though it was obvious her heart was not in it but she was only shuffling her feet to save her life.

Slash glanced at Pecos, who now stood glaring toward the fire himself.

"Let's get this done," Slash said.

"I hear that."

"Don't hit the girl."

"I hear that, too!"

Slash stepped out around the rocks and shrubs. He marched holding his cocked Colts straight down at his side. Pecos strode out to Slash's right and raised his Colt revolving rifle, aiming straight out from his right shoulder.

Billy Pinto had just screamed at and slapped the girl once more, who'd dropped to her knees, sobbing.

Gritting his teeth, Slash raised both his Colts, aimed, and punched a bullet through the kid's left leg. Pinto lifted his clean-shaven face and howled maniacally.

Pecos's rifle roared twice on the heels of Slash's first, still-echoing shot, blowing both Poncho Davis and Earl Willey off their feet with clipped screams, dying fast.

Slash drew a bead on Cletis Brown, who'd been sitting

atop a log near the strongboxes, swilling from a bottle. Brown had dropped the bottle when Pinto had yelled, and jerked his surprised eyes toward the two cutthroats walking out from the thicket on the north side of the clearing.

Slash's next slug punched into Brown's thick right shoulder, evoking a shrill cry and knocking the man back off the log, where he flopped, trying to unholster one of his three six-shooters.

Meanwhile, Pecos had just shot Tex Halstrom, who reached for his rifle as soon as Billy had screamed. Halstrom dropped his rifle, jackknifing forward from the bullet in his guts, fumbling for the pistol on his hip. Pecos fired two more rounds. One plunked into Halstrom's right knee, the other one into his left arm, making it flap out wide, like a broken wing. The tall Texan stumbled back and around and fell face first into the fire, howling and kicking.

Doc Peterson had just gotten himself tucked back into his pants after evacuating his bladder, and now as the Texan fell into the fire, Doc bellowed, "I'll be damned— it's them two old goats, Slash an' Pecos!"

Pecos's next shot missed Peterson, who grabbed his rifle and ran back into the trees, away from the fire.

"Dammit!" Pecos bellowed, and fired again as he strode after Peterson.

Both Slash's Colts bucked in his fists as he hurled lead toward the still howling Billy Pinto, who had just then run, limping, off to Slash's left, grabbing the Yellowboy leaning against the pine and stepping behind it, pumping a cartridge into the chamber. Slash slammed two more bullets into the side of the tree just as Billy had edged a look out from behind it.

The bark splattered into the kid's face, making him howl even louder.

"You go to hell, you old devil!" he screeched.

A gun barked to Slash's left. The bullet was a knife's nick across the outside of Slash's left ear. Slash turned to see Cletis Brown trigger another shot at him from behind the log. That bullet howled just wide of Slash's head. Flinching, Slash raised both his Colts, aiming at Brown's head.

Both Colts roared at the same time, planting neat, round holes in Brown's forehead, just above each eye. Brown's head bounced like a rubber ball against the log and then dropped out of sight behind the log. Just beyond the log, his legs and boots kicked spasmodically.

"Help me!" Tex Halstrom roared shrilly from where he was rising up out of the fire—a human torch running straight out away from the camp and into the darkening trees, apparently heading for the river.

The girl lay belly down in front of the fire, swatting at the sparks that had geysered out of it when Halstrom had landed in it.

The horrific vision of Tex Halstrom running into the trees engulfed in bright orange flames had stunned Billy Pinto, who stared toward him in shock. Slash saw the kid's rifle poking out from behind the pine. He triggered both Colts at it. One of the bullets tore into Billy's left hand. The kid shrieked and dropped the rifle as though it were a hot potato. He stared at his bloody left hand, howling.

"Damn you! Damn you!" Unholstering one of his two Remington revolvers, Billy strode angrily out from behind the tree. He was limping badly. He was squeezing one eye closed, the eye with the bark in it. He limped over to where Elsie lay on the ground and extended his pistol at her head.

Slash walked toward him, drawing a bead on him, firing.

Only, his right-hand Colt clicked empty.

"I'm gonna kill this little girl, an' it's gonna be all your fault!"

"Just like you did to the girl from La Junta?"

Billy didn't respond to that. He clicked his Remy's hammer back and pressed the barrel to the back of the girl's head.

Still striding toward the kid and the girl, Slash triggered his second Colt.

Billy screamed as the bullet tore into his left arm.

He stumbled backward as though drunk, grunting, staring at Slash in bright-eyed fear.

"No!" he cried, dropping the Remington as he got his boots under him and ran shambling off into the trees, in the general direction in which the human torch of Tex Halstrom had fled.

Slash dropped to a knee by the girl, who lay belly down, sobbing.

Slash placed a hand on her shoulder. "It's okay, honey. You're gonna be all right. We'll get you out of here soon . . . back to your grandpa."

She looked up at him in surprise, sobbing.

"That's right." Slash was punching the spent shells out of his first Colt and replacing them with fresh from his cartridge belt. "Everything's gonna be all right. . . ."

He turned to his right, toward where Pecos was exchanging shots with Doc Peterson, Peterson howling and cursing and Pecos bellowing back at him amidst the din of their gunfire.

Slash flipped his Colt's loading gate closed. He looked straight out toward the far side of the camp, past where the horses were frogging around, whickering anxiously and pulling at their picket line. Billy was running, stumbling toward the river, grunting and groaning.

"Just stay here and stay down," Slash told the girl.

Wincing against his sundry aches and pains, ignoring the blood showing through the makeshift bandage around his waist and the other one around his arm, Slash strode out away from the fire, heading in the direction of the fleeing kid. As he entered the trees sheathing the river, he stopped.

Billy knelt before him on one knee, his wounded leg extended out to one side. The eye that Slash had peppered with bark was half open now and weeping. The other eye wept, too, for Billy was sobbing as he said, "Don't kill me, Slash." The words had come in a hushed, pleading, sorrowful tone. "I'm sorry for what I did. Truly I am. . . ."

Slash walked slowly forward, rage a fist of fire burning just beneath his heart.

"Remember what I told you when you first joined up, Billy?" he asked, stopping ten feet away from the kid. "About killin'?"

"Sure, sure, I do," the kid said. "You said . . . you said . . ."

"No killin' unless it's your life or theirs."

"Yes, that's what you told me, all right."

"Remember what I said the punishment for killing in cold blood was?"

The firebrand stretched his quivering upper lip away from his small, white teeth, more tears streaming down from his light blue eyes. "Oh, please, Slash. Please, don't kill me! I'm sorry I let you down! I've learned my lesson! Oh, purely I have! I'll never kill again—honest!"

"No, you won't, Billy."

Billy stared up at Slash. Suddenly, his eyes hardened, and anger edged his voice as he said, "Now, dammit, I done told you I was sorry. Don't you kill me! I'm like a son to you—remember?"

"You're a lowdown dirty dog, Billy," Slash said evenly. "You're about to be put down like any other lowdown dirty dog."

"Dammit, I done told you, you stubborn old . . . !" Billy let the sentence trail off as he reached for the second Remington holstered for the cross-draw on his right hip.

He didn't get the gun even halfway out of its holster before Slash's Colt bucked and roared, drilling a bullet through the kid's chest, exactly over his heart.

"*Ohhh!*" the kid grunted in shock and horror, staring down, aghast, at the blood welling up from the ragged hole in his shirt, just above the V in his cracked leather vest. He looked slowly up at Slash, furling his brows as though deeply puzzled. "You . . . you done . . . kilt . . . me. . . ."

He flopped backward against the ground and lay quivering as his young life left him.

Running footsteps sounded to Slash's right. He whipped around, cocking the Colt again.

"It's me!" Pecos called. "You all right, Slash?"

Slash had whipped around too quickly. All the blood seemed to have rushed into his feet, leaving him light-headed and dizzy, the trees and brush and river swirling around him. He dropped the Colt. He staggered backward and to one side, raking a spur on a rock. He fell then, but he was out before he hit the ground.

He was only vaguely aware of time passing . . . of waking up briefly to find himself being towed on a travois that Pecos had apparently rigged for him and padded with spruce boughs and blankets. He saw his Appy following along behind him on the trail through a deep valley rimmed by high, craggy peaks. He vaguely recognized the valley as the one cut by the Animas.

Again, darkness closed over him.

The next thing he was aware of, after what had seemed a long, troubled time punctuated by intermittent agony, was warm, soft, female lips pressed against his own.

He opened his eyes to see the most beautiful pair of

hazel eyes he'd ever seen gazing lovingly down at him. His heart lightened. His pain slithered away. He was in a comfortable bed, in a hotel most likely. In Silverton, no doubt.

Fairly mesmerized by those soft hazel eyes, Slash felt his own lips shape a smile, heard his raspy voice utter the single word: "Jay . . ."

She smiled again, kissed him again, and sunk her fingers into his hair.

"You'd best get back on your feet soon," she said in her husky, feminine voice. "Don't forget—you're on Bledsoe's payroll now." Her smile broadened. "And you two old cutthroats finally have an honest job!"

Slash turned to see Pecos hold up the deed to the freighting business, grinning. But then the big blond cutthroat cut a frown at Jay. "There's that word again! Doggone it, Jay, it ain't a job. Why, we're proper businessmen, Pecos an' Slash is. Who would've *thought?*"

"Uh-uh," Slash said, gently wagging his head on his pillow.

"What do you mean—'uh-uh'?" Pecos asked.

"It's Jimmy Braddock and Melvin Baker, an' don't you forget it!"

He nodded off again, the laughter of Melvin Baker and Jaycee Breckenridge echoing softly inside his head.